POWER PLAY

Gavin Esler is one of Britain's best known television presenters and an award winning reporter for the BBC. He began his career on the Belfast Telegraph and with the BBC in Northern Ireland. For many years he lived in Washington D.C.  e White House as the Chief N e BBC. He has travelled wid winning a Royal Televisio award, and interviewing w and President Chirac to Ton Abdullah of Jordan. He is currently one of the presenters on *Newsnight* and on BBC World.

Praise for A SCANDALOUS MAN

'Esler understands power better than anyone . . . The suspense never slackens.'
                                                                The Times

'What enlivens the novel is its undoubted sympathy for the human condition . . .'
                                                            The Guardian

'While Esler's story is sweeping in scope and complex both politically and emotional, it's always accessible and fast-paced.'
                                                            Daily Mirror

'This is a cracking story, well told, with a conclusion that is as shocking as it is inevitable . . . Can't wait for the next one.'
                                                            Daily Express

'Tautly plotted and thoroughly entertaining narrative which neatly dovetails fictional characters with historical events.'
                                                            Daily Mail

'A compelling book, its sophistication made luminous with wisdom, sympathy and storytelling.'   BERNARD CORNWELL

By the same author

A Scandalous Man

GAVIN ESLER

Power Play

HARPER

Harper
An imprint of HarperCollins*Publishers*
77–85 Fulham Palace Road,
Hammersmith, London W6 8JB

www.harpercollins.co.uk

This paperback edition 2010
1

First published in Great Britain by
HarperCollins 2009

A catalogue record for this book is
available from the British Library

ISBN: 978-0-00-727811-4

Set in Sabon by Palimpsest Book Production Limited, Grangemouth, Stirlingshire

Printed and bound in Great Britain by
Clays Ltd, St Ives plc

Mixed Sources
Product group from well-managed
forests and other controlled sources
www.fsc.org   Cert no. SW-COC-1806
© 1996 Forest Stewardship Council

FSC is a non-profit international organization established
to promote the responsible management of the world's forests.
Products carrying the FSC label are independently certified
to assure consumers that they come from forests that are managed
to meet the social, economic and ecological needs
of present and future generations.

Find out more about HarperCollins and the environment at
www.harpercollins.co.uk/green

For Anna

They said, 'You have a blue guitar.
You do not play things as they are.'

The man replied, 'Things as they are
Are changed upon the blue guitar.'

Wallace Stevens,
The Man with the Blue Guitar

'Military necessity does not admit of cruelty . . . nor of torture to extort confessions.'

'Instructions for the Government of Armies of the United States in the Field,' commonly known as the 'Lieber Code', written by Francis Lieber and accepted by President Abraham Lincoln, April 1863

ONE

Please call me Alex. When you ask what happened to Bobby Black, I have a long and a short answer, depending on how much truth you think you can handle. The short answer is that the Vice-President of the United States wandered off. Whether this was by mistake, on a whim or some temporary insanity, the result is the same – we lost him out there in the mist in the Scottish Highlands. Now that the mist has cleared, this quiet little patch of Scotland is under American occupation, or so it would appear. From my bedroom window here on the top floor of Castle Dubh I can see a line of several hundred yellow-jacketed British police and Mountain Rescue teams on the heather. Above them four US Army Apache helicopters are beating across the hillsides. In the distance there is another line of perhaps a thousand or more British and American soldiers plus black-uniformed US Secret Service personnel quartering the bogland stretching down to Rowallan Loch. In the castle and its outbuildings there are teams from Scotland Yard, Grampian Police, the British government, the Scottish Executive, the US State Department, the Pentagon, the FBI, the CIA, and an alphabet soup of other American agencies, all searching for the Vice-President, or – more likely given the time that has elapsed since the disappearance – they are searching for his body.

I try to remain calm. It's what diplomats do. I console myself with the thought that even great public figures can die a banal death, or disappear on a Scottish hillside in the fog. Princess Diana was in a car that hit an underpass in Paris. President George W. Bush once almost choked on a pretzel. The world would be a very different place if George W. Bush's oesophagus had permanently embraced those awkward crumbs and Vice-President Dick Cheney had become President. It would have taken just a few weeks for the accidental death of the President to be turned into the Pretzelgate scandal, with a series of commissions of inquiry investigating the conspiracy and naming the usual shadowy figures – the CIA, the Cubans, the Communists, al Qaeda, Mossad and the pretzel bakery – as having connived at the killing. As I watch the Apache helicopters hover in mid-air or sweep down over the heather and, as still more busloads of American military personnel arrive at the castle, I also console myself with another thought, this one beaten into me since childhood: inside every crisis there is an opportunity, if you have the wit to seize it. That's the big question. Do I?

The longer answer about the disappearance of the Vice-President begins two years ago with a hurriedly arranged meeting between Bobby Black – who was then Senator Black from Montana – and Prime Minister Fraser Davis. I remember trying to persuade Davis to make time in his schedule, at first without success. It was just four weeks before the American presidential elections, and we had no sense of how profoundly the tectonic plates of history were about to shift. Prime Minister Fraser Davis was enjoying a honeymoon of sorts from the voters. They had not figured him out yet. Davis is, among other things, my brother-in-law.

'You have charm, Alex,' he told me when his youngest

2

sister, Fiona, accepted my proposal of marriage. 'And an air of menace. The combination appears to work on women. Perhaps it works on men too. It even works on me, up to a point.'

It was always 'perhaps' and 'up to a point' with Fraser Davis, and finding exactly where that point might be was a special skill of mine. I guessed that he never thought I was good enough for his sister, although it took some time for Fiona to come round to her brother's opinion.

In those first days of October two years ago, no one expected Theo Carr and Bobby Black to win the White House. The opinion polls had been consistent for months. Carr was way behind, more than ten points adrift against a comfortable, competent incumbent President. The American economy had at last picked up, and the smart people I knew in Washington – diplomats, journalists, members of Congress – dismissed Carr and Black as too extreme, too right wing, too out of touch with the mood of America. Their rhetoric was all from the past, talk of taking the War on Terror to 'the Bad Guys' and 'the Worst of the Worst', whoever *they* happened to be. When I raised the prospect of a meeting we were in the private sitting room in Number Ten Downing Street – the Prime Minister, me, his special adviser, Janey Masters, and the Director of Communications, Andy Carnwath. Fraser Davis joked that Theo Carr and Bobby Black talked as if they had an 'Enemy of the Month Club'.

'Y'know, a calendar of men with beards they plan to bomb. One Dead Beard a Month until the War on Terror is won.' Fraser Davis prided himself on his sensitive political antennae and expertise on the United States. He turned to me. 'Forget Bobby Black, Alex. Waste of my time.'

'Meeting Bobby Black is never a waste of time, Prime Minister,' I contradicted him. 'Trust me.'

3

You can get away with contradicting the PM's judgement about once per meeting. More can be perilous.

'I simply don't see why I should bother with Losers,' he responded, looking up from his briefing papers and pouting a moist lip in my direction, the way he did when he was annoyed. 'Fix me up with the Winners, for God's sake. Get the President or Vice-President in here. That's what we pay you for.'

I pointed out that unfortunately the incumbent President and Vice-President were not coming through London. Bobby Black was.

'Thirty minutes of your time,' I persisted. 'At Chequers.' Chequers is the Prime Minister's private retreat in the country-side just outside London. 'Tea and biscuits. A chat. It can do no harm, and it could do a lot of good. It will raise your profile in Washington and—'

'Nonsense,' he snapped, arching a prime ministerial eyebrow and pouting once more. Davis is a toff, of course, even though he tries to hide it. He makes a big thing of his love of football and is forever telling newspaper feature writers that his iPod is full of Kill Hannah and Nickelback, though I have never once heard him enquire about football match results, nor have I ever seen him listen to his supposedly beloved rock music. He's Eton to the core, Oxford PPE, once a City smoothie, a stint as a management consultant, and then time in a hedge fund where he made a lot of money and decided that he understood 'how the market works.' At moments when we disagree he and I are like two different species sizing each other up. My own background as a soldier in Northern Ireland gives me a bit of an edge. Davis likes to joke that his brother-in-law had 'strangled IRA terrorists with his bare hands.' Perhaps he likes this joke because the closest the Prime Minister ever came to serving his country in uniform was wearing a tailcoat at Eton and the Bullingdon dining club.

'Look, I simply haven't got time to listen to Yesterday's

Man.' Davis smiled that way he has which looks like a smirk. 'Black and Carr want to continue making the same mistakes in their War on Terror that we made thirty years ago in Ulster. Why, oh why, do these bloody Americans persist in thinking you can wage war on a *tactic*, for goodness sake?'

The British ability to suck up to the Americans and to patronize them simultaneously should not be underestimated. Janey Masters and Andy Carnwath shook with laughter at this Prime Ministerial *aperçu*. I didn't.

'Prime Minister, you are making a serious mistake,' I contradicted them all firmly. The chorus of laughter stopped. I was now on the edge of being rude, but I had the floor and so I used it. 'You should not make unnecessary enemies.'

'Unnecessary enemies?' Davis repeated, rolling the words around his mouth like a sip of unexpectedly good wine.

'Bobby Black wants to meet you,' I explained. 'And he is a man who plays favourites and bears grudges.' I advised that even if Black and Carr lost the presidential election, Senator Black would eventually have a position of considerable leadership, one day Senate Majority Leader. 'A good friend and a bad enemy. His reputation is as Washington's silent throat-slitter.' All eyes were on me now. Very busy people in power remind me of children: self-obsessed, in their own little world. Any device that catches their attention is legitimate. 'You cross Bobby Black at your peril. He's coming to London and we should be nice.'

The Prime Minister sighed and then agreed. Reluctantly.

'Very well then, Alex. If you say so. Fix it. Fix it. Please ruin my weekend at Chequers.'

And so I fixed it. I felt confident that ruining his weekend was the right thing to do and that Fraser Davis would soon be grateful. It really is what I am paid for.

On that day of Bobby Black's visit I drove myself down to Chequers from central London while Andy Carnwath, Janey

Masters and the Prime Minister travelled by helicopter. Another of Fraser Davis's routine jokes at my expense is that I was brave enough to interrogate IRA suspects face to face but too timid to get on a 'heavier-than-air machine'. He regards such schoolboy teasing as a sign of affection. I went to a different type of school.

The Chequers event was – how shall I put it in the language of diplomacy? – not a meeting of minds. Bobby Black and Fraser Davis had little in common, except for one fact: each of them always thought that in any meeting, in any gathering, he was the smartest person in the room. On that day, when we brought these two super-egos together at Chequers, at least one of them had to be wrong. Perhaps both of them. Bobby Black had flown from Washington to Heathrow and then helicoptered over to meet the Prime Minister. I remember it as an unseasonably warm day, early October, a day belonging more to summer than the start of autumn. The fine weather put everyone in a good mood. The American helicopter came down on the lawn, picture perfect. Unusually for Chequers, which is by tradition always private, we allowed a tight pool of British and American TV crews to film the occasion. What everyone saw on the evening news on both sides of the Atlantic was Davis and Black greeting each other with all the false *bonhomie* demanded on such occasions. The American network TV coverage – as I had predicted – helped raise Fraser Davis's profile in the United States.

We carry out confidential public opinion surveys in key allies once a year, and the most recent showed that when you asked Americans about British prime ministers they could name Churchill, Thatcher, and Blair. Fraser Davis, like the rest of our political leaders, simply did not exist. That night, thanks to me, for a few seconds on the American TV evening news, Fraser Davis did exist. The two men ran their hands up each other's arms to show how touchy-feely they were. They grinned. They exchanged pleasantries. The Prime Minister said he was 'delighted' to meet the grizzled Senator, more than twenty years his senior. Bobby Black, his owlish eyes glinting behind thick glasses, managed to appear as if he had just flown the Atlantic on the off chance he might catch a few words with our own esteemed Dear Leader, the Bright New Thing in London.

'I've come to learn how to win elections,' he joked for the cameras. 'Like you did, Mr Prime Minister.' Bobby Black's Chief of Staff, Johnny Lee Ironside, winked at me as we stood on the edges of the photo-opportunity, our faces split by broad grins. He's a tall, lanky southerner with a South Carolina accent that makes me think of the warmth of a hit of Southern Comfort.

'Good work on this get-together, Ambassador Price,' he whispered.

'Please call me Alex,' I introduced myself. He seemed like someone I could do business with.

'Johnny Lee.'

I had checked him out beforehand of course. Born Charleston. Rich Old South family, Anglophile, Harvard Law, Rhodes scholar. And now, as I could see, polite and generous. My kind of American. We moved to the main Chequers dining room. It was scheduled to be a half-hour visit before Bobby Black headed to a Republican fund-raising dinner in the City to tap rich donors resident in the UK. Afterwards he was flying to Paris and Berlin for quick photo-calls with the French President and German Chancellor, and more fund-raising, then back to Washington. Well, that was the plan. We sat across the big shiny walnut dining table on the opposite side to the Americans. Bobby Black started talking about the challenges of international terrorism. It was – disappointingly – a cut-down version of his standard campaign speech. I had heard it so often that, like the Lord's Prayer, I could recite passages by heart.

'Afghanistan . . . Taleban . . . hearts and minds . . . stay the course . . . democracy and freedom . . . al Qaeda . . . the Worst of the Worst . . . lessons of Iraq . . . shared values, shared sacrifice . . .'

It was warm and stuffy, Senator Black spoke quietly, and my mind wandered. I began to think of my own future.

Another two years as Ambassador to Washington and I would be in line for a knighthood, then promotion to Head of the Foreign Office, and eventually a peerage. Or – as Fraser Davis had hinted – I might be interested in quitting and thinking about going into politics. I could undoubtedly secure a safe seat under his patronage. As Bobby Black droned on, I started thinking of other things – of lunch, of the drive back to London, of seeing Fiona, and of the difficulties we had been having.

'. . . Iranian threat . . . shadow on the Gulf . . . oil supplies . . . nuclear proliferation . . . Islamic bomb . . . generations to come . . .'

I love and admire the United States, especially ordinary Americans, but so many of their top-tier politicians struck me as even worse than ours – difficult though that may be to believe. The kind of people with whom, after you shake hands, you feel you should count your fingers just to check none has been stolen. Bobby Black made me especially nervous, which was one of the reasons I wanted him to meet Davis. Besides, it helped me enormously back in Washington that Black and others knew how close I was to the Prime Minister. I tuned in again. Bobby Black was offering clues about a future Carr presidency. It struck me as unlikely that I would ever need this information. Theo Carr worried, he said, that 'Russia wants its Empire back and we're not about to give it to them,' but the main struggle would continue against 'militant Islam.' The new President would demand from all America's allies 'more commitment of blood and treasure' in this 'existential struggle against terrorism.' Prime Minister Davis rolled his eyes.

'Guts,' Bobby Black was saying softly, waggling a fat white finger in our direction. I watched the finger's reflection in the polished walnut of the table top. 'Old fashioned guts, when it comes to facing down the Russians, the Iranians or al Qaeda. Guts, and leadership, Mr Prime Minister. Moral fibre.'

I sipped the weak black coffee and nibbled at the digestive biscuits that mark British hospitality on these occasions. Suddenly the man Black had called 'Mister Prime Minister' sprang into life.

'Leadership demands Followership,' Davis snapped, the wet, pouty lip directed at Bobby Black. 'Don't you agree, Senator? And what kind of leadership are you expecting to offer that others will follow?'

Bobby Black winced and then smiled. He did not like to be interrupted, and I did not like his smile. He replied softly and deliberately, so you had to lean towards him to hear.

'There are some very Bad People out there, Mr Prime Minister, and—'

'Forgive me, Senator Black,' Prime Minister Davis interrupted again, with a degree of condescension that grated even on me. Johnny Lee Ironside shuffled uncomfortably in his chair and raised an eyebrow in my direction. The Prime Minister was in no mood to hold back. 'Forgive me, but most people across Europe understand that there are "Bad People", as you put it, "out there." We've had terrorist attacks for years – decades. We had them in Belfast from Nineteen Sixtynine, and in Glasgow, in London, Madrid, Amsterdam, Berlin, Istanbul, Rome. Our experience tells us that the challenge is to avoid creating more terrorists than you can possibly kill or arrest. So how do you propose to do that when the way you talk sounds like you are still making the same mistakes we made decades ago? The IRA taught us that subtlety and sophistication would help. That's why Ireland is now – mostly – at peace.'

Like Harrow, Fettes, and Winchester, Eton is a school that

produces many brilliant minds but very few humble ones. Bobby Black sat bolt upright and blinked behind his glasses at the Prime Minister. What I saw in his eyes was something akin to hatred. He did not like being interrupted and he certainly did not like being contradicted by a Prime Minister young enough to be his son. At that moment I hoped that the opinion polls were correct and that Black and Carr would lose the presidential election by a landslide. When he spoke, it was again so quietly I had to strain to hear him.

'Mr Prime Minister,' Bobby Black said coldly, stressing certain words as if they deserved to have capital letters, 'the IRA did not do suicide bombings or fly planes into buildings. This is a different world. Neutrality is immoral. Appeasement is immoral. Subtlety and sophistication – as you call it – to folks where I come from in Montana, are just European excuses to do nothing except wring hands, wet the bed, and complain about the wicked Americans. There was nothing subtle about your British citizens trying to blow up American airliners halfway over the Atlantic Ocean. And let me be clear. When Governor Theo Carr is elected President of the United States next month, the Carr administration will expect and require full cooperation on matters of national security from all allies of the United States.'

Expect and require. Your British citizens. Oh, shit. I put my coffee cup down. Now it was Fraser Davis who looked as if he had been shot. He began finger-pointing as he spoke. His lower lip was exceptionally moist, the way it gets when he is irritated and wants to start lecturing. I do not usually get these things wrong, but the informal Chequers meeting was unravelling before my eyes and I could do nothing to stop it. I looked over to Johnny Lee Ironside who nodded. He shared my pain.

'Senator Black, of course you will have our full cooperation and friendship. But for our part, we will expect the new President – *whoever* that might be – to lead an American administration that *listens* to its friends as opposed to lecturing them, and that upholds the way of life you say you want to defend. We urge you to look at the mistakes of the past and at your own country's record on human rights, the detention without trial of terrorist suspects – including British nationals – and matters that clearly fall under the United Nations' definition of torture.'

'Fuck the United Nations,' Bobby Black said softly. The room fell silent. Fraser Davis's lower lip dropped an inch. Bobby Black said it so quietly but with such unmistakable anger that I thought for a moment I had misheard him. Looking at the stunned faces I knew that I had not. Everyone held their breath. Bobby Black's eyes stared intensely from behind his glasses. The Prime Minister's pouty lip formed a single response.

'Pardon?'

'Fuck the United Nations,' Bobby Black repeated, without raising his voice. 'Fuck 'em. We'll do it alone if we have to. We'd like help. Everybody likes help. But we're the United States of America and we don't need it.'

Prime Minister Davis smiled although, yet again, the smile could look just like a smirk. He tried to make light of what we had just heard.

'Fuck the United Nations – would that be the official policy of the incoming Carr administration?'

I caught Johnny Lee's eyes again. They had an expression that said, 'Get us out of here.'

'If necessary,' Bobby Black answered, and brushed some imaginary fluff from his suit sleeve. 'On international terrorism, there is no middle ground. There is Right, and there is Wrong. Any country or organization that is not with Right is with Wrong. It would be a sad day if the United States had to withdraw from the UN. A sad day for the United Nations. The US would get over it.'

He stopped speaking. A silence fell upon us while we thought

11

about what he had said. The meeting was effectively over, after ten minutes of the allotted thirty. Bobby Black pushed his seat back so it scraped on the floor. Johnny Lee Ironside stood up.

'Thank you for your time, Mr Prime Minister. Our helicopter is waiting. I'm heading for the City of London.'

'And thank you for sparing time in your busy schedule, Senator Black.'

'No problem, Mr Prime Minister.'

A chill ran through me. Of course, Fraser Davis should have held his tongue. He should have listened to Black and nodded without being so sarcastic and condescending. For his part, Bobby Black should not have been so foul mouthed and imperious. You can bring people together, but you cannot make them like each other. The Prime Minister headed towards his study muttering under his breath about that 'awful bloody man'. Bobby Black strode briskly out of the room and across the grass to the helicopter, his lopsided grin firmly in place. On the way out, Johnny Lee shook my hand and whispered to me: 'Well, Ambassador, looks like we got ourselves a problem.'

'Yes,' I agreed. 'We'll talk.'

'Unless we lose,' Johnny Lee responded. 'In which case you'll never have to deal with either of us again.' He started to laugh. 'Which I guess Prime Minister Davis must be praying for right now.'

I smiled awkwardly and nodded. You won't win, I thought, as the helicopter took off. Ten points behind in the opinion polls with just a few weeks to go until polling day: without some kind of miracle you can't possibly win.

TWO

It wasn't a miracle, but it had the same transformative effect on the fortunes of Theo Carr and Bobby Black. The day after that catastrophic meeting at Chequers, I was woken early by Andy Carnwath, who called with the news that a bomb had exploded in an American airliner taking off from Manila Airport in the Philippines and bound for Los Angeles, killing everyone on board.

'You're going to be busy,' Carnwath said. 'Fraser wants you back in DC today.'

'Why?'

'The suicide bomber was British.'

I prepared to leave for the airport immediately. Fiona said she intended to stay in London for a few days longer.

'But Fiona . . .'

She pushed a strand of strawberry-blonde hair behind her ear and gave me the kind of pout that reminded me of her brother. I felt her slipping away from me.

'Don't start this, Alex. Don't do that *"but you are my wife"* stuff again. I have given up almost everything to follow you to Washington – almost everything – but I am entitled to hold on to something of my own life. I promised to meet Haley and Georgia for lunch, and that is what I am going to do.'

Haley and Georgia were Fiona's business partners in an interior-design consultancy they had set up after leaving Oxford, which owed at least some of its success to the idea that people could employ a company connected to the Prime Minister to renovate their homes.

'Fine,' I said, accepting the inevitable. 'That's fine.'

I headed to the airport alone, calling Andy Carnwath on the way for a further briefing about the Manila attack. It was the day we woke up to the possibility that every one of our nightmares might become true. All through the presidential election campaign, Carr and Black had consistently argued that the United States government and the President in particular were complacent about the terrorist threat. There had been no significant incident in the United States since 11 September 2001, and to many of us Carr and Black sounded like a pair of wackos: shrill, scaremongering, out of touch.

'Who was the bomber?'

'Name of Rashid Ali Fuad,' Carnwath said, 'from Yorkshire. Leeds.'

'Acting alone?'

'Our people doubt it, but that's all we have.'

'Definitely British?'

'Oh yeah. Definitely one of ours. Lucky us.'

As we drove into Heathrow, I could see, all around the perimeter, armoured troop carriers and fully armed soldiers. There were groups of police officers with Heckler & Koch sub-machine-guns at the terminal building, long lines at the check-in desks and serious flight delays as every piece of electronic equipment was checked. I skipped through the priority channel and into the first-class lounge where I sat in front of the BBC's 24-hour news channel. It said that Rashid Ali Fuad had climbed on board an American Boeing 747 aircraft at Manila, sat in a window seat and detonated a bomb in his laptop computer. It punched a hole in the plane and caused a crash on take-off followed by a catastrophic explosion.

The aviation fuel caught fire and the blaze incinerated everyone on board.

It was like being on the hinge of history. Everything after that moment was changed. The Manila atrocity confirmed to tens of millions of American voters that the world was just as dangerous a place as Governor Theo Carr and Senator Bobby Black had always insisted it was, and that the dangers came not just from countries with a long record of hating America, but also from people like Fuad who were citizens of the country most Americans thought of as a friend and ally, the United Kingdom of Great Britain and Northern Ireland. It was as if a switch went off in the heads of tens of millions of voters and, in that one instant, the out-of-touch scaremongers, Governor Theo Carr and Senator Bobby Black, suddenly seemed prescient and timely. Bobby Black cancelled the rest of his European trip. He skipped Paris and Berlin and flew instead to the Philippines. He stood on the tarmac in front of the charred hulk of the jumbo jet promising, 'No More Manilas.' It became the slogan that won the election. He pointed at the wreckage and at the body bags laid out on the tarmac, ready to be loaded on to a US Air Force C-5 transport plane with the ashes and dust of the American dead. With tears misting his glasses, Bobby Black promised that, 'America is grieving now, but there will come a time for vengeance, and that vengeance will be swift, brutal and just.' He stared straight at the cameras.

'There will be No More Manilas,' he repeated. 'I want everyone round the world to hear me. No More Manilas.'

'No More Manilas', they chanted in Boston and Houston and Fresno and Tallahassee and Atlanta and Baton Rouge in the closing days of the presidential campaign. 'No More Manilas' tee shirts, buttons and bumper stickers became best-sellers for street vendors from New York City to San Diego. The funerals of the dead from the Manila atrocity began just before election day, and America went to the polls in mourning:

15

resolute, defiant, wounded – and determined to secure justice. I admired, as I always do, the resilience and good sense of the American people, but I looked at the tracking polls with a degree of concern. The opinion polls measured a profound switch to Carr and Black, enough to win the presidency of the United States against all the predictions of the supposed experts. Bobby Black was about to become Vice-President of the United States.

On Inauguration Day the following January, I watched from the diplomatic stand on Capitol Hill as President Carr and Vice-President Black were sworn in at a sombre ceremony in a country that felt itself definitively at war. The crowds lining Pennsylvania Avenue and around the Capitol carried American flags and thousands upon thousands of banners repeating the same slogan time after time.

'NO MORE MANILAS. NO MORE MANILAS.'

President Theo Carr said as much in his Inauguration speech. He promised that his administration had 'no higher ideal, no greater purpose, than to ensure the life, liberty, and the right to pursue happiness of every American citizen by freeing our people from the shadow of the gunman, bomber, and terrorist. We will, as John F. Kennedy said on his Inauguration at this very spot, bear any burden, pay any price, to secure our great nation from those who would destroy us. They will not succeed. They will never succeed. They shall not pass.'

I stood to applaud when President Carr finished. After Manila, the whole world stood to applaud. We were, yet again, absolutely shoulder to shoulder with the Americans in their time of trouble; until, of course, the Carr administration settled into power with all the confidence of sleepwalkers, and the issue of Rashid Ali Fuad's British citizenship started to become part of the wedge between us, most especially in the mind of Vice-President Black. I could not believe how quickly relations deteriorated.

Just one day after the Inauguration, while the bleachers for the spectators watching the parade were still being dismantled all along Pennsylvania Avenue, the *Washington Post* published details of the argument between Prime Minister Fraser Davis and Vice-President Black at their Chequers meeting the day before the Manila bombing. The way the story was written made it look as if Fraser Davis and the British government were soft on terror, and that this weakness somehow contributed to the loss of all those innocent lives at the hands of what the paper kept calling 'the British suicide bomber, Fuad.' The reporter, James Byrne, claimed to have received a transcript of the Davis–Black row at Chequers from 'reliable Carr administration sources.' The report highlighted the section where Bobby Black said, 'Fuck the United Nations.'

The *Washington Post* story caused uproar in Britain, across Europe and at the United Nations. Black and Carr's popularity in the United States – which was very high in those first days – actually increased. Curiously, Fraser Davis's popularity in Britain increased too. I suspected it was because, unlike Tony Blair, nobody reading the story could accuse Davis of being an American poodle. But how did Byrne get the story, based on secret transcripts of a private conversation more than three months earlier? I considered the options and then called the Vice-President's Chief of Staff, Johnny Lee Ironside. I told him that it was very unhelpful to have this kind of leak.

'Makes it sound like someone in the White House is anti-British.'

'We didn't leak it, Alex.'

'But you benefited from it,' I told him. 'And it didn't come from us. The Prime Minister is livid. *Cui bono?*'

'C'mon, you guys did okay,' Johnny Lee retorted. He was in good humour. There was not a problem between the two of us. 'I read the British papers. Davis comes out of this just fine. Maybe you leaked it?'

'Me? For goodness sake, Johnny Lee, I am not a leaker—'

'Listen, Alex, lighten up. Who cares, all right? I mean, we both come out ahead. My man says fuck the UN, which plays to our home crowd. Your man says fuck the Americans, which plays to yours. So everybody wins.'

I didn't think so. But I let it rest.

I could not escape the thought that maybe Johnny Lee had leaked the transcript himself. He clearly suspected the same about me because I knew the reporter James Byrne quite well. Welcome to the Washington House of Mirrors. What you see reflects only upon where you decide to look. After just one day of the Carr–Black administration, I was beginning to worry that the next four years were going to be difficult. In that judgement, at least, I was correct.

THREE

'Fear', Vice-President Bobby Black said to me, 'works.'

It was now a week after the Inauguration and a week after the *Washington Post* had published the story about the row between Davis and Black. We were in the White House, and things were getting worse.

'Excuse me?'

'Fear . . . works,' he repeated, separating the words in his whispering drawl.

The Vice-President of the United States shrugged and blinked behind his glasses, as if that were explanation enough. I had been invited to the White House – 'summoned' might be a better word – for a bollocking. I had left early from the Ambassador's living quarters at the British Embassy on Massachusetts Avenue. I'd said goodbye to Fiona, kissed her and told her that I would be late – a long day at the White House followed by planned meetings with the new people in Congress, the new Speaker of the House of Representatives, Betty Furedi, plus two sessions on Capitol Hill, and then finally, around 6 p.m., a cocktail party to welcome the new Turkish Ambassador.

'Dinner? Eight?' I said as I kissed her. 'That's what we scheduled?'

'Yes,' she said, without enthusiasm. She pushed a lock of hair behind her ears. 'See you for dinner at eight.'

We entertained most evenings. That night I had planned a small dinner for a visiting delegation of representatives of British airlines to bring them together with two key members of a Congressional committee that was proving difficult about landing rights at JFK and O'Hare Airport in Chicago. There was no direct relationship between the problems we were having and the Manila attack, but Rashid Ali Fuad's British citizenship was mentioned repeatedly in the committee hearings, and constantly talked about on the US TV news networks.

'Dinner at eight,' Fiona repeated. 'You know, sometimes I feel less like an Ambassador's wife and more like a flight attendant. All I do is smile at strangers and serve them beverages.'

'We'll talk about it later,' I said.

'We always talk about it later.'

'You want out?' I snapped. 'This isn't much fun for me, either, being married to someone who treats me like I'm some kind of kidnapper.'

'I just want my own life back, that's all. Not just a part of yours. Is that too much to ask?'

'No,' I agreed. 'That's not too much to ask. We will talk about it, I promise.'

I kissed her on the cheek but did not ask how she was going to spend her day. At that moment, on my way to the White House, I had enough to deal with.

'Eight o'clock then.'

'Yes.'

There is a peculiar excitement about going to the White House, no matter how many times it happens. You remember the details. Every sense is on overload. It is like drinking from the Enchanted Fountain of Power. That day it was a small meeting which filled the Vice-President's tiny office – just Bobby Black, his Chief of Staff, Johnny Lee Ironside, the

20

White House Deputy National Security Adviser, Dr Kristina Taft, plus me, and a note-taker. A vase of lilies left over from the Inauguration celebrations sat on the Vice-President's desk, heavy with pollen. I still remember how the flowers gave off a pungent smell. Bobby Black had called me in to discuss the publicity given by British newspapers to the behind-the-scenes rows between the two governments, following the exposé in the *Washington Post*. It had become echo-chamber journalism, nothing more than the hollow sound of our worst prejudices as the British and American media had a go at each other. Johnny Lee Ironside had warned me that the Vice-President would bring up the related case of another British national who had been picked up by US special forces on the Pakistan–Afghan border. He was called Muhammad Asif Khan, and he had been arrested, detained, or kidnapped – you can choose your word – either inside Afghanistan, as the Americans claimed, or inside Pakistan, as his family and the Pakistan Government insisted. The American account said Khan was a British accomplice of the Manila bomber Rashid Ali Fuad, though we had no evidence of this and suspected the Americans didn't either.

Khan's family – from Keighley in Yorkshire – said he had disappeared while visiting relatives, and claimed he was being tortured by the CIA, or that he had been handed over to a 'friendly' country with a dubious human-rights record so that their intelligence agencies could torture him on behalf of the Americans. A number of British newspapers, politicians and human-rights groups, along with the Pakistan Government, protested that in its first week the Carr–Black administration was 'already even worse than that of George W. Bush and Dick Cheney.' The *Guardian* newspaper had called the Khan disappearance a 'blight' on 'all the hopes' for the new presidency. No one would confirm where Khan was being held, though some reports said it was in Egypt. Since the Manila atrocity, reports of this kind of treatment of suspected

21

terrorists had grown. Johnny Lee told me to think of it as 'outsourcing'.

'Like putting a call centre in Bangalore,' he said to me. 'You employ some real experts, hungry for the work, and you get more bang for your buck.'

'Is Khan in Egypt, Johnny Lee?'

'No idea, Alex. God help the sonovabitch if he is. The Egyptians don't do nice, from what I hear.'

The fact that Khan's father and uncles were from Keighley, geographically just a short drive from Leeds, the home town of Fuad, the Manila bomber, was asserted in the American media as evidence of a connection. The Khan family angrily denied it. They were politically well connected, friends of a British Muslim Labour MP who made a fuss, organized a series of well-publicized protests and asked awkward questions in Parliament. Fraser Davis was in trouble at Prime Minister's Questions, embarrassed by the Opposition, and also by some on his own side. Mostly he was embarrassed by being dropped in it by the Americans.

'Can the Prime Minister confirm under what circumstances he believes it is legal for the CIA or the American Army to kidnap and torture British citizens?' was just one of the unhelpful questions Fraser Davis faced in the Commons and on television.

'Can the Prime Minister confirm the whereabouts of Mr Khan?'

'Can the Prime Minister tell us how dispensing with due process of law and alienating the entire British Muslim community will help the Carr administration win their so-called War on Terror?'

And so on.

British newspapers showed pictures of Khan – clean shaven and smiling – helping a group of handicapped children on an Outward Bound course in the Lake District, a model citizen, apparently. The *Wall Street Journal* and *Newsweek* magazine showed a different Khan. This one was an Islamist fanatic, a

Taleban supporter and wannabe suicide bomber who had been recruiting young British men of Pakistani origin to kill – Americans and Jews preferably – without compunction. Khan, they claimed, was planning some kind of unspecified attack in the United States or against American targets 'along the lines of Manila.'

Where the truth lay in all this, I did not know. What I did know was that the row between London and Washington had now entered an even more aggressive phase. All the rest had been just foreplay. At least Johnny Lee Ironside and I had established a good relationship, I would almost say a friendship, in the months or so since the initial disagreement at Chequers. We met frequently and talked on the telephone almost every day.

'Heads up,' he said. 'The Vice-President wants to see you about Khan and other matters, and it isn't going to be pretty. Be prepared for Incoming.'

'Thanks,' I replied. I appreciated the warning.

'He's in need of a human sacrifice, Alex, and as the top Brit around here, you have been selected.'

I pretended to laugh.

'Ritual slaughter is one of the perks of the job. I'm looking forward to it. Obviously.'

That day of my White House visit I heard the morning TV weather reports predicting an ice storm all around the Chesapeake Bay. Flat blue clouds rolled in from the northeast, bringing a chill which drilled the bones. After I kissed Fiona goodbye, I came out of the ambassador's residence, around half past seven in the morning. I was swathed in a long black coat and I jumped into the embassy's dark green Rolls-Royce with the heating turned up full blast. I felt bad about Fiona; bad about the way it was going. On the journey down Massachusetts Avenue I tried to see things from her point of view. Yes, I had taken her away from her friends and career in London, but she knew all the drawbacks when she married me. Yes, I had a hectic job, but being the wife of the British Ambassador was not such a bad deal, was it?

And yes, yes, I wanted children. I'm young for an ambassador but when you hit late forties you are getting old for fatherhood. I felt time passing and the ticking of the clock that women are supposed to possess but men are not. Because Fiona is twelve years younger than me, perhaps she did not feel it so intensely, but I was slowly waking up to the idea that I might need a bit of diplomacy in my private life.

I got to the White House shortly before eight o'clock. Dr Kristina Taft met me near the media stakeout position at the West Wing door. That day she was still the Deputy National Security Adviser, though not for long. The newspapers called Kristina a 'Vulcan', one of the hyper-rational academics full of brainy ideas and yet apparently devoid of human emotion whom Carr and Black had brought in to run American policy. I could not square the newspaper hype with the smiling face that greeted me, though I admit I was slightly intimidated. Kristina was about the same age as Fiona and we stood shaking hands for the photographers. We exchanged a few words as the Marine Guard saluted and the machine-gun fire of lenses and flashguns went off in our faces.

Nothing happens at the White House by accident. Everything in the Carr presidency is scheduled into fifteen-minute slots, and there are therefore ninety-six of these across the President's twenty-four-hour day. Even 'downtime' – relaxation – is scheduled in fifteen-minute bites, though a sensible president will make sure he gets at least thirty-two of these a night. I used to wonder if some presidents – especially Kennedy or Clinton – had a fifteen- or thirty- or forty-five-minute schedule for sex. Anyway, Kristina Taft could have chosen for me to arrive discreetly, away from the cameras. Instead she picked the entrance designed to give the American media a full photo-opportunity of the British Ambassador being called in for his bollocking by Bobby Black. It was to be, as Johnny Lee had told me, an act of ritual humiliation. My humiliation. I shook hands and beamed. The 'special relationship' between the United States and the United Kingdom deserves no less than the occasional warm smile of hypocrisy.

'Welcome, Ambassador.'

'Dr Taft. Nice to see you. A pleasure.'

'I think the cameras have had enough,' she said out of the corner of her mouth as she steered me inside. 'You know, the Vice-President told me he is looking forward to meeting with you. He insisted we clear serious face-time.'

Serious face-time with Bobby Black? Diplomatic Warning Bell Number One went off in my head.

'Vice-President Black is a very busy man,' I replied carefully. In that first week he was more often on the newspaper front pages than the President himself, a pattern which was to continue for the next two years. 'I am grateful for the meeting. He's never out of the news.'

Kristina Taft smiled again, but her grey eyes didn't. She was wearing a sober dark suit, no discernible make-up, no jewellery. This was an attractive woman deliberately making herself look as serious as possible. She led me inside.

'We're going to have to wait a few minutes,' she said. 'He is in for a one-on-one with the President. Coffee?'

I accepted and we sat in a hallway watched over by two Secret Service agents. Kristina poured the coffee. I had of course done my homework, reading the briefing papers about the new Carr people. Kristina's said that her academic career had been stellar, and also that her supposed boss at the National Security Council was in trouble, accused of employing illegal aliens at his home in Virginia. It was just the first of the scandals that were to hit the Carr administration.

Kristina was from the start acting up, as National Security Adviser, with all the authority that implies, although in that first week the gossip was that she was too young for the job;

someone else would be brought in. She was, however, born to high office, part of a political dynasty. Her father had been Governor of California and the Tafts are Republican royalty, with a former President, William Howard Taft, to their credit in the early twentieth century. His main claim to historical fame is that he was so fat – 300 pounds – that he once got stuck in the White House bathtub. I looked over at Kristina and thought of a hummingbird: she was petite, hyperactive, with the figure of someone who exercises regularly. My briefing papers said *Washingtonian* magazine had voted her America's 'most eligible bachelorette', under a glamorous picture of her in a full-length evening gown. The *New York Times* reported that, during the transition, before Theo Carr was actually sworn in, Kristina Taft had a row with Bobby Black and had stood up to him. She had suggested, the story claimed, a White House reading list, including novels to help National Security staff understand how Arabs, Iranians, Pakistanis, and other Muslims might think.

The *New York Times* congratulated Kristina on her fortitude in taking on Bobby Black and also on being a 'civilizing influence' in the White House. It was a compliment that would not necessarily help her career.

'So,' I said, trying to figure Kristina out, 'what's this reading list I hear so much about? And can I get a copy? Or are the novels you read Top Secret, US Eyes Only?'

She had the grace to laugh.

'They are so secret you can get them from any bookstore, if you are open-minded enough to try.'

She explained about the row. During the transition, Theo Carr had held a brainstorming meeting of all his foreign policy advisers and challenged them to name the core failure in American policy in the past fifty years. Kristina stood up and said it was the 'United States' inability to understand the psychology of our enemies in the way we understood the psychology of the Russians during the Cold War.'

'Explain what you mean, Dr Taft,' Carr had asked, almost like a job interview. Perhaps it was a job interview. Kristina delivered a history lesson. She said that since the Iranian revolution of 1979 and the overthrow of the Shah of Iran, all America's troubles originated in an 'Arc of Instability' stretching from Palestine and Israel through Lebanon, Syria, Iraq, and Iran to Pakistan and Afghanistan.

'But we don't understand what we are doing,' Kristina insisted. 'So we blunder about like dinosaurs with powerful bodies and very small brains. If we don't change, we are going to be extinct.'

Theo Carr was clearly interested; Bobby Black less so.

'Give us an example of this dinosaur tendency, Dr Taft,' Black said. 'I want some facts.'

'Fact: Under George W. Bush the United States military destroyed Saddam Hussein in Two Thousand and three,' Kristina replied. 'Fact: the United States and its allies overthrew the Taleban in Afghanistan in Two Thousand and two.'

She paused.

'So?'

'So, what good did it do us? At great cost to ourselves in American lives, we took out Iran's two most dangerous enemies, and the Iranians still hate us. Fact: Under Bill Clinton in Nineteen Ninety-eight we saved the Muslim people of Kosovo from slaughter and get no credit from Muslims anywhere. So how dumb are we? We think tactics and ignore strategy; we screw up because we don't think through what the objective really is. No More Manilas means no more being dinosaurs.'

'The objective . . .' Bobby Black started to say something but Theo Carr waved him to be silent.

'How do we do better, Dr Taft?' Carr asked.

'By thinking like the people of the region, sir. By remembering the old Arab cliché, that My Enemy's Enemy is My Friend.

By getting smart. By getting others to do the dirty work for us.'

'But how?' Carr insisted.

That's when the White House reading list was born, despite Bobby Black's protests.

'Here's a start. Arabs and Persians watch our TV, our movies, read our books, listen to our rock music. We should do the same with their literature. They understand us and we do not understand them.'

'Through storybooks?' Bobby Black scoffed.

'One good novel revealing how ordinary Muslim people think,' Kristina responded, 'is worth a dozen CIA estimates about the opium crop in Afghanistan or political gossip on instability in Iraq or Pakistan or wherever.'

'She speaks Arabic, that's why she thinks this way,' Bobby Black responded. 'I speak American and, in plain American, we need to understand these people a whole lot less, and condemn a whole lot more.'

'I speak Human,' Kristina contradicted Bobby Black a second time, which is maybe where all the trouble between them started. 'And it's the human battle we need to win.'

The President looked at Kristina, then at his Vice-President, and decided the novels should stay on the White House reading list. As Kristina told me the gist of the story that day waiting for Bobby Black, she suggested some bookstore titles for me, beginning with an Egyptian novel called *The Yacoubian Building*.

'A young man from a poor background wants to become a police officer,' she told me, 'but he's from the wrong class and can't afford the bribes. So this decent young guy becomes a terrorist instead. The author says the real disease in the Muslim world is despotism. Terrorism is just one of the symptoms. He's right.'

I tried to digest this thought.

'So, has the Vice-President read this insightful book?' I asked mischievously. Kristina Taft laughed again. I had broken through. I could see her visibly relax in my company, and I sensed an opportunity. Bobby Black was shaping up to be the most powerful Vice-President in US history, even more powerful than Dick Cheney. After Manila, Theo Carr announced that Black would be in charge of anti-terrorism policy. It was difficult for me to see how his approach and Kristina's ideas could ever work together in the same administration. She would need allies. So would I.

'More than two hundred American dead,' Bobby Black had said in speeches in the dying days of the campaign. 'Two hundred and forty seven of our people; thirty-nine of other nationalities. Two hundred and forty seven of *Us*. Every American will be avenged. You have my word. No – More – Manilas.'

All through the transition, London had badgered me to find out what this sabre-rattling talk actually meant. The most important question for any British government is always to figure out what the Americans are up to, and I am the person who is supposed to know.

'The Spartacus Solution,' I told Andy Carnwath when he contacted me at Fraser Davis's insistence.

'What the fuck is that?' he said. Phone conversations with Andy Carnwath are typically littered with so many expletives that within the Civil Service they are known as 'The Vagina Monologues'. I explained that the British military attaché had heard whispers in the Pentagon that Bobby Black had been very impressed by a discussion paper written by an obscure US Army General, Conrad Shultz. General Shultz – according to the DoD, the Department of Defence buzz – had written a paper during a year's sabbatical at West Point calling for '*The Spartacus Solution*' to terrorism.

I had no idea what the paper was about but I reminded Carnwath that Spartacus led the slave rebellion against the Romans. He and his fellow rebels were crucified on the roads into Rome.

29

'Jesus fucking Christ,' Carnwath said. 'Slaves? Crucified? You'd better get a copy of this fucking fairytale, Alex. Top priority.'

The urgency of getting a copy of 'The Spartacus Solution' became even more obvious when Theo Carr announced that General Shultz was to become the new Director of Central Intelligence.

'So, come on, has the Vice-President been reading anything on your booklist, Dr Taft?' I teased. 'I mean, anything at all?'

'Vice?' Kristina replied mischievously, sipping her black coffee and using a nickname for the Vice-President that was already current in Washington, even though he had been in the White House for such a short time. 'Vice boasted to me that he hasn't read a storybook in thirty years and did not need fiction to tell him that, once you've got people by the balls, their hearts and minds will follow. So I guess I have some work to do.'

She watched for my reaction. I nodded, sympathetically. Diplomatic Warning Bell Number Two went off in my head. Dr Kristina Taft had now clearly signalled to me that there was serious tension in the White House, and the Carr administration was less than ten days old. Perhaps she was also signalling that she herself was out of her depth, but I was less sure of that. It would take me a long time to find out what her depth might be.

We were interrupted by an aide who came through to say that Bobby Black had finished his meeting with President Carr and was now ready to see us. We walked down the corridor. The Vice-President was behind his desk. He did not get up. He did not apologize for keeping me waiting.

'Ambassador Price.' We shook hands. His fist was cold and moist, like wet dough. The air smelled strongly of lily pollen.

'Mr Vice-President.'

'You know Johnny Lee.' Johnny Lee Ironside nodded. I was glad to see him. He was to become a guide into the Heart of

30

Darkness that is the OVP, the Office of the Vice-President. I congratulated Bobby Black on the election.

'I'm very pleased to see you here in the White House, Mr Vice-President,' I said. 'The Prime Minister has instructed me to pass on his personal congratulations and his sense of awe', I continued, 'at your ability to confound conventional wisdom. Prime Minister Davis would like to learn your election-winning secret.'

Bobby Black smiled the way a car salesman does with an irritating customer.

'Our secret is that winning the War on Terror isn't the most important thing,' he said. 'It's the *only* thing. The voters of this country understand that. I'm hoping to get your Prime Minister to understand that too. It's kind of like missionary activity on our part you might say. Spreading the word.'

The November election had been a split decision. Carr and Black had won the White House but the Democrats scraped through to keep control, narrowly, of Congress. That was one of the reasons I was so keen to meet the new House Speaker, Betty Furedi, later that day, to try to gauge how much she would cooperate with Carr, and how much she might get in the way. Vice-President Black looked across the desk at me and blinked. A slack, lopsided grin appeared across his face.

'Fear', he said, by way of further explanation of the election victory, 'works.'

I took a breath. If Bobby Black thought fear was a useful weapon to use upon the American electorate, then perhaps our discussions about the treatment of British terrorist suspects like Muhammad Asif Khan might not be about to go so well. I looked at Kristina Taft. She pulled out a Montblanc pen and gazed at the yellow legal pad in front of her. She did not catch my eye. The Vice-President launched into a short speech.

'Newspaper stories in your country about torture', he began softly, 'are not helpful: not helpful to President Carr and this

31

administration, not helpful to my people, not helpful to the fight against terror, and not helpful to the close cooperation between our two countries.' Bobby Black went on to explain that in what he called 'exceptional circumstances and exceptional times' the 'exceptional' use of torture was justified. 'You do not need me to remind you that, since Manila, these are exceptional circumstances,' he emphasized, 'which is why the President as Commander-in-Chief has authorized enhanced interrogation techniques. Some people choose to equate these with torture. I don't care what word you use. I care that we get the job done.'

He hit a doughy hand on the table in front of him for emphasis. The Vice-President did not equivocate. Nor did he talk about 'robust treatment of detainees', which is the phrase that a beleaguered Prime Minister Davis had used in the Commons. And he did not try to pretend all this was simply some rough stuff that had got out of hand. Bobby Black confirmed to me that one of the first acts of the Carr Administration had been to sign what was known as National Security Directive 1402227. He clasped his hands together in an attitude of prayer and calmly explained that this directive specifically authorized the use of 'highly coercive methods of interrogation by the United States', which might be considered to fall within the United Nations definition of torture. This time he did not say 'fuck the United Nations', though I suspected he was thinking it.

'The presidential authorization', Black said, 'comes with safeguards.'

'Safeguards?' I repeated. 'What safeguards can you have on highly coercive interrogation, Mr Vice-President?' He tapped his fingers together. His ruthlessness had an honest face. He never pretended otherwise.

'All highly coercive procedures must be carried out under the supervision of a designated senior CIA officer. Only the Central Intelligence Agency – not the US military – only the CIA is authorized to carry out these enhanced interrogation procedures.'

I gulped. So, those were the safeguards? In their entirety? There was a pause while I was allowed to digest these statements.

'Well, in the Khan case—' I began, but Bobby Black cut me off. He said it was 'just one of those things' that the story had got into the British press, and that he did not bear grudges about that.

'In fact, I'm mighty grateful the British media are reporting we are playing hardball with al Qaeda and their British supporters like Mr Khan,' he said. 'Because we are. We are serious. Committed. Determined. We do not do this lightly. It shows the nature of the exceptional threat we face.'

He had the franchise on the word 'exceptional'.

'Legally Mr Khan is not—'

'Legally we have a Golden Shield, Ambassador Price. A Get-Out-Of-Jail-Free card. The President, under the Constitution of the United States, has absolute authority to manage a military campaign as he sees fit, including whichever enhanced interrogation techniques he chooses to authorize, notwithstanding any definitions of torture used by foreign powers or multinational organizations.'

'But the United Nations' definition . . .'

He grinned. 'You know what I think of the United Nations.'

I tried to change the subject. 'Specifically, when it comes to British citizens like Muhammad Asif Khan—'

'Well, let me tell you about British citizens,' Bobby Black interrupted again, 'including the British citizen who was the Manila suicide bomber, your Mr Fuad . . .' He paused for effect. 'The fact that British citizens might be subject to coercive interrogation techniques shows that we do not discriminate in favour of our closest friends and allies. Look around this room.' I did as I was bid. Kristina Taft still did not catch my eye. 'There's a new team in Washington, Ambassador. We have a mandate from the American people to go after the Bad Guys, to implement what some of us are calling "The Spartacus Solution", and I intend to see we do it.'

'The Spartacus Solution?' I leaned forward with real interest now. 'I have heard the term but I . . .'

'Yeah,' Bobby Black said, and nodded to Johnny Lee Ironside. 'Give the Ambassador a copy, Johnny Lee. With my compliments.'

Johnny Lee handed me a short bound document of maybe fifty pages of A4. I felt thrilled, as if I had just been handed the Holy Grail, but I tried not to look too pleased. The document said on the front: 'The Spartacus Solution – how the United States will win the War on Terror.' The Vice-President looked over at Kristina.

'This is the kind of bedtime reading that might get us somewhere against these SOBs, even more than storybooks, isn't that right, Dr Taft?'

Kristina looked up and smiled. It did not take much emotional intelligence to understand what she was thinking behind that smile.

'Thank you, Mr Vice-President,' I said, to break the awkward silence.

'You're most welcome,' Bobby Black responded. 'Anything and everything for our British friends. Now, before you go, Ambassador, Johnny Lee tells me you had experience in the British Army in Ireland?'

'As a very young man in Northern Ireland, yes, Mr Vice-President. I had a short time in Military Intelligence and—'

'So, if you and your British Military Intelligence buddies could have prevented a terrorist attack, let's say the bombings on the London Tube, by torturing one or two bad guys, would you have done it?'

'If,' I replied, clutching at 'The Spartacus Solution' document, as though it might be taken away as punishment for giving the wrong answer. 'It's a big "if",' Mr Vice-President.

When you begin to torture someone, you can never know for certain if—'

'Of course you damn well would use torture,' he answered his own question definitively, snapping at me but again never raising his voice. 'Torture works. Fear works. Read Spartacus and tell me you agree.'

I blanched. It sounded like an order.

'Mr Vice-President,' I responded, keeping as calm as possible, 'I will of course read "Spartacus", and thank you again for the documents. But I also read American history. De Tocqueville wrote that America is great because America is good. In the worst days of your Civil War in Eighteen Sixty-three, President Lincoln signed into law instructions to the Union Army that torture and cruelty were not to be permitted. With great respect to you, Mr Vice-President, if Lincoln could win a war for the very existence of the United States without using torture, so can we now in the twenty-first century. I prefer Lincoln over Spartacus.'

Everyone in the room was looking at me now, including Kristina. Bobby Black stretched his neck like a turtle emerging from its shell.

'Well, thank you kindly for the historical lecture, Ambassador,' he said slowly. 'But I think you will find that in Lincoln's day nobody was blowing up airliners with C4 plastic explosives or crashing them into skyscrapers filled with civilians. The Confederates were not suicide bombers. The people we now have to face down – well, they inhabit a different moral universe from the rest of us normal folks, and your Prime Minister needs to get out front and centre of this and get your own citizens into line. The human-rights question people oughtta focus on is the right of normal folks to go about their business without getting blown up by some British fanatic like Rashid Ali Fuad in Manila or your friend, Mr Khan. If you don't see your problem, well, we do. And if you don't act, we will.'

35

Bobby Black gently slapped both wet palms down on the desk. He was white with anger and it was clear that the meeting was over. I said something about democratically elected governments not being able to pick and choose which aspects of human rights to support, which to abandon, depending upon apparent necessity. I said this not because it would change anything, but for the weakest of diplomatic reasons – so that I could report back to Downing Street that I had made a protest on behalf of the UK government. They could spin it to the press and in the Commons. Bobby Black looked at me with pity on his face, as if I had farted, and out of a generous spirit he'd decided to ignore the smell. His eyes were glazing over with indifference.

'Thank you for your time, Ambassador,' he said, reaching forward to shake my hand. Wet dough again. 'Enjoy your bedtime reading.'

Johnny Lee Ironside nodded at me. 'Good to see you, Alex. Let's get caught up soon.'

Kristina Taft showed me out.

'You're brave,' she whispered. 'Not many do that.'

'Is it always like this?' I replied, putting the copy of 'The Spartacus Solution' in my attaché case and presuming on a connection with her that I sensed I had now made. Kristina did not reply until we were almost at my car, which – I noticed – was now parked at the more private south entrance, away from the cameras.

'Pretty much,' she said. Then she tugged gently at my sleeve. 'Maybe we should talk,' she whispered. 'We seem to be on the same page on all of this.'

I nodded.

'You were brave too. Over the books.'

She shrugged. 'It's not brave to do what you think is right.'

I looked straight into her grey eyes and a moment of recognition passed between us. One of the peculiarities about being British Ambassador in Washington is that there are always factions within US administrations, and sometimes they see you as a potential ally, a useful tool or even as an intelligence asset for use against the other factions. It is a difficult and dangerous game to play. It's also thrilling. Being allowed to play it at all makes the British a little bit special in the diplomatic corps in Washington.

'Of course, let's talk,' I responded. 'Any time. You say when.'

'Not in the White House,' she said. 'I'll figure out someplace. I might need more help than you think. Later today they're announcing that I'm being promoted to National Security Adviser.'

'Congratulations!' I was genuinely pleased for her, though I was not sure she would survive. She was too young, too inexperienced, and Bobby Black already had his tanks on her lawn. He was already doing her job.

'I'll call you,' Kristina said.

I understood. Or at least I thought I understood. If the meeting I had just endured was a sign of things to come, then relations between Britain and the United States were about to take a serious turn for the worse, mostly as a result of one man. Kristina would need friends and so would I. I was also flattered and intrigued to be asked to spend time with one of the rising stars of the Carr administration.

I climbed back into my car and told the driver to take me to the rest of that day's meetings on Capitol Hill – but he informed me of a surprise hitch. While I had been meeting Vice-President Black, Speaker Furedi's office had called the embassy to cancel. She had to be in the House chamber for an emergency session to discuss the Carr administration's demands for a huge increase in defence funding. The Carr team wanted to rewrite the entire budget as an emergency antiterrorism measure. Carr and Black were talking about Spartacus and vengeance for Manila, while Betty Furedi and the Democrats in Congress were reluctant to pay for whatever it was they had in mind.

'We're sorry, Ambassador,' Furedi's Chief of Staff, a soft-voiced Californian called John Crockett said to me when I rang him for details. 'I hope you understand. We'll reschedule.' I always thought Crockett was a decent man.

'Of course, John. Not a problem. I know how busy Speaker Furedi must be. Call me.'

Suddenly I had a two-hour hole in my day. I felt like a schoolboy who is told that lessons are cancelled. I had nothing planned, nothing to fit in, and I realized that I also had a longing to see Fiona. I would apologize and tell her that I would no longer try to hurry her into motherhood, and that perhaps she should spend more time in England. I sensed that she felt trapped. I would make the peace and buy flowers on the way back to the embassy. I replanned my day very quickly. First, I would call Downing Street and tell them about Bobby Black and the Khan case. Then I would mention – just in passing – that I had obtained from the Vice-President himself a copy of the document that we all were so desperate to see, General Shultz's report on fighting terrorism, 'The Spartacus Solution'. Then – after receiving the well-deserved congratulations of a grateful British people from Downing Street – I would give Fiona a big surprise.

FOUR

By the time I stepped out of the Rolls-Royce at the embassy
with the copy of 'The Spartacus Solution' in my attaché case
in one hand and a bunch of flowers for Fiona in the other,
the ice storm had rolled in over the Potomac and all down
the Chesapeake Bay. The roads were slick, the air bitterly
chilled, the sidewalks mostly empty. Dampness seeped through
my coat like cold fingers. I stopped off at a florist's near
Dupont Circle to buy Fiona as large a bunch of flowers as I
could find. I forget what, exactly. Roses. Maybe tulips. They
were just closing because of the ice storm, and grateful for
the business.

When I reached the Great House, as the Ambassador's residence is sometimes called, I walked into the living quarters.
I put the attaché case down. I had the flowers in my hand
and I bounded up the red-carpeted stairs two at a time, like
an eager suitor, anxious to make amends. Fiona sometimes
worked at her interior designs in the library, and so I tried it
first, but there was no sign of her. I checked my watch and
decided that she might be exercising on the treadmill in the
small gym next to the main guest bedroom, but there was no
sign of her there either. I turned the flowers in my hand. I
was about to head towards the final possibility, that she was

still in our own bedroom, when I heard a noise from the guest quarters. I turned. You never know what twist of fate, what nerve or synapse drives you to take a decision, but I suddenly threw open the door of the guest quarters.

Fiona and her lover were in front of the three large mirrors above the dresser. They had angled the mirrors so they could watch themselves. He was naked. Fiona wore a black bra, nothing else. Their clothes had been discarded carelessly and were strewn on the floor. He was behind her, holding her hips with his big hands. She was grasping the table top of the dresser in front of the mirror and gasping. I could not see Fiona's face. Her hair was stuck to her skin with sweat. The man turned and I recognized James Byrne, the *Washington Post* columnist, immediately. He had been over for dinner at the embassy a number of times, to parties and diplomatic receptions. I had known him since before I was Ambassador, and before he had been given his syndicated column. Byrne was standing upright, his hips moving. He is a big man, bigger than me, over six feet, slim and muscled, a Bostonian who had played American football for one of the Ivy League college teams. He had hair on his back and shoulders, like a monkey. The hair was slick with sweat and it disgusted me.

I said, 'Get your dick out of my wife.'

Byrne looked at me and stepped away from her. Fiona turned too. She stood up slowly and put her hands to her face in shock. She gasped something which I did not catch, clasped her breasts and ran towards the bathroom. I heard her slam the door, but all the time I was watching Byrne. I walked towards him and hit him once, hard, in the throat with my fist. He fell to the floor like a puppet whose strings have been cut, gasping for breath. I stood for a moment and thought about killing him, but the moment passed. Instead I turned him over with my foot and looked at him gagging on the floor, then I walked out of the room. I had to step over the flowers, which were scattered all over the floor. Despite the ice storm, Fiona left for London that very same day, on the overnight flight from Dulles to Heathrow. Tulips. The flowers were definitely tulips.

FIVE

Some people are in the fund-raising business. I am in the friend-raising business. When you are a British diplomat in the United States, you look around and decide who the future leaders and opinion-formers might be, and in the words of Prime Minister Davis's Communications Director, Andy Carnwath, 'You get up their arse, Alex, and you stay there.' Diplomacy is political proctology. *Up the arse and stay there.*

I am regarded as being good at it. A few years back, just before Fiona and I were married, I was Number Three at the Washington embassy. I sensed that Governor Theo Carr was preparing a run for the presidency as soon as I heard he had hired Arlo Luntz as his Chief Political Adviser. Luntz is a world-class operative. Like Bobby Black, I don't much like him, but I do respect him. All three of us – Black, Luntz and me – have one thing in common: we came from nowhere, we were born to nothing, and we try to do the best we can. I respect that. Anyway, at the time I persuaded the then British Ambassador in Washington that I should go down and meet this Theo Carr before he hit the big time. Luntz called me back straight away.

'Sure,' he said, sensing an opportunity of his own. 'Governor Carr always makes time for our British friends.'

I hurriedly made arrangements. Luntz greeted me at the Governor's Mansion. He is unimpressive to look at, a badly dressed, shambling figure with scuffed shoes and an appalling jet-black wig, but what lies beneath the bad wig has made him one of the most sought-after political consultants anywhere in the United States. Luntz walked down the central staircase in the mansion towards me wearing a stained blue suit, which fitted him the way a horsebox fits a horse. We shook hands and I followed him upstairs to meet Governor Theo Carr. We sat on the porch at the back of the mansion, the three of us, drinking iced tea and chewing over world affairs.

'To what do we owe this honour, Mr Price?'

'Please call me Alex, Governor. I was just passing through on my way west and I thought it would be good to say hello.'

I offered to host a visit to London, guaranteeing that Governor Carr could speak to Members of Parliament, my future brother-in-law (who was then the Leader of the Opposition,) government ministers, and maybe even the then Prime Minister, Fraser Davis's predecessor.

Carr and Luntz nodded that it would be a good idea. Of course it was a good idea. A convenient friendship was born.

'Passing through our state capital? No way,' Theo Carr told me as I prepared to leave. He had that famous twinkling in his eyes and a cheeky grin. 'Delighted as we are to see you, Mr Price, no one just passes through here.'

Theo Carr was Governor of a state of 'flyover people' – the people you fly over on the way between the east and west coasts.

'Busted,' I admitted, holding my hands up in mock surrender. 'I made a point of coming to see you, Governor Carr. You are worth a deliberate detour, as they say in the tourist guidebooks.'

He laughed. 'Yeah, like a National Park. And why might the – what's that title again? – Minister Counsellor at the

43

Embassy of the United Kingdom in Washington be sufficiently interested in Governor Theo Carr to make a detour?'

'Talent spotting,' I laughed along with him. 'I think you might be President of the United States one day . . .'

'You – and Arlo here – and my momma, God bless her,' he interrupted with more twinkling and more of a grin. 'Makes three of you. Just a couple of hundred million American voters to go.'

'. . . and I thought we should do what dogs do in the street, and sniff noses.'

Theo Carr laughed uproariously. So did Luntz.

'Let's just leave it at noses,' he guffawed, and slapped me on the shoulder. It was a Gateway Moment. Fast-forward a few years, and now here I am promoted to Ambassador and he is what the US Secret Service calls POTUS, President of the United States, and Arlo Luntz is the most highly regarded and devious political consultant on the planet. It was worth the deliberate detour.

'We didn't do so badly, Alex,' Theo Carr told me at the White House reception for the Inauguration, 'for a coupla country boys.'

In those first months of his presidency – and despite all the trouble I was having with Vice-President Black – President Carr, building on that early familiarity, always called me by my first name.

At diplomatic functions or G8 Summits he would point at me in that friendly way of his, and call out, 'Yo, Brit Guy, how's the nose-sniffin' comin' along?'

None of this *bonhomie* made any impression on the Vice-President. Month after month it seemed to me that Black had a moat around him, like an old-fashioned castle.

'The drawbridge is up, the portcullis down, defences primed to repel invaders, Alex,' Johnny Lee Ironside once told me. Johnny Lee has many talents, of course, including a fine turn of phrase. He's loyal. Discreet. Clever. And unlike those who talk behind the Vice-President's back, Johnny Lee genuinely admired and respected Black, yet even he sometimes called his boss by the Churchillian phrase once applied to Soviet Russia – a riddle inside an enigma, wrapped in a mystery. What makes Johnny Lee special is that he is part of a dying breed within American politics, a gut-instinct Anglophile who does not just *think* relations between Britain and America are the most important rock for the United States, he breathes and eats it. Once when we were talking about the aloof nature of his boss, Johnny Lee confided that he had been reading the works of Evelyn Waugh and they provided a clue.

'The Vice-President is an Englishman,' Johnny Lee informed me, bizarrely.

I did not understand. 'The Vice-President is from Montana,' I blurted out. 'Couldn't be further from English in every way.' The centre of gravity in American politics had shifted from East Coast anglophiles like Johnny Lee to people like Theo Carr, Bobby Black, and Kristina Taft. They were all from the West or Midwest. Johnny Lee shook his head.

'Your Mr Waugh says that an English gentleman understands two social states – Intimacy and Formality. Intimacy is for family, lovers, and close friends. Formality is for everybody else.' Johnny Lee smiled. He delights in being more learned about English culture than those of us who happen to be British. 'Whereas we colonial-American types are capable of three social attitudes – Intimacy, Formality – but also *Familiarity*.'

I congratulated him. It was a great insight into Bobby Black's character. Unlike many Americans, he could not do Familiarity. Theo Carr is the administration's backslapping baby kisser. Bobby Black isn't.

'So how do you explain it?' I wondered.

'British genes,' Johnny Lee said. 'The Black family is from Scotland, 'parently.'

Ah, I thought. A useful clue to the heart of Bobby Black's darkness. Not Englishness after all, but Presbyterianism. The Vice-President was some kind of dour Scot from the mountains of Montana, with a chip on his shoulder about the English. I filed this piece of information away for further consideration.

As Arlo Luntz tells it, friendship in Washington, like that between me and Johnny Lee, is a 'power resource'. It enables you to get things done. The more friends you have, the more stellar the cast list at your dinner parties, the more influential you are . . . therefore the more friends you have . . . and so on, in a virtuous circle of power. Luntz is full of little observations and proverbs like this, rules for conduct in modern politics. He told me once that Washington DC Rule Number One is 'Don't Make Unnecessary Enemies.' Rule Two is that 'the bigger your friends, the more juice you have', 'juice' being Washington slang for power or influence, though not always in a good way.

'And you have plenty juice, Ambassador Price,' Luntz said to me, almost as an aside. 'Anybody whose brother-in-law happens to be Prime Minister has plenty juice.'

In that first year of the Carr presidency, Vice-President Bobby Black had more juice than anyone in DC, except perhaps Carr himself, and yet he routinely broke Arlo Luntz's basic rules. Bobby Black stomped on people. He made enemies, necessary and – like Kristina Taft and me – unnecessary enemies too. His own friends were anonymous corporate types from his previous business past, middle-aged balding men in grey suits who ran oil companies, high-tech businesses and private security corporations, plus lawyers and lobbyists from what Washingtonians call 'Gucci Gulch' – a corridor of nastiness along K Street in northwest Washington. It takes its name from the inhabitants who wear $500 tasselled Gucci loafers along with their $2,000 suits.

'Friends in the shadows,' Johnny Lee Ironside once told me of his boss, without explanation. 'FOBs.'

FOBs meant 'Friends of Bobby'. I knew some of the names. Just the names. Ron Gold of Goldcrest, the energy and private security consortium, was a long time FOB. So was Paul Comfort, the CEO of Warburton, the high-tech military and construction contractor. Warburton had somehow snagged all the latest contracts for rebuilding Iraq. This caused more bad feeling with Downing Street, much more than the public row about torture, Manila, Muhammad Asif Khan or the United Nations all put together. Fraser Davis was furious. He shouted at me on the secure line that the Americans had their snouts in the trough. More importantly, we did not.

'British jobs are at stake, Alex!'

He demanded an explanation of how $7 billion in Iraqi contracts went to just one company, Warburton, on a no-bid basis, meaning no British firms could compete.

'A billion dollars worth of these infrastructure projects is in the south – Basra – that's supposed to be our bailiwick, Alex!'

'I don't think the Americans see it like that, Prime Minister.'

'But . . . the Vice-President gave you a copy of that Spartacus document. He must think highly of you, yes? And of his relationship with the United Kingdom government? And yet he did not talk about the Iraq contracts?'

'You know what it is like dealing with the Vice-President, Prime Minister. It's not easy.'

I lamely tried to explain that no American firms were allowed to compete for the contracts either, and that Speaker Betty Furedi had promised a Congressional investigation into what she called the 'Iraqi sweetheart deal scandal.'

'But investigations in this town are like belly buttons, Prime Minister,' I said, 'everyone's got one.'

Davis was apoplectic but impotent.

'It's just not right,' he bellowed, 'just not right.'

* * *

Warburton's CEO Paul Comfort, like Bobby Black, was from Montana. They were childhood friends. People suspected something in their relationship, but could not get to the bottom of it. Campaign contributions? Soft money? I'd heard Comfort was a 'bundler' – one of the people who 'bundled' contributions together from many sources and provided Bobby Black with serious and above board cash. But Gold and Comfort were just names to me. I read about them in the *Wall Street Journal* business pages. I knew they were members of NEST – Bobby Black's National Energy Strategy Taskforce – set up to map out US energy policy for the twenty-first century, but you never saw them on TV, they never gave interviews, I never had the pleasure of meeting them. Men, as Johnny Lee said, from the shadows.

Johnny Lee Ironside also says that outside the White House there are five permanent Washington Tribes – Diplomats, Congressmen, Lawyers, Journalists, and Lobbyists. The Five Tribes overlap. Their people sleep with each other and sometimes marry. They play golf and poker, entertain together, commit adultery, and their children go to the same schools. Members of all Five Tribes know that, like the Carr–Black administration, the people in the White House come and go, but the Tribes go on forever. Superficially the Tribes defer to the Office of the President, and to the Office of the Vice-President, but all the time they know that the President and Vice-President will only trouble the permanent Tribes at most for eight years before being replaced by the next incumbents. The Office of the Vice-President is, of course, proverbially 'one heartbeat away' from the most powerful job in the world, but those of us in the permanent Five Washington Tribes feared Bobby Black, because he was much more important than that.

Here's an example. A Wednesday morning, just after 11 a.m., six months after the Inauguration. An intruder, a deranged man from West Virginia, leaped over the White House fence

48

and ran towards the Oval Office, threatening to kill President Carr. He set off the alarms and was stopped by the Secret Service before he could get more than twenty metres. The deranged man had a gun, an old Smith & Wesson revolver, and the Secret Service shot him in both legs. He was lucky they did not kill him immediately. The gun turned out to be empty. Not a bullet in the chamber. I was in the library of the Great House at the embassy on Massachusetts Avenue where I like to work.

CNN were live in the White House pressroom where Sandy McAuley, the Communications Director, was fielding reporters' questions about the incident. I put my papers to one side and watched.

'Where was the President – and the Vice-President – at the time of the incident?' one of the reporters asked.

McAuley twitched a little. 'Vice-President Black was at his desk in the West Wing, working on papers.'

Pause.

'But where was President Carr?'

McAuley twitched some more. 'President Carr was in the family quarters.'

'Doing what?'

'President Carr was exercising on a rowing machine in the gym.'

You could hear the intake of breath from the journalists, and a few titters of laughter. Even those of us who are not professional workaholics usually put in a few hours work in the mornings. It was just after 11 a.m. on a weekday, six months after President Theo Carr's election, and when a nutty assassin tried to get in to the White House, the President was on a rowing machine? And Vice-President Bobby Black was in the West Wing, at his desk, working on papers? Running the country? Told you something, didn't it?

*   *   *

49

Kristina Taft understood this quicker than anyone. She had been confirmed as National Security Adviser and called me a couple of days later. She decreed that our first private meeting would not, under any circumstances, take place at the White House. She suggested breakfast one morning at her apartment in the Watergate.

'At six.'

I gulped. 'Six a.m.? Sure.'

Kristina explained that she usually woke at five, sat on an exercise bike for thirty minutes, read some papers, and then left in time to get to the White House before seven every morning. I considered the private meeting a show of trust and an honour.

'I don't want word to get out to anyone,' she warned me.

'Anyone?' I responded.

'Especially not the Vice-President. I'll send the help away.'

By the 'help' she meant her security staff as well as her maid. When we met she was alone.

'I'm the new kid on the block,' she said over poached eggs and muffins. From the start there were whispers that Kristina was too young for the job, and that it was not much of a job anyway – just 'executive assistant' to the Vice-President who was driving national security policy himself. In Washington it's like this. You can go from being 'up-and-coming' to 'has-been' without any intervening period of success. I could feel Kristina's nervousness.

'Until this administration, I only ever came to DC as a tourist,' she said. 'You have been here for years, Alex. I need advice on how to handle it. How to get it right.'

'Arlo Luntz will tell you that there are no second acts in Washington life. You have to get it right first time.'

'Luntz is extraordinary.'

'Yes,' I said, 'take time to get to know him. He'll also tell you that the best people know what they do *not* know, and strive to fix it.'

Maybe that was the reason I liked Kristina from the start. That was what she was like too. In that first breakfast meeting I suppose I showed off a bit. I told her how administrations had functioned in the past. I had been in Washington for part of the Clinton years and part of the George W. Bush debacle, and I knew people who remembered Bush senior, Reagan, and Carter.

'Who was it who said that happy families are all alike, but unhappy families are each unhappy in their own particular way? Anyway, the same is true for political administrations or governments. In my experience, they always end unhappily.'

'Always?'

'Always. Sometimes, like now, they begin unhappily. Unhappy does not mean ineffective. DoD, State, Justice, and the CIA are always at each other's throats. That's normal. That's life. That's power. You – as National Security Adviser – have to act as referee. Honest broker. That's why President Carr wants you around. He trusts you to be honest and fair. Sometimes the infighting will suck in Treasury as well, but all of that's manageable. The problem . . . well, I'm not sure how you can fix a problem like Bobby Black.'

'Me neither,' she admitted, brushing a few crumbs of muffin from her lips.

'You want people to read novels on Muslim culture; he wants to bomb somewhere. Almost anywhere will do. There's not a lot of give and take here, I'm thinking. He's a problem for us too.'

'Fiction', Kristina shrugged, but her face remained impassive, 'is always a kind of Lie, but it only works because it is also a kind of Truth. And it is a Truth we all need to hear, even Vice. I have been talking to Arlo about this. Arlo is in on everything, and he jumped in on my side about the reading list. It was a small thing, but it helped.'

'How exactly?'

'Arlo told the President that all power demands a degree

of fiction. The way Arlo sees it, people in power are not supposed to lie, but they cannot tell the truth all the time either. We require believable stories, simple explanations, myths, what the newspapers call "spin". A convenient fiction, Arlo calls it, and he says it is better than a complicated truth for most voters.'

'The real question is, whose spin, whose fiction, or whose myth gets accepted,' I said. 'Whose truth or version of the truth do we trust?'

'That's why history always belongs to the victors,' Kristina said, offering me another toasted bagel, which I declined. 'Winners dictate the truth. More coffee?'

'Please.'

'So, anyhow . . . Spartacus,' she switched tack as she poured. I watched her carefully, not sure what to make of her. She spoke fast; she thought fast; she did not suffer fools gladly, or at all. And I confess that from that first conversation she wound me into her. I would gladly have stepped inside her brain with a flashlight and have a look around.

'Yes, Spartacus.'

'Well?' Her grey eyes were steady as they looked into mine. 'You were in Northern Ireland, right? Would the Spartacus Solution have helped?'

She arched an eyebrow. She already knew my answer.

That night of the ice storm, the night I had discovered Fiona with James Byrne, Fiona had immediately packed her bags and headed to the airport in the teeth of the bad weather. She caught the overnight British Airways flight back to London. We did not say goodbye. After she left I sat in the study at the ambassador's residence, poured myself a large whisky and read through General Conrad Shultz's document. Page after page of it promised a relentless war on terrorists, their supporters, and the regimes that gave them space to operate.

'Well, Spartacus is a view, I suppose,' I told Kristina. 'A

one-eyed, one-dimensional approach – let's kill bad people. If only life were that simple, and that all the Bad People wore black hats so we knew who they were. What we learned in Northern Ireland is that nobody is born a terrorist. We are all born as babies. So you need to have a two- or three-dimensional approach – fight, kill if you have to, but also persuade, cajole, bribe, whatever it takes to stop the baby growing up wanting to kill you . . .'

'Exactly!' she clapped her hands together and poured me more coffee. 'Exactly! Do you think it sends the right signal when the new Director of Central Intelligence says we should treat terrorists like ancient Rome treated rebellious slaves, crucifying them on the streets? And the Vice-President buys into it? It's just another Faith-Based Initiative – you do it and you pray to God it might work. Well, what happens when this is leaked? When some of it gets in the newspapers? You know what the reaction on the Arab street will be? "Here come the Christian Crusaders one more time." It plays into every prejudice about us and our motives. Dinosaurs. Goddamn dinosaurs.'

Now it was my turn to shrug. 'I don't understand why Black and Shultz seem so determined to piss off a billion Muslims, most of whom do not want to be our enemies.'

'Me neither,' Kristina shook her head. I could feel her mind whirring with ideas. 'Spartacus will tear us in two,' she said, indiscreetly. 'You are either for it or against it, and . . . I guess I've said enough.'

It was time for me to go. I asked to use her bathroom while she cleared the breakfast dishes. I have always been nosey about other people's lives. At parties I sometimes open bathroom cabinets and take a peek. In Kristina's case perhaps I was looking for signs of human habitation. Did she have a man? Why did I care? As I peed, I looked around. There were no signs of male habitation, but I noticed a polished steel cabinet on the wall. I don't know why I tried to open it, but

I did. It was locked, of course, and with no sign of a key. Perhaps Kristina expected from her visitors precisely the kind of nosiness I was demonstrating. When I came out of the bathroom Kristina walked me to the door. She gazed straight into my eyes and gave me that smile of hers.

'Can I ask you something else?'

'Of course,' I said.

'I hear you and Fiona split up a couple of months back.'

I swallowed. 'I . . . we . . . have things to . . . work out.'

Kristina looked at me with sympathetic warmth. 'Washington is a killer for relationships. Harry Truman said that if you want a friend in Washington, get a dog.'

I laughed. 'Harry Truman also said that if you tell someone to go to hell you should be able to see that he gets there. An observation which is lost on the Vice-President, I think.'

'Does the Fiona thing affect your relations with the Prime Minister?'

'No. At least I don't think so.'

'That's good.'

We kissed each other goodbye, on the cheek, chastely, European style.

'Let's do this again,' she said.

'Definitely,' I replied.

It was by now seven thirty on a Monday morning and by her standards Kristina Taft was already late for work. I wanted to see her again, even if the reasons why were jumbled up in my head. I caught a cab from the Watergate up Embassy Row, my mind buzzing from the meeting, wondering whether I should call Kristina back and if so when.

I had no time to take a decision because the moment I arrived at my desk I received a hand-delivered letter from a lawyer employed by James Byrne. I suppose I should have expected it. If anything, after I hit him, I had expected something even worse. I am not sure how he left the residence that day. After the punch to the throat he would have needed medical treatment. I assumed that he might call the police and cite me for assault, but he didn't. What Byrne did do was to get his lawyer, Dan Feingold, to write a threatening letter. It said that I had caused 'laryngeal trauma'. His smashed voice box, according to a specialist's report that the lawyer had helpfully included, meant Byrne faced a permanent impairment in his ability to speak. I confess it made me laugh out loud. The lawyer's letter said Byrne had been 'forced to give up a lucrative career' on the Sunday TV talk shows and would be seeking 'punitive damages' from me. I stared at the letter for a while and when I calmed down, I called the lawyer on the telephone number at the top of the headed notepaper.

'Mr Feingold? Alex Price.'

'I would rather deal with your attorney, Ambassador Price,' he said smoothly.

'I'm sure you would, Mr Feingold,' I replied. 'But you're going to have to deal with me. I regret that Mr Byrne has a voice problem.'

'You do?'

'Yes, I regret it so much that I intend to drive over to his home later today to talk things over with his wife and family. I'll apologize to Mr Byrne and explain matters in detail to his wife and four-year-old son, and then to his editor at the *Washington Post*.' I heard Feingold suck in air. 'In particular I will explain to his wife and child why I am reluctant to pay Mr Byrne financial compensation for fucking my wife in the main guest bedroom of the British Embassy residence.'

Feingold coughed into the telephone. He apologized and said he suffered from allergies. Then he said that before I did anything that could be construed as 'harassment' of his client, he would like to talk to Mr Byrne.

'Of course,' I said. Two hours later, Feingold called me back.

'Ambassador Price, good news, Mr Byrne accepts your apology,' he said, his voice full of defeat. 'Everything is now resolved between you. No further action on your part is necessary.'

'Thank you,' I said, and put down the telephone. Fear, as Bobby Black says, works.

SIX

In the days following our breakfast meeting, I thought a lot about Dr Kristina Taft. When you are the British Ambassador in Washington, when your marriage is breaking up, and your wife is the sister of the Prime Minister, you have to ask yourself whom you can trust, and the answer is almost no one. But from the start I trusted Kristina. Maybe it was a matter of instinct. There was also an obvious attraction, though we kept it hidden. Perhaps at first we even kept it hidden from ourselves. I was intrigued by her intelligence and I particularly liked her observation that Fiction is by definition always a Lie but it only works because it is also a kind of Truth. It hit a chord.

My father ran out when I was a child. My mother found a job, but I was raised mostly by my grandparents and there was never much money. I won a scholarship to a private school where I was always the kid who could not afford to go on the foreign trips, despite my talent for languages. To help pay my way through university I became an officer cadet in the British Army. I studied languages and linguistics, and at first I thought that humans invented stories to show off their language skills. Gradually I came to realize that it is exactly the opposite. Humans invented language because we are bursting with stories to tell, and because that is the way we make sense of, control, and organize our world. We invent stories to play god. *In the beginning was the Word.* Luntz was right too. Everyone complains about political 'spin', but a coherent Lie is much more valuable than an incomplete Truth. That's why governments need people like me, like Luntz and Johnny Lee.

And so I began meeting Kristina regularly. We never called it 'dating', though that was what it became. Sometimes we met formally at White House meetings, semi-formally at dinners or cocktail parties, and occasionally we met in her apartment for a working breakfast. We shared confidences, gossip, and ideas – at least up to a point. She never told me any secrets, she never betrayed anything that would have compromised her position or the Carr administration, though we did frequently consider what we should do about our mutual problem with Bobby Black. Then came the night I drifted into Blues Alley, and our relationship took a different turn. It's a jazz club near where Wisconsin meets M Street in Georgetown. As the name suggests, it is down a back alley, though being Georgetown it is a well-kept, bijou back alley. Once Fiona left, I entertained less often and drifted into Blues Alley a little more, always alone, for the late show and a few beers.

I could guarantee that I would never see anyone I knew. The Washington workaholics – which is most people – are, like Kristina, at their desks at six or seven in the morning, and that means they are in bed by ten. If they happen to be jazz fans, they might take in the early 7.30 p.m. show, but you never see them at anything that finishes after midnight. As for me, I no longer seemed to need much sleep. Jazz past midnight was just fine.

The night I met Kristina in Blues Alley, it's difficult to say which one of us was the more surprised. It was a Friday. Herbie Hancock was playing, and the late show began at

11 p.m., way too late for the kind of people I like to avoid. I was wearing a dark shirt and black jeans and I sat at the corner of the bar in the back with a bourbon on the rocks and a beer. Kristina was already there when I arrived, also alone, at a corner table. I did not see her, but she watched me for a while as I sat at the bar. She said she worked on the same logic as I did – that with a show past midnight, no one she knew would be there. During the second or third Hancock number I felt a movement by my side.

'Like to join me at my table, Ambassador?' Kristina whispered in my ear, so close I could feel the heat of her breath. I was shocked to see her. She giggled with pleasure at my surprise, then I moved over with her and took a seat. She was wearing dark clothes, a black dress and heels. She had let her hair fall down her face and had a touch of jewellery and make-up.

'You look . . . different,' I said lamely. 'You look very nice.'

She smiled and touched my arm. 'I like to remember I am a woman,' she replied. 'Sometimes.'

I signalled for another round of drinks: beer and bourbon for me; vodka tonic and a glass of water for her. We listened to the jazz together with only a few whispered conversations between numbers, though she glanced at me and smiled as if to check that I was enjoying things as much as she was. We had to sit close to talk, and her hair brushed my face. I was aware how good she smelled.

'I love it here,' she whispered in response to one of my questions, 'partly for the music, partly because it is so . . . anonymous. Jazz in Washington is an unnatural vice. A taste of freedom. Or anarchy. A reminder that this is a black southern city, not the uptight place we work in. Everything else is so . . . controlled.'

'You like being naughty?'

'Doesn't everyone?'

By the break in the set, past midnight, I was already slightly drunk. I think she was drunk too. We sat so close together I could feel her breath on my face and neck.

'It's late for you White House people. You turn into pumpkins after dark.'

'Whatever you think of me, Alex, I am a California girl, and my body runs on California time. We wake up three hours after the rest of the country and never catch up.'

Her laughter tinkled over me. She asked me about my background and I told her.

'I have all the lower-middle-class insecurities about never quite fitting in,' I laughed. 'That's why I overcompensate by working so hard.'

'Not fitting in? You're a chameleon, Alex. You blend in everywhere.'

I shook my head. 'Any time soon they will offer me a K, a knighthood – I'll be Sir Alex. It comes with the job. Then, when I go back to London, I get the peerage – I'll be Lord Price of Somewhere-or-Other. And yet . . . people like Fraser will never see me as one of them. Because, deep down, I'm not.'

The whisky was talking.

'Does that matter?' she said, laying a hand on my arm. 'Your Lordship?'

'I guess not,' I shrugged and looked around the nightclub. 'Not in this great democracy.'

She tactfully changed the subject.

'The army must have been rough for a twenty-two year old,' Kristina said. 'Especially Northern Ireland.' I nodded.

'That's why Spartacus gets to me,' I said. 'Because it's like Northern Ireland for slow learners.'

'Meaning?'

'When an IRA sniper took out one of our boys we'd round up a few Republicans and beat the shit out of them. Show them who's boss. Revenge was always a relief, but it didn't help us as much as it helped them. It gave them another grievance and helped them recruit more to the cause.'

60

I drank my whisky.

Kristina was full of questions that night, I think because our relationship really had changed. She asked me directly about Fiona. I told her the whole story.

'You hit Byrne! In the throat! So that's why he sounds like a frog on acid!'

'Shhh. Not so loud.'

She punched the air. 'Yes! At last! On behalf of the government and people of the United States,' Kristina shook my hand in mock seriousness, 'thank you for silencing that major-league asshole. How about you break his typing fingers too, yes? Let me buy you a drink.'

'So, what about you?' I wondered. Herbie Hancock was walking back on stage for the rest of the set. 'What are your secrets, Dr Taft?'

She was drinking a lot of vodka, but then I was drinking a lot of bourbon. I felt her leg shift next to mine as she leaned towards me.

'I have no secrets,' she laughed. 'None. Blameless.'

Her grey eyes danced with amusement behind the cocktail glass.

'But you do have a private life?'

She laughed again. 'Yes, but it's private, Ambassador. Private. Se-cret. It's so private it's a secret even from me. But I . . . I understand why Fiona used Byrne.'

'Used?' I was puzzled by the word. She shrugged.

'Oh, come on. You must have heard the feminist joke? What's the difference between a man and a vibrator? One is cold, mechanical sex. The other runs on batteries? For *some* women at *some* times, a man like Byrne is just something to fill the void – though I don't know why Fiona would hook up with a guy who spends more time on his appearance than she does.'

'The . . . void?'

Kristina looked at me impatiently. 'You know the difference

between the White House and a nunnery? In the White House you get to wear your own clothes. Otherwise, we get up in the morning, pray to God all day we're doing the right thing, and go to bed late at night. Alone. The nunnery of Pennsylvania Avenue.'

'Power's supposed to be an aphrodisiac,' I said.

'Only for those who do not have it,' she said. 'For the happily married, the White House is a strain. For the rest, it's death. Game over.'

'So there is no one in your . . .?' I blurted out.

She shook her head. The music started to grow louder. 'Not any more. It ended when I accepted the job from the President. I'll tell you about Steve sometime, but maybe not tonight.'

She turned away and we watched Herbie Hancock. Steve, I thought. Lucky Steve. We sat through to the end of the set, but I was less interested in the jazz than in her. We stood up to applaud and then sat back down to talk.

'Okay,' she said, as if steeling herself for what she was about to say. By now we had both drunk way too much. Kristina told me that before coming to Washington to talk about the Deputy National Security Adviser job, she had been dating a history professor from Stanford, Stephen Haddon. Haddon was an expert on Germany in the interwar years and the rise of Hitler. They had considered living together. At one point they even talked of marriage, until Carr's people head-hunted her to join his campaign team.

'I couldn't resist,' she said. 'But Steve could. Big time. Maybe if I had known how much I was going to get fucked over by Bobby Black . . .'

She did not complete the thought. Instead she explained that Professor Haddon refused to move east. He wanted nothing – absolutely *nothing* – to do with Washington life, the scrutiny it would bring, or the Carr administration.

'Steve's idea of heaven is to sit in the Public Record Office in Berlin and write about how decent people in a civilized country like Germany became so scared that they allowed their society to be hijacked by Nazis,' Kristina said. 'And who could blame him? Steve isn't even a Republican. Why would he put up with this shit?'

'You loved him.'

'Yes,' Kristina said. 'Part of me still does.'

'Ah,' I said. 'I know the feeling.' Blues Alley was closing and they wanted to clear up. We drained our glasses and walked out into the Georgetown air, which was warm and humid in the late summer heat.

'I need to get a cab,' she said. 'I gave my adult supervision the night off.'

'I'll walk you back . . .'

'There's no need . . . oh, 'kay, what the hell, a walk will clear my head.' She laughed and took my arm. 'I need it to be clear. It's what I'm good at. Newspapers say I'm a Vulcan, 'parently.'

We turned right on M. It was about a mile to the Watergate building. It must have been one o'clock in the morning. Washington is an early town, except for the tourists. The streets were empty.

'I talk to no one about my private life,' Kristina told me as we walked, raising an eyebrow as if the idea startled her. 'And now I have talked to you, Ambassador Alex Price. It's weird.'

'Weird that you trust me?'

'Yes. Even more weird that I want to.'

Her hair fell a little to one side. I put my hand on her, gently. She did not move away.

'Sometimes, I just want to hold someone,' I said softly. 'To put my arms around a woman and hold on. But I . . . have something that keeps me back . . . A fear of failing again.'

We had stopped in the street where M forks towards Pennsylvania Avenue. Kristina looked at me and I felt her hand grasp mine with a quiet desperation.

'Me too,' she said, squeezing hard. 'Me too.'

Her fingers were small, but her touch made my heart pump hard. We stared into each other's eyes and said nothing, did nothing.

'Maybe I made a mistake about Steve.'

'You mean you'd prefer to be the wife of a history professor in California than to work in the White House?'

She laughed. We were still holding hands.

'Maybe I'd prefer to be the wife of a history professor than to work with Bobby Black.'

She laughed again and kissed me suddenly on the lips, just a peck.

'I guess not,' she said.

We stopped holding hands and walked on, briskly. We started to talk about business, once more about what we could do about Bobby Black, and then about the problems Carr was having with Speaker Furedi and the Democrats in Congress, but I remember the grasping of our hands and that peck on the lips as one of the most erotic encounters of my life. We reached the Watergate.

'I'd invite you up but . . .'

'No,' I protested, taking the hint. 'I have to get back.'

'Early start.'

'Yes, always an early start. Sleep is for cissies.'

'We should do this again,' she said. I nodded.

'Pursue our secret jazz vice together.'

''S a deal.'

'Deal.'

We stood silently again for a moment by the doorway to the Watergate, knowing that something important had passed between us but not fully understanding what it was. She put her arm again on mine and it was as if I had been connected to some kind of energy source. I wanted to kiss her properly, but I stopped myself from trying. It was impossible, I decided. Don't even think about it.

'Thank you for the drinks,' she said as I kissed her on both cheeks.

'Thank you for our conversation,' I replied. 'I . . . really like your company.'

I felt like an adolescent.

'Me too.'

I watched her hit the keypad on the building and fumble in her bag for keys. When she was on the far side of the glass she turned and gave me a sad little wave, and a smile. Don't even think about it, I repeated to myself several times in my head. I decided I would walk the mile and a half back to the embassy.

Don't even think about it, I told myself with every stride. *Don't even think about it. Don't even think about it.*

But that meant that I *was* thinking about it. I could not stop thinking about it.

I walked fast, to clear my head. Plenty of cabs tooted but I let them pass, until I reached the Great House and my bed just after two in the morning, which is around 7 a.m. British time. Just as I was ready to switch off the lights, my secure phone rang. At least by now I was sober. It was Andy Carnwath, the PM's Communications Director.

'Alex, we have a problem.'

'I'm listening.'

'Several problems.'

One problem that I already knew about was that the Prime Minister was scheduled to fly to Washington for an IMF meeting in a couple of weeks time. London told me that my 'absolutely top priority' was to secure a one-on-one with President Carr, and it would be regarded as a humiliation for all of us if I failed. In the current mood of anti-British feeling I had not nailed it down yet. I thought that might be the reason for the call. It was something worse.

'Our security people say it is very important that we all

back off on the Khan case. All of us. Immediately. And especially you, Alex. We don't want Khan mentioned in any way
to the Americans; we don't want him talked about publicly;
we want none of this to cloud the Prime Minister's visit. Most
especially we don't want any more fucking aggro with the
Vice-President.'

Andy Carnwath stopped talking.

'Delighted as I am to hear your voice Andy, why does this
require a two a.m. phone call and not an email?'

'I don't know all the details,' Carnwath said, 'but I do
know that Khan is a dirty little fucker. And his family is. It's
complicated, Alex, but I needed to stress it to you in person.
Our people are on top of it.'

'Manila?' I started to feel very uneasy.

'No, thank fuck,' Carnwath sounded relieved. 'Something
else, something slow burning and, according to our people,
something even worse than Manila – if you can believe that.'
I could believe anything. 'Khan's relatives are on the Watch
List. The PM's been told that being too robust in the defence
of Muhammad Asif Khan will blow back and haunt him. So,
back off – but, here's the thing, under no circumstances must
you tell the Americans why you are backing off. You got that,
Alex?'

'Of course.'

The 'Watch List' was the Security Service list of people
thought close enough to staging a terrorist attack to demand
up to twenty-four-hour-a-day surveillance.

'And one other thing I need to tell you,' Andy said. 'Brother
Yank has been asking questions about you. You'll hear it from
the embassy security people. Discreet approaches from the US
Secret Service to our people to check and make available all
your security clearances and background.'

'Oh, fuck,' I said. And then, despite myself, I smiled. Maybe
Kristina was checking me out. And then I stopped smiling.
Maybe someone else was checking us both out.

'Any reason we should be worried, Alex?'

'Not that I know of.'

'Goodnight then, Alex. Sorry to wake you, but I'm heading to Berlin right now with Fraser for the Euro-fucking-bollocks, and you can see why this would not keep.'

'Yes, of course. Goodnight, Andy.'

I was completely sober now, and unable to sleep. I lay and looked at the ceiling, thinking about the implications of the Khan case, and about whether Kristina might help me out of a jam by fixing the one-on-one meeting between Davis and Carr that Downing Street so desperately wanted. I finally fell asleep. As I did so I dreamed about Kristina's hair brushing my face.

As we were eventually to find out following the publicity over the Heathrow conspiracy trials, the British Security Service, MI5, really was on to something with Muhammad Asif Khan. A cousin of his, Hasina Khan Iqbal, had been flagged up as a security risk after she applied for a job at Heathrow Airport. MI5 started looking at Hasina and then at other members of the family, including her older brother, Shawfiq. It turned out that Shawfiq already had a file fat enough to ensure that the whole family was put on the Watch programme. The Iqbals' father was dead, but the brother and sister, mother and maternal grandmother lived in Hounslow in west London. Shawfiq – and this interested our security people a great deal – chose to go out of his way to attend a mosque in Slough that was well known for the extremism of some of its members. For her part, Hasina, as is obvious from the newspaper pictures during the trial, is a strikingly statuesque woman. At the time I was tipped off by Andy Carnwath about the Khan family, Hasina would have been twenty years old. In the newspaper pictures her face is always set off by a black hejab and abaya. By her own later account to counter-terrorism police officers, it was shortly after the disappearance of Muhammad Asif Khan, and the Carr administration talk about vengeance against the perpetrators of the Manila bombing, that Shawfiq instructed Hasina to get a job at Heathrow Airport, Terminal One. Shawfiq was now head of the family and Hasina did as she was told. She applied to a confectionery and newspaper chain, but was told the only job vacancies were in Terminal Five.

'Go along for interview anyway,' Shawfiq instructed. 'Take the job. You can get a transfer later.'

On the day of the interview, a Saturday, the watchers recorded that Hasina Khan Iqbal appeared to have dressed with special care. She had put on her dark kohl eyeliner and a hint of make-up, repeatedly making sure that not a single stray hair emerged from her tight-fitting black headscarf. Shawfiq was filmed by the watchers as he drove her from the family home in Hounslow to Hatton Cross Tube station. Hasina caught the Piccadilly Line to Heathrow. The newspaper store manager offered Hasina a job in Terminal Five immediately. The police reports showed that later he claimed he had had one minor reservation. Looking at her CV it was obvious that Hasina Khan Iqbal was overqualified for the position of shop assistant.

'You could go to university,' the store manager had said.

Hasina had replied that her family did not want her to study any more and that they needed the money. Shift work was ideal, she said, because it enabled her to look after her elderly grandmother. She might go to university 'sometime', she said, if the family agreed. It did not seem much of a big deal.

After he dropped Hasina at the Tube station, the watchers followed Shawfiq Iqbal to Twickenham. He was filmed parking his dark blue Subaru near Harlequins rugby ground, known as 'The Stoop', a place he was to return to repeatedly over the next year or so as the Heathrow Airport bomb plot developed.

The Stoop lies about half a mile from Twickenham. Shawfiq walked with the crowds streaming along the pavement towards the big game, the Heineken Cup Final, the biggest club rugby event in Europe. Shawfiq had bought a ticket to see London Wasps play Toulouse. In his martyrdom video, Shawfiq explained that he felt weird in the rugby ground, completely foreign. He was uninterested in sport, had never seen a rugby game before, and the ticket for the West Stand was expensive, which he resented.

'Rugby', Shawfiq declared aggressively, waving his hands in the martyrdom video, 'is not a game played by people like me or for people like me.'

He quoted something he had read in a book, a quote attributed to the historian Philip Toynbee. Toynbee was supposed to have said that blowing up the West Stand at Twickenham would set back the cause of English fascism by decades. Shawfiq laughed on the martyrdom video as he jabbed his fingers towards the camera in accusation.

'When you mess with the Muslims,' he said, bouncing jauntily at the camera, 'the Muslims come and mess with you.'

On that day of the Heineken Cup Final, Shawfiq Iqbal was recorded on surveillance cameras and by the watchers walking around inside the ground, taking photographs on a digital camera. Crowds in their tens of thousands streamed towards their seats. The pictures show that Shawfiq photographed the fans drinking beer. He walked around at various levels inside the stadium, photographing the underside of the West Stand and the reinforced concrete pillars on which it stood. At one point he filmed a short movie. He asked a couple of Wasps fans in their yellow-and-black hooped shirts how many people were inside Twickenham at maximum capacity. One fan, with a pint of Guinness in his hand, mugged for the camera as he said it was 'about eighty thousand.'

'Eighteen thousand?'

'No, EIGHTY thousand,' the fan repeated. 'Eight-zero.'

'Wow,' Shawfiq said, genuinely impressed. He had no idea what was normal for an international rugby match, but, as he said in his emails to Waheed, Umar, and the other conspirators: Eighty thousand is twenty-five times as many as died on 11 September.

'Eighty thousand,' you can hear Shawfiq repeat on the camera footage, as if he cannot quite believe it. 'Wow.'

Shawfiq shot pictures of the bars, souvenir, and programme stands, the hamburger and pie stalls. He confessed in the emails to Waheed and Umar that he had never seen anything like it. When the teams ran out just before kick off he was in his seat. He noted in one email that there were more non-white people among the thirty players on the pitch than among the 80,000 people in the ground. It was all-ticket, all-white; no Asian fans that he could see, anywhere.

'Where are the Muslims?' he asked in the email. 'Where are the Muslims? Muslim Free Zone!'

Shawfiq watched only part of the game. He found the play confusing, brutal, incomprehensible, typical of the worst of Western culture. On that I agree with Shawfiq. Rugby is organized violence broken up with committee meetings. The security cameras and the watchers recorded that he left the ground during the first half after around thirty minutes of play.

Before he did so he was filmed looking up to the sky and watching the long, slow descent of a passenger aircraft towards Heathrow Airport, a few miles away to the west. It was, he wrote in an email to Waheed, an extraordinary sight. Three hundred tons of metal, flying at 250 miles an hour, hanging as if suspended in the air. The possibilities, he decided, were incredible. Shawfiq left the ground and returned to his Subaru near The Stoop. The vehicle by that time had been fitted with listening devices and cameras, and so was the family home. The watchers at first used a white van that they moved near the house; later they rented a small apartment nearby for the months of surveillance that followed as the conspiracy unfolded.

As he drove away from The Stoop, Shawfiq called Hasina on her mobile phone. I suppose he must have been wondering how she had got on in her job interview, but Hasina's mobile was switched off. Then he switched on the radio to the Five Live commentary which called the Wasps–Toulouse Twickenham game a 'real thriller'. After a few minutes he turned the radio off and played a CD of a man singing verses – sura – from the Koran. When he arrived home in Hounslow half an hour later, Shawfiq Iqbal spent that evening sending JPEGs of the pictures he had taken to a number of email addresses in different parts of the United Kingdom, with a few annotations and a brief commentary. He prayed. He checked his maps of Heathrow and Twickenham, and then smoked half a dozen cigarettes, lost in thought. Some time later that night his mother told him that Hasina had indeed got the job. She would start work at Heathrow Terminal Five the following week.

That night Hasina took off her make-up and sat by the mirror in her bedroom, brushing her long black hair. In her later statements to police she said that she tried to read a book while lying on her bed, but could not settle. When police raided the house just over a year later they found the book still by her bedside. The novel, *White Teeth* by Zadie Smith, a story about race relations in multi-cultural England, was still unfinished. Hasina said from the moment she got the job at Heathrow she could not concentrate on reading, and instead kept wondering why the manager in the shop where she was to work had asked her about her plans for the future and university. At that time, Hasina told the police, she did not know exactly what her brother was planning, but she knew enough to recognize that the future was like a foreign country, which she was not planning to visit. She too prayed before she went to bed.

SEVEN

Details of 'The Spartacus Solution' were not leaked, as
Kristina and I had feared. They were publicly announced,
boasted about by Bobby Black at a news conference two
days before the Prime Minister's visit to Washington. It was
as if he had taken a brick and thrown it into a calm pond.
I sat at my desk in the embassy watching the Spartacus
news conference – as it came to be called – on television,
open-mouthed. It began normally, as the regular daily White
House press briefing, introduced by the Communications
Director Sandy McAuley, who said the Vice-President had
a short statement to make. There would be a press handout
and the Vice-President would then take questions. An aide
passed around a two-page document which turned out to
be an executive summary of 'The Spartacus Solution'
pamphlet that Bobby Black had given me in confidence at
the start of the Carr administration.

The news conference led all the TV and radio bulletins,
and would ensure that Bobby Black made the cover of *Time
Magazine*, *Newsweek*, *The Economist*, *Der Spiegel*, and the
front pages of the main European and American newspapers. He delivered a short statement on the need to meet
terror with 'appropriate severity', and then called for questions.

The BBC's White House correspondent asked whether – in the light of the Vice-President's comments about Spartacus – it was pointless the Prime Minister raising the issue of the alleged torture of Muhammad Asif Khan on his visit to the American capital. Bobby Black offered a lopsided grin.

'My good friend the Prime Minister of Great Britain is welcome to raise any issue with us,' he said. 'Any issue at all. That is what friends do. Doesn't mean to say we are going to agree.' Then he started to repeat the kind of things he had told Fraser Davis at that disastrous meeting at Chequers the previous year. He went through his 'Neutrality Is Immoral' speech, coupled with the instruction that America's allies were all expected to help win the 'War on Terror'.

'Be clear: if you are in the business of harming American citizens, or of helping those who do, you will pay a price and the price could be your life.'

The declassified version of 'The Spartacus Solution' that was handed round to White House journalists argued that the United States could never completely defeat all its enemies in the War on Terror, but it did not have to. What America had to do, General Shultz argued in his essay, was to punish to the utmost those terrorists it could catch, without mercy, even at the risk of being thought cruel and imperialist.

The handout included what I thought was the essay's most controversial conclusion, in full.

The Romans in the Roman Republic and later in the Empire knew they could never be sure to deter a slave rebellion. There was always the chance that somewhere, someone would rise up violently against his master. But when it happened on a grand scale under Spartacus, each of the captured rebellious slaves was crucified on the roads around Rome, their bodies left to rot and be feasted upon by vermin. In the twenty-first *century, Roman methods are inappropriate, but Roman psychology is useful. There will always be rebellions, always trouble-makers, always potential suicide bombers. The Spartacus Solution will ensure that terrorists are kept alive long enough to confess, to betray their comrades, and pay the full penalty. The United States in the* twenty-first *century must be a good friend. We must also be a ruthless and implacable enemy.*

One other conclusion was also made public:

The more hostile media we receive for perceived human-rights abuses, the more discriminate our deterrence and the more potent the Spartacus Solution. Hostile media works for us. It is an effective communications tool. The Romans understood it best: Fear works.

'But just talking of a Spartacus Solution, Mr Vice-President,' one of the White House reporters asked, waving the extracts in her hand, 'isn't that inflammatory? Crucifying terrorists on the road to Rome? Is that seriously going to be American policy in the twenty-first century?'

'You are, with respect, confusing a metaphor with a policy,' Vice-President Black retorted. 'What is inflammatory is blowing up American airliners on takeoff from Manila.'

Another British reporter, Jack Rothstein from *The Times*, stood up. I liked Rothstein and had in the past briefed him about our side of the rows over torture and Muhammad Asif Khan.

'Mr Vice-President, diplomatic sources say this kind of talk is not in the best traditions of the United States. Abraham Lincoln . . .'

'And I have explained to "diplomatic sources" that

75

Abraham Lincoln did not have to deal with your British suicide bombers,' Bobby Black interrupted scornfully.

'We will not rest until all the people attacking us are in a place where they can no longer do any harm. We will do what it takes. Abraham Lincoln would understand that, even if a few diplomats in striped pants don't get it.'

Black went on the offensive. He said that since 9/11 you were 'either with the United States or you were against it. There just is no middle way. There is no split-the-difference between Right and Wrong.'

'Aren't things a bit more complicated in the real world than simply black or white?' a woman from CBS suggested.

'On the contrary: since Manila, there is no such colour as grey,' Bobby Black shot back. 'International leaders, diplomats, journalists who see the world in terms of grey are deluding themselves, or, worse, they are deluding the people who elected them – or, in the case of some TV news anchors, they are deluding the people who watch their news programmes.'

I listened to the interview with sinking heart. My job is a study in shades of grey. I sent Kristina a text message: 'You watching this?' She did not text back. A couple of hours later, FOX News quoted an unnamed 'American official' describing me personally as 'a leading appeaser of terror' for my intervention in the Khan case, and saying it was 'not expected' that Prime Minister Fraser Davis would 'waste time during his upcoming Washington visit' arguing on behalf of the rights of a terrorist, 'unlike Ambassador Alex Price.' We started to take hostile calls at the embassy. The people at FOX News gave out our number on the air, which meant that every right-wing wacko with access to a telephone dialled in to shout abuse at what one caller described as the 'pansy-assed British faggots.' Ironic, you might think, given that at that very point I was no longer pressing Khan's case at all.

Late that night, Kristina called me on my mobile. 'I guess you saw it?' she said.

'Oh, yes.'

'What did you think?'

'Any statement which pisses off your friends and encourages your enemies is not a good idea.'

'That good, uh?' Kristina said.

'Are you coming to the dinner for the Prime Minister?' I wondered. I was hosting the event at the ambassador's residence.

'Yes.'

'Will you be my partner for the evening?'

Kristina thought for a moment.

'Of course.'

Then she rang off.

The day before the Prime Minister was due to arrive in Washington, I had yet another run-in with Bobby Black. It was becoming increasingly difficult to deal with him, even though I had managed to ensure – thanks to some deft footwork from Kristina – that Fraser Davis would indeed sit down with President Carr for his allotted fifteen minutes of 'special relationship' face-time. I had promised that Davis would not raise the Khan case. Johnny Lee Ironside called me.

'I see you got your man in,' he laughed. 'Despite the best efforts of me and my man to keep him out.'

'I don't know what you're talking about,' I replied.

'You and me need a serious talk, Alex,' he said.

'You coming to the dinner for the Prime Minister? It's over at ten. Stay behind afterwards and have a few beers with me. We need to do something to make all this better before it turns into a festering sore.'

'Talking 'bout festering sores,' he said, 'the Vice-President wants to see you again. Wants to whup your English ass.'

This time it was about Britain's reluctance to provide locations for part of the anti-ballistic missile shield the newspapers call 'Star Wars'. Fraser Davis had been back-pedalling. The Poles and Czechs had been threatened with Russian nuclear obliteration for their part in playing host to the American radar network, and there were political problems too. As soon as the Spartacus Solution news conference ended, you could feel the wave of unpopularity towards Carr and Black hit Britain, Europe, and most American allies.

It was profoundly dispiriting. Carnwath told me it was starting to rival the way the United States was seen during the Bush/Cheney administration at their worst. Fraser Davis could read opinion polls. He did not like the new wave of anti-Americanism. None of us did. But he also knew he had to be careful. Carnwath told me that at all costs Fraser wanted to avoid what he called 'the poodle factor' – being seen to jump to every American demand; being thought of as the new Tony Blair. On the way to the White House, I skimmed through my briefing papers on missile defence in the back of the Rolls. This time it was just Bobby Black, Johnny Lee, the British military attaché Lee Crieff, and me. No Kristina. As she feared, she had been sidelined in matters that she should have played a part in.

Bobby Black sat at his desk and scowled. He delivered a terse lecture on the 'need for urgency in the creation of the missile shield, and the need to live up to commitments.' When he finished talking, I prepared to argue back, saying that we accepted the urgency but the British people were not persuaded about the nature of the threat requiring a space-based antimissile system.

'There is a clear danger to Britain,' I said, 'and no clear benefit.'

It would always be cheaper for the Russians to build more missiles than it ever would be for the Americans to keep increasing the power of the supposed missile shield – even assuming that it did work. Our scientists said that, so far, it didn't.

Suddenly Bobby Black snapped: 'Thanks, Ambassador.'

'B-but . . .'

Then he said, 'Goodbye.'

That was it. Vice had spoken. I was ushered out by Johnny Lee who said, 'We'll talk after the dinner.' He said it in a whisper. Later that evening, I read on the wire services that the White House had briefed journalists that 'the British have been consulted' about Strategic Missile Defence and that the British had 'agreed with the Carr administration that they would make radar early warning facilities fully available in the United Kingdom in a timely manner.'

It was nice that he told us.

Woof, woof.

By the time of Fraser Davis's visit, Bobby Black was so obviously the driving force in the White House that late-night comedians were joking that it was *Theo Carr* who was 'one heartbeat away' from the presidency of the United States, and I decided I needed to try to get Black and Davis together again, under tight supervision. James Byrne, in one of his *Washington Post* columns, said Black had become 'like one of the Dementors in a Harry Potter novel – he sucks the souls from those who meet him', and that he represented the Carr administration's 'Dark Side'.

The day after our discussion about Star Wars, Prime Minister Fraser Davis arrived in Washington for his forty-eight-hour visit. He met President Carr without a hitch, and then on the last evening the Vice-President and his wife Susan were guests of honour at my dinner at the embassy. Much thought from Johnny Lee and me went into the choreography of the evening. Davis and Black were never to be allowed to meet each other without significant adult supervision. We brought them together at the cocktail party, where they stood awkwardly side by side and allowed a few photographs to be taken alongside one of the other guests, the comedian Mike Myers. They smiled at each other, shook hands, said nothing. Then, just as we moved into dinner, Bobby Black turned to Fraser Davis.

'Now is the time,' he said softly. There was such a hubbub of people moving into the dining room that I barely heard the words.

'The time for what?' the Prime Minister smiled affably.

'Now is the time for you to crack down on that group of your citizens who are the seedbed for terrorism. These Pakistani people have to be dealt with.'

To his credit, Fraser Davis remained calm. 'If you mean British citizens of Pakistani origin, then they are of course British and need to be treated with equal—'

Before he could finish, Bobby Black said, 'We are actively considering making all of these Pakistani–British people apply in person to the US embassy in London should they ever wish to get on a plane to this country. And if you do not help us in this, Prime Minister, we may take the same steps with all British citizens.'

'There is only one class of British citizen, Vice-President Black,' Davis responded. 'You must do what you need to do, but you must treat all of our citizens alike, whatever their background.'

'If that's the way you want it,' Bobby Black scowled and walked in to dinner, shepherded by Johnny Lee Ironside. I led the Prime Minister to his seat and took a deep breath. At least they had not actively come to blows. At the end of the dinner I made a short speech about the importance of British–American friendship in a dangerous world, about the fact that our values and interests were so often the same. I ended by trying to tease the Vice-President in a neighbourly way. As part of the bad publicity about me being supposedly a 'friend of terrorists', someone had leaked my fear of flying in helicopters to various news outlets. Presumably more evidence of my role as a pansy-assed Brit. *The Washington Post* printed a gossipy piece suggesting that the British diplomat who was not frightened to stand up to the wrath of Vice-President Bobby Black over Muhammad Asif Khan was nevertheless terrified of a heavier-than-air machine. Towards the end of my speech I joked about it.

'If you read the papers last week, you will know that I have a thing about helicopters. I confess that they are my personal hell – especially the ones that bring my esteemed neighbour Vice-President Black to and from official engagements.'

There was an intake of breath around the table as people began to calculate whether the British Ambassador was about to have a go at Vice in the company of the British Prime Minister. I should explain that the Vice-President and I really were neighbours. The ambassador's residence is next door to the US Naval Observatory, which is the official vice-presidential residence. This accident of geography did not mean we were the kind of neighbours who drop in for coffee or climb over the fence to borrow a lawnmower or a cup of sugar. If you go on to Google Earth and zoom in on Massachusetts Avenue on the satellite photographs, you will see that – uniquely for Washington – Bobby Black's home in the Naval Observatory is blanked out, pixelated. The White House isn't. You can see it clearly. You can even look at some major US military facilities around the world; but one of the few places where Google Earth cannot shine is Bobby Black's official home, next door to my own home, which, of course, Google Earth does show in every last detail, almost down to the rose bushes and fireflies in the garden.

'Even though our two nations do not agree on the Kyoto Treaty on carbon emissions, Mr Vice-President,' I smiled, full of diplomatic good cheer, 'may I respectfully suggest that the small sacrifice of switching off the helicopter engines when the Chinooks sit idling on your lawn would signal we are more in harmony on global warming than people think—' I paused for effect – 'as well as being good neighbours and friends, of course, with the heli-phobe next door.'

There was much laughter and then applause. Susan Black threw her head back and hooted with amusement in that easy Montana way of hers. So did the Prime Minister. Mike Myers laughed too, and then said 'Groovy, Baby,' in his best Austin Powers accent, so everyone got the joke. I stared over at Bobby Black, who was sitting opposite Mike Myers. His lopsided grin was fixed on his face. He turned his spoon towards his tiramisu dessert, did not look at me, and said nothing. My own tiramisu tasted of sulphur. There was to be no change in the pattern of helicopter emissions over the next year.

When the guests left at ten o'clock, the hour that most Washington events finish, I said goodbye to the Vice-President and Prime Minister, and had a few words with Kristina. Then Johnny Lee Ironside and I headed outside for a beer on the porch. The night was still warm, though we were heading towards autumn. The last moths of the year danced around the garden lights.

'Clusterfuck,' he replied, using one of his favourite words.

'Unbelievable. Does he mean it about making British citizens of Pakistani origin apply for special visas?'

'First I heard of it,' Johnny Lee said, sucking on a bottle of Sam Adams beer. 'Doesn't mean to say it won't happen.'

We began talking about the eccentric ways of those we were paid to serve.

'I mean, Davis and Black,' Johnny Lee went on, 'two men, great on their own, who just can't stand each other. You know what the Vice-President said to me the other day?

He said the British are even more of a pain in the ass than the French. You hear me? How does anyone handle that?'

I swallowed a few mouthfuls of beer and asked Johnny Lee whether he thought the Vice-President of the United States and the British Prime Minister – men who spend their whole adult lives seeking the highest levels of power and then obtain it – were truly different from the rest of us.

'You bet,' Johnny Lee said, pulling the beer bottle from his mouth. 'Different as spare ribs from a spare tyre.'

'But how come?' I persisted. 'Do they start different or do they become that way because of the job?'

'The rich are different from you and me,' Johnny Lee suggested, 'because they have more money. Presidents and Prime Ministers are different from you and me, because they have more—'

'Juice,' I said. 'They have more juice.'

'Hang-ups,' Johnny Lee contradicted, with a laugh. He made a sign with his finger at the side of his head to suggest mental illness. 'More psychoses. Frickin' nut jobs. All of them.'

'Okay, nut jobs,' I agreed. 'But does power attract nut jobs, or does it create them?'

'Hmmm, we're getting in deep here, brother,' Johnny Lee nodded vigorously, grabbing yet another beer. 'For my money, they start off fucking weird. They might get weirder, sure. But they *always* start off fucking weird. You never really *know* them, you know?'

I disagreed. After years of watching government ministers close up, members of Parliament, prime ministers, Congressmen and presidents, I had concluded that normal people do want to serve their country, but they *became* peculiar when they achieved power.

'I have never met an evil politician,' I said, 'but I have met plenty who are delusional. The chief delusion is that they need to stay in power otherwise the country will go to hell.'

Johnny Lee laughed.

'In this town,' he gestured with the beer-bottle neck towards the lights of Washington DC, 'politics attracts freaks just like your light here attracts bugs. Normal folks have lives. Abnormal folks have political ambitions. Normal folks go to bars. Abnormal folks go to political meetings. My mama always told me politics is just show business for ugly people.'

'Then your mama was as cynical as you are,' I scolded him. 'Plenty of decent people enter public service, but it twists them inside out. It's like living in a fishbowl or a cocoon.'

Now it definitely was the beer talking. It was near midnight and I was getting drunk. I poured us two fingers of Jack Daniels over ice.

'*Fishy-bowl? Co-coon?* Ambassador Price, I do believe you are talking what we Washington Tribesmen call bullshit.'

'No, no, hear me out,' I protested, passing him the whisky. 'Hear me out. A fishbowl because people in power have no privacy any more. None. Everything Vice-President Black or President Carr or Prime Minister Davis says or does, is written down, photographed, recorded, and dissected. They got blamed for the great food they ate at the IMF banquet, right? Because half the world is going hungry. But if Davis or Carr refused to eat the fancy food set in front of them, they'd get blamed for lousy gesture politics, a stunt that makes no difference to the poor. Politicians can't win, Johnny Lee. The press asked President Reagan about a cancerous polyp in his colon, for God's sake.'

Johnny Lee took a sip of the Jack Daniels. 'United States media – finest in world,' he responded, jabbing the whisky

84

glass at me. 'Our journalists have a goddamn *constitutional right* to peer up the president's ass.'

A doctor or psychologist would say that Johnny Lee and I were engaged in 'relief drinking' as a way of dealing with stress. Like me, Johnny Lee was in theory married but in practice separated. The rumour was that his wife, Carly, had remained in Charleston to pursue her career as a lawyer, but mostly – or so I was told – to pursue her golf instructor, her tennis coach, her pool boy, and various other diversions. Johnny Lee and I never discussed this, or Fiona leaving me. Some things are best left unsaid.

When you are married to the younger sister of the Prime Minister of the United Kingdom, you cannot afford a scandal. When you are the Chief of Staff to the Vice-President of the United States, you cannot get a divorce until it is politically acceptable to get one. The two of us argued in good-humoured drunkenness until Johnny Lee got up to leave. I walked him to where his car and driver were waiting. He burped.

'So what we gonna do, Alex? We can't go on trying to keep your man and mine apart. And we can't get them together without worrying about it coming to a fistfight. So what we going to do?'

Suddenly, standing unsteadily in the embassy driveway, I explained an idea I had been turning over in some dull recess of my brain. Johnny Lee listened and said it sounded like a 'neat idea'. He burped again and told me we should sleep on it and talk in the morning. We said goodbye and I sat on the porch for another half-hour, having one more beer and one more whisky, thinking through the idea. Early the following day, when I still had a pounding head and a bad stomach, Johnny Lee Ironside called and said he had been thinking over my idea, and we should try to make it work. I had suggested – though it would take months to organize – that we should invite Vice-President Bobby Black to Scotland for a private visit, to shoot grouse in the Highlands with members of the British royal family. He could explore his roots, and along the way meet the Queen and key members of the British government, including the Prime Minister. He and Fraser Davis would be told that mutual self-interest meant they had to kiss and make up. Had to. Imperative. They would be instructed to joke about their rough words at Chequers and to insist that, despite the occasional differences, they were truly the best of friends.

'Let's do it,' Johnny Lee said. And so we did.

EIGHT

Plans involving heads of state, kings, queens, presidents, vice-presidents and prime ministers are like plans involving oil tankers. They take a long time to execute. The idea of bringing Bobby Black over for a kiss-and-make-up trip to the Scottish Highlands took a while to ferment, and then required agreement from everyone you can think of: the Office of the Vice-President, the White House, the State Department, Downing Street, the Foreign Office, and Buckingham Palace.

The date was eventually set for the October of the Carr administration's second year, two weeks before the mid-term elections when most of Congress is up for re-election. It seemed a long way in the future, but just the fact of the acceptance by Bobby Black helped improve relations between London and Washington. The Vice-President was interested. Enthusiastic. He asked Johnny Lee to get him books on grouse shooting. He knew that the birds fly at speeds of up to eighty miles an hour and he wanted to prepare himself as best he could. He commissioned family research from a genealogy company and instructed Johnny Lee that he needed to visit churches in the Aberdeenshire area to find graves of his ancestors. Perhaps most importantly, the plan to require British citizens of Pakistani origin to apply for special visas if they wanted to travel to the United States was quietly dropped.

'At least for now,' Johnny Lee Ironside told me. For me, 'for now' was good enough.

Susan Fein Black's desire for the trip also helped. She quickly realized that the Queen was genuinely interested in horses and called me one evening to ask if Her Majesty would like to know about Mrs Black's own rare-breeds programme for horses on her ranch in Montana. I said I would find out. It is one of the curiosities of the world that the more republican the country, the more fascinated the citizens are about the British royal family. After all their exertions to get rid of the monarchy, you might have thought Americans would be different, but they are not. Susan Black sounded unbelievably girlish on the phone.

The plans for the trip to Scotland started to develop. The Blacks were to go shooting, they were to have tea with the Queen – informal – and then come to a dinner – formal – with Her Majesty, other members of the royal family, and the Prime Minister. Then Davis and Black were to spend a whole day together trying to work through all their differences. Well, as I say, that was the plan.

The biggest thaw in US–UK relations came when I heard from the Queen's Private Secretary, Sir Hamish Martin, that the Queen would be delighted – ('absolutely delighted, Alex,') – to hear about the Montana rare-breeds programme, and Her Majesty wondered if, instead of joining her husband on the shoot, Mrs Black would care to visit a horse-breeding bloodstock facility near Balmoral in the company of the Queen herself.

('Very, very informal,' Sir Hamish whispered to me.)

When I phoned the Naval Observatory to relay this request, a secretary passed me over to Susan Black in person, and I could again feel the excitement in her voice. I imagined her turning cartwheels across the floor. A little royal stardust had been sprinkled on the visit. Even the dark heart of the Vice-President began to melt under its influence.

Over the next months, as I spent more and more time organizing these few days in Scotland, things with Kristina changed completely. From the moment Fiona had left me I had been busy and lonely, although the busy part usually helped me forget about the lonely part. I soon realized that, at every stage, seeing Kristina seemed to help. Perhaps it was that my friends and family were all in London, hers all in California. Whatever the reason, we became closer and closer. She confided in me how she continually felt sidelined. She had been specifically forbidden by Bobby Black from playing any part in his National Energy Security Taskforce, even though it dealt with areas – the Arab world and Iran, mostly – in which Kristina spoke the main language and had special experience.

'It's like I'm the National Security *Wife*,' she told me bitterly, biting energetically at a bagel with cream cheese at one of our regular breakfasts. 'I get allowed to dress up and look good, but when it comes to anything important, the men go talk somewhere else. I need to find a way around this.'

We both knew there was no way, not unless Kristina was prepared to take on Bobby Black directly. But that would be a battle she was destined to lose.

'Can't the President . . .?' I wondered.

'He doesn't want to lose his impeachment insurance,' Kristina joked. She was helping herself to scrambled eggs. I said I didn't understand. She rolled her eyes in mock exasperation.

'We have a Democratic Congress, Alex,' she explained, her eyebrow arching skyward, 'you with me so far? The Democrats are hoping to pick up seats in the mid-terms, big time.'

I nodded. The American political process, to outsiders at least, seems like a series of permanent elections. Presidents are elected every four years, but Congressional elections take place every two years, and in the 'mid-terms' all of the House and a third of the Senate is up for re-election.

'Arlo Luntz says the polls look bad and that Bobby Black is to blame. Vice is very unpopular, Arlo says. A vote-loser. And the Democrats are claiming he was at the heart of the corruption in the Iraq contracts. They say there were kick-backs from Goldcrest and Warburton to the Carr campaign. But even under a flaky liberal like Speaker Betty Furedi, no Democrat will ever impeach President Carr, no matter what he does wrong, if they know he will be succeeded by President Black.'

I must have looked stunned at this impeachment talk. 'Theo Carr hasn't done something really bad, has he?'

'It's a joke, Alex,' Kristina laughed, and I felt her hand gently on my arm. She paused for a moment and scowled. 'Kind of.'

I laughed too, as much at my own inadequacies as at her humour. She poured me a fresh black coffee. I always had gossip to trade, and Kristina usually listened more than she spoke, but that morning it was like some kind of therapy for her to get it all out.

'Luntz told me he advised the President to make sure Bobby Black goes to Scotland on your shooting trip in the run-up to the mid-terms,' Kristina told me. 'Says the further Vice is away from the campaign, the better. I even think Arlo wants the President to drop Bobby Black from his own re-election ticket, but that's real tricky.'

For me this was all heady stuff. Knowing who was up and who was down at the White House was a key part of my job. I had some gossip of my own to trade.

'Vice *enjoys* being thought of as the President's Dark Side,' I said. 'Did you know that?'

Kristina looked at me, stunned. 'What do you mean, enjoys?'

'Johnny Lee Ironside told me. We have a few beers from time to time. We talk.'

I had mentioned the Congressional hearings into the Iraq contracts to Johnny Lee. The Vice-President had been described in all kinds of ways, usually beginning with the prefix 'Un-' – *un*cooperative, *un*forthcoming, *un*reliable, *un*willing to appear before the Joint House and Senate Investigative Committee, and then – when he was sub-poenaed and had no choice but to appear, he pleaded executive privilege, refusing to say on what basis the contracts had been awarded to Warburton, except that it was a 'national security matter'. He was declared *un*communicative and *un*helpful.

'That shit makes his goddamn day,' Johnny Lee laughed. He told me the Vice-President routinely asked his staff to search out any negative comments in newspapers that suggested he represented President Carr's 'Dark Side', so he could have the best ones framed for his Ego Wall. An 'Ego Wall' is the wall in the private office of any Washington politician dedicated to the qualifications and citations that mean the most to the Big Political Beast – military honours, photographs showing the Big Beast shaking hands with a past president, a world leader or Hollywood movie star, plus university degrees and military citations.

'You want to put the Boss in a good mood,' Johnny Lee Ironside had told me, 'tell him some pinko Democrat bed-wetter like Hurd or Furedi called him a mean SOB: that'll do it. The sun comes out all over Planet Black.' Johnny Lee giggled like a schoolboy. 'Ma-aaan, he *Baaa-aaaad*!'

Kristina looked at me, fascinated, as if I was reporting on a new species of ape from the African jungle or an alien civilization discovered on a distant planet.

'Un-fucking-believable,' was all she said. Then she traded one further important piece of insider gossip. She handed me a draft speech that Vice-President Black was about to deliver at the US Naval College at Annapolis, Maryland, to a class of midshipmen. I pushed my scrambled egg to one side and started to read.

'The next stage in Spartacus,' Kristina suggested.

'All options remain open', the Vice-President was scheduled to say, 'when dealing with Iran.' In case journalists were too stupid to get the point, he added, 'Including military options. Neutrality on Iran's nuclear programme is immoral. The programme itself is immoral. It has to be stopped. It is a threat to Israel, to other countries in the region, and to world peace. An Iranian regime determined to acquire nuclear weapons is a nightmare for the entire world. The administration of President Theo Carr will end the nightmare. We will do so by all necessary means.'

'Oh, fuck,' I said. ''All necessary means' is the phrase diplomats use when they want to threaten a war. 'We need to tone this down.'

Kristina nodded.

'He's getting ahead of where the President is,' she said. 'Vice says that unless we are prepared to at least *threaten* an attack, the Iranians will not take us seriously, and the Israelis will go ahead anyway, with extreme prejudice.'

'Not necessarily,' I said. 'The Israelis would need to fly through Jordanian and Iraqi airspace. If you didn't want them to do so, they couldn't.'

Kristina shook her head impatiently. 'That's not my point. Once Vice makes public any kind of threat against Iran, we will end up going to war. I know how he operates. He will argue that our credibility is at stake and we have to follow through. It's like World War One – you have train timetables and you start mobilizing your soldiers and in the end you can't stop the war even if you want to. But that's not the worst. The Israelis are letting it be known that the bunker-busters that we supplied them cannot get the job done.'

Bunker-busters are bombs or missiles capable of causing an explosion a long way underground.

'Exactly,' I said, 'which is why negotiations are the only way . . .'

She interrupted again, very impatiently. 'Which is why there are those within the Israeli government who are talking about Canned Sunshine.' My jaw dropped. 'Canned Sunshine' is a military expression for a nuclear bomb. 'They are calling for nuclear pre-emption.'

'Nuclear pre-emption?' I blurted out. 'That's . . . that's like committing suicide because you fear dying. They couldn't possibly drop a nuke . . .' She waved me quiet.

'Vice says Spartacus applies to states as well as to individuals, and if ever a regime needed to be crucified, it's the Iranians. He wants to hit them after the mid-terms. Or to get the Israelis to do it.'

'Oh, fuck,' I said.

'And if we do go in, we will call on all possible support from all our allies. Which means you, Alex.'

I didn't feel like eating breakfast any more. I drank my coffee and left to return to the embassy, where I called Downing Street immediately on the secure line.

'How do we feel about being sucked into war with Iran?' I said to Andy Carnwath.

'What the fuck do you mean, Alex?'

I explained about Canned Sunshine. For once Andy Carnwath could not think of any expletives appropriate to the information.

Later that night, around midnight, I was lying on my bed reading a book, sipping whisky and water and listening to a CD of Charlie Parker. Kristina called me on my private cellphone.

'You're up late,' I said.

'You got time to talk?'

'Of course.'

I pushed the book I was reading to one side. It was called *Sleepwalking to Hell,* a recently published history of the Weimar Republic and the rise of the Nazis, written by Kristina's former lover, the University of California history professor Stephen Haddon. A liberal, I guessed, with a strong libertarian streak. Haddon argued that the transition from a sophisticated and prosperous Weimar democracy to a Nazi dictatorship was not one catastrophic leap. It was a series of little steps.

Any one of these steps might seem sensible by itself because the German people wanted to escape Bolshevism, anarchy, and economic collapse, but taken together they led decent people inexorably towards the Nazis. Haddon wrote in his preface that it could happen again. Terror produced terrified people, and terrified people made bad decisions.

'Is that jazz?' Kristina said.

I turned it down.

'Charlie Parker.'

'Perfect,' she said. 'Just perfect.'

Kristina was on her way home. President Carr and the First Lady, Rosa Carr, had invited her to the private White House movie theatre to watch a film with the Carr family, Bobby Black and his wife Susan, Arlo Luntz, and a couple of Democratic senators that Theo Carr had decided he should get to know better. The senators were on the Armed Services Committee, and Carr was still after more money for the Pentagon budget. It was a huge mark of confidence in Kristina to be invited to share private time with the President, and she was bubbling with enthusiasm. I wasn't really listening. I had something I had been meaning to say, and that night I said it.

94

'Instead of going home, Kristina, why not come here right now. Spend the night with me.'

She giggled. Then the line went quiet.

'You mean it, Alex?'

'Yes, I mean it,' I said. 'I have meant it for months.'

NINE

The visit of Bobby Black to Scotland took so long to organize I sometimes thought it would never happen. But it did happen, almost exactly two years after he and Prime Minister Davis had their first row at Chequers and just two weeks before the US mid-term elections which, yet again, all the experts, polls, and pundits claimed were going to offer a very sharp rebuke to the Carr administration. In preparation for the shooting trip, Vice-President Black insisted that the visit be kept as private as possible, and that his entourage be as small as possible. I spent hours on the telephone with Andy Carnwath in Downing Street and Sir Hamish Martin at Buckingham Palace fixing exactly who would meet Bobby Black at which point, who would shoot grouse, when he would meet Her Majesty the Queen, when Susan Black would go off to see the horses, and when Fraser Davis would turn up. I also talked repeatedly with Lord Anstruther, who was a Junior Defence Minister in Fraser Davis's government and whose estate was right next to the royal estate at Balmoral.

Anstruther had agreed to host the visit, though if he had realized exactly what he was in for, he would have told me to get lost. I tried to explain that when the President or Vice-President of the United States moves anywhere, it is rather like a medieval pope moving around Christendom – up to a thousand staff, journalists, hangers-on, advisers of all kinds – but, until Anstruther experienced it, I don't think he quite understood how big a 'small entourage' really was going to be. In the week before the visit I had called the Prime Minister to warn him, yet again, that it must not fail.

'We cannot afford a repeat of the row at Chequers,' I said. 'You and Bobby Black are fated to like one another, whether you want to or not.'

Fraser Davis was very positive. He asked me to go over the arguments he should use with Bobby Black to deflect him from a confrontation with Iran without causing a row, and the kinds of things he should say if the question of special visas for British citizens of Pakistani origin were to be raised.

'We say it is unfair, unworkable, discriminatory and the twenty-first century equivalent of the Jim Crow laws,' I said. Then I reminded the PM that the policy details were not significant. What was significant was the tone. The policy would come right as long as he was nice. Very nice.

'But I'm always nice, Alex,' Fraser Davis replied, sounding rather hurt. I could imagine his wet, pouty lip. 'As you well know.'

'It has taken us months to bring this off.' I refused to be deflected. 'We mustn't blow it. You mustn't blow it.'

'Well, it is different now,' Fraser Davis responded, brushing aside the possibility of failure. 'It's not as if he is just some obscure senator. He is representing the American people. I promise you, Ambassador Price, that I will represent the interests of the British people, with every courtesy. Is that good enough for you?'

It was good enough. And so one day in late October it finally happened. Bobby Black's White House motorcade swept into Lord Anstruther's great house of Castle Dubh in the Scottish Highlands shortly before eight in the morning for the start of the grouse shoot. Castle Dubh is a massive Victorian pile with false battlements built over Jacobean foundations. From the faux-ramparts you can easily see twenty miles over the Scottish mountains, up into the hills and down to Loch Rowallan and Rowallan village, and even across to the royal estate at Balmoral. As the cars swept into the driveway, the leaves were turning autumnal reds and golds. The air was clear and cool, the skies that morning empty of cloud and full of the sounds of songbirds. The Americans arrived to the roar of a dozen police motorbikes, nine saloon cars, two stretched limousines, plus communications vehicles, and two identical four-by-fours scrunching up on Anstruther's gravel drive, like a gigantic metal snake uncoiling in front of us.

'You told me a small entourage,' Anstruther whispered to me as we stood in front of the house and watched the cars arrive.

'This is a small entourage,' I replied. 'You don't want to see the full works, believe me.'

Anstruther blinked. I think it began to dawn on him what lay ahead. The Vice-President stepped out, not from one of the limousines as you might expect but, for security reasons, from one of the bulletproof four-by-fours. Anstruther greeted him warmly and invited Bobby Black and Johnny Lee inside for a quick breakfast, while the servants fussed around the Secret Service and other members of the vice-presidential party.

'I can't wait to get out on the mountains,' Bobby Black said, clapping his pudgy hands together and looking genuinely happy.

'Me too,' Anstruther agreed with a nod of recognition. 'Just a quick coffee then.'

The rest of us tried to look pleased. Diplomacy, like politics, requires acting ability. Blair knew it. Clinton knew it. So did Ronald Reagan, obviously. Reagan once said that politics was just like being on the stage – you have a helluva opening, you coast a little, and then you have a helluva close. You meet people you do not like, but you act in whatever way is necessary to win them over. You meet people who despise you, and you bear their hostility with fortitude.

On that day of Bobby Black's hunting trip, we joked and laughed as we dressed in the shooting gear handed to us by Lord Anstruther: jaggy brown and green tweeds which abraded the skin and chafed the knees. We brought our own walking boots. We looked the part as we sipped coffee and watched the American communications teams set up in one of the large Castle Dubh outhouses, Bolfracks Bothy. Our mood was upbeat. We were doing the best for our countries and we were having fun doing it.

'My daddy used to say that a man should avoid any enterprise that requires the purchase of new clothes,' Johnny Lee quipped as he struggled to pull on his tweeds. 'The old man had a point.'

'You should pass it on to Arlo Luntz,' I said. 'Sounds like one of his pieces of wisdom.'

'Arlo came out with a knockout phrase the other day,' Johnny Lee smiled. 'He said, "Sincerity in public life is the most important political virtue. Fake that, and you got it made." Guy's a freaking genius, you ask me.'

In a good mood of banter and fun we shouldered our day-hike rucksacks filled with food, water, and small metal flasks of whisky, then we strode out to the front of Castle Dubh and climbed into a fleet of freshly washed Land Rovers arranged by Anstruther. Secret Service and British police teams had spent the previous forty-eight hours checking the grounds, the neighbouring glens, and the mountainside as best they could. The presence of armed protection officers was to be kept to a discreet minimum and only on the perimeter of the shoot, for fear of scaring away the whole point of the trip, the grouse themselves. In our mood of jollity we behaved as if it were a *Boys' Own* adventure, on which nothing could possibly go wrong. Anstruther had winked when he handed the whisky flask to me.

'Salvation from Speyside,' he said.

We parked the Land Rovers at the side of a muddy track and started hiking up the mountain as the sun split through a clear blue Highland sky. It was cold, with the edge of the moon visible over the hills, like a poster from the Scottish Tourist Board, and I was nervous. The Queen, the Vice-President, the Prime Minister, at least two other government ministers, staff from Number Ten, the Foreign Office, and the Office of the Vice-President were all being brought together over the next forty-eight hours in the Scottish wilderness, thanks to what Downing Street was calling Alex Price's 'great idea'. I wasn't sure what would come of it, but I hoped for a footnote in the history books, if I was lucky, and a few headlines for my own Ego Wall. *The Balmoral Understanding. The Aberdeenshire Entente. The Scottish Special Relationship.* Something had come of it already.

In the thaw leading up to the trip, the Americans had announced that Muhammad Asif Khan, the British detainee we had all made so much of a fuss about, was to be released. The release of Khan was privately regarded as very useful by the British security service, MI5. They wanted him out of jail so they could watch him. They needed to know if he was indeed connected to what they were now convinced was a major conspiracy that included his cousins, a plot that was leading towards what Andy Carnwath told me was an imminent attack involving Heathrow Airport.

'Imminent?'

'Within the next month or so,' he responded. 'That's what I'm told. That's all I know.'

'Not during Bobby Black's visit?'

'Not during the Vice-President's fucking visit,' Carnwath replied, exasperated, 'as far as we know, Alex. Though I will obviously have to get bin Laden on the blower to ensure al-fucking-Qaeda cooperates so as not to interrupt your fucking plans.'

100

Carnwath repeated his instructions that on no account must I mention anything about the Heathrow plot or Khan's family to any American, any member of the Carr administration, any US government official.

'The Americans have no fucking patience when it comes to things like this,' he said. 'They will want to charge in and put their big boots all over everything. Our people say we need to give them time to get a result in court. The Prime Minister is putting everything on the line for this, Alex. You understand how important this is?'

I said that I did understand. If it went wrong, Fraser Davis's political career would melt. Khan's arrival in Britain was expected to include some kind of hero's welcome from his handful of supporters. It was scheduled for the same day as the beginning of the Vice-President's shooting trip.

'Accidental timing,' the Foreign Office said. 'A coincidence.'

'Coincidences,' Johnny Lee whispered to me with a wink, 'are God's way of reminding folks he's still around.'

Coincidental or otherwise, on the Scottish moors none of us thought very much about anything – except the grouse and whether Bobby Black was enjoying himself. Anstruther took the Vice-President with him to hunt on the right of the shooting party.

'Best if we keep him on the far right,' Anstruther whispered to me with a knowing wink. 'If you see him or his gun heading leftwards, don't forget to duck. I hear in the Carr administration that the right hand sometimes doesn't know what the far-right hand is doing.'

'Not so loud,' I hissed, worried that all our good work might be undone with some feeble joke at Bobby Black's expense. The Vice-President's problems on shooting trips in the past had been well publicized. There had been a minor scandal in his first year in office when the Vice-President had mysteriously shot one of his hunting companions in the backside on a quail shoot in Texas.

The hunting companion had been Paul Comfort of Warburton, the long-time FOB, Friend of Bobby, who had to spend a painful night having buckshot removed from the cheeks of his bottom. Details were hard to come by, although Comfort appeared on TV and publicly blamed himself for stepping into Bobby Black's line of fire. Kristina said to me at the time that it was a display of true loyalty.

'Greater love hath no man', she smiled, 'than to lay down his ass for his friend.'

Princess Charlotte was also to be with Bobby Black on the right of the shooting party. I was pleased because she was a charmer, and Black warmed to her immediately. The Princess and Anstruther had a closeness that I never figured out, a closeness despite their marriages to other people and the fact that she was fifteen years his junior. There was gossip. Possibly it was an aristocratic affair that oiks and retainers like me would never be told about.

I looked around and thought how far I had come from my grandmother's little three-bedroomed semi to this walk in the Highlands with the great and the good and the not-so-great and not-so-good. At least Bobby Black was on good form. He breathed the clean air and said how much he liked Scotland. It made him feel 'at home.' He smiled in his owlish way, and muttered about 'ancestral roots'. When I saw him in his green and brown shooting gear I realized that I had never before seen him without a dark suit, white shirt, and sober tie, and I had never seen him happy either. For his age, mid-sixties, Black was fit, wiry, with a hint of a suntan on his face from the golf course and the quail hunts.

After an hour's walk from where the Land Rovers dropped us off, we reached a high valley with a stream – a burn – flowing through the heather. Anstruther suggested that Prince Duncan and some of the others stay in the middle or move to the left. Prince Duncan had every sign of a hangover. We headed to the shooting butts at a place called Shap Fell.

Everyone fell in line and deferred to Anstruther. I was told he could trace his ancestry back to Robert the Bruce and the de Brus family from Normandy sometime after 1066. In aristocratic circles this was regarded as more impressive than the Battenberg family of mere British monarchs who had been imported from Germany when the British royal line was in danger of dying out. Since I was unable to trace my own ancestry on my father's side even by one generation, I suppose I should have been in awe of Anstruther, but I wasn't. I liked him. He told me he had joined the Labour Party at university only because there were already 'too many Anstruthers in the Conservative Party.'

When Fraser Davis was elected, Anstruther switched sides and was offered a job at the Ministry of Defence.

'Ah,' I told him, 'we have something in common.'

'Which is?' Anstruther cocked his head sideways with curiosity.

'We are both class traitors.' He had the good grace to laugh.

Barbara Holmes, the Foreign Secretary, walked with us for the first couple of hours. She had a pair of worn hiking boots and an impressively battered Barbour jacket. She was a vegetarian, which meant she had to swallow some of her supposed principles for the pleasure of a hunting trip to meet Bobby Black and the Queen, though she seemed to manage the process of political indigestion with reasonable grace. Johnny Lee and I walked behind the main hunting party, alongside four of Bobby Black's US Secret Service bodyguards and a couple of our own British protection people – the minimum possible. After their survey of the hills over the previous two days – mostly by helicopter – the security services said they were satisfied, as the Americans put it, that the probability of anything bad happening to the Vice-President 'tended towards zero.' It was a phrase of perfectly duplicitous precision.

* * *

Lord Anstruther and Vice-President Black hit it off immediately. Every time I looked to where they walked together or whispered in the shooting butts, they were deep in animated conversation, sometimes pointing out local landmarks and sometimes jabbing their fingers towards where they thought the grouse might be. Anstruther is a tall, handsome man, early forties, a contemporary of Fraser Davis's at Eton. Davis and Anstruther both have Scottish ancestry, but they fit perfectly into the English upper classes. Anstruther, with a shock of black hair that flicks across his forehead, has a passing resemblance to the actor Hugh Grant, but instead of Grant's blinky-stuttering foppishness, Anstruther has steel about him. He had served in a Guards regiment in Northern Ireland and the 1991 Gulf War, and was famous for being a member of the Dangerous Sports Club. Apparently it involves jumping off mountains, leaping down waterfalls, and sitting in underwater cages waiting for great white sharks to appear. As I watched him and Black in conversation it occurred to me that Anstruther might be in line for promotion. We could use him in the Foreign Office, in charge of the Americas. I'd put in a word with Downing Street.

He was telling Black that the grouse season began in Scotland on 12 August – the 'Glorious Twelfth' – and lasted until December.

'How Glorious is this Glorious Twelfth?' Black wondered.

'A bloody nonsense,' Anstruther scoffed. 'Marketing ploy. Not the best time to shoot.'

'When is the best time?'

'Right now,' Lord Anstruther said, looking proudly over the endless expanse of purple heather that formed his estate. 'When the birds are fat, sleek, and fast. These are the best days on the moors, Mr Vice-President. I've been shooting since I was a wee lad, and these are the best days . . .'

'Bobby,' Black said. 'Please call me Bobby.'

'Dickie,' Anstruther replied, with a smile and a handshake,

immediately reciprocated by Black. 'You can never be sure when you will have a good day or a bad day with shooting, but . . .'

'Well, yeah, right,' Bobby Black chimed in. 'Like in government.'

It was as if I was watching two people fall in love. In ten minutes they had formed a stronger bond than I had managed with either of them. I caught Johnny Lee's eye, and he winked. Our job was done. He took a first pull of whisky from his flask and held it towards me in a silent toast. The invisible hand of British and American diplomacy was chalking up another triumph – unless, of course, the Prime Minister actively blew it, which was well within the capabilities of Fraser Davis.

'Khan has arrived in London,' Johnny Lee told me. He had been getting messages from the Secret Service. 'He's on the train to Keighley. With his posse.'

'Did he say anything at the airport?'

'Thanked his family and his MP for standing by him and warned there would be more to say later about American brutality and hypocrisy. He said he was going on a peace march against American imperialism towards Iran.'

I shrugged.

'There's always more to say about American brutality and hypocrisy,' I told Johnny Lee. 'You know we're not going to arrest or charge him?'

'I guessed,' Johnny Lee said. The Metropolitan Police had concluded that there were no crimes committed by Mr Khan that were prosecutable in the United Kingdom. 'The majesty of the English law,' Johnny Lee shrugged. 'Let's just hope Khan doesn't bomb someplace.'

I wanted to tell him that we were doing a little more than just hoping, but at that point the guns started to fire and the Vice-President took his first grouse of the day.

*   *   *

At lunchtime we sat on groundsheets on the heather and had a picnic by a burn, as the clouds came in. The colour leached from the land. 'Vice' had now taken two grouse in the butts and was in a good mood. Barbara Holmes stayed long enough to attempt to lecture Bobby Black on G8 responsibility to Africa being tied to the implementation of good governance. She had apparently read and partly understood one of her briefing papers, the one that said President Carr was scheduled to meet the Prime Minister of Nigeria and the Congressional Black Caucus to discuss that very subject. Johnny Lee Ironside winked at me.

'She thinks Bobby Black gives a shit 'bout frickin' Africa?' he whispered. 'Is she for real?'

''Fraid so,' I replied. 'And we have more like her, male and female.'

'So do we.'

We munched game pie and cold beef sandwiches. Johnny Lee and I sipped red wine. Anstruther stood up and said that the weather was closing in, so we should get on with the shoot. Anstruther's two favourite dogs, a dun pointer called Sandy and a chocolate retriever bitch called Meg, were at his feet as he chatted with Bobby Black about hunting in Montana and Wyoming, everything from moose, elk, and mule deer to pronghorn.

'But this sure is a great day, Dickie, thank you. It's a good time to be here.'

'I hear now is a good time for you to be in Scotland for other reasons, Bobby,' Anstruther teased as we set off again.

'You mean the mid-term elections? Jeez, yes,' the Vice-President agreed, shouldering his shotgun. Then he laughed. 'No doubt about it. The President wants me out of the way. He's got this creep-o Svengali called Arlo Luntz who says I frighten the children. Well, I guess he's right. I'm the administration boogie man, no question. So maybe the President is happy for me to spend time in Scotland. The longer the better. Two days – maybe two years.'

'Maybe you should ask for political asylum, Bobby,' Anstruther laughed. 'I'm sure we could come to some arrangement.'

He and Anstruther guffawed again. I had never heard Bobby Black joke about himself before. It was a remarkable day.

As we walked on, we sipped hot coffee from flasks. There was a damp chill from the lowering clouds as the weather started to change. Anstruther explained that there were several traditional ways of shooting grouse. The easiest way was for the guns to be hidden in shooting butts, as we had done in the morning. The word 'butt' had caused momentary amusement to our American guests.

'Well, perhaps putting you in a butt might not have been the best move for this morning, Bobby,' Anstruther called out, and again Bobby Black laughed.

'Not my thing at all,' he responded.

A new Bobby Black was emerging from the shadows: self-deprecating, salty, human. Anstruther announced that we were now going to try what he called 'walking up', which he pronounced to be 'much more the ticket.' Johnny Lee and I zoned out of the explanation, but it seemed to mean that the dogs would figure out where the birds were, and instead of driving them towards the guns in the butts, we would walk to the birds as they were flushed from cover.

'Means you get a chance to see more of the countryside,' Anstruther drawled.

'Whatever you say, Dickie,' Bobby Black responded, checking his shotgun. The lopsided grin split his face. He patted Anstruther on the arm. 'I can't thank you enough.' Then he turned to me. 'And thank you, Ambassador Price.'

It was the first time Bobby Black had thanked me for anything.

We sweated with effort and the increasing humidity. From time to time we whispered between us, watchful for the rise of a covey or a sign from the beaters and the dogs. I learned that coveys are little family groups of grouse. The birds stick close to the ground and eat young heather shoots. Their stone colouring enables them to blend in, and they are difficult to spot until they rise up at an extraordinary speed, so it is like shooting at the Red Arrows display team. Even though I was not shooting, I could understand the challenge and excitement in the hunt. Like cooking with fire and smoke on a barbecue, hunting is hard-wired into the male head.

I could also see that, despite his glasses, Black was a good shot. He concentrated hard and blanked out everything else. Good politicians are always like this. They divide their lives into a series of boxes. Compartmentalization. For Black, politics was in one box, the War on Terror in another, and the box marked 'Grouse Shoot' was the only one he had open that day. By mid-afternoon Bobby Black had bagged another two birds to add to the two he had taken that morning in the butts. Then another one. Five now in total. Anstruther and Black maintained their distance on the right of the party. Anstruther politely let his guest make the shots, and only rarely fired his own gun. He was the perfect host, acting like a high-class beater. The chocolate retriever, Meg, brought the birds back, tail wagging energetically with pleasure. If the Vice-President of the United States had a tail, he would have wagged it too.

'My guy is one happy puppy,' Johnny Lee whispered to me, taking a mid-afternoon pull of his whisky. 'Well done, Ambo.'

'Well done, Chief of Staff.'

We each took a bow. I pulled Anstruther aside.

'Thank you,' was all I said.

Anstruther nodded. He knew he had done well. 'For Queen and country, yes?'

'Indeed,' I agreed, and looked over the hillsides to a large patch of whin bushes stretching into the distance. We had walked about ten or twelve miles and were pleasantly tired, far from any road or track. 'What do you reckon to the mist?'

'Coming down,' he agreed. 'But Our Guest said he'd like to hunt until he couldn't see. Maybe another hour? He's got grit. And a good eye. I've no idea how he shot someone in the backside in Texas, because he is not careless. He's not the accident type.'

'Oh,' I replied, and thought nothing more of it.

By late afternoon, Johnny Lee Ironside and Barbara Holmes had decided to turn back to Lord Anstruther's home, Castle Dubh. Johnny Lee said he had work to do, but he whispered to me that he was bored stiff. He had drunk his whisky and wanted to make phone calls and check emails. His Blackberry did not work on the hillside and he felt naked without it. The Blessed Barbara said she would hitch a ride because she needed to get back to her boxes to prepare for a European Union ministerial.

'I don't trust air I can't see,' Johnny Lee told me. 'Too clean up here. No broadband. No Internet. No cable TV. 'Sides, I want to hear more about our friend Khan and check out the latest on the mid-terms. I'm groused out.'

Half an hour after they left, there was suddenly air that you really could see. The mist came down hard. It started as the flat grey of the Highland sky sucking all the remaining colour from the heather and the whin bushes. It was as if the lights were put out. I thought of calling to Anstruther and suggesting we go back to Castle Dubh, but I did not want to seem like a middle-class wimp who couldn't handle himself on a grouse shoot. Anstruther was two hundred metres ahead looking up the hillside. Bobby Black was standing alone near the biggest of the thick patches of yellowing whin bushes with his shotgun under his arm. I took a sharp pull from my whisky flask. The mist swept down and I felt disorientated enough to put the whisky away.

I thought it might pass but in the cloud I lost sight of Anstruther. And of Black. And of the shooting party at the centre. I felt a thrill of fear. Anstruther yelled something, a warning, possibly, though I could not make out the words. The mist deadened sound as well as vision. Moments later he emerged sweating, a lumbering man, pulling hair from his wet face.

'I told the beaters to call it a day,' he gasped. 'No fun in this.'

We were on a sheep track near a burn. Anstruther moved off to call out to Prince Duncan and the others, and tell the beaters to pull everyone back down the hill. The next minute the mist closed in again and I could see nothing, except the yellow-tipped whin bushes dripping water right in front of me. The sheep track led downhill to a stile and then a mud road. At no time did I worry about my own safety, or that of anyone else. Why would I? I assumed that somewhere on the mud road beneath us the Land Rovers would be waiting, engines running, with flasks of hot coffee and cold beers. Civilization. Anstruther had gone over our planned route several times for the benefit of the Secret Service, the British police, and the beaters.

I could hear yelling, though it was not clear who was calling to whom. I walked downhill keeping the burn on my left as the mist seeped through my clothes. The dampness in Scotland is like midges, the biting flies of the summer months. It gets in everywhere, into the clothes, sticking on the hairs in the nose and eyebrows. Everything was damp and insufferable under a blanket of wet grey. I had a sudden memory of my childhood.

This kind of mist had happened to me before with the *haar* on the Pentlands, and when low cloud came down while I skied with my school at Glenshee and the Cairngorms. One of my teachers, a maths teacher called Mr Erick, had gone missing for a night in the mist and snow in Glencoe.

Clever man, he dug himself a makeshift igloo and had been picked up in the morning by the Mountain Rescue teams, none the worse for his ordeal except cold and hungry, but for months afterwards he had had to suffer the indignity of his school pupils, including me, drawing igloos on his blackboard and nicknaming him 'Eskimo Erick'. Lost in my thoughts, I was suddenly knocked off the path. Two US Secret Service agents, a big man and a wiry, much smaller woman, ran past, going up the hill, breathing hard. They were very alarmed. I could hear them calling out.

'Mr Vice-President? Sir? Mr Vice-President? Mr Black? Vice-President Black? Sir?'

I stopped and listened, not knowing what to do. In a fog, panic is infectious. Two more Secret Service agents ran past, and then two of our own Diplomatic Protection officers puffing behind them.

'What is it?' I called out. They were in a hurry and did not answer. I could hear half a dozen voices yelling out the Vice-President's name with increasing insistence. They spread out and moved up the hill in a line.

'Mr Vice-President? Mr Vice-President? Mr Black? Vice-President Black? *Sir?*'

The damp air dulled the sound. There were no echoes. We were licked by the grey, wet tongue of the fog. If I turned uphill towards where everyone seemed to be running, the chances were that I might end up lost, too, so I kept walking down the widening track towards the mud road. I came across Princess Charlotte and two of the beaters. We started to make our way down the track together.

'What happened?' Princess Charlotte fretted. 'Where's Dickie?'

'I have no idea. But they are calling for the Vice-President.'

'It's easy to get separated in this weather,' she said. 'I hope he sits still and waits for a moment, not wanders off. The mist always clears. You are in no danger, if you are patient.'

It was treacherous underfoot, and we had to take great care on the rocks. We came to a stile and I helped Princess Charlotte over it. It felt good to stand on the mud road after the bleakness of the moors. I still could not believe that anything serious had gone wrong. I could see the lights of the Land Rovers blasting into the fog, engines running. Thoughts of hot tea and coffee followed by a shower at Castle Dubh filled my head. The Princess and I sat in the back of one of the Land Rovers with the heating full on, warming ourselves. We put our hands round cups of tea poured from vacuum flasks, wondering what was going on further up the hillside. There was more shouting and the blurred outlines of running figures. Every sense was confused by the mist; every sight, sound, smell, touch, and taste was shaken by the fog.

Princess Charlotte raised an eyebrow. 'This could get nasty,' she said slowly.

I did not reply. The Princess, I should say, is one of the calm members of her family, late twenties, a horsewoman of formidable skill. I've watched her at three-day eventing, guiding her horse over walls two metres high. She is not given to panic. 'I hope nothing has happened to him,' she whispered to me.

'Me too, ma'am,' I responded. The thought of the Vice-President with a broken arm or leg sent a chill through me worse than the fog itself. 'Me too.'

Prince Duncan also found his way down. He poked his head into our Land Rover and mumbled something about a 'proper bloody pea-souper, yes?' It was heavy fog rather than mist now. Unlike his cousin, Princess Charlotte, Prince Duncan is regarded as a fool. He divides his time between a pretend-career in the army and a real vocation for swilling back free vodka in nightclubs. The tabloids have taken to calling him Prince Smirnoff.

'Yes, indeed,' I agreed, and Prince Duncan walked off

towards his own Land Rover while Princess Charlotte and I sat in silence for another fifteen minutes or so in ours.

'This really is *not* good,' she said insistently. I did not bother to respond. I could see the lights of more cars bouncing along the mud road and I could hear the radios of the police, though the mist deadened the conversations.

'I hope he has the sense to squat down and wait to be found,' I said. I told her the story of my teacher Eskimo Erick. Princess Charlotte shrugged.

'He's from the Wild West. I expect he's used to this sort of thing.'

I thought of using my mobile phone to call the Foreign Secretary or Johnny Lee or Kristina or Downing Street, but there was no signal on the hillside. Besides, what would I say? That I had brought the Vice-President of the United States to Aberdeenshire and lost him in the fog? I took a deep breath and decided that it was all going to turn out fine. He would reappear, perhaps shamefaced at yet another embarrassment following the shooting incident in Texas. We would go down to Castle Dubh, shower and prepare for dinner, and he would regale Her Majesty the Queen with stories of what had happened. We would praise his skills as a hunter and admire his sagacity on surviving the wild mountainside. It would be fine. I looked outside the Land Rover. In the darkness the mist was as thick as you can imagine. Even with engines running, the stink of diesel and the lights of the cars, I could no longer see across the track to the barbed-wire sheep fence at the other side where the stile had been. The headlight beams dissipated in the mist.

'You should go back, ma'am,' I suggested. 'I'll wait.'

Princess Charlotte would have none of it. 'We arrived together and we shall return together,' she said slowly. I liked this woman.

After a further hour of frustration, Dickie Anstruther himself appeared, dishevelled and alarmed.

113

'We've lost him,' Lord Anstruther said, handing his gun to one of the beaters and pulling at his Barbour jacket. He swept the hair back out of his eyes. His mouth was set grimly. 'We've lost the Vice-President of the United States of America.'

TEN

In Washington, the White House was alerted to the disappearance almost immediately. It was early evening in Scotland, and just after noon on the eastern seaboard of the United States, with the October sun arching over the dome of the Capitol. Kristina told me that from very early that morning the White House staff had been digging in for a crisis, but it was a completely different kind of crisis. When she arrived at 7 a.m., Kristina looked out on a group of journalists who had gathered on the lawn outside the press room in the West Wing, waiting for a scandal. The wolf-pack was ready to attack the weakest of the herd, and they had the scent of a straggler, the Transportation Secretary, Harry Concini. Concini had been pictured receiving what was described coyly in news reports as 'a sexual service' from a woman identified as a 'lap-dancer' in the back of a government vehicle. Pictures had been posted on the Internet. You could see that Concini had a smile on his face. In the puritan prurience of the news media, the idea that he actually enjoyed it seemed to make it worse.

'Social conservatives are outraged by the sex,' a commentator said, with a smirk, on one of that morning's TV talk shows. 'Fiscal conservatives are outraged by the misuse of a government vehicle. Concini is just the latest in what's being called here a long line of "blows" to the Carr administration.'

During those first two years in office, Theo Carr, like many a president before him, was considered by the Washington media to be unlucky, scandal prone, and clumsy. The TV shows recited the evidence. Vice-President Black was a malign influence and a vote-loser. He had also shot one of the biggest donors to the Republican Party, Paul Comfort, in his rear end. Theo Carr himself had hit a golf partner in the face with a ball at a course in Maryland, slicing a fairway shot into the teeth of the Governor of Iowa. Carr had also served awkwardly in a doubles tennis match, hitting his partner on the back of the head. The unfortunate victim was the CEO of a New York banking conglomerate that later needed to be bailed out by federal funds. None of these things would matter except that, taken together, the journalists had a metaphor for what they increasingly believed was really wrong with the Carr administration – and maybe even for what had gone wrong with the United States itself in the two years since the Manila attack. For all the greatness of the country, the genius and essential goodness of the American people, voters were beginning to wonder whether the United States was on the wrong track, run by the gang who could not shoot straight.

President Theo Carr walked into the Oval Office shortly after seven o'clock that morning. He was in a bad mood.

'Harry Concini and a hooker,' he said aloud, but to no one in particular. 'Anything else I need to know about?'

His Chief of Staff, Stephanie Alejandro, shook her head.

'Not that I know of, sir. Nothing except routines until the Nigerian President and the Congressional Black Caucus at noon.'

Alejandro was a corporate lawyer from Albuquerque, New Mexico, and a long-time friend of the Carr family.

'I'll need my cards on that,' Carr said. He liked to be briefed for all meetings with a series of notes, double-spaced, on six-by-four-inch cards.

'Yes, sir. On their way.'

The President moved from his desk to the lectern, where he stood to improve his circulation as he looked over his papers. He read the digest of that morning's headlines with increasing irritation. The one that most annoyed him was a signed commentary from James Byrne which called President Theo Carr '*the Accidental President*' elected only because: 'our nation was in a funk after the terrorist incident at Manila Airport. Now, funk over. Let us use these mid-term elections to curb the excesses of the Carr presidency – and especially to curb the power and influence of Vice-President Bobby Black. Yo, People! Put a Brake on Black!'

'"People, put a brake on Black!"' President Carr said out loud. 'How much he get paid for this shit, Arlo?'

Arlo Luntz was finalizing the six-by-four card briefing on the Nigerian President's visit.

'Byrne? He earns just a shade over three hundred thousand dollars a year. Used to be more but they don't use him on the Sunday talk shows since his voice problem.'

'Maybe he should run the country,' President Carr grunted. 'Seems to know all the goddamn answers.'

'Sometimes I wish I was as sure about anything as these press boys are about everything, Mr President,' Arlo Luntz responded, pushing a stray hair from his bad wig back to the top of his head as he shuffled the notecards. Carr looked over at him.

'I like that, Arlo. Mibbe I'll use it, next time I get asked some bullshit question. Which could be later today.'

'Yes, sir.'

'Polls?'

Luntz looked up from the cards. 'Same old, same old.

Latest puts us ten points and more behind nationwide and we got serious state-wide problems in Missouri, Kentucky, Oklahoma, Ohio, Pennsylvania, and Florida. Those last three states—'

'Uh huh,' Carr responded, waving at Luntz to be quiet. Carr knew all about those last three states, and did not want to hear it again. He had won all three of them in the presidential election two years ago, and Luntz told him repeatedly that he would need to win all of them again in two years' time to stand any chance of re-election, but they were states in which Bobby Black was particularly unpopular. Carr flicked through more of the newspaper digest. The front page of the *Washington Post* carried pictures of Harry Concini tastefully cropped so it was not clear exactly what was going on, and yet even in the blurred pictures, shot on a mobile phone, it was possible to make out a young woman in her underwear kneeling over the Transportation Secretary in the back seat of a limousine, and the Secretary's obvious pleasure at the encounter.

'Why can't these guys just keep it in their pants?' Theo Carr wondered. 'I mean, just for two years?'

He felt the blood pump in his forehead. Despite giving up red meat, bacon, French fries, eggs, cheese, cakes, and pastries – all the foods that made life worth living, despite the exercise and standing at the lectern as instructed, the president's cholesterol levels had risen considerably since taking office. So had his blood pressure.

The doctors told him he was in increasing danger of a heart attack or a stroke. They prescribed statins, more exercise, and less stress. Carr swallowed his morning pills standing at the lectern. He just loved the concept of 'less stress'.

'You were elected to change America, Mr President,' Arlo Luntz replied, assuming the question was directed at him. 'You were not elected to change human nature. There's plenty

118

of folks who can't keep their pants on. You only employ some of them.'

'Well, hell, that's good news that I haven't got the monopoly of them, Arlo.'

'Yes, sir. There's plenty in the private sector. And in the legislative branch.'

President Carr threw the newspaper digest into the trash. He turned to the television and fiddled with the remote. The reporters on the White House lawn tried to hide their own obvious pleasure as they continually discussed what they repeatedly called 'yet another blow' to the Carr administration.

'And it could not have happened at a more crucial time,' one of the reporters intoned. 'Just two weeks ahead of the "make or break" moment for President Carr in the midterm elections, with all the talk in this town that Theo Carr will not be a one-term president – he may only be a half-term president, cut off at the knees after just two years in office.'

Carr felt his blood pressure rise and switched off the televisions.

'Well?' Carr asked, turning towards his senior staff.

'Fire him immediately, Mr President,' Stephanie Alejandro said. 'No excuses.'

Carr disagreed. He said he wanted to hear Concini's side of the story, face to face. Alejandro looked at Kristina and rolled her eyes. Luntz sat impassively. He had finished arranging the briefing cards about the Nigerian visit and was scribbling on a notepad. Both women liked Carr personally, admired his warmth and strong personal qualities, but they thought his softness was an irritation. Whatever their dislike of Vice-President Bobby Black, if he were in the room instead of being in Scotland, Kristina and Stephanie Alejandro both knew that Concini would be gone already. Toast. Decision taken.

'As you wish,' Alejandro said. She scheduled fifteen

119

minutes face-time with Concini and the president late in the afternoon, when Concini's flight got back from Louisiana.

'At least he'll be fired in time for the evening news and the morning papers,' she whispered to Kristina.

'The hooker looks African American,' Carr suggested.

'Yes, Mr President, I do believe she is. Though that fact is not going to be helpful with the African American vote. Or any vote. Concini's got to go, sir. You have got to—'

'I know what I have got to do, Stephanie,' Carr said. 'All in good time.'

Kristina moved away to prepare for the arrival of the Nigerian President. Stephanie Alejandro returned to her own office and began finalizing a short list of three possible replacements for Concini. Luntz sat in the Oval Office talking through the campaign and fund-raising schedule he had organized for the president up to the mid-terms. Stephanie Alejandro was wondering how her day could get any worse when she was suddenly interrupted by a call from the director of the Secret Service. His voice was usually flat calm. This time he sounded shaken.

'The Vice-President has gone missing in Scotland, Ms Alejandro.'

'Missing?' she repeated in astonishment. 'What do you mean, missing?'

The director of the Secret Service explained what he knew of the incident on the Scottish hillside, which wasn't much.

'Missing,' he said, 'as in, lost.'

'Jesus Christ,' Stephanie Alejandro said. The Transportation Secretary with a hooker. The Vice-President missing in fog on a shooting trip. 'Say it ain't so?'

The director of the Secret Service told her exactly the opposite. 'It's a very serious incident. We are doing all we can.'

Stephanie Alejandro pushed aside the files concerning the

possible new Transportation Secretary. Nobody would care about that now. She herself did not care about it now. She stood up and checked her clothes in the mirror, a dark blue suit with a discreet silver brooch on the lapel. She looked good, she thought. She'd need to: it was going to be a long day.

'This is where I pretend I know what the hell I'm doing.' She checked her hair and make-up, shaking her head in despair. 'Even though nobody knows anything in this town. Nobody.'

The words of Theo Carr when he offered her the Chief of Staff job came to mind: 'Some folks get paid to panic, Stephanie. You get paid *not* to panic. So do I. This is a calm White House. A calm presidency.' Calmly she called Kristina.

'Yeah, I just heard,' Kristina said. 'I called an emergency National Security crisis team meeting in Sit. Room Alpha. Joint Chiefs. Director Shultz. In one hour.'

'I'll get the President,' Alejandro said. Kristina liked Stephanie Alejandro because she was straight, she was organized and, unlike most of the men in the White House, she appeared to submerge her own ego and interests into whatever was best for the President and the country. 'If everyone around here did that, we wouldn't have so many problems,' Kristina once told me.

Stephanie Alejandro walked towards the Roosevelt Room to interrupt President Carr in his scheduled meeting with the President of Nigeria and the Congressional Black Caucus. They were discussing aid to Africa. Kristina was already there. They were sitting on sofas, taking fifteen minutes to discuss how to spread democracy. Carr's interest in the subject had hitherto been thought close to zero, but it increased considerably when Arlo Luntz told him that being seen to host a delegation of African American Congressional leaders two weeks before the mid-term elections would help with voters.

'Big time.'

'You kiddin' me, Arlo? Like there's Republican votes in Sudan and Zimbabwe? Who knew?'

Luntz shook his head. 'You need to be more user-friendly, is all,' he insisted, brushing back the bit of stray hair that continually fell in his eyes. President Carr never understood why his Chief Political Adviser had purchased such a bad wig. He paid him well enough, and yet the hair flopped in his face like a raccoon's tail.

But then, Carr decided, choosing a good wig would have meant he would not have been Arlo Luntz, with his trademark bad suits, mismatching polyester shirts and ties, worn shoes, bad grooming, and good advice. You had to take the whole Luntz package.

'You can count the African American votes I get for my party,' Carr said laconically, 'on all the fingers of one hand . . . of Captain Hook.'

'That's not the point, Mr President,' Arlo Luntz argued back. One of the reasons Carr liked Luntz was that he robustly contradicted him. Luntz called it 'speaking Truth to Power.' Carr thought allowing Luntz to be borderline rude showed that he himself was a strong and confident President, despite what the newspapers suggested about him being Bobby Black's puppet.

'It's not the point, Arlo?' Theo Carr snapped back. 'You telling me that outside a few evangelicals I get any African American votes at all? You been smoking that shit again? Why you waste my time with this?'

Luntz had a twenty-five-year-old conviction for smoking marijuana when he had been a postgraduate in political science at the University of Virginia. Theo Carr never let him forget it. Carr himself had an even older 'driving while intoxicated' conviction from his time at Princeton. For his part, Luntz never mentioned it.

'We focused it, Mr President,' Luntz said, meaning he

had conducted a series of focus groups with ordinary voters on the President's strengths and weaknesses. 'Voters *want* to like you. They *love* your warmth. But they don't want to hug you close. Folks don't think you *care* for people who're not so lucky. The downtrodden. Cosying up to an African president and the African American Congressional leadership is not 'bout getting black votes. It's 'bout getting white votes. Folks'll see that despite all the mean things said about your administration, there's a message. And the message is: *You Care*. You Care about Africa.' Carr nodded. This made sense.

"Course I care, Arlo.'

'Yes, Mr President. Evangelical churches, white and black, have projects to help out our African brothers and sisters, so our people care about that too,' Luntz continued. "Sides, it'll take about half an hour, tops, and when the Reptiles bring up the subject of Harry Concini getting a blow job from the New Orleans hooker, you tell them you're fixing world poverty and suchlike and all the Reps can talk about is sex, the dirty-minded sons of bitches.'

Luntz chuckled. Theo Carr nodded and smiled. Luntz was right. Luntz was usually right. 'The Reptiles' or 'the Reps' was Luntz's phrase for the White House press corps. Theo Carr beamed. A light switched on in his head. *Of course* he would like to meet with the President of Nigeria. He would be honoured to visit with the Congressional Black Caucus. Sit awhile. *Sure he would*. And he would be *pleased* to remind Americans that a billion people in the world – many of them Africans – lived on less than a dollar a day. All that moral high ground made him feel dizzy. Political vertigo. And Luntz was right about one other thing too. It meant the Reptiles asking about Harry Concini's dick in the lap-dancer's mouth would be beneath contempt. *Message: He Cared*. Oh, yeah. He cared a bunch. President Carr cleared his throat and smiled at the Nigerian President.

'Bad governance is a bigger killer in the continent of Africa than Ebola or AIDS,' Carr said, turning his 100-watt gaze towards the members of the Congressional Black Caucus, as if he had just thought of this particular insight. 'That is the real sickness. And democracy is the cure.'

Arlo Luntz watched from the side of the room. He marvelled at the political skills of the President of the United States. Whatever his limitations, there was a bizarre alchemy that made people like Theo Carr. It also made Theo Carr desperate for affection. If there was a hand, Carr would grasp it. If there was a baby, he would kiss it. If there was a fist, he wanted to turn it away and change it into a handshake. For Carr an Enemy was just a Friend he had not yet made. That optimism and apparent good nature was part of his undoubted political genius.

'Soft words turneth away wrath,' Luntz lectured Carr approvingly on one occasion, 'as the Good Book says.'

'And if soft words don't work, Arlo?' Carr wondered.

'Then we kick ass.'

Arlo Luntz's focus groups were consistent. When asked to choose who they would like to have for supper or to invite to a family barbecue or to share a pitcher of beer with, independent and non-committed voters would choose Theo Carr every time.

Folks liked his bad golf swing. They liked the time he hit a tennis ball into the back of his partner's head, especially since it was a Wall Street banker. The focus groups compared Theo Carr to Homer Simpson or *Family Guy*, a Regular Joe who made embarrassing mistakes, but was basically good hearted and solid. Sure he fucked up. Who didn't? But Luntz had for months privately told the President that he had a problem. Most voters, even Republican Party loyalists, hated the mean streak they sensed running through the Carr administration.

'I'm not mean, Arlo,' Carr had protested, with genuine surprise.

'They don't think you are, Mr President. They think the Vice-President is mean enough for both of you. His reputation could cost you re-election and he will cost you votes in the mid-terms. Time for a change.'

'Bullshit,' Carr protested. 'Bobby's a great asset to the team.'

'He's a drag on the ticket, Mr President,' Luntz told Carr, and repeated it at every opportunity. 'Folks think he's your Dark Side. Hell, *he* thinks he's your Dark Side.'

'That's just TV talk. It doesn't play in the real world.'

'Yes it does, Mr President. And I have the focus groups to prove it. Ohio, Pennsylvania, and Florida . . .'

The President just smiled.

'You tell Bobby Black this, Arlo?'

'No, Mr President. I work for you, not him. But do you want four more years in office or not? You need to think about that.'

'And what do *you* think *I* think about that?'

Luntz sucked in a deep breath. He knew that the next thing he said could cost him his job and his career in Washington. He decided to say it anyway. Speak Truth to Power.

'Let's see how these mid-terms play out,' he said. 'See how bad a hit we take. But you want to be re-elected for a second term, you need to get rid of Bobby Black. Find someone . . . less brittle. A woman. Or an African American. Or both.'

If Theo Carr was surprised by this suggestion, he did not show it. He thought for a moment. 'Without Bobby and the way he handled the Manila bombing, I would not be president now.'

'And with Bobby,' Luntz interrupted, 'I mean, with the Vice-President, you won't be elected again. If there's another terrorist attack, then folks'll blame him for fucking up, and if there isn't a terrorist attack, they'll wonder why you need

125

a junkyard dog around the White House yappin' at everything in sight. It's time for him to go. With dignity. I'm thinking, what about his undisclosed health issues?'

Theo Carr looked at Luntz all the way down from the bad haircut to the badly polished shoes and smiled.

'What about them?'

'Well, we need to get him some.'

President Carr took a deep breath. He was the one with the undisclosed health issues.

'Best keep this conversation our little secret, Arlo,' he said. 'Just you and me.'

'Yes, Mr President,' Luntz replied. 'It's not like I'd care for the Vice-President to hear about it.'

Theo Carr put his hands together in an attitude of prayer, and he nodded.

'Me neither.'

In the Roosevelt Room, Kristina looked across to where Theo Carr was smiling. His face was lit up with a new-found passion for Africa. It was one of the marvels of the modern political world. Theo Carr had discovered a continent. No matter how often Kristina witnessed this presidential enthusiasm, it always astonished her. She also marvelled that the President of the United States could make every scripted and rehearsed comment seem off the cuff. Carr had spent just ten minutes reading his prepared remarks aloud and memorizing them as he habitually did, in front of the mirror in the bathroom at the side of the Oval Office. It was a little trick Luntz had taught him years before when he was a state governor.

'I look weird reading in the mirror,' Carr had protested the first time.

'If you look weird reading in the mirror,' Luntz answered him, 'then you look weird. If you look good in the mirror, then you look good. So I want you to do it till you look good.'

Carr did as he was told. After years of practice, now he always looked good. His remarks on Africa had been crafted as usual by Carr's speech-writing team, exactly the way Luntz and Carr liked them. Luntz insisted on a series of simple, declarative sentences. He always demanded active verbs, except if the president had to admit a mistake in which case it was what Luntz called 'the Fucked-Up Passive'.

'*Mistakes have been made*,' was Luntz's most obvious example of the Fucked-Up Passive. It was absolutely forbidden to use an active verb for failure. Nobody in the Carr White House would ever say, 'I made a mistake.' Any White House scriptwriter who wrote such a thing would be fired. The whole point about mistakes, Luntz lectured, was that they are impersonal. They were visitations from Heaven, fatherless bastards, except if they were made by political opponents who, of course, did actively make mistakes. As for Carr himself, he did not care as much about the grammar as he cared about layout. He insisted that every speech was double-spaced fourteen-point on his six-by-four-inch cards, each numbered in the top right-hand corner. In his ten minutes of rehearsal that morning he committed the words to memory and put the cards in the shredder. Word perfect. It was a remarkable performance, day after day.

'You do not *deliver* a speech, Mr President,' Luntz constantly told Carr in one of his many political aphorisms. 'You *live* it. That's what makes it live for other people too.'

The day that Bobby Black disappeared, as the President talked about the problems of African democracy to his invited guests and the Washington press corps, Theo Carr appeared to be living out his deeply held beliefs. Luntz taught that this ability to believe was crucial. Carr was a natural. Bobby Black was not.

'Believe,' Arlo Luntz frequently told Carr, quoting more of his favourite political maxims, 'and you never need to fake anything. Tell the truth, and you never need to remember anything. Win, and you never need to apologize for anything. And never, on any account, ascribe to malice what you can blame on stupidity.'

'You wanna update Machiavelli's *The Prince* for the twenty-first century,' Carr had told him. 'That's what you gotta do, Arlo. Share the wisdom.'

'Maybe I will,' Luntz had replied. 'I intend to write a book when we're done with this.'

'Yeah, but remember it's when we're *done with this*, Arlo,' Carr insisted. 'Not until I leave the White House.'

Luntz nodded. He had two other maxims for Carr to learn that day. 'Campaign in Poetry,' he instructed, 'Govern in Prose.'

'Makes sense,' Carr agreed. 'And the other one?'

'As president you need to tell people that "Bad planning on your part does not necessarily constitute an emergency on my part."'

Theo Carr laughed. 'That one, I can remember. That one I can use.'

As Carr worked through his prepared remarks in the Roosevelt Room, without notes, the members of the Congressional Black Caucus, all but two of them Democrats, nodded along with the caring, poetic eloquence of the Republican President.

'The way I see it, bad governance and disease in Africa are directly related,' Carr went on. 'We're talking two faces of the same monster. Those countries that have the worst of one, 'most always have the worst of the other. Take how things have changed in Uganda, f'r instance . . .'

Kristina received a message that the emergency National Security team had now assembled in the Situation Room. She nodded at Stephanie Alejandro.

'We're ready,' she mouthed, as she left the room and gave a thumbs-up out of sight of the press. The President kept talking but he caught Kristina's eye and then Stephanie Alejandro's face and immediately knew something was wrong. Alejandro moved to the side and stood beside Sandy McAuley.

'. . . those countries that have the best systems of government also have the best record for public health and ending poverty. The worst African governments have the worst public health records. Coincidence? No way. I like to think, Mr President, that democracy in Nigeria makes your country healthy, and it makes your people healthy . . .' He looked towards the Nigerian President who beamed in response.

'Sandy,' Stephanie Alejandro hissed, nodding in the direction of the pool TV crews and reporters. The pool, as usual, was completely ignoring the visiting African dignitary and the Congressmen. The Reps had no interest in foreigners from No-News Zones like Nigeria. They were waiting for Carr to finish his homily about Africa and preparing to ambush him with questions about the Transportation Secretary and the lap-dancer.

'Sandy,' Stephanie Alejandro hissed again, 'get the Reps out of here.'

'Okay, that's it,' the press secretary clapped his hands and called out loudly at the TV crews and journalists. 'Time to go, people.'

'. . . indeed, the provision of anti-malaria mosquito nets in West Africa increases the chances of survival of the newborn, by more than . . .'

'People! Time to go, okay . . .'

'. . . saving babies is God's work . . .'

The White House press corps sullenly began to move. They knew the Carr team called them Reptiles. They could take abuse. What they could not take was being moved on from a boring no-news photo-op with a bunch of foreigners before their chance for a drive-by interrogation of the President of

129

the United States on Harry Concini's sex life. Did Sandy McAuley really think they were going to get a story out of Africa? Jesus. The woman from AP butted in.

'Mr President, how does the conduct of Secretary Concini fit with this administration's rhetoric on family values?'

'. . . clean potable water transforms . . .'

James Byrne started to shout out in his hoarse, shattered voice. His larynx had not recovered from being struck and his words had a squawk to them, as if he was still going through puberty.

'Can the Transportation Secretary keep his job', he shrieked, 'if he can't keep his pants on?'

Carr put his hand towards his ear and inclined towards Byrne, shaking his head as if he could not quite make out what he was saying. Then he kept to his script.

'When it comes to Africa, the message is simple. Message: I care, America cares,' President Carr said suddenly and loudly, winding up the meeting.

'. . . having oral sex with a lap-dancer in the back of a government limousine?' Byrne croaked, as he felt Sandy McAuley's hand on his arm.

'Thanks, James,' McAuley said. 'Thanks everyone.'

Carr smiled engagingly, as if the questions were being asked in a foreign language. He turned to the Nigerian President.

'You have these folks in your country?' he whispered.

'Not yet,' the Nigerian leader whispered back with a grin. 'The advances of democracy take time.'

The two Presidents giggled. Carr slapped the Nigerian on the knee. A bonding moment for the cameras. The Congressional delegation beamed. Arlo Luntz looked on, delighted.

'That's it, people,' Sandy McAuley bellowed again to the remaining journalists. 'Puh-lease!'

The press pool finally left. Stephanie Alejandro nodded

towards the Congressmen and walked towards the two Presidents.

'Excuse me, Mr President . . . Gentlemen,' she flashed an insistent smile at the Nigerian and the others, then whispered in the ear of President Carr so only he could hear. 'The Vice-President has disappeared,' she hissed.

'What?'

'On a Scottish mountain.'

'What do you mean, disappeared?'

'Gone. Missing. No sign.'

Carr frowned, remembering something. 'The shooting thing? With Queen Elizabeth?'

'Yes, sir. We may have to leave the White House, Mr President. Right now.'

Theo Carr's face collapsed into a heap of disbelief. 'But . . . I . . . my guests . . .' He gestured towards the Nigerian and the others. A genuinely courteous man, he hated to be thought rude. He employed others to be rude for him.

'*Now*, Mr President. Saving Africa is some other day. We have to leave for Sit. Room Alpha right now. And potentially leave Washington. We have no reason to believe this nation is under attack, but Dr Taft says this is being treated as national security emergency, Code . . .'

She whispered the code words for a profound strategic emergency facing the United States. The room filled with Secret Service agents, ushering people away. Carr stood up. He remembered to smile, almost as a reflex action. He apologized to the hapless Nigerian leader and the African American congressmen. He shook hands and put his own arm around their shoulders in a gesture of affection.

Stephanie Alejandro acquiesced in the short delay. There were various stages in Carr presidential affection, some of which he had copied from Bill Clinton, another president who had been desperate to be loved. There was the simple handshake, sometimes with a double hand-grasp.

131

There was the handshake plus elbow-squeeze, which Carr reserved for the more junior congressmen. Next up was the handshake and rub of the upper arm, which was being offered right now to the Senator from Michigan. Finally came the ultimate in Theo Carr's political foreplay, the handshake, upper-arm rub, followed by the arm around the shoulder, which he employed briefly on the President of Nigeria. Bill Clinton often used similar techniques, though after the Monica Lewinsky affair, Theo Carr joked to Luntz and his senior staff that, 'Unlike me, Clinton was just wiping his hands.'

'Thanks for visiting with me,' Theo Carr called out with a cheery wave. 'Thanks so much. Thank you. Sorry it's been cut short, but something's come up. Thank you. Yes, and thank you. G'bye now.'

Everyone left the room smiling. Luntz insisted that cheering people up was often the sole purpose of a White House visit.

'Make 'em happy and they never forget to tell their friends,' Luntz said. 'Piss 'em off and they never forget to tell the Reptiles.'

The Congressional delegation was escorted towards the Old Executive Office Building, a massive grey, French-inspired structure on the edge of the White House grounds where, to fill in time, they were promised a hastily scheduled meeting with the only person available, Kristina's Deputy National Security Adviser. He knew very little about Africa. He was a Europe specialist. Following a hurried telephone call from Kristina, at that precise moment he was demanding a rapid briefing on the 'Millennium Goals' for Africa and complaining to his Senior Staff Assistant that his knowledge of the entire continent was largely confined to PBS wildlife films involving wildebeest being eaten by crocodiles as they crossed the Masai Mara.

'Message: we don't know jack,' he shuddered.

In Situation Room Alpha, Kristina called the emergency meeting to order.

'The Vice-President is missing in the fog on a Scottish hillside,' she said. 'The President will be with us momentarily. We need to assume the worst. So I'd like you all to tell me what you think the worst might be. Give it to me.'

ELEVEN

The White House is the best-known building in the world; beautiful, perfectly proportioned, a neoclassical gem. It is also small and vulnerable. Like the massive Department of Defence building, the Pentagon, on the other side of the Potomac River in Virginia, the White House contains more secrets underground than above it. The Situations Rooms are part of the secure, concrete, steel, and lead-lined subterranean basement system constructed under the White House during the Cold War, beginning in the early 1950s. The basement system leads to tunnels that fan out in every direction to facilitate escape in case of emergency. Some of the tunnels lead into the Washington underground Metro system. All are kept at a constant 68°F. Each has generators, communications systems, emergency doors, food, and oxygen supplies capable of lasting at least a month, depending on how many staffers need to be housed.

By the time President Carr and Stephanie Alejandro arrived in Sit. Room Alpha, it was already full. Half of those inside wore military uniforms. Everyone stood up. The military officers saluted the Commander in Chief. Carr motioned them to sit. Kristina was a splash of colour in a sea of drab, surrounded by staff from the OVP, the Secret

Service, the Director of Central Intelligence, General Conrad Shultz, and the two of the four Joint Chiefs, who happened to be in Washington. The Marine Corps Commandant was in Japan and the Chairman of the Joint Chiefs, USN Admiral Henry Walters was in California, though he joined the meeting by secure video link from an aircraft carrier in San Diego. The emergency meeting lasted less than ten minutes.

'What do we know?' Carr asked.

Kristina ran through the facts, counting them out on the fingers of her left hand.

One: Fog on the mountain.

Two: Probably an accident.

Three: No way of knowing.

Four: The Vice-President has disappeared.

'Perhaps dead, injured, or kidnapped.'

'Kidnapped?' Theo Carr looked devastated. Morale seeped from him as if down a drain. 'Two weeks before the mid-term elections, Bobby gets himself kidnapped?'

'Unspeakable at any time, Mr President. But it is obviously a possibility.'

'Jesus.'

The President of the United States slumped in his chair and did not speak. He rubbed his face and did not ask questions either. Kristina Taft ran through the response so far.

'Before you arrived, Mr President, we discussed how we would plan for the worst and hope for the best. Best – he's wandered off and will turn up soon. Worst – hostile activity. He's been murdered or kidnapped. Sandy is working on a hoping-for-the-best statement for the press. The Brits have scheduled a full news conference for eight a.m. tomorrow. Nothing on the record before then except news about search activity. The British say he's just wandered off. They are hoping to keep a lid on it.'

'Jesus,' Carr said again, digging his fingers into the skin on his forehead. 'Might as well hope to keep a lid on a nuclear explosion.'

'Yes, Mr President,' Kristina Taft agreed. 'Now for the worst.'

She asked for a rundown of the troop alerts. Since 9/11 the plan for a major domestic national security emergency included fighter-plane deployments over all major US cities and an alert in all major public buildings and transportation facilities. Then Kristina turned to the Director of Central Intelligence, and asked Conrad Shultz to say a few words.

'We are efforting a full intelligence assessment and prepared for every contingency, Mr President,' Shultz began. He was known for his brilliance in navigating the dark waters of Pentagon politics but also for the opacity of his verbal opinions. Arlo Luntz said when Conrad Shultz spoke it was 'Tofu Talk' – you could chew it but at the end you were not entirely sure what it was you were eating, and five minutes later you were hungry again. At Bobby Black's insistence, Shultz had been rewarded for his 'Spartacus' paper with the CIA job, and now, almost two years later, it had sucked the life out of him. He had sallow, etiolated skin and dark circles around his eyes from overwork.

His large, hunched shoulders gave him the appearance of a panda bear, though pandas have claws and teeth. Shultz called himself the Worrier-in-Chief.

'NSA reports no unusual chatter,' the Worrier-in-Chief said. The NSA was the National Security Agency, the eavesdropping arm of American intelligence, not to be confused with the space agency, NASA. 'Nothing unusual around the time of the disappearance. Nothing suspicious from the Aberdeenshire region. No reason to believe hostile intent. No detectable al Qaeda movements, though it's a big religious festival day in the tribal areas of Pakistan, and there has been a suicide bombing at a dog-fight in Kandahar.'

'What kind of dog-fight?' Theo Carr said, puzzled, thinking it was some kind of slang expression.

136

'Literally a dog-fight, Mr President,' Shultz explained. 'It's a sport down in that part of the country. Dog eat dog. Bottom line: we have no reason to believe anything other than the British version, that the Vice-President has gone missing or been involved in an accident. But I agree with Kristina. Assume the worst, including celebrations—'

That word also puzzled Theo Carr. 'Celebrations?'

'Yes, Mr President. There will be celebrations. Folks'll take to the streets in Gaza, in Tehran and among extremist Muslim organizations in other countries. The usual suspects. People delighted that anything bad has befallen the leadership of the Great Satan. Within twenty-four hours, I'd guess. Like I say, Mr President, assume the worst and you will not be disappointed.'

'And what is the worst, Conrad? The real deal here?'

The Director of Central Intelligence sighed and turned his panda eyes towards the President. The Worrier-in-Chief looked very worried.

'The worst, Mr President, would be if it's kidnap.' There was a sharp intake of breath around the room. 'I repeat, we have no evidence of kidnap at this time. Everything up to and including assassination of the Vice-President would be survivable. Regrettable but survivable. A kidnap and a hostage situation would be . . . a nightmare.'

There was a murmur of conversation. Carr silenced it with a wave of his hand and then continued. 'Explain, Conrad.'

'Vice-President Black is . . .' He rubbed his tired panda eyes for a moment. '. . . He's fully briefed on everything.'

'Everything?'

'More or less, Mr President. You tasked the Vice-President specifically to become one of the keepers of the crown jewels of US intelligence, and to implement with me elements of the Spartacus programme. We have been working . . . *very* closely together. You . . . you personally have not been informed of all the details of Spartacus because the Vice-President decided it was better that way. But now, if we've lost him, then we have lost . . . one of the gatekeepers.'

General Conrad Shultz stopped talking. There were forty people in Sit. Room Alpha. No one dared breathe.

'You mean Bobby knows more about what's going on than I do?'

'About some things, yes, Mr President.'

'Go on.'

'If Spartacus is compromised, then we're in deep shit.' Shultz coughed a little. 'I mean we're in deep shit, *sir*.' People breathed out. The gloom in the room deepened. 'Fact is,' Conrad Shultz continued, opening a leather notecase, 'in consultation with the Joint Chiefs, with Dr Taft, and the Attorney General's office, I have taken the liberty to produce a Presidential Intelligence Finding.' He put a piece of paper in front of the President. 'I'd be grateful if you would read and sign it before you leave Washington, Mr President. It's of the utmost import-ance and sensitivity.'

Kristina Taft caught the eye of Stephanie Alejandro. Carr looked at the document but did not read it.

'Which says?'

Conrad Shultz sucked in a breath. He read from his own copy.

'The directive says that in the event the Vice-President of the United States is being held against his will by forces hostile to the United States, and in the event that a rescue operation is deemed by the Director of Central Intelligence or his deputies to be not possible with a high probability of success, the Commander in Chief instructs the Joint Chiefs and all other US forces, military and civilian, to do whatever may be necessary to ensure that the Vice-President cannot become an asset to the enemies of the United States, such necessary measures to include but not be limited to deliberate termination of the subject.'

President Carr looked at his CIA Director. The room was silent again.

'*Whatever may be necessary*,' Carr repeated. '*Deliberate termination of the subject*.' He understood but wanted it spelled out. 'In plain man's talk, Conrad?'

'In plain man's talk, Mr President, we are seeking authorization to ensure that the Vice-President's knowledge of Spartacus or any other programme cannot be used against the United States.'

'You are asking me to authorize you to kill Bobby Black.' It was not a question.

'Yes, sir. If we locate him but rescue is impossible.'

Theo Carr stood up slowly. Then he banged his right fist on the desk. His face was suffused with anger. 'How in God's name am I going to look Susan Black in the eye after I have given the order to execute her husband? You ever think on that? Well, did you?'

Conrad Shultz shuddered and turned his dark eyes to his papers without answering directly. Kristina Taft broke in.

'Mr President, after you sign this Finding you are going to be able to look Susan Black in the eye because you can look every American in the eye. You can say that you did the right thing for the security of the United States. It is the unanimous view of this meeting that you should sign the Presidential Intelligence Finding before you leave Washington.'

Theo Carr glared back at her. This young woman was scolding him and he resented it.

'Unanimous?'

'Yes, sir.'

'Then you're all wrong,' he growled, and looked at the faces surrounding him. Theo Carr took a deep breath. 'Y'know what people outside of here say about me, Dr Taft?'

Carr only called her Dr Taft when he was really pissed. She said nothing.

'All of you. D'you know?' No one answered. But they all knew. 'So nobody here reads the papers? Except maybe the funny papers? Nobody? Well, here's a clue. They say Theo

139

Carr is a nice guy but a dumb ass.' President Carr took a deep breath. 'And I am here to tell you that both parts of that statement are untrue. I'm not so dumb. And I am not so nice. Arlo Luntz is forever telling me that Franklin Roosevelt had a second-rate intellect but a first-rate temperament. And that's what Arlo tells me people vote for. It's what they are comfortable with. And my first-rate temperament tells me that I will not sanction the death of the Vice-President of the United States at this time, even as a theoretical possibility, until one of you comes up with some better reason to persuade my second-rate intellect than I have heard so far; and I will not leave the White House until the search parties have had a chance to find Bobby, or you come up with something else that we should worry about. I will reconsider both matters in twenty-four hours. Unless there's anything else, I am heading back to the Oval Office, which is where I can do most good. And I suggest that you all get back to wherever it is that you can do likewise.'

TWELVE

By the time of Bobby Black's disappearance, Kristina and I had been lovers for more than a year. We told those who needed to know. The President knew. Kristina decided that she had to tell him personally. Stephanie Alejandro knew. The Secret Service knew. I am sure that others, including Bobby Black, also knew, but I never troubled to find out. On our side, I informed the embassy security staff and the Foreign Office, although I asked them, if possible, not to tell the Prime Minister. There was no security reason for them to do so, and I expect that they followed my wishes, though they were noncommittal. I did not tell Fiona. In matters where public and private lives collide you can never really be sure what people are going to do. From the start, that first night making love in the ambassador's residence, Kristina set the rules for the twilight world in which our relationship was to live.

'Don't move,' she instructed fiercely as we lay in bed that first time, and so I did not move. She gripped me with quiet desperation. Her eyes stayed closed for what seemed like a long time, and when they opened they flashed with contentment. Then she cradled my head between her hands and stared straight at me.

'No,' she gasped, looking into my eyes, 'no, no, no.'

'No what?'

She sighed. 'The thing is, Alex, what you have got to understand, is that this is a *totally, totally* bad idea.'

Over the next months, right up until the disappearance of Bobby Black, in pursuit of our totally, totally bad idea, Kristina and I met twice a week, sometimes more often, and mostly at her Watergate apartment. She gave me a key, under strict instructions that I was never to go to her apartment without telling her first.

'I don't like surprises,' she said, 'unless I expect them.'

'You know that Mae West said there was a difference between fooling around and screwing around?' I teased her one night as we lay together in her enormous Japanese-style bed.

'And that is?'

'With screwing around you don't get dinner.'

'Well, we had dinner.'

'It was a takeaway. That doesn't count.'

We did very little except be together. Occasionally we returned to Blues Alley and sat in some dark corner. Other times we cycled on the Potomac trail out to Great Falls, or drove to small towns in Virginia or on the Chesapeake Delmarva coast. Mostly we stayed in the security of Kristina's apartment, playing at domesticity, trying to recapture something of a normal life. I suspect that for both of us in Washington, a city of secrets, part of the attraction was the secrecy itself. We made love as if we knew it was fated not to last, which meant that every moment was as precious as the final touch, the last kiss.

'Some day it will be,' she said to me, and I did not disagree. Our entire professional lives were filled with plans about the future. Our personal lives were conducted almost entirely in the here and now. After a few weeks, Kristina found out that I had won a poetry prize at university and brought me

142

selections from her favourite American poets, including Wallace Stevens. We would sit reading together and saying nothing. I enjoyed a surprising contentment in her company, although there were tensions. Sometimes I saw her go into the bathroom when she was stressed by work, or by Bobby Black, or both, and she would reappear and her mood would have changed. She would be supremely calm, or at other times she would speak very fast and become hyperactive and decisive, as if on caffeine overdrive. I began to figure out why. One night she left the bathroom door ajar and I saw her pop pills from the steel bathroom cabinet. She quickly closed the door on me in embarrassment and annoyance. We never talked about what I had seen, but from time to time I checked her steel cupboard, and it was always locked. I never asked about the key. One other time she left the bathroom door open and I wanted to pee. I thought she was in the kitchen and pushed the door open as she was swallowing pills with a glass of water. That time she slammed the steel door shut and angrily threw me out.

There was an edge to our lovemaking that thrilled and sometimes unnerved me. Kristina would enjoy the act of surrendering her body, as if she needed to compensate for being so decisive and in charge in her work and relished the idea of being used as a plaything in bed. But then at moments of tenderness she would turn vicious, shocking me by biting me on the hand or arm or chest until I yelped with pain. She drew blood. She scratched at my face. Sometimes she bruised down the inside of my arm and left teeth marks. One time I hit her back, a hard slap, and was surprised by my own violence. She burst into tears but, in truth, she did not seem to be annoyed.

The best of it was when we stopped the world. We switched off computers, laptops, pagers, Blackberries, mobile phones, televisions, radios, unplugged land lines, and locked ourselves in her room with its big Japanese bed and that became our everywhere. For an hour or two the Mexican army could invade Arizona, Fraser Davis could resign and Theo Carr be impeached, but in those moments, I did not care. Kristina wanted me to enfold her, and I did.

'Will this work out between us?' she asked me one time, as we lay in each other's arms in her bed at the Watergate. She fitted into my armpit and held my body as if I was her only source of rescue or protection from a storm.

'I doubt it.'

'Why?'

'Look at the stats,' I replied. 'One hundred per cent of our previous relationships have failed. Plus, we are both Washington workaholics. You'd have to say the prognosis is poor, Dr Taft.'

She sat up on her elbows and put a pillow behind her. I watched her hair fall across her shoulders and the cup of her breasts. I stroked her skin. Kristina smiled.

'Power-fuck,' she said softly.

'What?'

'That's what some of the women in the White House call it. Not getting involved emotionally. Ever. Just Washington power-fucking.'

'That's what we are doing.'

'Then let's not change anything. Not get in any deeper.'

'You can never make rules and draw lines about things like this.'

'Sounds like you're about to write a Country song. Anyway, yes, you can make rules and draw lines if you have to. Triumph of the will. Washington power fuck-buddies. No commitments, no promises that we have to break. No planning for the future. We live in the "here and now", as you call it, and have our own special relationship.'

I was not sure she was entirely serious. Perhaps she was not sure either. She pulled a pillow towards her and hugged it as a child would hug a favourite toy. 'I spent a semester

144

in my sophomore year at the University of Hawaii,' she told me. 'One of the local women, a campaigner for the Hawaiian language from the Big Island, told me about the word "aloha".'

'Aloha?' I scoffed. 'You mean "hi" in Polynesian?'

'That's just the point,' Kristina answered, puffing up the pillow, irritated. 'In the Hawaiian language, aloha means what tourists think it means – hello. Or it means friendship. Or it means love. The Hawaiian woman told me it literally means the mingling of "*ha*", the word for breath. *The mingling of breath*, you get it?' Her breath was hot on my neck. Of course I got it. 'But white people – you and me – we're what they call *ha-oles* . . . the people who have all the power and who steal your breath. Washington is like that. A town of *ha-oles*.'

'It's usually pronounced ass-holes.'

'I'm serious Alex. This town steals your breath. We do it every day. The only way to survive is to recognize that fact. *Aloha*. It's a pity we don't have a word with such a sense of ambiguity.'

I did not understand exactly what Kristina meant, but I sank back into the comfort of her body and we fell asleep in each other's arms like kittens in a basket.

'We should keep as much mystery in this as we can,' Kristina told me, a few weeks after we first became lovers.

'What does that mean?'

'You'll see.'

What it meant was that when I arrived at Kristina's apartment I was never entirely sure what I would find, never sure which of the many sides of Kristina would be waiting for me. By day we lived the lives of public certainty that people in positions of power are expected to show to outsiders, the pretence of competence. By night, things were different. The way it worked was that I would call her office at four o'clock most afternoons to decide whether we could spend the night together or not. Four o'clock was the time when Theo Carr scheduled an hour's downtime for himself in the family quarters, and Bobby Black also always had a gap in his diary until five. President Carr usually exercised and had frequent medical checkups. Sometimes he took a nap. No one knew what Bobby Black did in what the White House staffers called 'Vice's Missing Hour'. Some thought he might have a mistress, though that seemed unlikely. Others thought he read his papers and took time to think. Still others thought he exercised at a private gym. Personally, I began to suspect that he might hang upside down with his leathery wings over his face and await the darkness.

Kristina would juggle her own schedule to make a few minutes every day to talk with me at four o'clock.

'Tonight?'

'Yes.'

I would come over to the Watergate around seven thirty. Sometimes we would cook together for relaxation; mostly we existed on takeaways.

'Make it eight o'clock tonight,' she might say, with anticipation in her voice. 'I need to get ready. Bring wine.'

The later we met, the more mysterious the evening. At eight o'clock I would walk into the Watergate building, come out of the elevator at Kristina's floor, my heart pounding with anticipation. I would turn the key in the lock, not sure what I might find. On some occasions it would be nothing out of the ordinary. She would be reading a magazine or attending to paperwork. She would push it to one side and rush to the door and kiss me like a 1950s housewife, delighted her man had come home.

'Martini? Glass of wine?'

We would switch off the telephones and everything else for an hour and make love. On other occasions she would be waiting for a call or be busy at her laptop and would signal to me to make myself a drink while she completed work that she was unable to discuss, locking the papers away in her secure safe in the piano room. I rarely went in there. The room was soundproofed, and Kristina would enter it sometimes just to practise a little on the piano, but more often to take private telephone conversations. She never told me not to enter, but I knew it was out of bounds. Sometimes – and I never knew exactly when, which added to the sense of anticipation – sometimes when I arrived and opened the door to the apartment, Kristina would be naked in the bath or shower, or wearing something cheap and deliberately provocative that she would never wear in public. On those occasions, she wanted to play.

'Kristina?' I would call out.

'In the bedroom.'

The first time like this, I gently pushed the door, expecting the usual kiss of greeting. Instead she was standing in front of a full-length mirror like something from a soft-porn mag – in precipitously high heels, a cheap black dress cut too tight and too short, Victoria's Secret lingerie, too much make-up. I could hear her take a deep breath.

'How much?' she said softly. I smiled and moved forward to kiss her bright crimson lips but she pushed me away.

'Not the lips!' she cried out. I was stunned. I put the wine on the bedside table.

'How much?' she repeated. I was slow on the uptake. 'I asked you how much you will pay to do what you want with me?'

'I've never . . . never paid,' I laughed.

'Tonight that will change. I asked you how much?'

'I don't know what is . . . expected of me. But I . . . I like the make-up.'

I put my hand on her hip and pulled her towards me. She did not resist. She coiled her body into mine and smiled. 'I'm sure you will think of something.'

I was suddenly very aroused. I grabbed her breasts in

my hands. Now she was startled, which I suppose was the point, although of course she was manipulating everything. She slapped me hard on the cheek.

'Don't touch,' she insisted. 'Until we agree on a price.'

'A hundred dollars,' I blurted out a figure at random, rubbing my face, 'and I stay the night.'

'Five hundred, and you use a condom.'

'Two fifty. And you do exactly as I say.'

She nodded. 'Now you are getting the idea. Two fifty, it's a deal.'

I pushed her on the bed and we made love violently. All I know is that in an hour of playing games we escaped our lives of certainty and strategy and plunged into the abandonment and the enjoyment of the 'here and now'. I think I hoped that I would hurt her, but her own anticipation meant that it was not so. Encouraged by her submissiveness, I pulled at her body and threw her across the bed. In the end it was as if everything in our lives had been moving towards that one violent release. Perhaps we were both more damaged than either of us realized. We lay together, gasping, arms wrapped round each other, game over. She switched on her Blackberry, quickly scanned the messages, and came back to bed. I realized that at some level she wanted to be hurt, to be controlled, and it aroused me.

'You're right,' she said suddenly as she got up from the bed, and prepared to cleanse away the cheap make-up.

'Right about what?'

'Right about the fact that we spend all our lives planning for the future and a few hours together is the only time I truly live in the present tense.'

'Leave it,' I ordered her. She stopped with the cleansing wipe poised near her face. 'If I'm paying, you do as you're told.'

She smiled and put the wet wipe in the trash.

'Sure,' and I knew she was pleased. 'Whatever you say.'

I ordered the meal – Chinese – and opened the wine, Gewürtztraminer. We ate quickly and returned to bed with the bottle and our glasses. That night I lay on Kristina and held her tightly. I could feel her chest heave. I pulled back. She was crying.

The tears – relief, sorrow, I had no idea – were running down her heavy make-up, and there were stains of mascara and powder on the pillow. I moved to kiss her again and she resisted for a second until I grabbed her hair and pulled her lips towards me. It was the warmest of kisses, but as if remembering something, eventually she pushed me away. We lay together for a while in silence.

'You know I had you checked out,' Kristina said. 'The Secret Service insisted on it.'

'Downing Street told me there had been an approach to the security service. I guessed it was you.'

'You angry?'

'No,' I replied. 'I'm just relieved it was not someone else. It's inevitable you'd check me out. You'd be crazy not to.'

'Did you check me out?'

'Only on Google and Wikipedia.' I paused. 'But I told the British security people about you. If there was something I needed to know, they would tell me. They haven't.'

We lay in silence again. I could feel her breathe softly beside me.

'What's up, Kristina?'

'You want to tell me what you were doing in Northern Ireland that was redacted from the files?'

I took a deep breath.

'Northern Ireland was twenty years ago. Best forgotten.'

'Not by me.' Kristina got up on her elbow and looked at me in the darkness. Then she switched on her bedside light. 'I need to take this cheap make-up off and have a shower. And you need to think about what you just said. It could be difficult if I don't know everything.'

'It could be difficult if you do,' I said. I watched her undress. The sight of her body aroused me, but she quickly pulled on a robe and stepped into the shower. Twenty minutes later she was back beside me, rubbing cream into her naked body. We said nothing until she put out the light and stretched beside me. I turned to touch the mound of her belly. She grabbed my hand and held it tightly.

'Well?'

'By the age of twenty-five I was a Captain, and seconded to army intelligence,' I said softly. 'Gough Barracks, County Armagh. By the age of twenty-seven I had left and joined the diplomatic service.'

'We did get that much from the files, Alex. Thank you. What we did not get was why one section was marked "British Eyes Only", and then cut out.'

'It's a long story. I became . . . disillusioned.'

'A lot of people become disillusioned in long wars with no prospect of winning, but that does not explain why you were subject to an internal inquiry and why the files were redacted when the US Secret Service specifically requested sight of all matters relating to you.'

'There is nothing in my past that will embarrass you,' I said slowly, 'though there are things that embarrass me.'

'Such as?'

I sighed and lay back in the darkness, looking at the ceiling.

'Kristina, despite what we agreed, maybe I am falling in love with you.'

'Don't.'

'I don't want it to happen but it is not under my control.'

'Yes it is. I control my emotions.'

'Then you are not completely human.'

There was a long pause and she turned away from me in the darkness. I put my arms around her and she did not resist.

'Look,' I whispered, 'Northern Ireland was our War on Terror, and sometimes we didn't know which side the United

150

States was on. Americans – law-abiding, solid Americans – shipped money and guns to the Provisional IRA to kill British soldiers and police. Just like the Libyans. We would pick up guys in south Armagh, I would interrogate them and then be told to lay off. When I tried to pursue it too far, I'd be told that some of the IRA people we most wanted to break had links to important Irish Americans, which we all took to mean the CIA. Your people were not always helpful.'

'Way before my time,' Kristina said. She turned back towards me. 'Go on.'

'My Military Intelligence file is in part UK Eyes Only, I would guess, because we did not want to tell the Americans exactly what we were up to. We had plenty of reasons not to completely trust the United States on matters to do with Ireland. I still don't. For some Americans a Muslim terrorist with a beard is a terrorist and an Irish terrorist with a beard is a patriot. All I can tell you is that there is nothing I have done, and nothing in my file, which should cause you to lose any sleep.'

'How do I know that, Alex?'

'You'll just have to trust me. Like I trust you.'

We did not say any more that night, but I felt her stiffen beside me and go to sleep. A few hours later, in the middle of the night, Kristina's hand searched out for mine and I moved towards her and kissed her. In a sleepy voice, she said, 'Don't fall in love with me, Alex.'

'I'll try not to.'

A few moments later she spoke again. 'We need to be up early.'

'We do?'

'You need to leave by six. I'm having breakfast with someone at seven.'

'Should I be jealous? Who's the lucky guy?'

'Conrad Shultz.'

There was a long pause while I thought about all the reasons why the Director of Central Intelligence was coming to breakfast. I put my arms around her and tried to go to sleep.

'You can leave the money on the dresser on your way out,' Kristina said, then she kissed me, and rolled over to face the wall.

In our last face-to-face conversation in Washington before I left for Scotland, I had joked that with all the plotting in the White House she was fated to end up like Lady Macbeth.

'Lady Macbeth?' she shot back at me, offended. 'You mean dead, after a lot of hand-washing?'

'No,' I replied. 'But like her you're clever, ambitious, ruthless, devious. Otherwise you would not be having secret breakfasts with Conrad Shultz.'

'Are you turning into Mr Jealous?' she teased. 'Of Conrad?'

'Jealous of your time,' I admitted.

'Clever, ambitious, ruthless, devious, and you want to spend more time with me?' she laughed. 'Times have changed. Lady Macbeth did what she did for her husband. If I am any of those things, it's for myself, not for some man. If Bobby Black won't invite me to all the meetings I think I need to go to, then I will improvise. Conrad and I are getting along just fine, thank you. He needs friends too.'

'I'm glad to hear it. I have one other question for you.'

She looked at me. 'I'm not going to like this, but go on.'

'The pills.'

Kristina was not embarrassed. 'What about them? When I need help, they help. When I don't, I don't use them. It's not a problem. They make me sharper, calmer, quicker and harder working. On prescription. And they make me sleep better, when you are not around. It really is not any of your business, Alex.'

'I care about you. That's my business. Some of these things are very addictive.'

'Not to me,' she said offhandedly. 'I can take them or leave them. I can do that with most things. Trust me.'

THIRTEEN

That moment when Anstruther told us that Bobby Black had gone missing, I felt physically sick, the way you do when you are a child and you get caught by a teacher doing something bad. I returned to Castle Dubh, exhausted and glad to be off the mountainside. I wanted a hot shower and a drink. Princess Charlotte and the royal party returned to Balmoral. The US Secret Service stayed on the hills and called for backup. Police, soldiers, dogs, Mountain Rescue teams were all dispatched in the fog. On the way back, Anstruther and I sat in gloomy silence in the Land Rover, bouncing in our seats as one of his gamekeepers drove us at ten miles an hour over the potholes and through the mud and mist. Ten miles an hour seemed too fast for the appalling conditions. We had two Grampian Police officers with us, and I was aware of the Secret Service and the British police talking on their radios, but I was not listening. I was trying to think what to do.

Some prime ministers handle bad news well, but Fraser Davis was not one of these, despite having had a great deal of practice. The economic projections were still bad. Inflation up. Unemployment up. House prices down. There were daily scandals about military overstretch from our commitments abroad and lack of equipment for our troops, plus there was a very tricky referendum on full independence coming up the following year in Scotland. Fraser Davis did not want to be the prime minister who presided over the break-up of the United Kingdom, and yet the polls were against him. That was one of the reasons why Davis had put his weight behind the 'Island Race' rugby games kicking off at Twickenham in two weeks' time, involving England, Scotland, Ireland, and Wales, in the hope of re-emphasizing the historical and cultural ties between the different parts of the British Isles. It was also part of the reason he had been so enthusiastic about Bobby Black coming to Aberdeenshire. Anything that appeared to tie Scotland firmly into every aspect of the Union with England and British government policy, including sport, foreign policy, and defence, was a good idea as far as Davis was concerned. Until now.

I dreaded the phone call I would have to make. I took a deep breath and leaned my hot forehead on the chilled glass of the Land Rover window. There was a brief respite as we came off the mountains. I repeatedly checked my phone, but still there was no signal. As we bounced along, I noticed cars moving towards the mountains through the fog, mostly four-by-fours from the local constabulary with garishly flashing yellow lights, plus a few unmarked Toyota Land Cruisers bearing grim-faced, square-jawed men staring out into the darkness.

'They'll be getting the Mountain Rescue people out now,' Anstruther told me out of the side of his mouth. 'Fat lot of good it will do in this weather. You can't find what you can't see. Nothing will happen till first light.'

'What are the chances he's alive?' Anstruther did not respond. I repeated the question. 'You know these hills better than anyone, Dickie.'

He shrugged. 'But not well enough.' I could see the glow from the lights in the mist etching Anstruther's face a shade of jaundice. 'Evidently.' He was feeling as sick as I did, and he wanted to confess. 'It just took me by surprise, Alex, the speed of it all. One minute we were talking about shooting mule deer and pronghorn in Montana and Wyoming, then I got distracted. There was a covey towards our centre. It was our last chance of the day, and I took it. You always take it. We moved apart, Black and me, and he was up by the big patch of whins. The next thing you know, I looked up and couldn't see him. Gone. I called out his name and listened for a reply, but heard nothing. Not even an echo. I wasn't sure which way the rest of you were, but instinct kicked in and I turned and found the burn and followed it down, calling out all the time. It's what you do. Everybody knows that. You follow the burn down the hill.' Anstruther shook his head. He sighed and tugged nervously at his thick matt of long brown hair. 'He must have turned the wrong way. Started *up* the hill instead of down. Easy to do if there isn't much of a gradient. Or maybe he moved away from the burn completely. Once you're in the heather and in the mist it all looks the same . . .' I took a deep breath. He did not need to finish the thought. 'I'm his host, for Chrissake,' he murmured with an air of self-pity. 'How could I be so . . .?'

'Dickie, I asked you what were the chances he's alive?'

'Realistically,' Anstruther replied, pulling himself together, 'good. A fit man will survive a night on the mountains at this time of year provided he is wearing decent clothes and boots. He needs to keep still and not make things worse by wandering off down some corrie and breaking his bloody neck.' He sighed with exasperation. 'But this search is putting other lives at risk, even though I understand why the Americans are insisting on it. There was no reasoning with them . . .'

'I know, but . . .'

'They say that you can always tell the US Secret Service,' Anstruther snarled. 'It's just that you can't tell them much.' He sighed, rubbing a hand nervously over his hair. 'In their position I would do the same, of course. You have to, don't you? Try everything. On the plus side, it's wet but it isn't cold, so if he stays put – even without shelter, he will survive. Hypothermia is a possibility, but the real risk is panic.'

The sweet heather is soft underfoot, but in the mist and the darkness there are all kinds of dangers: hidden corries, jagged rocks, slippery granite, stream beds, burns that appear underneath the purple heather to twist an ankle or break a leg, springs that spurt out and then are lost.

'He's an outdoorsman,' Anstruther clapped his hands on his thighs to cheer himself up. 'A practical man. He'll know what to do.'

'Yes,' I agreed.

By the time we got to Anstruther's castle it had already been turned into the headquarters for the search teams and the expanding American diplomatic and security delegation, as if it had been invaded. There were a dozen marked police cars, two fire engines – I never understood why they sent fire engines, but they did – and two ambulances, plus several large white vans and cars parked on the gravel driveway behind the American limousines. Lights were burning in all the windows of the big house, and in the offices known as Bolfracks Bothy in the estate grounds, which was now the US Communications Centre. Armed police were sheltering at the gate. I saw two dog patrols in the grounds – again, I was not entirely sure of their purpose – and there were two more officers and one of Anstruther's staff at the front door to greet us. I now had a signal on my mobile phone and so I called Andy Carnwath immediately we arrived. I wanted privacy, and walked out to the rear of the big house. There's a conservatory filled with ferns and ficus. I sat in a wicker chair and stared out at the darkness and fog.

'Andy?'

'Is Fraser available?'

'No, he's with the Home Secretary. What is it?'

I shocked him into silence.

'Bad news, Andy. Very bad. You are going to have to disturb the PM from whatever he is doing and tell him.'

I took a deep breath and ploughed on. 'We have lost Vice-President Black. It was all going well until two hours ago when the mist came in quickly. He was on the right of the party. I could see him clearly. And then he was gone. He must be there somewhere, out on the hills, but it's very dark and very foggy.' I stopped for a moment. I thought we'd been cut off. 'Andy? You still there?'

'Yes,' Carnwath responded in a weary voice. 'Go on.'

'The mist is very heavy. The Secret Service, our own people and Anstruther's ghillies began searching immediately, and we called the police and Mountain Rescue, but it is simply impossible. On the hills you cannot see your hand in front of your face.'

'B-but,' Andy Carnwath tried to grasp the situation, 'you called out to him, right?'

'Of course, But there was no reply. Nothing. The Secret Service are still up there. He couldn't have been more than fifty or sixty metres from Anstruther, who also called out, but . . .'

'I don't understand.'

I sighed. 'Neither do I, Andy. Just tell Fraser, will you, that Bobby Black is missing. The search has begun. We're doing all we can. I'll keep you informed.'

'I see, I see,' Carnwath repeated, the way you would if you did not see at all. 'I'll interrupt him . . .'

The conversation trailed off. We hung up and I left the conservatory to return to the main part of the house. People were moving at speed through the corridors and I followed half a dozen Grampian Police officers to the large baronial kitchen at Castle Dubh, which they had taken as their main base. Police caps were resting on an old pitch-pine table in front of a warm Aga; jackets over the back of chairs. The kitchen smelled of damp wool and sweat. The men and a couple of women sipped black coffee and talked to head-quarters in low, confidential voices. Anstruther walked in behind me.

'You got all you need?' he said to the Assistant Chief Constable.

'Yes, Your Lordship, except maybe for daylight and sunshine,' the man answered laconically. Anstruther introduced me.

'Alex Price, our Ambassador in Washington.' I shook hands and accepted a mug of hot coffee.

'Can you do much?' I asked. The Assistant Chief Constable nodded towards a red-faced sergeant who, he said, was the most experienced in the force in terms of mountain rescues.

The sergeant came over and slowly shook his head. 'Not really, sir. We can be in place for when it lifts. We can get the Mountain Rescue boys into position. But if the Vice-President is not answering when we call out and he has no whistle – I always recommend a whistle, sir – well, if y'know these hills as well as His Lordship here, then you know the most important thing is not to rush it. That way you risk more lives. Though . . .' Here he paused and looked around him. '. . . though I'm not so sure that message got through to our American friends. Lost in translation, you might say.'

'Are there any Americans still here in the castle?' I asked. 'Or are they all out on the hills?'

One of Anstruther's staff, a maid, explained that the Secret Service personnel had headed for the hills despite the fog and darkness and had taken their mobile, secure communications four-by-four so they could contact Washington directly. But the maid said that one or two Americans remained behind. Some were in the bothy at the main communications post, and one man was in the library. I guessed who that would be. When I walked in, Johnny Lee Ironside was alone, sipping tea behind a large mahogany desk in front of ancient bookshelves with glass fronts crammed with leather-bound volumes that looked at least a hundred years old. Johnny Lee had a laptop, a Blackberry, two other mobile phones and two land-lines in front of him. He was talking to someone on one of the land-lines. His face was contorted as if in pain. When he hung up, he turned to me, angrily.

'What a goddamn clusterfuck, Alex,' he said. His hand thumped the table so hard the phones shook, then he stood up and walked towards me. 'How could you lose the fucking Vice-President of the fucking United States? What were you thinking?'

'How could the Vice-President just wander off?' I replied. 'And if he needs constant adult supervision, then where were you? Surfing the Net? Keeping dry and warm here in the library?'

We were standing almost toe-to-toe confronting each other. He waved a finger in my face. 'Don't start the blame game, Alex, because it is a game that only you can lose. This was your idea. This is your country. And you have let us down . . .' I had never seen Johnny Lee Ironside angry before. It was a volcanic performance. After a few seconds he was literally rendered speechless by his rage.

'There is a huge search effort going on already,' I tried to reassure him, calmly. 'But until the fog lifts we just have to be patient and . . .'

'I talked to the White House,' Johnny Lee snapped back at me. 'They don't do "patient". I am as good an American friend as this country will ever have and I have to tell you, Ambassador Price, that I am mightily, mightily disappointed in you and the way this has been handled.'

'But—'

'Kristina says they are assuming hostile intent.'

I was astonished. 'What do you mean? Who is assuming hostile intent?'

'Everybody. The Joint Chiefs, the White House, the CIA,

160

anybody with a fucking American passport and half a goddamn brain, for Christ sake.' Johnny Lee's voice was almost like a scream. I tried to keep my response as calm and even as possible.

'Johnny Lee, he's lost, that's all.'

'And we should trust your judgement on this? You lost him in fog, for fuck's sake.' He sat back in a chair and sighed like a balloon being deflated. 'How could you, Alex?'

'So what exactly did Kristina say?'

He recovered his composure and began to talk slowly and calmly.

'She said that an accident would mean we would have an injured man or even a body, and we don't. Consequently they are assuming hostile intent on the part of some person or persons unknown. Kidnap. Forcible detention. Sequestration. Possible ransom or blackmail. Words you do not want to hear in the same sentence as the Vice-President of the United States. The Pentagon has upped the threat level for a potential terrorist attack. Right now there're F16s over New York, Washington, LA, and God knows where else. Peoria. Des Moines. The President met with the brass and if Bobby Black doesn't turn up within hours he will leave Washington for somewhere more secure. All US armed forces are being placed on battle alert.'

'B-but why?' I repeated. There is a paranoid style in American public life, and the way they snapped into Fear Mode astounded me. 'This is total overkill. It's ridiculous. Bobby Black wandered off in the mist. With his steamed-up glasses, he wouldn't be able to see anything. He's lost but he can't get far. We'll find him. Maybe we've found him already.'

'Prrr,' Johnny Lee shook as if a chill had just hit him.

'It's . . . just an accident,' I persisted, lamely.

Johnny Lee jabbed at me, beating out every word with his fingers. 'There's no such thing as "just an accident", and no time for patience when bad things happen involving the President or Vice-President of the United States.'

161

This was no longer the man I drank beer and swapped gossip with. All pretence at affability was gone.

'They are scrambling in Washington to send two more Secret Service teams to Scotland, at least one FBI team, and other agencies will be involved as well. CIA, NSA. Half the London Embassy is trying to get up here by plane and train. I've been told to prepare for five hundred people. You got that? *Five hundred*, Alex. All US combat troops in Western Europe have been put on alert. They have sent up planes from Lakenheath and Mildenhall. AWACs from Germany. Incirlik. Naval forces in the GIUK gap. Two aircraft-carrier battle groups are already heading towards the Gulf.'

Incirlik is the massive US Air Force Base in eastern Turkey, used to monitor the entire Middle East. GIUK is the acronym for the strategic sea-lanes between Greenland, Iceland, and the UK, which were a top defence priority during the Cold War to bottle up the Russians and keep the North Atlantic open.

I was astonished. How could Kristina think any response to the disappearance of Bobby Black would involve strategic shipping lanes, Turkey, and aircraft carriers heading to the Gulf? Maybe I knew her less well than I had thought.

'B-but . . .'

'Alex,' Johnny Lee Ironside said, repeating each word slowly as if speaking to someone with a minor retardation, 'we . . . don't . . . do . . . fucking . . . accidents.'

'But it's not a war,' I protested. He looked at me as if I had just argued that the Earth was flat.

'Of course it's a fucking war. Where have you been these two years since Manila? We were elected to fight the Bad Guys. The American people picked us – *us*, Alex – because they know we will do anything to win, and fuck the consequences. That's what they expect, and they have a right to expect it.' He stood up and gestured out of the window to the darkness of the mountains. 'Whatever this is, whatever

162

happened here, President Carr demands full cooperation from the United Kingdom at every level.'

I swallowed. 'Of course.'

He sat down. 'The FBI want to talk to everybody on the shooting party.'

'Yes.'

'. . . plus everybody who arranged it and everybody who knew about it.'

'Yes, absolutely.' That would be hundreds of people. But I was trying to be helpful, and I was feeling contrite.

'Including you and me. And if the Vice-President turns up in the meantime, we'll laugh long and hard, just like we laughed about him shooting Paul Comfort's scraggy ass in Texas. But until we can laugh, we're gonna cry.' He jabbed at me again. 'One hundred per cent fucking cooperation. At every fucking level.'

I nodded. Did Johnny Lee really expect some FBI agent was going to be allowed to question Prince Duncan and Princess Charlotte? Lord Anstruther? The Foreign Secretary?

'I need to clear it with the palace . . .'

Johnny Lee glared at me. 'Everyone,' he said slowly, again jabbing his fingers. 'No exceptions. Clear it with whoever. Whatever. Just get it done before the FBI arrive. They are sending Deputy Director Marian Killick. It's a full court press, Alex.'

I nodded once more. I'd met Killick and found her intimidating, an African American woman in her mid-forties with a reputation for not suffering fools gladly. Or at all. In an administration with few African Americans, Killick was tipped to take over soon in the top FBI job. She was already being written about in American newspapers as if she were the Elliott Ness of the twenty-first century. Maybe she was.

Listening to Johnny Lee tell me what I had to do, I felt like some nodding dog in the back window of an American car. I was not used to taking instructions like this, especially not

163

from someone I considered a friend. I told him I needed to make a few phone calls. Johnny Lee did not respond, nor did he look as if he was prepared to let me have use of any of the array of telephones immediately in front of him. I excused myself and returned to the kitchen, as if I was returning to British soil from a foreign land. It was late in the evening by now, almost midnight. Anstruther had gone to have a shower. The police officers were all on the telephone or radio. Andy Carnwath had not called me back. Maybe he had better things to do. I called Balmoral and alerted the Queen's private secretary Sir Hamish Martin to the possibility that the FBI would wish to talk to members of the royal family. There was an intake of breath followed by a sudden stillness on the line.

'Sir Hamish . . .?'

'Yes,' he said eventually. 'I'm still here . . . I'll do what I can, Alex. This will have to go to . . . to Her Majesty herself. She may still be awake. If not, it will be left until morning.'

'Of course. I understand.'

'Her Majesty is very upset. She likes Mrs Black enormously. They spent such a pleasant day with the horses. And now this. It's so . . . distasteful.'

He put the phone down. I went to find the Foreign Secretary, Barbara Holmes. She was in her bedroom at Castle Dubh, sitting in an old-fashioned leather armchair, on the mobile phone to London, briefing papers strewn out in front of her, her stockinged feet on the pouffe in front of her.

'Downing Street,' she mouthed at me. She was talking to Andy Carnwath. This time it was *The Vagina Monologues* for real. I could hear him shouting and swearing at her. He functions as Fraser Davis's enforcer when it comes to dealing with ministers. The words were indistinct but I could make out a few phrases. The volume and tone were clear. Barbara Holmes went pale. Each phrase was a physical assault.

'Fraser wants . . .'

'Of course, Andy.'

164

'Fraser needs . . .'

'Yes, Andy.'

'Fraser expects . . .'

'Right away, Andy.'

I returned downstairs to get more coffee. I wondered why Carnwath had phoned Barbara Holmes instead of me, and then it struck me. He was protecting Fraser Davis. It suited Downing Street to take the blame away from the Prime Minister's brother-in-law and put it instead on the Foreign Secretary, the Blessed Barbara. I was at least temporarily grateful to be short-circuited. One of Anstruther's maids brought me a cafetiere and two cups on a tray. I returned to the library, bearing the coffee as a peace offering for Johnny Lee. He was still on the telephone but appeared to have cooled down. He signalled for me to come into the room and accepted the coffee gratefully. No table-banging. One of the most important rules of power is that no one can remain angry in perpetuity. You let them shout, if that's what they have to do, and you wait until they calm down. Then there is an opportunity to do business and close the deal. I had watched it happen many times before, and I had learned it from the best. In Northern Ireland, President Clinton sent over Senator George Mitchell as his special envoy.

With the patience of Job in the Bible, Senator Mitchell would listen to the Ulster Unionists as they ranted at him, and then he would listen as the Irish Republicans ranted at him. Then he would let the Unionists berate him again, and so on, taking it in turns for weeks on end. When they had ranted themselves to exhaustion, Senator Mitchell began to bring them together. Eventually he helped persuade them to sign a peace treaty.

I poured coffee for Johnny Lee as he put the phone down.

'I just talked briefly with President Carr,' he said, 'and then again with Kristina. Kristina told me to make it clear to the British authorities that President Carr holds them –

you – absolutely responsible for the safety of the Vice-President of the United States.'

I pushed a cup towards him. 'Well, we're doing our best.'

'Your best might not be good enough.' We stared at each other in silence for a minute. Then he said, 'This is very fucking bad, Alex.'

'I know it's bad,' I replied irritably. 'For everybody. You're part of it.'

Johnny Lee raised an eyebrow. 'If anything happens to Bobby Black,' he said, 'God might forgive you, but President Carr never will. It's like he's lost his father. And his chief adviser. And the person who is next in line, all at once. Kristina is mightily – mightily – pissed.'

'At me?'

'Yes. Among others. At me too.'

I swallowed. My plans for improving relations with the Carr administration had become a stinking corpse, decomposing in front of me, not to mention the problems I had caused Kristina.

'Next in line?' I said, picking up the phrase he had just used. Johnny Lee nodded. He had slipped into the British expression for the royal succession. Now he delivered the American equivalent.

'Chain of command,' he said. His eyes were not with me in the room. I could feel his mind making an abrupt political calculation.

'Alex, President Carr is facing personal crisis, a national security crisis, and now a constitutional crisis, all at the same time.'

I wrinkled my face. My understanding of the US Constitution is wide but imperfect. I marvel at the genius of the document. It combines two of the things that I most admire: the certainties of Newtonian physics and the doubts about the devious nature of mankind found in Calvinist theology. The Constitution, created in Philadelphia more than

166

200 years ago, is like a perfect machine for governing, a ticking timepiece with every bit in perfect harmony. Checks and balances, different branches of government, the separation of powers between the president, the Congress and the Judiciary, all resolved through sweet reason. At least in theory.

Tick, tock.

The American Constitution is a document of profound optimism. The executive, the legislative, and the judicial branches contend for power, but no one branch has a monopoly of it. A dictator cannot arise. And yet it is also riddled with Calvinist gloom. The basic presumption of the US Constitution is that government can be made perfect but the people who run it are fundamentally wicked, fallen creatures, capable of doing wrong; politicians have eaten the Forbidden Fruit and tasted knowledge and power. The people who aspire to lead America, the US Constitution clearly implies, need to be watched. A president or vice-president is not a king, a divinely appointed being. He or she is just another flawed mortal capable of very bad things, like President Nixon, or lesser failings, like President Clinton, or enormous intellectual laziness, like George W. Bush. They all need to be kept under control.

Tick, tock.

'A constitutional crisis?' I persisted. 'Why?'

'Two words,' Johnny Lee answered, holding up two fingers to make his point. 'Betty Boop.'

'Oh, Christ,' I replied. It hit me like a wave of nausea. If something terrible happens to the president of the United States, the Constitution is clear. In the assassinations of Lincoln and Kennedy or the resignation of Richard Nixon, the vice-president becomes president and commander in chief. *The chain of command. A heartbeat away.*

But if something – God forbid – should happen *both* to the president and the vice-president, then the chain of command rule means the next in line, Number Three as it were, is the speaker of the House of Representatives. It had never happened before, but then a vice-president had never gone missing like this before. By default, Congresswoman Elizabeth 'Betty' Furedi, Democrat, of San Francisco, would become the first woman president of the United States.

'Betty Boop,' I repeated. 'Of course!'

To those on the political Right, Furedi was a hate figure, a West Coast liberal with a billionaire husband, a life of privilege, out of touch with the American values of Joe Sixpack. To those on the Left, Betty Furedi was exactly the opposite, a bright, talented woman at the core of what American values might mean. As an earnest young lawyer, she had worked for the impeachment of Richard Nixon. As a young Congresswoman she had called for investigations into Ronald Reagan's foreign policy in Latin America and his possible impeachment over the Iran-Contra affair. She had voted to censure Bill Clinton for his affair with Monica Lewinsky, but had stopped short of endorsing impeachment. If the opinion polls were correct and the Democrats were to win a big Congressional majority in two weeks' time, then the whole political landscape of the United States of America was about to change profoundly in an anti-Carr direction – even before the Vice-President's disappearance. The Washington Punditocracy were now writing off Theo Carr after just two years as 'not even a one-term president but a half-term president.'

'Oh, fuck,' I said.

'Oh fuck is right,' Johnny Lee agreed. In a recent campaign speech, Betty Furedi had described Theo Carr as 'the worst President in American history, a man who makes George W. Bush seem like an overachiever; a man who takes money from defence contractors to run his campaigns and then takes money from taxpayers to buy more weapons than we could ever need from those same defence contractors. How stupid does he think we are? He's bribing us with our own money.' Carr had shot back that Furedi was the 'shrill spokeswoman-in-chief for the Blame America First brigade.'

Kristina's joke that Bobby Black was so awful he functioned as 'impeachment insurance' for Carr came into my head. With Bobby Black missing, the impeachment insurance was gone.

Speaker Furedi might even now threaten to remove President Carr – as the Constitution prescribes – for 'high crimes and misdemeanours'. She had already suggested that Carr's policy of authorizing torture constituted a crime against humanity which would fit into the definition of an impeachable offence. Johnny Lee rubbed his tired eyes with the fingers of his right hand and then stretched out for his cup of coffee.

'Starting with the best case first,' Johnny Lee broke in to my thoughts, 'as I tried to tell Kristina, the Vice-President will be found real quick, thanks to the diligence of our British hosts. And when he does turn up, we will call a news conference, praise his Montana backwoods skills and the courage of . . . bullshit, bullshit, whatever.'

'Search and Rescue. Grampian Police.'

'Yadda yadda. Or, not so good, but almost forgivable, Bobby Black will be found injured, maybe dead. The President moves to find a successor by the weekend. Senator Ruskin from Colorado. Governor Mills from Indiana. Arlo Luntz and the President's political people are talking to their people right now, trying to put another warm body with a pulse between him and President Boop. But . . .' and here Johnny Lee looked out into the wood fire burning in the library grate. The licking flames seemed too festive for the occasion.

'But?' I prompted Johnny Lee.

'But if we do not find Vice-President Black dead or alive within the next few hours, then . . . things are about to get difficult. Everything will ratchet up. And if the Vice-President is missing, the catch is, he can't immediately be replaced.'

'I understand,' I responded. 'Fuck.'

169

'The Secret Service have deemed that in the event of a kidnap of the Vice-President,' Johnny Lee went on, 'the White House is not safe for the President. I'm guessing they'll take him to NORAD, or Offutt Air Force Base, Nebraska. Some place a thousand miles away from the coast. Air defences are on critical. F15s have been scrambled on the north slope . . .' The north slope is part of Alaska, a sensitive military area for the United States ever since the Cold War.

'Kristina doesn't imagine that the Russians—'

Johnny Lee cut me off. 'Kristina doesn't do "imagine",' he said. 'What she does do is figure things out. And the way she figures it, now would not – repeat, *not* – be a good time for the North Koreans, the Iranians, the Russians, the Chinese or any other member of the Enemy of the Month Club to start playing grab-ass. Not a good time.'

I swallowed hard. NORAD was the kind of place where Americans hid away their president when they were about to launch World War Three. After the attacks of 11 September 2001, George W. Bush was spirited away from Florida to the Presidential Emergency Operations Center Bunker at Offutt Air Force Base in Nebraska. His Vice-President, Dick Cheney, had been taken to 'an undisclosed destination'.

'Your people are overreacting,' I suggested. 'God, do you overreact?'

'No, we damn well are not overreacting,' Johnny Lee corrected me with the utmost vigour. 'If anything happens to President Carr, we're fucked. You're fucked. Fraser Davis is fucked. The world's fucked. Speaker Furedi will be sworn in as President of the United States, and with Betty Boop in the White House you can bet your skinny Brit ass that American engagement abroad will be confined to saying prayers, knitting throws for the Dalai freakin' Lama and sewing fucking quilts for Africa. We need Bobby Black back. And we need him now, Alex. You got that?'

Our friendship was in peril, his and mine. So was the

friendship between our countries. There was one bit of good news. Sir Hamish Martin called from Balmoral. Despite the late hour, he had discussed matters with the Queen. Her Majesty said she was 'distraught' that 'an accident' had befallen the Vice-President of the United States. Sir Hamish said the Queen wanted to 'tell the Americans' that all members of the royal family would make themselves available to be interviewed by the FBI or anyone else connected with investigating the disappearance of Vice-President Black, at any time, without preconditions, and she had offered Susan Black a cottage in the grounds of Balmoral should she choose to use it.

'We will do what we can. Her Majesty is most insistent that we will help in any way that we can. There will be no problems at this end, Alex,' Sir Hamish said, and then paused for a second. 'Though I wouldn't like to be in your shoes.'

'Thanks, Hamish,' I replied.

Hamish Martin was a Diplomatic Service contemporary of mine, although he chose the courtier route rather than the ambassador route. It suited his personal life better. In Buckingham Palace, homosexuality is not compulsory, though it often seems advisable. The Queen Mother once famously interrupted an argument between two of her flunkeys by yelling, 'Would one of you two old queens like to get this old Queen a gin and tonic?' I put the telephone down and passed on the news.

'The Queen,' I said to Johnny Lee Ironside, 'wants to assure you that anything you need, at any time, will be granted.'

Johnny Lee offered the hint of a smile. 'Thank you,' he said softly. 'God Bless Queen Elizabeth. At least she gets it.'

As he said that, one of his many telephones rang. It was the Director of Central Intelligence, Conrad Shultz. From the look on Johnny Lee's face, my presence was no longer welcome. I returned like an upmarket waiter with the coffee tray to the baronial kitchen in Castle Dubh. Lord Anstruther was there, his thick dark hair slick from the shower. He was wearing a loud country check shirt, deep red cord trousers, and old Church's brogues. He was sitting at the massive pitch-pine table in front of the Aga, enjoying the heat that radiated throughout the room like sunshine. Stretched out before him were the dogs Meg and Sandy, giving off that unmistakable smell of wet fur. On the table, four shooting bags had been emptied by his staff. Twenty red grouse lay on the table. One of the staff, his butler, Norris, was preparing to take the birds outside to the game store to hang for a few days before plucking. Anstruther motioned to me to sit down. It might have been the greatest crisis between Britain and the United States at least since Suez and possibly since the American Civil War, but the routine of the great country house ground onwards inexorably. A maid poured coffee. I took a cup even though I was already floating on a sea of caffeine and adrenalin.

'I didn't get the chance to tell him,' Anstruther said mournfully, as one might speak of a dead relative or lover.

'Tell who what?'

'I didn't get the chance to tell Bobby Black that he shares the same name as my home, Castle Dubh. It's Gaelic for Black Castle. There are several Black families around this area. Maybe he is related to one of them.'

'Maybe,' I repeated, mournfully. Anstruther looked at his hands.

'Perhaps there will be time later,' he suggested.

'Perhaps.' I turned to the coffee. My mobile rang. It was Kristina Taft. I stood up to take it.

'Well?' she asked. Just one word.

'We're doing our best, Kristina.'

'And?'

'Nothing. The fog is so thick that anyone out in it is risking their lives. We have no idea what happened to him. The mist came in suddenly, and when we looked round, he had gone.'

I could hear her sigh. 'Where are you?' she wanted to know.

I started to move out to the conservatory. 'I've been sitting in the baronial kitchen of one of the largest estates in Scotland looking at a pile of dead birds, smelling wet dogs, and feeling like a piece of shit. You?'

'I can't say, exactly. On the move. Calling you will be difficult for now. Everything will be difficult for now. Perhaps for a long time.'

'I'm sorry that—'

'Which is why I am calling now.' She hesitated. She told me how the news had been received in the White House and what the impact would be if we did not find Bobby Black soon. Kristina's voice was calm, but very cold. From her tone I realized that, if anything, Johnny Lee had understated the sense of emergency in Washington. After ten minutes or so she stopped and said, 'One other thing, Alex.'

'Yes?'

'What makes this even more difficult . . .' She hesitated again and then continued. '. . . is that, despite everything I said and everything we agreed, I think I have become closer to you than I wanted to be, which could cause us both problems.'

I took a deep breath. 'The only relationships worth having are those where there is a risk of getting hurt. If there is no chance of hurt, there can never be any love. You can hurt me, Kristina.'

'And you can hurt me,' she said. Then she hung up. I walked outside through the conservatory into the grey darkness. I realized I was trembling. I was shocked by the sense of panic in Washington, and by the tone of Kristina's voice.

The mist had dropped even further down the hillside and I could barely see the Castle Dubh walls across the lawn. It was like being licked by the tongue of some cold, dead thing, which touches your very soul. It's why the Scots invented whisky. In Gaelic they call it *usquebaugh*, or *uisce beatha*, the water of life. I wanted a whisky now. I remembered reading about all those unfortunate people hijacked on 11 September, and in particular the ones on United Flight 93. They knew they were about to die and called their loved ones before disaster struck. I was under no particular threat now, unlike, maybe, Bobby Black. But I had always wondered if it came to being in real danger, who I would call. Who would I want to share the worst things with? Once upon a time, it would have been Fiona. And now? Would it really be Kristina? Or some faceless, nameless desk officer at the embassy in Washington, or in Downing Street?

The wetness of the fog crept into my lungs and I started to shiver. I texted one word to Kristina on my mobile phone then returned to the warm glow of the big house. As I stepped inside I saw that she had texted me back with the same word I sent to her.

'Aloha.'

FOURTEEN

A red dawn was breaking over Castle Dubh. Fingers of pink and scarlet poked through the rising mist to the east. A red sky in the morning, shepherds' warning, as my grandmother would have said – except that in Aberdeenshire all the shepherds were in bed, keeping out of the rain. Anstruther and I had spent a sober night without sleep in the castle kitchen, as if at a funeral or a wake. We did not talk much. After my conversation with Kristina I kept telling myself not to smile, not to think how those few words with her had cheered me. We waited for news from the search teams, and made repeated pots of coffee. I would stare at the cup or the fire or out through the window into the blackness and realize that whatever had happened to Bobby Black, it blighted everything. There would be an inquiry. We would all be judged, not just on what we had done but also on how we appeared, our demeanour. Was I sad enough? Sorry enough? Concerned, active, and compassionate? However it turned out, whatever they found up the mountain at daybreak, I faced, with dread, months of interrogations, media scrutiny, conspiracy theories, inquiries. Everything about me would become public knowledge, including my relationship with Kristina – and, however much she felt for me, Kristina could not risk being associated with someone who had precipitated such a disaster. A thrill of fear hit me. The first whisper of public scandal.

'The brother-in-law of the Prime Minister of the United Kingdom, the one responsible for the disappearance of the Vice-President, has been having an affair with the United States National Security Adviser.'

But it wasn't an affair. It was something else. Water in the hand. The more I tried to grasp it, the quicker it ran away.

Throughout that first night, Anstruther and I were repeatedly summoned to speak with Downing Street, the Ministry of Defence or the Security Service on a secure telephone. We relayed the same stale news and heard the same stale nostrums played back to us. Nothing. At dawn I went out to stretch my legs. It was slate grey at first light, with a rim of pink and red spreading on the eastern horizon towards the North Sea, a Scottish tequila sunrise. The rain had turned heavy for a few hours which helped clear the mist, though it did nothing to lift our mood of gloom. The clouds rose slowly up the mountains, like an old woman's grey skirt being modestly lifted.

Mostly it was too wet to stand outside for more than a few seconds, but I let raindrops refresh my face and brushed them away like tears. I walked back through the castle. From the upper floors you could see hills all around, and the magnificence of the Highlands. There was a covered terrace behind the Victorian faux battlements, which had been built round the ruins of the original Jacobean fort by one of Anstruther's relatives, a colonial sahib who had made his fortune in India. Inside the main house, Anstruther had fitted out one room as a gym for his own use. There were flat benches, a sit-up bench, a rack of free weights, a Nautilus set and boxing equipment. I looked at the speed bag and could not resist the bright red boxing gloves in the corner of the gym. I put them on

176

and pounded away, thumping as hard as I could. It had been years since I had boxed and I hit the speed bag for five minutes, bobbing and weaving until I felt completely breathless, then turned back and thumped the punchbag again until my wrists and shoulders started to ache from the effort. I was angry at myself, above everything, for having got us into this mess, and I pounded on the bag until the sweat stung my eyes and my breath came in gasps.

I stopped and felt the bag on my shoulder and grasped it to me. I took the gloves off and walked to the window, breathing hard and staring over the hills to where the mist continued to rise until only the summits of the highest peaks remained in cloud haloes. The rest of the hillsides were brown, green and yellow, fresh like new paint. The Mountain Rescue and army search teams had been out through the night, under strong pressure from the Americans to do something, or to be seen to be doing something, which as far as the media is concerned is much the same thing. Anstruther told me that two men and one woman had already been injured in the search. The woman was a US Secret Service agent who broke her collarbone when she slid off a damp granite slab and pitched head first on to the rocks below.

'Lucky she wasn't killed,' Anstruther muttered. 'Damn fools searching in the fog and dark.'

The injured men included one of Anstruther's ghillies, a young volunteer who split his head open in circumstances that were still unexplained. The other was from a Mountain Rescue team. This man had fallen on his backside on the granite and was stretchered off the mountain with a suspected fractured coccyx.

The media siege of Castle Dubh had already begun. The first two TV crews had taken up station on the public road by the main entrance to the driveway, and others were on the hills. Even without binoculars I could make out lines of men in high visibility bright yellow tops fanning across the hillsides. The pictures of the search would be seen around the world within an hour. I felt a thrill of fear and anticipation. There is something terrifying and yet energizing about knowing you are to become part of the biggest news story on Planet Earth. It is like preparing to surf a forty-foot high wave, or that old Japanese Hokkusai print of the small boat with the wave about to pound it from above, and the slenderest of hopes that the boatman can somehow surf the wave to safety. I swallowed hard. If waiting for the wave to strike was bad for me, I tried to imagine what the overnight phone calls from Washington must have been like for Johnny Lee and the Americans. Pressure does not always lead to success, and it frequently leads to mistakes. 'Mistakes had been made,' in the jargon of Arlo Luntz's fucked-up passive. And I had made them.

Early that morning, Anstruther mobilized his estate staff – forty in total, all volunteers – to back up the by now exhausted Mountain Rescue teams. One of the maids, a teenage girl, told me everyone volunteered because they were 'scunnered' that 'our American guest' had got himself lost. Workers from three neighbouring farms and from Balmoral also turned out, plus Princess Charlotte and several of her friends on horseback. She was also involved in the Balmoral coordination efforts. Prince Duncan had yet to bestir himself. Another vodka hangover, I assumed. The civilian volunteers were supplemented by 400 soldiers from an infantry barracks in Aberdeen. Busloads of police were on their way from Edinburgh and Glasgow, and so were extra troops, St John's Ambulance Brigade, and even boy scouts who had volunteered for duty, with the enthusiastic support of the Scottish National Party government in Edinburgh. The cavalry were on their way. Literally. A detachment of US Air Cavalry in Apache helicopters was flying northwards from East Anglia, plus – Johnny Lee Ironside informed me – a jumbo jet full

178

of US law enforcement, Secret Service, and intelligence personnel had taken off from Andrews Air Force Base near Washington. It was expected to arrive late morning at Prestwick Airport on the outskirts of Glasgow. Another jet was on stand-by at JFK in New York, ready to take off later in the day. At least a dozen caravans and temporary buildings were being dispatched from Glasgow, rented by the Americans to be used as offices by the search teams and investigators.

'I'd better clear some room,' Anstruther muttered, not used to being ordered about in his own home, but taking it with good grace. He went out in the lightening rain with two of his staff to work out where to put the newcomers and how to provide them with electricity without blowing the wiring of the castle. A team of engineers from the power company had already turned up, at Johnny Lee's insistence, and began uncoiling massive cables across the castle lawn and plugging them into Bolfracks Bothy. I sympathized with Anstruther, but I had problems of my own.

'Prime Minister Fraser Davis for you sir,' Anstruther's family butler, Norris, a cadaverous figure of indeterminate age, called out to me as I tried to take the morning air on the battlements as soon as the rain cleared. 'Says it's urgent.'

Davis was very angry, though I confess that even in a rage there always seemed to be something not quite authentic about him. It was as if he had learned to be cross from one of the housemasters at school.

'What the hell is happening up there?' the Prime Minister yelled at me. I imagined a major wet-lip-pouting moment. I started to brief him, and then realized my answers were redundant. Davis already knew what was happening. Andy Carnwath had told him everything. Several times. The more angry Davis became, the more pronounced his patrician accent, the more patronizing he sounded. 'I've had President Carr on the phone – at four in the morning – telling me that we have been acting like a banana republic, and that if we do not get our act together and find Black then he will say as much publicly on American television.'

'President Carr won't say anything of the sort, Prime Minister. He is just venting his—'

'We are all venting, Alex, all of us. But this is the most serious breach in British–American relations in my lifetime, or in any history book, maybe since George the Third. And I am holding you directly responsible.'

'But—'

'. . . because you *are* directly responsible, Ambassador Price. This was your plan. Your bloody disaster.'

Curiously, instead of being concerned with the deep shit that I was in, I was thinking about the vocabulary of the Prime Minister.

In the space of two minutes I had become 'Ambassador Price', not his brother-in-law Alex. And only a pedant would speak of 'British–American' rather than Anglo–American relations. The Prime Minister was a very odd fellow indeed; as odd, in his way, as Bobby Black.

'And now I've got that buffoon Dougal Hastie calling me before daybreak to tell me that the Scottish police are doing their best to track down the missing American VIP lost by our incompetence,' he spluttered. The Scottish First Minister Dougal Hastie is Fraser Davis's oldest political rival, the Auld Enemy. They were contemporaries at Oxford. Fiona's version of their mutual dislike was that they both competed to be editor of the student newspaper and President of the Oxford Union. Fraser Davis won on both counts, leaving Dougal Hastie rejected and defeated. He returned from Oxford to Edinburgh a committed Scottish nationalist.

'Hastie is a well-balanced Scotsman,' Fraser Davis had once said to me. 'He has a chip on both shoulders.'

Hastie and Davis had been involved in another, more

intimate, competition, for the affection of the woman who was to become Fraser Davis's wife, Abigail.

'And not before Abby sampled both rival products,' Fiona had informed me. 'She told me Dougal did not measure up.'

Nowadays Dougal Hastie had put on a bit of weight and risen to become the Scottish National Party leader and First Minister, the bumptious Numpty-in-Chief of the Scottish Executive. Hastie was that most dangerous of things in politics: a Big Man in a small country. Six months ahead of the vote on Scottish independence that might mark the end of the United Kingdom, reversing the history of the previous four centuries, you just knew Hastie was salivating over the opportunity presented to him.

'Forget Dougal Hastie, Prime Minister,' I said soothingly. 'He's a chancer. Chancers always overplay their hands. Think only of the Americans. We need to convince them to calm down. Anstruther calls it a "grey out" and the likelihood is Black has got lost, unless we find something which says otherwise.'

'*You* didn't get lost,' Davis snapped back, accusingly.

'No, and I was not under Secret Service supervision either,' I reminded him. 'The Americans are in this too. There is plenty of blame to go around. Shared adversity. Shared responsibility. President Theo Carr and Prime Minister Fraser Davis, shoulder to shoulder. Yes?'

Davis liked people who brought him answers rather than those who brought him questions. In power, as Arlo Luntz himself always says, you do need a convincing story, what Luntz calls a 'narrative'. It almost doesn't matter what that story is, so long as it is consistent and you stick to it. Fraser Davis was soothed by my narrative. He could use it. His tone thawed.

'My security people tell me Bobby Black specifically asked for the Secret Service to hang back from the shoot so as not to spoil things. Is that right, Alex?'

'Correct, Prime Minister,' I agreed. 'The Vice-President's decision. Not ours. It might be useful to make that fact known to the media through Andy, and to the Americans.'

'Indeed. But why is President Carr calling me at four in the morning yelling at me that we have allowed his Vice-President to be kidnapped?'

'He's overwrought. He's about to be uprooted and flown off to some godforsaken air force base in the far West for security reasons. He's also facing up to a huge constitutional problem.'

'A what?'

I explained about Betty Furedi, the chain of command, and the mid-term elections. Davis got it immediately.

'Good God, Alex, I hadn't realized.'

'None of us realized, Prime Minister.'

Leaders of governments instinctively know about problematic elections facing fellow leaders, as if there is a trade union of People in Power who prefer to stick together against all those Not in Power.

'Of course, of course. Furedi. Frightful woman. Always banging on about human rights. No wonder Carr was edgy.'

I pressed home my point.

'Bobby Black must be on these hills somewhere, and we shall find him – or his body – within the next few hours, in which case the Americans can stop panicking. Anstruther is sure of it.'

'Anstruther'd better be right,' Davis said, ending the conversation. 'I have JIC at seven, COBRA at eight, then the Saudis all morning. And I have another formal dinner in the City tonight, if I live that long. No wonder I can never get anything done. Bloody nightmare. Call me when there's news.'

'The Foreign Secretary . . .' I began.

'No,' Davis replied firmly. 'I don't have time to waste on the Blessed Babs. She's there in case things . . . go pear-shaped.

But you are the only one I want to hear from. And you are the one I want briefing the press. Do me a favour, Alex.'

'Yes, Prime Minister?'

'Don't fuck up.'

'I won't, Prime Minister.'

'. . . unless you wish your next posting to be in a country whose name ends with -stan. Understood?' He paused for a second. The thought of sending me somewhere awful made him think of something else. 'How are things between you and Fiona?'

I took a deep breath.

'Difficult,' I conceded. 'Bad.'

'Terminal?'

I sighed. 'We should have had children.'

'Perhaps there is still time,' he said slowly. 'Children would be good. For all of us. Might you get back together again?'

'I doubt it,' I said.

Children would suit Fraser Davis. Children are always good for politicians. He'd like to be a doting uncle. A divorce would not be good for him, not when he had stuck his neck out to have me appointed as ambassador.

'You need to make a decision, Alex.'

'I know.'

'Soon.'

'I know.'

I had a feeling he would try to force a reconciliation with Fiona, something which neither of us would want.

'You know the Americans have been asking about your security files again, Alex? Going back to Northern Ireland?'

'I had heard, Prime Minister.'

'Do you know why they are so interested?'

'They have their procedures, Prime Minister. I have no problem with it.'

'Goodbye, Alex.'

'Goodbye, Prime Minister.'

I could hear the click as he put the telephone down. I breathed deeply several times until I was fully calm. At least he did not ask me directly about Kristina, and I did not directly lie to him, but from the tone of the conversation it was obvious that he knew, and that I would have to make a decision, soon, about my personal life. But not now. Now I had to get back to business. I thought about Fraser Davis's scheduled meetings. JIC was the Joint Intelligence Committee, which brought together the Secret Intelligence Service MI6, the Security Service MI5, the police Counter Terrorism Command and Government Communications Headquarters, GCHQ. COBRA was our response to being attacked. Except that we were not being attacked. Or were we? Panic was infectious. The paranoia virus had been caught by the Prime Minister on a transatlantic telephone call when the American president sneezed. Now he was passing it down the line to me in Aberdeenshire. It had been a long day already and it was just eight o'clock in the morning. I switched on the radio and listened to the *Today* programme in the castle kitchen. They reported the 'stunning news', as one of the presenters put it, that Vice-President Bobby Black had 'gone missing in mysterious circumstances' in Scotland.

Then they tried to turn it into a political crisis of credibility for Fraser Davis in what they called 'the run-up to the crucial Scottish referendum next year, which could signal the end of the United Kingdom.'

'A virtual news blackout has been declared in Aberdeenshire,' the *Today* presenter said, then he 'empty-chaired' the government, as they call it, announcing with considerable fanfare that: 'We asked Number Ten, the Foreign Office, the Home Office, Grampian Police, Scotland Yard, and the Scottish Office to put up someone to explain the situation. Unbelievably they all said that no one was available.'

But someone was available. Step forward, Dougal Hastie. The Scottish First Minister sounded like the cat that got the cream as he did the rounds of the morning talk shows. Hastie told the *Today* interviewer that the British government might have lost the American Vice-President but the Scottish forces under his personal direction were coping magnificently, right down to the boy scouts in Aberdeenshire. They had – by special order from him – been given a day off school to help in the search, and the people of Scotland 'looked forward to welcoming the Vice-President back to the country once full independence had been secured.'

Hastie made me want to puke. I began to hate the chancer as much as Fraser Davis did. Andy Carnwath was listening to the same interview in London. As soon as it was over he called me and demanded that I make sure the 1 p.m. news conference was 'a definitive response' to Hastie's comments, as well as to the Americans.

'Yes, Andy,' I said.

'Definitive,' he repeated. 'I want that motherfucking bastard to fucking well—'

'I heard you the first time.'

By ten in the morning, the sun had come out fully. I had told Andy that there was no point in holding the news conference – definitive or otherwise – before all the TV satellite trucks arrived from Glasgow and Edinburgh, which meant I had even more time to kill. Crises are like warfare. Most of the time you feel you need to be doing something, when the hardest part is recognizing that you simply have to wait.

Again I went for a walk outside. I bumped into Anstruther, who said he had completed arrangements for the invading American army of investigators, military personnel and others.

'Jesus, look at that, will you!'

He pointed to where the Apache helicopters of the US Air Cavalry, four of them, suddenly appeared, beating over the mountains, quartering the hillsides. They were contour flying at a height of no more than twenty-five metres. As they approached you could feel the shock waves from their rotors hitting the earth. Anstruther said that American thermal-imaging aircraft were buzzing overhead, and they could spot a warm body. The Americans were also using spy satellites, and there were two Chinooks from a USAF base in Suffolk and some kind of ELINT – electronic intelligence – which monitored short-wave signals and other radio broadcasts from a spy plane launched from a US Navy aircraft carrier somewhere in the north Atlantic. There is a difference between activity and progress, and all this activity had delivered nothing, but at least it was a properly organized nothing, a nothing that we could talk about in the news conference and which we could defend when the inquiries started and the blame was spread around. I took Arlo Luntz's wisdom to heart and started to construct a convenient fiction to explain it all away.

After our hurried conversation Anstruther left to go out on the hills. I returned through the kitchen where Grampian Police and British military commanders stood together, drinking coffee, studying maps and planning how to move men and machinery. I wanted to find Johnny Lee Ironside. He had spent the night in the library but now he was no longer alone. He had been joined by a growing team of Americans, including a shaven-headed USAF colonel who introduced himself as Martinez and who had flown up from East Anglia in one of the Chinooks, plus half a dozen staff from the US Embassy in Grosvenor Square, four men and two women, all of whom looked like CIA. One of the men had taken the time to print out a piece of paper with the words: '*U.S. SIT. ROOM – Knock Before Entry.*' It meant KEEP OUT if you happened to be British. He pinned it to the library door. It felt to me like an unnecessary insult.

Johnny Lee and I exchanged a few words. He told me that a convoy of FBI special agents, intelligence officers, search specialists and media-briefers was on its way to Aberdeenshire by road and that a second jet-load of security and other personnel had already left Andrews Air Force Base. Martinez interrupted us.

'Mr Ironside? We need to get on . . .'

'Now, if you'll excuse us, Alex . . .'

I took the hint and left. Down below another six coaches pulled in through the gates, up the drive and onto Anstruther's castle grounds. It reminded me of the arrival of the circus in a small village. I went down to look.

'Four hundred secure telephones and other communications equipment,' one of the newcomers told me when I asked what he was doing. He was from Texas, by the sound of him. 'Most of them going over there.' He signalled towards Bolfracks Bothy, the other big building in the estate grounds.

'Houston?' I guessed.

'Galveston,' he responded, looking around in amazement at the hundreds of people who had arrived. 'We're out of Iraq. It's one war zone to another I guess.'

I nodded towards where two enormous satellite dishes were being set up, linked to the coaches and caravans.

'So you can see American TV just in case you get homesick?'

The engineer laughed. 'So these guys can talk directly to Washington.' He nodded to the growing number of Americans climbing out of the coaches.

'Without the need to go through British telephone lines?' I completed his thought. The engineer shrugged. Maybe he had said too much.

'I guess so.' Did the Americans think that GCHQ would start bugging their conversations from Castle Dubh? Perhaps things really had sunk so low. The trust had gone. There were long-standing agreements preventing us from bugging each other, but if the biggest question in British diplomacy was always 'what are the Americans up to?', maybe we were no longer able to trust one another on the answer.

I walked back inside Castle Dubh, sat down with a pad of A4 and began making notes for the news conference as more British reinforcements began to arrive, led by half a dozen staff from Number Ten, including Janey Masters, the Prime Minister's 'special assistant', plus another half dozen from the Foreign Office, and a few intelligence and plain-clothes police officers from the Counter Terrorism Command. I took over the castle's main drawing room. It was enormous and comfortable, with two large tables and two desks, though only one telephone socket. We commandeered chairs from the castle chapel and Janey ordered new telephone lines to be put in. A British Telecoms truck was already outside. As I looked round, workmen were inserting cables into every available orifice of Castle Dubh and of Bolfracks Bothy.

By eleven that morning, with the telephone lines now installed, Janey Masters breezed into the drawing room.

'Right, Alex,' she said, clapping her hands. 'We need to talk.'

Janey can be a major distraction. As my grandmother would say, 'She hasn't got much, but she makes the best of it.' She had been up all night, dealing with Fraser Davis's calls to the Americans, then she had flown to Aberdeen, without sleep and probably without much to eat. She looked fresh. She always looked fresh. She wore a well-cut business suit, clickety-clackety heels and no tights, which in Aberdeenshire is not standard dress, but Janey sets her own standards. Her idea of a woman's magazine is *The Economist*, and she's also one of the True Believers, in her early thirties, determined to make it to the very top, to find a safe seat and get into the Cabinet before she's forty. Her transparent desperation to succeed reminds me of one of those Chinese child gymnasts who begin training for the Olympics when barely out of the womb.

'Fraser wants this,' she yelled at some poor hapless unctionary setting up her computer in the drawing room. 'Andy wants this,' to another. Then she turned her attention to me.

'Andy wants to know why the news conference has not yet begun. He told me he wants you on the American breakfast shows, and to put Hastie in his place.'

I sighed. One of the worst things about my job is having to explain the same things over and over again as people talk to each other in a circle of half-understood information. Sometimes it is almost a kind of insanity.

'I told him already that the news conference is scheduled for a few minutes after one o'clock,' I responded, with controlled exasperation. 'That would be eight a.m. New York and Washington time. I understand Fraser's sense of urgency, but there is no point in doing it until the networks are all set up and ready.'

'And Andy understands that you have to do it right,' she snapped back at me. 'And so does Fraser. But they want you to do it soon to reassure the American public that we—'

'Shut the fuck up, Janey.'

'What?'

'I said shut up. Just shut . . . up.'

The room went quiet. People looked at me, and blinked at my unaccustomed rudeness. From the look in her eyes, I think Janey Masters would have killed me. But my own eyes were drawn towards the television set.

'Give me the remote!' I yelled. 'And keep the noise down! All of you!' I switched up the volume on the BBC News Channel. There were pictures slugged 'Dewsbury, Yorkshire'. Muslim men with long beards and placards reading 'Death to Satan Black' were jumping up and down and celebrating outside a local mosque. It was difficult to see how many there were, probably only a couple of dozen demonstrators, but as usual on television, everything looked more dramatic than it really was. Shots of a dozen chanting men tightly bunched together could be made to look as significant as tens of thousands of demonstrators on the streets of Gaza. The voice-over cranked up.

'At Dewsbury's Green Mosque, demonstrators cheered the news that Vice-President Black has gone missing. While not representative of the wider British Muslim community, these self-confessed extremists say that the disappearance of the Vice-President of the United States is the will of God. One of those demonstrating today is Muhammad Asif Khan, who only yesterday arrived back in the United Kingdom after being released from detention in Guantanamo Bay.'

They cut to pictures of a man with five-day-old stubble on his chin. He was wearing traditional Pakistani clothes and spoke in a Yorkshire accent.

'Black is a war criminal,' Muhammad Asif Khan said. 'Black authorized the kidnapping and torture of our brothers in Afghanistan and Iraq. Black put innocent people, including me, into the hands of thugs acting on behalf of the United States. He deserves whatever fate awaits him now – and, by God's will, those who attack Islam shall perish . . .'

'Can you not forgive him?' the interviewer said. 'After all, you've just been released.'

'Turning the other cheek is part of the Christian religion,' Muhammad Asif Khan snarled, jabbing his finger at the interviewer like a dagger, 'but it is not part of mine.'

They cut to pictures of a different demonstration, this time in north London. Men with placards accused Vice-President Black of complicity in torture and war crimes.

'At the North London Mosque in Tottenham, small groups of Muslim men also celebrated the disappearance of Bobby Black.'

A demonstrator was interviewed. He had a long black beard and he repeated the charges that Bobby Black had publicly endorsed the use of torture to obtain evidence, authorized the disappearance of detainees into secret CIA prisons, and backed rendition flights by which some detained terrorist suspects were flown to countries allied to the United States.

'Where good Muslims can be tortured under American law,' the man yelled out, 'there is no justice. And where there is no justice, there is no peace. If Satan Black is missing, that's good. If he's dead, that's better. If – *inshallah* – he has been kidnapped by good Muslims to be brought to Islamic justice, then that would be best of all.'

The chanting began.

'*Death to Satan Black! Death to Satan Black! Death to Satan Black! No Justice, No Peace! No Justice, No Peace!*'

The words hit the drawing room like a fist. Everyone was struck dumb, even Janey Masters.

'Oh, fuck,' she said, and slumped behind a desk.

'I'm going down to the Rowallan Hotel,' I said. Anstruther had arranged that it would be the base for the news media and the location for the news conference. As I moved out of the door, the chanting changed.

'*Behead Satan Black! Behead Satan Black! Behead Satan Black!*'

At least I now had an idea what the journalists would want to talk about. I walked up to my bedroom in Castle Dubh and checked my watch. Noon. Seven in the morning Washington time. I knew Kristina would be awake. When I called she was already in the White House. She said she had spent a mostly sleepless night in a cot in her office. I started to tell her about the demonstrations and about Khan, but she had already seen the reports on CNN. She told me some details from that morning's 6 a.m. emergency National Security Council meeting.

'It's going to be difficult to talk to each other if we head out west,' she said. 'Everything is going to be difficult from now on, Alex.'

I told her I understood. We hung up after a few minutes

191

and I changed into a dark suit, fresh shirt and tie, grabbed my coat and ran down the stairs to get my car. As I walked out of the main doors of Castle Dubh, I bumped into Anstruther who was rushing in.

'Where are you going?'

'The news conference.'

'Not yet,' he said breathlessly. 'You've got to come with me first. They've found something. Something big.'

FIFTEEN

The way Kristina told it to me, the emergency National Security Council meeting reconvened with President Carr in the White House at 6 a.m. on the morning after Bobby Black went missing. Most of the National Security team had been together in Sit. Room Alpha throughout the night.

'Well,' President Carr demanded as soon as he walked through the door. 'What progress?'

Kristina was chairing the proceedings. The disappearance of the Vice-President gave her the space to do so. She asked the director of the US Secret Service to offer his account of the search so far.

'Nothing?' President Carr said. 'What do you mean, nothing? Are you sure?'

'Yes, Mr President. Nothing.'

'No shotgun? No clothes or day pack or . . . whatever?'

'No, sir.'

'Conrad?'

Conrad Shultz began the intelligence assessment which was an echo of the day before, very guarded, with a few words about celebrations in the places he had predicted – Gaza and Tehran – and some he had not mentioned, Dewsbury and Tottenham.

'Options? Kristina?'

'Mr President,' Kristina Taft replied, 'the unanimous view of this meeting is that you should no longer stay in Washington. We can discuss the Presidential Intelligence Finding on route.'

'On route to where?'

'SAC,' Kristina replied, for Strategic Air Command. 'NORAD. Nebraska or Colorado. The joint chiefs are still finalizing where would be best and safest.'

'So I'm to go into a cave?' Theo Carr laughed bitterly. 'Like Bin Laden?'

'Colorado Springs, Mr President. It's a lot better than a cave.'

'Yeah, a cave,' Carr repeated. 'Been there, done that. Well, I guess that's the way we're gonna have to do it.'

Kristina was pleased with his agreement.

'Yes, sir. We have already made arrangements to fly you . . . out.'

As she said the word, as if by a hidden signal, everyone rose and the meeting adjourned. Kristina took a copy of the Intelligence Finding from Conrad Shultz and placed it in her own leather file folder. They exchanged whispered words. Kristina returned to her office while President Carr felt a gentle pressure at his elbow from the Secret Service guys, directing him down the long white-tiled tunnel which ran under Lafayette Park. The tunnel forked. One fork led to the Commerce Department basement, the other to an exit that surfaced in the empty kitchen storeroom of a five-star hotel overlooking the White House grounds. President Carr was led towards the hotel storeroom. It opened out into a sub-terranean parking lot, which was full of agents pushing files and equipment into vans. They guided the president into a Chevy four-by-four with dark tinted windows, one of four identical vehicles kept on permanent stand-by in the rear of the hotel's basement garage.

The convoy shot out of the parking lot and turned at speed

past the Old Ebbitt Grill on to Pennsylvania Avenue. The Secret Service have their own traffic control system which enables them to pre-empt the Washington D.C. traffic computer. They altered the timing of the lights between 10th and 15th Streets and on F, G, H and Eye Streets to speed the president on his way. The convoy swept towards the Capitol and then out to Andrews Air Force Base in the flat Maryland countryside on the outskirts of the District of Columbia. The plan was for Air Force One, with a fighter escort, to head for Cheyenne Mountain, near Colorado Springs, one of the places a president was supposed to go to in the event of a nuclear war.

'But we're not at war, Kristina,' President Carr said as he left the White House. 'Are we?'

'No, Mr President. At least, not yet.'

Kristina travelled to Andrews AFB in a separate Secret Service four-by-four. On route she took a call from Secretary of State General Andrew Baker who was at the Asia-Pacific conference in Beijing.

'I feel like I'm out of the loop,' he complained. Kristina could hear the wheels in Baker's brain turning, thinking through his options. 'Bottom line?' Baker wanted to know.

'The bottom line, Andy, is you need to come home,' Kristina Taft said, trying to keep the exasperation out of her voice. She had other things to worry about beyond the delicate ego of the US Secretary of State. 'My advice would be to get on a plane. Now.'

Baker agreed. Kristina thought she detected some kind of delight or at least anticipation in his voice, as if he was calculating how far he could benefit from the disappearance of the Vice-President. Maybe he thought Black was finished and there might soon be a vice-presidential vacancy. That was the trouble with Washington, Kristina had often told me. The US government had become like a giant log floating down the Mississippi River with a hundred thousand ants on board, each one of which was convinced that it was steering, and each one of them resentful because Bobby Black had been doing most of the steering until now.

At Andrews, Kristina scrambled to join President Carr, White House Chief of Staff Stephanie Alejandro, and the president's special adviser, Arlo Luntz, in the Airborne Sit. Room at the front of Air Force One. They took off more or less immediately, and within a few minutes sat around the table running through the problems ahead and the options for dealing with them. Every twenty minutes or so, as they flew westwards, the President asked if there was 'any news from Scotland'. Every twenty minutes the answer was the same.

'Not yet, sir.'

'Elsewhere?'

'No unusual military or terrorist activity,' Kristina Taft reported. 'Director Shultz says the NSA continues to report no unusual chatter from any of the presumed terror cells. No demands, no claims.'

Carr shrugged. 'So far so good,' he said. Then he caught sight of Arlo Luntz's face. Luntz was doodling on a pad, his face pained with anxiety.

'Whassup, Arlo?' he said. 'You got a problem?'

'We all got a problem, Mr President. You, mostly.'

Carr sighed. 'I have you around, Arlo, 'cos you're such a ray of sunshine. The Roman emperors had some guy with a pig's bladder on a ride-along on their chariots to hit them with the bladder from time to time and remind them they were mortal. You're my goddamn pig's bladder, Arlo. This Spartacus deal—'

Luntz interrupted. 'Forget Spartacus, Mr President. Enough Romans, okay? Shultz'll figure it out. Forget what Bobby Black has locked up in his brain. Spartacus is not the problem. Or not the immediate problem. The ball-crusher for you is this, Mr President. Until we get the Vice-President back, dead or alive, if anything happens to you, the next President of the

United States is Speaker Betty Furedi, and you cannot allow that, sir.'

'And how do I "not allow" that, Arlo? How do I get round that minor technicality that folks call the Constitution of the United States?'

Luntz realized that his doodles looked like pill bottles from a pharmacy. He'd been thinking about the fact that they had not disclosed publicly all President Carr's health records. They had said nothing about the statins, the high cholesterol count or the high blood pressure. He put the pen down and stopped doodling. Sometimes, when Luntz looked at his boss, he wondered if he would last the next few years. He pushed a wisp of squirrel-like stray hair from his wig back across his forehead. 'You wanna laugh but it ain't funny. Mr President, the Secret Service would gladly take a bullet for you. Your staff would take a bullet for you – hell, I would take a bullet for you. But to prevent Betty Boop getting to the White House, half the country would take a bullet for you.'

Despite the air of banter, Arlo Luntz's face was completely serious.

'What you saying, Arlo?'

'Mr President, I am saying that if we don't get the Vice-President back within forty-eight hours, you need to declare him missing and presumed dead. You immediately move to nominate a successor. I'll have a short list. Otherwise . . .'

His words trailed away. Carr completed the sentence himself. '. . . Otherwise, hail to the Boop.'

'Jeez,' Stephanie Alejandro hissed, rubbing her forehead.

Luntz said, 'And just the whisper of that increases her juice coming up to the mid-terms. If the Constitution says Betty Boop's good enough to be your successor as President of the United States, the voters of this country might figure she's good for a ten-point lead in the polls. We have a Democratic landslide in the making. And in Ohio, Pennsylvania and—'

'Shut the fuck up about Ohio, Pennsylvania and Florida,

Arlo, will you?' President Carr stood abruptly and walked over to the refrigerator in the Air Force One galley. 'You fucking pig's bladder.'

Pottering around in the kitchen, even at 35,000 feet in Air Force One, almost felt like home. It was a short glimpse of normality in the otherwise abnormal life in the White House fishbowl. He pulled at the tab on another Diet 7 Up.

'Anyone else?' Carr held a can towards them. 'Steph? Bladder Boy?' No one took up his offer of a drink. 'Now listen up,' President Carr said slowly. 'In the past twelve hours or so I have been asked to declare the Vice-President of the United States dead, without any evidence – or politically dead, which is much the same thing, and to allow – to order – US forces to kill him, if necessary; though I have to ask myself how he could be terminated if he can't be found.'

'It's in case he can be found but can't be rescued, Mr President,' Kristina explained. 'We're just trying to cover all bases.'

'Yeah, right, all bases.' Carr shook his head dismissively. 'Do any of you have any idea what you are saying? Do any of you have a sense of perspective about this?' There was a silence in the presidential quarters. After a full thirty seconds, Kristina cleared her throat.

'Mr President, not everyone in this administration was a close personal friend of Bobby Black,' she began. 'We all had our run-ins with him. But we do have a sense of perspective when we are telling you that for the good of the country, as Commander in Chief, it is necessary for you to authorize all necessary means to make sure that the knowledge the Vice-President carries cannot be used to weaken the security of the United States.'

'Kristina, don't . . .' He waved the can of 7 Up towards her. Uncharacteristically, she refused to be quiet.

'The information in Bobby Black's head puts your administration and this entire nation at risk. No serving president of

198

the United States has had to face a crisis of this magnitude, sir. Not ever. It's your Pearl Harbor, except at least in 1941 we knew it was the Japanese. You can't duck it, go around it, or avoid it. You have got to make this authorization.'

Carr looked at her. He seemed stunned. Kristina went on. 'You need to sign the Presidential Intelligence Finding authorizing the . . . termination of the Vice-President if necessary, Mr President,' Kristina Taft insisted, pulling out the document from her leather folder. 'If a rescue cannot be mounted with a reasonable chance of success.' She handed him a pen. Carr did not move. 'Mr President, if this goes wrong, never mind Susan Black, not one of us – not one – will be able to look *you* in the eye.'

Carr blinked.

'And you need to think about a successor,' Arlo Luntz insisted. 'Mr President, there is simply no other way. If anything happened to you, we can't have . . . You know who.'

They sat looking at the President of the United States as he sipped his soda, a row of stony faces. Air Force One headed due west towards the mountains of Colorado. Theo Carr slowly read the paragraph on the page in front of him. He stopped at the word 'termination'. Then he took the pen and signed on the line where it said: 'President of the United States.' He stopped and closed his eyes for a moment, and mouthed a silent prayer. When Theo Carr finished, he opened his eyes, sat back, and looked at his staff. Kristina met the President's gaze and gave an encouraging nod, then she stared out of the window to the square lines of the fields of the Midwest, giant rectangles of corn and wheat. Iowa, probably. More Flyover People. Within a year the presidential candidates, including President Carr himself, would be out in these fields seeking the first endorsements from the Iowa caucuses, in Des Moines and Davenport and Winterset, way down in Madison County, in all the little towns where the chief concern was the price of corn, soy beans, and pork bellies. By then, Kristina thought, maybe she would do as she had planned and tell Theo Carr that she was going to quit as soon as he was re-elected, as soon as it was politically convenient to go. Maybe, Kristina thought, maybe she would return to university life. To California.

Or maybe her new relationship would . . . would amount to something if she gave it a chance. As she looked at the fields, Kristina kept telling herself that Carr was right. The United States was truly not at war, though it might look that way. It made her think of a tee shirt she had been given early in the Carr administration. She had visited the US Air Force Base on Shemya, Alaska, a tiny speck of heavily protected rock in the Aleutian Islands, a long chain of bogs and hills facing towards Russia, full of electronic early warning systems in case of a nuclear attack from the Russians. The tee shirt said: *Shemya: It's not the end of the world. But you can see it from here.*

Kristina looked back at President Carr. He had reclined in his seat and was taking a nap, the cares of the day parked somewhere in his mind. It was another of his great political skills. He could delegate and then switch off. She received a message to say that Harry Concini had resigned as Transportation Secretary. Everyone had forgotten about him. The hooker had sold her story to a New York tabloid. It turned out Harry Concini was what she called 'one of my regulars', but nobody cared any more. On a less stressful day, Stephanie Alejandro would have wakened the President to tell him, but not on this day, not with Bobby Black gone. As she looked out over the cornfields of Iowa, Kristina thought that the Vice-President's disappearance was not the end of the world, but she could see it from here, and she could see it with remarkable clarity.

SIXTEEN

'What do you mean they've found something?'

'On the hills,' Anstruther replied. 'Get in the car.'

He nodded towards a Land Rover with one of his ghillies in the driver's seat. I did as I was told and we headed back up the road we had driven along in much happier circumstances the day before. Anstruther told me that at first light the searchers had fanned out over the hillside but found nothing – no shotgun, no ammunition, no clothes, no rucksack, no game-bag, no glasses, no tracks; nothing whatsoever. You could be forgiven for thinking Bobby Black had never existed or that he had been spirited away by aliens. Aerial reconnaissance also drew a blank. The thermal-imaging devices were capable of flagging up anything significantly hotter than the ambient temperature down, apparently, to the size of a grouse, which meant they'd found plenty of red deer and other wildlife, but nothing of any use in the hunt for Bobby Black. As we drove, Anstruther pulled an Ordnance Survey map from his Barbour pocket and pointed to the spot where Bobby Black had disappeared. He had drawn a series of concentric circles around the location to show the main search zones.

'This is the maximum perimeter a fit man walking in a straight line could achieve,' he said. 'If the Vice-President disappeared here and then walked solidly for twelve hours or so, then at the very utmost he would have reached the edges of this circle.' Then he pointed to a much narrower inner circle. 'This is the more likely distance a not-so-fit and disorientated man would cover, assuming he decided to move at all,' he said. 'We concentrated our efforts in this inner perimeter which, as you can see, is about a kilometre wide. And that's when we got lucky.' He turned to the Land Rover driver. 'Put your foot on it please, Mr Campbell.'

The man did as he was told and we sped along the surfaced road and then turned on to a dirt track, which I recognized as leading us towards where Bobby Black had been last seen. The sight on the mountains was now eerie. A dozen or more white transit vans, plus innumerable Land Rovers and police cars were parked on the roadside. Some had been bounced up on the verge to allow traffic to pass. I could see more than five hundred people fanned out across the hills immediately ahead of me, plus a large group of perhaps 150 focused on an enormous patch of yellow whin bushes.

'Over there,' Anstruther pointed. We got out and started walking at a breathless clip up to the whins. 'I told the SAS search team commander to tell his men to think out of the box. They did.'

Anstruther said that instead of considering the disappearance in the way the police and Mountain Rescue teams had been doing, the SAS thought about how they could most easily have done harm to Bobby Black. How would they have set about kidnapping him? One of the SAS teams decided they would have hidden on the periphery of the shoot, waited for their opportunity, preferably when darkness fell or the mist came down and then they would have attacked, dragging their victim into the biggest patch of cover they could find. The whins. After twenty minutes they had found signs of a camouflaged pathway in the whin bushes. Another twenty minutes and they had found the hide.

'What do you mean, a hide?' I asked Anstruther, as we arrived at where the police were establishing a cordon round the bushes. 'For birdwatchers?'

He shook his head.

'For long-range insertion teams,' he said.

In Northern Ireland, and of course in Iraq or the Falklands, British special forces, the SAS and SBS, were repeatedly inserted behind enemy lines. That's their job. The common view of special forces from newspapers and TV programmes is wrong. They are often portrayed as the heavy mob, the people who crash in through windows and shoot the bad guys or engage in dramatic hostage rescues, and of course sometimes they do. But mostly the role of special forces is to gather intelligence by going where the enemy is, finding a place to hide, sit, watch, wait, and then report back without being discovered. American long-range insertion teams have been in Iran undetected for years. The Americans have teams right now in Afghanistan, Iraq, tribal areas of Pakistan, and in Syria. Typically, the team digs a hide in the middle of a bush or under sods of grass, in a ditch or out in the desert. They scoop out the dirt, stake a sand-coloured groundsheet over the hole, put the sand back on top, and watch. Done properly these hides can be almost impossible to spot, and digging in the centre of a massive patch of jagged whins would be a near-perfect location. I breathed in deeply. The crisp highland air was so clean it hurt. The whin patch was being treated as a major crime scene. Anstruther and I were not allowed to get close.

'What does it look like?' Anstruther asked a uniformed SAS Major in mud-stained combat fatigues. 'You've seen it?'

The Major nodded.

'Seen it? I nearly fell into it,' he said, pointing to the centre of activity in the whins. 'A big hole, almost two metres deep and about three metres square, dug with spades or entrenching tools in the middle of the bushes. Sods pulled back and marks on the ground as if three or four people were there. Everything carefully replaced and very difficult to spot.'

'Poachers?' I suggested.

'Not likely,' Anstruther answered. 'Poachers come in, take the game, and leave. They don't spend time digging holes, and certainly not two metres deep.'

'Why wasn't it found during the security sweeps'?

The SAS Major, thin faced and wiry, wiped at his brow.

'Not easy to find,' he said. 'Not under bushes like this. It could even have been dug weeks ago for all I know, with no one in it until after the sweeps. Just an empty hole. All I can tell you is that it's professional. If one of my teams was monitoring activity on these hills and came up with this location, I'd tell them, good job, well done. Three hundred and sixty degree vis. Near enough that track to get down the hill. Half a klick from the road. Very hard to spot, even from the air, and nobody would wander into a patch of whins like this by accident. Top marks.'

'But why would anyone . . .?' I started to say, and then let the question die on my lips. I checked my watch. It was half past twelve. I needed to get down to the hotel for the press briefing. At that moment there was some excitement from the Scenes of Crime Officers in the hide. The SOCO team was all in white, to prevent contamination of the site, and I could hear American voices in among them. One of the Scenes of Crime Officers was signalling that she had found something. I was not allowed to get close, but someone called out that it was a button. I thought at first it might have been from the Vice-President's coat or hunting jacket, but I found out later it was something quite different. The button had been ground into the mud of the hide, probably by a boot. There were boot prints in the mud consistent with three or four people, possibly five. There was no body, no sign of Bobby Black, nothing directly to connect him to the button or anything else.

I was not sure how important all this would prove to be, but we had to leave for the news conference. Anstruther and I ran down the hill to the Land Rover, and Mr Campbell drove us at speed to Rowallan village. I felt my feet wet with morning dew from the hillside, and saw that fresh mud had spattered up my trouser legs.

The Rowallan Hotel car park emerged amid a forest of aerials and satellite dishes, a newly constructed media city with journalists babbling at cameras in half a dozen languages, technicians plugging and unplugging equipment and checking their satellite transmissions. All around the world, the digital tower of Babel of twenty-four-hour news networks, American breakfast shows and others would want to join us live. We walked through crowds of reporters towards the banqueting room, Anstruther in front like an ice-breaking ship pulling me in his wake.

'Lord Anstruther! Ambassador,' a sharp-faced reporter in an Armani suit yelled out. 'Any chance of a one-on-one for Sky News?'

'Not now. After the news conference.'

'But—'

'Not now. After the news conference.'

The Rowallan Hotel is a gaudy Victorian watering hole, all granite and heavy wood, the kind of place where it seems compulsory to eat red meat and drink red wine. The corridors were dark, the carpet ruby red and covered with stains, the kind of carpet that never quite gets clean enough. I headed for the men's room, grabbed some toilet paper and wiped the wetness and dirt from my shoes and trousers as best I could, then I checked how I looked in the mirror. Tired. Stressed. I smiled grimly. It did not look right. I would avoid smiling in the news conference. Ninety per cent of these events is not what you say but how you look. Calm. Composed. In control. Get it right, and you set the agenda for opinion formers and governments all around the world. All the following day's headlines are good. Get it wrong and you spook the markets, watch your currency fall, your credibility gone, and you lose your job. I joined Anstruther in a back room next to the banqueting suite. A one o'clock news live conference in practice usually begins a few minutes after the hour to allow the TV networks to headline the news and introduce the event.

We planned for six minutes after one, exactly.

'What do we say about the hide?' Anstruther asked me, his face etched with uncharacteristic worry.

'Nothing,' I insisted. 'Absolutely nothing. We have enough to tell them without telling them everything.'

Anstruther nodded.

'Sufficient unto the day is the panic thereof,' he murmured, shaking his head.

'What's the matter? You worried that the security sweeps did not spot it?'

'Not so much,' he said. 'That would be very difficult, I suppose, given the vast area that they were covering. It's the location that's been eating away at me. Strange.'

'Stop speaking in riddles, Dickie. We haven't got time. We're on in two minutes. Strange in what way?'

He wrinkled his brow.

'Look, my dogs are damn fine dogs. If any of them caught scent of people in whin bushes they would raise the alarm. But they didn't. And they didn't because the location of the hide was five hundred metres from the furthest edge of where we were supposed to be hunting.'

'So?'

He pulled at his fringe of long brown hair.

'Thinking aloud here, but we stuck to our agreed plan for the shoot because that's the way the US Secret Service wanted it. I was very careful about that. The people who dug the hide were either incredibly lucky to position it just right or . . .'

206

He stopped talking and shook his head again in a manner I was beginning to find irritating.

'Or?'

'Or they knew. They knew exactly what our plans were likely to be. They kept themselves just far enough away, beyond the dogs . . .'

His voice trailed away.

'Who would know enough?'

Anstruther looked perplexed. 'I suppose it's possible that the hide has nothing to do with the disappearance.'

'Not really,' I said.

'Or maybe . . .'

'Go on.'

'Could it be the Americans?'

'The Americans?'

'Well, maybe they wanted to keep an eye on the Vice-President but did not want us to know that they did not trust us with his security? The US Secret Service had a full plan of everything we were doing, down to the last hundred metres. They were most insistent . . .'

'What about us? What about our people? Could they have been watching from the hide?'

Anstruther shook his head. 'I'd have known if it was any of the Funnies,' he said. 'It's not us. Our people would need political clearance in case it went tits up.'

I took him at his word. He was, after all, Minister of State at the Ministry of Defence. I checked my watch. Time.

'We need to talk further about this,' I told Anstruther, 'but not now.'

'Agreed.'

My head was buzzing with tiredness and adrenalin and, I suppose, with fear – fear of what we were about to discover. I walked along the corridor to the banqueting room behind Anstruther and alongside Johnny Lee Ironside, who nodded to me but said nothing more. Behind us was Katie Fisher, the spokeswoman for the search and rescue effort. In front, chairing the meeting, was Andy Carnwath. He had just arrived from London.

'You know about the hide?' I asked him in the corridor. He had been briefed.

'Yes,' he said. 'Janey just told me. We need to say nothing about it. Absolutely nothing.'

'Of course.'

As we entered the banqueting room, it was as if we were taking incoming gunfire. The cameras, flashes, and lenses popped and shot at us. It reminded me of the perp. walk staged by US prosecutors in high-profile murder cases in which the District Attorney insists that the accused – supposedly innocent until proven guilty – walks past the assembled media scrum, to ensure that he looks as guilty as sin. That day I felt guilty, too, although I was not sure exactly what I was guilty of. Two people in the front row caught my eye. Jack Rothstein of *The Times* at one end, and just along from him, in the middle of the front row, James Byrne of the *Washington Post*. The last time I had seen Byrne in the flesh was when I stepped over him after hitting him in the throat. Seeing him now made my stomach churn with nausea. He was unshaven, tie-less, with a crumpled shirt and a scruffy brown cord jacket. He had caught the red-eye from Washington Dulles just for the pleasure of tormenting me. He looked up, without emotion. I glanced back at him, as if at dirt on my shoe, and a wave of hatred flowed over me. I wanted to punch him again.

'Welcome, ladies and gentlemen,' Andy Carnwath said as the room fell silent. Networks all over the world cut to us live. Carnwath made a businesslike introductory statement, outlining the format of the news conference and introducing those of us taking part. Then he read out a short statement from the Prime Minister stating the absolute determination of Her Majesty's Government to find out what had happened to Bobby Black and to return him to his family as soon as possible. Carnwath is a class act. He's early forties, spent fifteen years working on right-wing tabloid newspapers before switching to his role as party and then government spin doctor, although he really functions as Fraser Davis's chief confidant. Fraser once told me that Andy Carnwath is the only person he knows who does not want anything from him, except simply to serve.

'You have no idea how valuable that is, Alex,' the Prime Minister told me.

Carnwath was a reformed alcoholic by the time he reached thirty, but when he gave up the booze he replaced it with other addictions, mostly exercise and intimidation. In one of his columns in *The Times*, Jack Rothstein had described Carnwath as 'a marathon runner with the temper of a wolverine.'

In the news conference, Carnwath went through some of the facts on the Who, What, Where, and When of the incident – who was on the shooting party, what we thought had happened, where it took place, and when those present realized that something was wrong. Then he handed over to Katie Fisher, who told the journalists about the search efforts.

'Just the facts,' Katie Fisher said in response to speculative questions about what had happened. She said there were already 2,000 searchers of various types with more arriving hour by hour, and then she outlined the areas where they were concentrating their efforts. 'But I don't want to answer you by speculating on matters which I simply do not know about.'

'Facts,' Carnwath repeated. 'That's right. Facts.'

In my experience it is always the why and the how questions that catch you out. They were mostly directed to me and Johnny Lee Ironside.

'Why was Bobby Black here, Ambassador Price? What exactly were you trying to achieve by inviting the Vice-President to Scotland?' Jack Rothstein asked. 'And how far was it to repair relations because there has been a high-level falling out between two men who just can't stand the sight of one another?'

'No,' I replied simply. 'In a word, it was not. It was a private visit to Scotland by a good friend and ally of this country.'

James Byrne stood up. 'But what was the reason for the invitation at this time?' Byrne croaked. 'Why now?'

His voice was even more hoarse than I had expected. It made me smile.

'Sorry, can you speak up?' I said. 'Didn't quite catch that.'

Byrne knew that I understood him perfectly. His face flashed scarlet with anger.

'It's an open secret,' Byrne went on, straining to speak as loudly as he could, 'that Vice-President Black and Prime Minister Davis did not get along. The British government, and you in particular, Ambassador Price, backed off criticism about the Khan case, and as a quid pro quo the Carr administration released Khan from custody. That's what this is about, isn't it?'

'If I heard you correctly,' I replied, 'then you have got it completely wrong. As I have seen in the past from reading your column, Mr Byrne, you confuse your personal prejudices with the facts. So here are the facts. The Prime Minister and the Vice-President are friends. Good friends. They speak as friends do, frankly and honestly to one another. It's a robust relationship, but a good one. The shooting trip was arranged to be at the best time to shoot grouse – which is now.'

I could see Byrne's throat tighten as he prepared to rasp some more. 'So why the get-together, if it was not to repair . . .?'

'This visit was a courtesy invitation extended to an old friend of this country,' I interrupted. 'Vice-President Black had made it clear to me months ago that he would like to explore his family roots in Scotland. The motive was personal friendship, not political calculation.'

'Two weeks before the mid-term elections?' Byrne croaked, sarcastically.

'I am not sure the grouse are aware of the American political calendar, Mr Byrne.'

'Next question?' Andy Carnwath said. It was Don Reid, a dwarfish man from the *LA Times* who took up the microphone.

'Can Mr Ironside confirm if the visit was agreed because President Carr wanted the Vice-President out of the United States in the run-up to the mid-term elections? White House private polling shows the Vice-President is an unpopular and divisive figure.'

Johnny Lee shook his head and pulled a disappointed face. His voice was, as always, warm and southern, but his tone unmistakable.

'That, Mr Reid, is misinformation. Private polling means "private". I don't know what's in it. Neither, with respect, do you. The Vice-President is not a candidate in the mid-term elections. His presence or absence in the United States at this time is irrelevant. He and the President decided he could best serve our country by coming to Britain to be with friends . . .'

'But the President has been campaigning hard in what everybody knows are knife-edge election races,' Don Reid persisted. 'And while the President is doing a series of whistle-stops, the Vice-President takes four days off to shoot small birds in Scotland? For fun? Are you serious?'

'I am always serious,' Johnny Lee retorted. 'And fun is allowed in the Carr administration. It may even be allowed for reporters at the *LA Times*.'

'But is it true that the President is considering dropping Vice-President Black from the ticket when he faces re-election in two years' time?'

'Not to my knowledge,' Johnny Lee Ironside replied. Don Reid sat down.

'When was the Vice-President scheduled to meet the

Prime Minister?' John Coxon, the BBC political editor, chimed in. He is an awkward and angular man whose questions have all the subtlety of a dentist poking at teeth with a pitchfork. 'And are you really expecting us to believe that the Prime Minister and Vice-President are somehow best mates, despite all the rows about torture and extraordinary renditions, about Mr Khan, about Star Wars, about Iran, and that notorious meeting at Chequers two years ago? If this is best mates, I'd hate to meet someone the Prime Minister does not get along with.'

My turn. 'Mr Coxon, were you present at what you call that "notorious meeting"?'

'No, but . . .'

'Well, I was, and it was not as you have characterized it,' I insisted. 'As for this visit, the Prime Minister was scheduled to meet Vice-President Black over dinner at Balmoral this evening, then tomorrow they were going for a walk in the hills together. The dinner has of course been cancelled.'

'The Prime Minister and Vice-President were going to shoot grouse together tomorrow?' Coxon said. There was an air of sarcastic disbelief in his voice as he said this.

'I said for a walk in the hills. I said nothing about grouse. The Prime Minister does not shoot.'

'Does he object to others doing so?'

I thought: for God's sake man, get a grip. Andy Carnwath turned towards Coxon like a snake intrigued by a particularly fat mouse.

'The BBC is – sadly – yet again trivializing a very serious situation. This news conference is not about the ethics of grouse shooting. It's about finding the Vice-President of the United States, who will have spent a very difficult night on the hills. Is it too much to hope that at least some of you can show a glimmer of humanity, and professionalism, and stick to the point?'

Even the dimmer Reptiles understood that a red line had

been drawn. A British journalist working for Al Jazeera asked Johnny Lee Ironside whether Bobby Black had a 'history of wandering off.' Johnny Lee baulked at the question.

'I do not believe so, sir,' he responded calmly. The journalist should have understood the word 'sir' for what it was. A polite American way of saying, 'back off'. He didn't.

'But Mr Ironside,' the journalist persisted, 'given the incident last year when Vice-President Black shot one of his fellow hunters at a quail shoot in Texas, he seems a particularly accident-prone member of a highly accident-prone administration, especially when it comes to shooting trips.'

I could see the veins in Johnny Lee's forehead pump with blood. He kept his voice calm.

'How dare you say such things? How dare you insult a man who represents the United States and who has gone missing in circumstances that we can only guess at?' You could hear the roomful of journalists suck in their breath. Johnny Lee kept going. 'How dare you, sir? How dare you impugn the integrity of Vice-President Black or any member of the US administration? It is unworthy of you and of Great Britain and the friendship that so far we have enjoyed between us.'

The room went silent. I did not like the words 'so far'.

'Next question,' Anstruther suggested, and we moved on. Dickie cleverly selected a journalist on the local Aberdeen newspaper who wanted to know about the identities of the volunteers on the search teams and the role of the boy scouts. Thank God for local news. But then a few minutes later it was Byrne, again.

'Ambassador Price,' he croaked, 'from your extensive experience in the United States, can you understand how angry and disappointed ordinary patriotic Americans are right now when they see the misfortune of our Vice-President treated as cause for celebration and gloating by British citizens?'

'No one is celebrating and gloating,' I responded.

'On the contrary, Ambassador. We have seen the outrageous

213

pictures . . .' Byrne interrupted, his croaky voice filled with what sounded like phoney anger.

'You mean small demonstrations outside two fringe mosques representing a tiny minority of a religious minority in the United Kingdom?' I replied, waving my hands as if swatting a fly. 'You don't have any sense of perspective, Mr Byrne. There are sixty million British people and a couple of dozen of them are behaving inappropriately.'

Another journalist stood up, Sam Balz of the McCain Group Newspapers.

'Ambassador, the British people who were celebrating the disappearance included Muhammad Asif Khan, who was released from US custody under pressure from you personally and your government. Do you think it wise—'

'Then he is despicable,' I interrupted. 'All of those who gloat over human misfortune are despicable.'

'Should you personally have campaigned so hard to release despicable people from American custody?'

I could feel the sweat begin to stipple on my forehead. I did not want to talk about any aspect of the Khan case.

'These few demonstrators do not represent our society, or the majority of British Muslims. I repeat: sixty million British people want the Vice-President to be found safe and sound. A few dozen do not. Their views are odious. And irrelevant.'

'But why did your government pressure the US to release from custody a man who clearly hates Americans? Odious, despicable – your words.'

'The release of Mr Khan and the disappearance of the Vice-President are not in any sense related.'

'How do you know?'

I didn't, of course. I was winging it.

'We have absolutely no evidence whatsoever of any link. None. If anyone does have such evidence, I should be glad to hear it.'

Byrne was still on his feet and Balz handed him the microphone as he came back for another go.

'What about the Respect MP, Graham Guest?'

I scoffed. 'Respect is a tiny anti-war party, with one MP. Mr Guest—'

Byrne cut in. 'Mr Guest is a Member of Parliament for a London constituency. He said on the *Today* show on BBC Radio this morning – and I'm quoting now – that he "celebrated" with those who hoped that the "world's greatest unconvicted war criminal – the evil Bobby Black" – had met his just fate on the Scottish hillsides. This is a Member of Parliament who—'

'Mr Guest does not speak for anyone except himself. He certainly does not speak for the British government.'

'He was elected—'

'He speaks only for himself, one of more than six hundred Members of Parliament,' I interrupted. 'The Prime Minister speaks for the British government and the British people. Her Majesty the Queen, I should say, is also deeply concerned. At this moment I am told she is meeting again with Mrs Black and has offered her accommodation in Balmoral until Vice-President Black is found. That is the true spirit of this country – from farmers and boy scouts to ghillies and police officers to the Queen herself, all doing their best to help. If Mr Guest chooses a different route, settling old political scores, then that is a matter for him and his conscience, if he has one. The handful of Muslim extremists making all the noise have been repudiated by mainstream British Muslim organizations.'

Byrne was still on his feet. 'Nice and dandy, but this has got to further damage relations with the United States.'

'Absolutely wrong. The Prime Minister has frequently said that there is no more important bilateral relationship for the people of Britain than that with the United States of America. Does anyone other than Mr Byrne have a question?'

Some of the journalists started to leave to phone their stories through to their desks. Ten minutes later we wound up and left. When we reached the back room behind the ballroom, Andy Carnwath was already on the phone to Fraser Davis in Number Ten. When he came off he held up his hands for a high-five and congratulated me.

'Fraser says you did well to take no shit,' he said. 'He was watching. Not an inch. *Despicable. Odious.* Fraser liked that. Good man.'

'The Prime Minister would do well to get out in front of this story,' I replied brusquely, seizing my opportunity while Andy was temporarily in a benign mood.

'Meaning?'

'Meaning, get back on the phone, Andy, and tell Fraser that he needs to speak publicly to the American people and the British people. A speech would do, but a series of one-on-one interviews with the US networks would be even better. He needs to defuse the Khan thing. Get him interviewed on ABC evening news, live from Downing Street. Show his concern. It's on at eleven thirty p.m. our time. I'll fix it.'

Carnwath said he would think about it.

'Don't think too long, Andy. We need to be ahead on this, before the discovery of the hide becomes public knowledge.'

'I said I would think about it, all right?'

I decided to return with Anstruther to Castle Dubh.

'Any more word from the scene?' I asked him as we jumped back into the Land Rover. Anstruther checked his Blackberry. He had also been in contact with the search teams.

'No,' he answered. 'Nothing more than when we left. The SOCO boys are still turning it over.'

'You think he's been kidnapped?' I asked directly. Anstruther wrinkled his brow and shrugged. It was answer enough. We walked into Castle Dubh and I planned to call Downing Street myself with some suggestions for what the Prime Minister might say if he granted the US networks an interview, but before I could do so, Johnny Lee Ironside sought me out.

'Alex, you have to go right now to . . . what's the place called?'

One of his helpers from the US embassy in London told him. 'Bolfracks Bothy.'

'Bolfracks Bothy. Down the track past the rhododendron plantation.'

'I know it,' I said. 'Why?'

'That's where the FBI have set up,' Johnny Lee offered by way of explanation. 'They're waiting for you. Marian Killick herself.'

'Am I allowed a lawyer?' I grinned.

'No,' he said. His voice was matter of fact, without humour. 'No lawyers. Good luck.'

'Good luck? Do I need it?'

Johnny Lee held his hands open, palms upwards.

'From what I hear of Marian Killick, yes.'

SEVENTEEN

Bolfracks Bothy is where the Castle Dubh estate workers used to live. It was constructed as a large Victorian dormitory by a philanthropic ancestor of Anstruther's, who wished to offer the best accommodation for his single, seasonal, male workers, the ones who came from Ireland to pick potatoes and to help with the grain harvests. He also wanted to keep an eye on them. Like most Scottish landlords of the nineteenth century, he was suspicious of subversive Irish Popish ways, and preferred to keep the Catholic Irish away from his Presbyterian permanent workers. Anstruther had refurbished the bothy into an office complex for the management of his estate. Half the office ran the farming and shooting businesses, the other half was involved in claiming grants from the European Union, the Department of Environment Food, and Rural Affairs, and the Scottish Executive.

'Triple-dipping,' Anstruther told me it was called. 'You dip the snout into three separate troughs of taxpayers' cash – Scottish, British, European.' He shrugged. 'Welcome to twenty-first-century European agriculture.'

I walked through the grounds until I came to the checkpoint of armed American guards. They had put barbed wire around the bothy so that there was only one entry point.

The guards were dressed in the black of the uniformed US Secret Service and carried sub-machine-guns and pistols. They asked me for proof of identity. I had nothing except credit cards and my driver's licence. They refused to let me in. I blinked in disbelief. At times American bureaucracy is unfathomable, and even worse than British. I once had to take up the case in Washington of a British-born professor of agricultural sciences at a university in Iowa who was applying for American citizenship. The US authorities threatened him with deportation because he refused to provide them with a full set of fingerprints. The professor had sent them the fingerprints of his left hand, but not the right, with an explanation about why he had done this. His explanation was repeatedly rejected by the Department of Homeland Security, which threatened to deport him as an undesirable alien. It took two years to persuade the US authorities that the reason he could not supply the fingerprints from his right hand was that it had been amputated in a farming accident. I looked at the Secret Service guards.

'Look, I'm here by invitation,' I said gently. 'The FBI wants to see me. Special Agent Lindsey and Deputy Director Killick. But if you do not want to let me in, I am happy to go about my other business, and you can explain the problem to Marian Killick yourself.'

At the name of Marian Killick, the Secret Service guards visibly perked up. They called inside for instructions. After a short wait, I was escorted to the estate manager's office, where four special agents were sitting beside computers. Special Agent Lindsey was a slightly overweight red-headed woman in her thirties. She brought me through to Marian Killick's temporary office, which had been the estate manager's office for Castle Dubh. Killick was wearing a black sheath dress and a black cardigan; slim, soignée, in her forties, African American, carefully coiffed straightened hair. She looked me over with the kind of curious eyes that appeared to bore through to your very soul. She spoke with what sounded like a Tennessee accent.

'Please sit, Ambassador. Coffee? Water? Cookies?'

'Memphis?' I said.

'Close,' she replied, with a quick smile which faded almost as soon as it began. I had surprised her, which was good. 'West across the Mississippi from Tennessee. Helena, Arkansas. My father was a pastor there, until we went north to Chicago. Obama territory. You have a good ear for American accents.'

'Thank you, Deputy Director.'

I took coffee and picked up a cookie. I'd visited Helena, Arkansas, a few years back. It was a poor, run-down shit-hole of a Mississippi delta town. Killick had done well to get out of there and to reach where she now was. The cookie tasted good. I couldn't remember when I had last eaten. I had been sustained by caffeine, adrenalin, fear, and now sugar. Killick introduced her team and said they would record the interview. They would also take notes.

'You comfortable with that, Ambassador?'

'Of course.' As if there was an alternative.

'Before we begin, and off the record,' Killick said, 'I know I speak for most of my colleagues at the bureau when I say I admire the stand you personally took on exceptional interrogation methods.'

I was completely taken aback by this, and I showed it. 'You do?'

'We don't like torture either,' she said, matter of factly. 'It's wrong, and it doesn't work. I hear you raised the example of President Lincoln with the Vice-President. If it was good enough for Lincoln, I guess it's good enough for me.'

I looked at this woman in front of me and did not know what to say. She had wrong-footed me completely, and I think I may have blushed, possibly for the first time in years. I agreed completely with Killick that torture is immoral and almost certainly illegal, but more importantly, under torture people will admit anything, say anything, do anything. It often just does not work. What does work in interrogations is rapport, and control. The best interrogators have it, and so do those who are best at resisting interrogation. That's what the US and British military teach in what they now call SERE training – Survival, Evasion, Resistance, and Escape – and in R2i 'Resistance to Interrogation' courses. I have had enough experience of all this from my days in Northern Ireland to know that when Marian Killick praised me, she immediately established rapport, and also established her own control. I shifted uncomfortably in my seat. This was going to be more challenging than I thought.

'Lindsey?' Killick said, nodding towards one of the three other agents in the room. Special Agent Lindsey looked up from her notepad towards me and began asking questions, questions not very different from those posed by the news media outside. I answered as affably as I could, all SERE and R2i. It was the warm-up. Then it turned to something much less pleasant. Marian Killick took over.

'Who organized it so Vice-President Black came here?'

'Me,' I said. 'At least, at first, along with Johnny Lee Ironside. And then of course our staff here, at Number Ten, Castle Dubh, and at Balmoral.'

'How many were involved?'

'I already handed over a list. I'd guess two hundred people.'

'Your idea?'

'Yes.'

'Thank you for your list. You are aware of the term "snow job", Ambassador?'

I was puzzled. 'Of course.'

'What does the term "snow job" signify?'

'It's when someone produces a vast amount of information in response to an enquiry.'

'Making a pretence to be helpful, whereas the aim is to get in the way,' she interrupted, her Helena, Arkansas accent no longer sounding quite so charming. The eyes bored into me again. 'Two hundred names is a snow job. Why are you wasting my time?'

I scoffed at this. 'You want an incomplete list, Deputy Director Killick, so you can complain I am hiding something? Or you want a complete list so you can complain about it being a snow job? You choose. You can have whatever you want to fit into your best idea of a complaint, if that's your starting point.'

She sat back a little. We were each staking out our territory.

'We want information we can use and use quickly. This is time urgent.'

'Deputy Director Killick, that is disrespectful to me, offensive, and way out of line.'

She was not deflected. Icily polite. 'Ambassador, I'd be most grateful to hear who you think are the key people who knew most about the Vice-President's itinerary from your two hundred names. Gimme your top ten.'

I gave her about a dozen names, including myself, Johnny Lee, Anstruther, the three who did most of the planning, plus the Secret Service and our Diplomatic Protection officers.

'But including estate staff,' I went on, 'civil servants, the royal household, all of whom gossip and have friends, wives, and husbands, plus local people, the butcher and baker and candlestick maker in Rowallan village – we could be talking of hundreds and hundreds of people. Thousands. There's your snow job, Deputy Director. It's called the truth, the whole truth, and nothing but the truth.'

So help me God, I thought.

'But who knew the precise details of the visit?' she persisted. 'The schedule? The route the shooting party was likely to take? Where exactly the Vice-President would be standing at any one point relative to the rest of the shooting party?'

222

'Even I did not know all that,' I snapped. 'Just Anstruther and his ghillies, maybe the Secret Service and Diplomatic Protection unit, and anyone they told. The general principles were known to hundreds of people, but Anstruther made up the precise route on the day in response to conditions.'

She looked at me and raised an eyebrow. 'We will need you to think on this some more,' she said.

'Of course. I'll see what I can do, and so will Lord Anstruther. But I don't believe that thinking on it will change anything.'

Killick looked at her notepad and then at me. She was a dog with a bone and she was not going to let go until she had chewed me up to her satisfaction.

'Remind me again whose idea this was?'

'I told you. Mine.'

'Yours alone?'

I swallowed. 'I . . . Yes. Mine alone. But everybody thought it was a good idea.'

'Everybody? You discussed it?'

I sucked in a lungful of air and told myself to be polite. 'I discussed it widely, with many people in Downing Street, the Foreign Office, and of course in the White House and OVP, including Johnny Lee Ironside.'

'Anyone suggest it to you?'

'No.'

She said it the way people at airports ask you if you packed all your own luggage, and could anyone have tampered with your suitcase.

'*What* suggested it to you?'

'I don't understand.' I thought we were going round in circles.

'How did the idea come to you? You were standing in line at the supermarket and it hit you? You were in your office? A flash of inspiration in the shower?'

I took a breath. 'Why is this important?'

'Because I say it is,' she shot back.

'I don't remember exactly, except that after the disastrous Chequers meeting with Fraser Davis, there were so many problems between our governments made worse by the nasty atmosphere between Black and Davis that Johnny Lee and I knew we had to do something to get things back on track. It took us two years to figure out what to do and to do it. Two years of niggling arguments between Washington and London that benefited nobody except our enemies. I still don't understand why you think it is important to know when inspiration struck.'

Her eyes flashed at me and she slapped the table hard with the flat of her hand. 'Because I need to know everything, Ambassador, and I will know everything. President Carr has tasked me with this, and I will not let him or my country down. I don't do half-assed. It's not how I was brought up. This whole thing is out of whack and I want to trace the out-of-whack part back to the source. And I'm thinking that source might be you. Something's up here, don't you think? Something smells bad. Now what or who suggested this visit to you, Ambassador Price?'

'What suggested it to me, Deputy Director Killick, was that something needed to be fixed. Davis and Black were divided over everything important – Iran, detention, rendition, the anti-missile shield, the contracts for the rebuilding of Iraq, particularly when that occurred on a no-bid basis.'

'My understanding is that the new contracts were awarded by the democratically elected Iraqi government,' Marian Killick said.

'Indeed,' I responded sarcastically. 'And the democratically elected Iraqi government democratically came up with the view that only Warburton should get the business, when Warburton is run by one of President Carr's biggest campaign contributors, and one of Vice-President Black's best friends. Well, there's democracy for you, as I explained to the Prime Minister. Completely unconnected to the forty-five million dollars in bonuses and so-called facilitation payments made by Warburton to members of the Iraqi government. Some people would consider that money to amount to bribery.'

Killick refused to be deflected. I admired her style.

'And there was that telephone conversation a couple of months ago between the Prime Minister and the Vice-President on that issue.'

'Yes.' So she knew about that as well. I took a deep breath. One of the best interrogation techniques is to make the prisoner feel as if his information is more or less superfluous because the interrogator already knows all the answers. Even though I understood what Killick was doing, I was still impressed.

'What did they say to each other?' she demanded.

'I'm not at liberty to . . .' One of the agents handed some papers to Killick. She glanced at them and read the quotes.

'Did the Vice-President say to the Prime Minister, "Don't fuck with us, Fraser. You're fucking with the big boys now"?'

'I believe he may have used words like that.'

'And did the Prime Minister respond, "You have delusions of competence, Mr Vice-President. If the competence of the Carr administration matched your own personal arrogance, then we would not be in this mess."'

I squirmed with embarrassment.

She went on. 'And then there was another exchange, with the Vice-President telling the Prime Minister that this was not the time to start going all grey on him and having misplaced European doubts, and the Prime Minister responding . . .'

I finished her sentence.

'. . . responding that Vice-President Black reminded the Prime Minister of those Muslim extremists who claim they are doing God's will when in fact they are merely operating in their own best interests, and the Vice-President telling the

Prime Minister to – I believe I am quoting correctly – go fuck himself.'

'Yes,' Killick said, glancing at the transcript in front of her. 'I see you are familiar with the conversation, Ambassador.'

I nodded. The quotes were engraved in my head.

'And then there's the matter of Rashid Ali Fuad and Muhammad Asif Khan.'

I began to sweat. 'What about them?'

'Did the Vice-President at one point ask why the Prime Minister insisted on calling Fuad and Khan "British citizens"?'

'You know all this, why do you ask me?' I blurted out. Marian Killick just looked at me in silence. 'All right,' I said. 'Yes. As you know, the Vice-President had threatened to make sure that all British passport holders of Pakistani background require special visas for travel to the United States, and the Prime Minister . . .'

'. . . said that was racist and inflammatory and if pursued could lead to race riots in British cities,' Killick said.

'Correct. The Vice-President said he didn't give a fuck so long as . . .'

'Go on.'

'. . . so long as what he called "no Paki terrorist blows up any American aircraft."'

The room seemed to be silent around me. I held my breath.

'How do you think the Prime Minister took that comment, Ambassador?'

'About as well as you might expect, Deputy Director, given that the word "Paki" here in Britain is usually considered a racist insult. It is not a word that any British politician would ever use, in public or private. I believe you have similar racially charged terms in your own country.'

She ignored that comment.

'And your personal view? I take it you were listening in to the conversation.'

'Yes. My personal view is that if Vice-President Black's

comments were made public they would persuade most British people he is a racist. I don't see that there is any other interpretation. We only have one class of British citizen: black, white, Asian, Christian, Muslim, Jew. One class. The message appears to have reached the Vice-President. As you know, in recent months the special visa idea was quietly shelved.'

Killick sat back and looked at me thoughtfully. She glanced over at Special Agent Lindsey who introduced another line of questioning.

'Why was the Secret Service protection for the Vice-President scaled back?'

'Ask the Secret Service.'

'We did.' A young white male agent who was standing leaning on the wall to my left butted in. 'And the Secret Service told us that it was Prince Duncan and Princess Charlotte who specifically demanded an end to what they called the "heavy–handed" American presence on the hills. They said it was against the spirit of the shoot.'

'How the protection was organized is not my thing. I cannot confirm . . .'

'But you were told about it,' Special Agent Lindsey butted in. I sighed again. I was feeling increasingly hot and uncomfortable. My shirt stuck to my back with sweat. They were treating me like a criminal and I had begun to feel like one.

'Yes. I was told about it. But not consulted.'

'So let me get this straight, Ambassador,' Lindsey summarized. 'Vice-President Black agreed to scale back his Secret Service detail on these mountains in response to a direct request from a member or members of the British royal family?'

Special Agent Lindsey looked at me and tapped her pen on her notepad impatiently.

'You may be correct in that, yes.'

'So as not to offend his hosts?'

'Possibly. I don't know his motives. But I don't believe any of us thought that thirty Secret Service agents on the Scottish mountains would do much good on a grouse shoot. Johnny Lee told me that in Texas—'

Killick interrupted. 'Texas isn't Scotland. This is a foreign country.'

'Not to me,' I shot back. 'And it is also a remarkably safe country. A lot safer than Helena, Arkansas, Deputy Director – or Texas. I understand that in Texas the Vice-President hunts with just two agents. The Secret Service raises no objection.'

'That's not what the Secret Service tell us about the situation here. They say they protested vigorously but were overruled by the Vice-President under direct pressure from Prince Duncan, and that you knew about it. Funny how in this business all roads lead back to you, Ambassador Alexander Price. Your fingerprints are all over this.'

At first I said nothing.

'The President's adviser, Arlo Luntz, is fond of telling me that you should not ascribe to malice that which can be put down to stupidity,' I suggested. 'Pretty sound advice, it seems to me. I'm sure I get things wrong. So do other people. I don't claim to be perfect.'

Killick's eyes bored into me. Dropping Arlo Luntz's name and reminding her that I had access to the President's staff was a smart move on my part. I decided to go on the offensive.

'Can I ask you something, Deputy Director?'

Marian Killick shrugged.

'Sure. Go ahead. We've nothing else going on here.'

'The hide that was discovered this morning. Was that something dug by the US Secret Service or some other US agency to keep an eye on the Vice-President?'

She glared at me. She had obviously been considering the same thing. Special Agent Lindsey stopped tapping her pen and was pretending to look at her notes. We all wanted to hear Killick's answer.

'I honestly do not know,' Marian Killick said, and I believed her. 'Though, like I keep saying about a bunch of things, I intend to find out. Why do you ask?'

I told her about the conversation with Anstruther.

'He said that the hide was in exactly the right place to monitor the Vice-President's movements but just far enough from the shooting party to escape detection from the dogs. Maybe that's just luck, but Anstruther suggested to me that only someone with intimate knowledge of the planned movements of the shooting party would be able to dig a hide at that point.'

She looked at me thoughtfully. Rapport, control.

'Do you think British special forces dug the hide?' she asked. It was the first and only question during my entire interrogation to which she did not already know the answer. 'Perhaps to keep an eye on the shooting party?'

'I wondered about that too,' I replied. 'But Anstruther assures me he would have known if anything like that were contemplated, and it was not.'

We paused and looked at each other. I think we were both frightened that we were stepping into some bottomless chasm. I started to imagine the potential for catastrophe if either the British or the Americans really had dug that hide and the Vice-President had disappeared in the fog under the noses of the watchers. I was fairly sure Killick was contemplating the same thing. She had a sour twist to her lips for a moment and then regained her composure. I did not know what to believe any more, except that I would not be the fall guy for everything that had gone wrong.

'And what of the button?' I wondered.

'What of it?' Killick replied, and then thought for a moment.

'W-well?' I stammered. 'I was up there this morning when they found it. Is it useful?'

She raised an eyebrow. She obviously knew something. The question was whether she was going to tell me.

'We think it's Iranian,' she said eventually. 'It's a Chinese-manufactured button of a type used for combat fatigues, but with slivers of cotton thread of a type sourced to Iran, and not exported. The consequences of this could be enormous, Ambassador.'

'I-Iran . . .?' I stuttered again.

She nodded.

'Thank you for your time, Ambassador,' Killick said, closing her notebook. 'We will need to call you again. Please say nothing of what I have just told you, although our British counterparts have the same information and have reached the same conclusions, so I guess you will be formally briefed soon enough. And please let us know where to reach you.'

'Of course. I'll be here for the foreseeable . . .' I nodded towards Castle Dubh. 'The Prime Minister wants me to stay until . . . it's over.'

The lead agent, Lindsey, handed me a card. 'Call this if there's any change of plan,' she said.

'Let me walk with you a-ways,' Killick said, this time with a smile. 'I could do with some fine Scottish air.'

I looked at the card. It said Special Agent Debra Lindsey, Federal Bureau of Investigation, and gave the address of the FBI in Washington DC plus a cellphone number. Killick walked me through the Secret Service cordon and part of the way towards Castle Dubh.

'The cellphones work just fine here,' she said. 'Call Debra Lindsey if you think of anything that might help us, or if you want to speak to me again. I am always available. I guess I'll be staying here for a while.'

I promised I would call if I could think of anything. Then she stopped. Marian Killick was driven by curiosity, and that made me nervous. She really did want to know everything.

'One last question for now, Ambassador.'

'Go ahead.'

She looked at me, scanning my face for a reaction.

'How exactly would you characterize your relationship with Dr Kristina Taft?'

EIGHTEEN

Air Force One began its descent towards the Rocky Mountains. In the presidential suite, President Carr was shuffling through the six-by-four-inch cards that contained his speech of reassurance to the American people. He was, as usual, quickly memorizing every word. There would be no teleprompter, but that encouraged him. Carr thought teleprompters were the seed of the Devil. He worked best when the words were ingrained inside him, not written on a glass screen in front of the camera. President Carr was wearing a brown leather flight jacket with the presidential seal on his breast. All major US military facilities have their own TV crews and TV channels for base communications, and when he stepped off the plane he was filmed by a US Air Force crew, saluting, shaking hands with the top brass at the airfield, looking calm and confident. The President of the United States was taken underground immediately for a briefing on the military and security situation, chaired by Kristina. All quiet. Four American soldiers had been killed that day on the outskirts of Kabul in Afghanistan by an IED – an improvised explosive device. Two other US personnel were killed in Iraq when their Humvee was in collision with another vehicle. There was no connection in any of this with the Vice-President's disappearance. As the President sat in the underground TV studio ready to broadcast to the American people, he received one further short briefing from Arlo Luntz on his delivery.

'Slow and calm. Not sombre. It's not a funeral. Not a war. Or not yet. Just slow and calm,' Luntz said soothingly in a hypnotic voice. 'It's all under control. You have it all under control.'

'All under control,' President Carr repeated. 'Slow and calm.'

An assistant gave him a touch of make-up to raise the colour on his pallid cheeks and to emphasize the line of his eyebrows, which were naturally blond and did not show up well on television. Luntz had, at one point, tried to insist that Carr dye his eyebrows dark brown, something Carr had so far resisted. He sat in the USAF TV studio and waited for the link to be established, surrounded by uniformed Air Force officers and White House staff. I was in the gym at Castle Dubh punching rapidly at the speed bag when the broadcast came on the BBC News Channel. I stood, panting with effort, and stared at the screen. My sports clothes were drenched with sweat as I took off the red boxing gloves and switched up the volume on the remote.

For the first time since he took office, I thought that President Theo Carr looked and sounded every inch the Commander-in-Chief with his troops in time of war. There was a strength in his voice and in his bearing that surprised me. Arlo Luntz had once told me that no other democracy in history had so glorified the military at the highest levels of power as the United States in the twenty-first century. But that was okay, Luntz said, 'Because we are the *Good Guys.*' The President sat calmly for three seconds and then he was cued. The words were exactly as Luntz had ordered – soothing, slow and calm.

'My fellow Americans,' President Theo Carr began, 'we are still awaiting news from Scotland on the search for

Vice-President Black. We are hopeful. We pray that he will be found soon, safe and well, perhaps after a difficult time in bad weather on the Scottish hills. The British authorities are giving us every assistance, and I have directed the FBI and other agencies to send personnel to Scotland to help with the search and to determine what has occurred. Queen Elizabeth and Prime Minister Fraser Davis are aware of the situation and watching developments. We have no evidence of hostile activity. We have no credible evidence of any direct threat to the Vice-President or to the security of this country. However, due to the serious nature of this incident, as Commander-in-Chief I have ordered US forces worldwide placed on a high state of readiness to respond to any threat to our national security from any source at any time. Our thoughts and our prayers are with the Vice-President and his family.' President Carr stopped talking and paused for a few seconds. He looked straight into the camera.

'Come on home safe, Bobby. We need you here.'

Arlo Luntz had suggested the folksy peroration. He knew it would be the headline clip used round the world. He was right.

'He's their Vice-President,' Luntz had said, 'but he's your friend. You got me?'

The broadcast ended. The lights in the studio were switched off and the President's microphone was unclipped from his leather jacket. Luntz had watched the performance with intense satisfaction, and could not restrain himself from giving President Carr two thumbs-ups.

'Terrific,' he said. The President nodded, turned on his heel and left for a medical check-up from USAF doctors before another series of national security briefings.

'Well?' Kristina asked. Luntz said he was quietly satisfied. It was the kind of news broadcast he liked. No Reps to ask awkward questions. No sceptical journalistic filter, no pesky point-scoring. It was the way things ought to be. The President of the United States talking with his people. The broadcast would be seen or heard by an estimated 100 million Americans, plus hundreds of millions of other people around the world. Every television news bulletin in the United States and every newspaper the following day would choose the same clip for a headline, as Arlo Luntz knew they would. That night's news bulletins all over the world opened with the same nine words:

'*Come on home safe, Bobby. We need you here.*'

I switched down the volume on the TV, put my boxing gloves back on, and began hitting the punchbag as if my life depended on it.

The meeting of the President's Emergency National Security Team took place immediately after the broadcast. Kristina outlined the results of the search in Scotland so far. President Carr arrived from his medical check-up and asked for more information on what Kristina said was potentially an extremely significant development.

'This "hide" thing,' Carr said. 'What do we mean by a "hide" here?'

The room fell silent. Kristina read from the US Secret Service report, which described a small tunnel dug under a patch of spiky yellow-flowering mountain gorse, which covered a large part of the Aberdeenshire hillsides.

'In Scotland they call it "whin", Mr President.'

She explained that the tunnel had been discovered by a British special forces team, the SAS; that the very large patch of whin, near where the Vice-President had disappeared, had looked impenetrable until the searchers found the hide beneath. The tunnel did not go deep. It did not go anywhere.

The Secret Service report concluded, just as the British report did, that the hide was large enough to conceal three or four average-sized men, that it had been recently dug and recently used, and that it was consistent with the kind of hides used by US and other special forces, including those of Britain, most European armies, Russia, Israel, and elsewhere in the Middle East.

'The British special forces found the hide,' Kristina read from the report, 'because that is exactly where they would have put it if they had wanted to kidnap the Vice-President of the United States on a shooting trip in Scotland.'

Theo Carr appeared puzzled. 'Are you telling me that special forces were on the ground watching Bobby?'

'Not US special forces, Mr President,' Kristina said. 'And not British special forces either, from what they tell us. All we know is that the hide is consistent with the type of—'

'I get it,' Carr sighed. 'So the Vice-President has been kidnapped? Is that what this hide is about?'

'We do not know for sure, Mr President,' Kristina replied. 'But my advice from General Shultz and from the Joint Chiefs is that we should affirmatively act on that possibility.'

She explained about the button and the Iranian thread.

'We need more than a button and a piece of thread,' Carr said calmly, 'if this is leading to Iran.'

'Yes, Mr President,' Stephanie agreed. 'It is by no means definitive.'

Stephanie Alejandro butted in.

'You need to think actively about a replacement for the Vice-President right away, Mr President. We need to act decisively.'

'Decisively is one thing,' Theo Carr said. 'Precipitately is another. What's the legal position? What do I have to do and when do I have to do it?'

Alejandro rolled her eyes. She was sure he wanted to delay again. Carr always wanted to delay. She dug her nails into her leg in frustration. Arlo Luntz cleared his throat and tucked his hair back from his forehead.

He had prepared two weeks of political campaigning for Theo Carr, crisscrossing the country to raise funds for Republican candidates in the most hotly contested House and Senate seats, and now he was going to have to bin it, costing the party at least $20 million. But Luntz was not downhearted. He, too, had been brought up to recognize that there was an opportunity in every crisis. Exploiting that opportunity was what a crisis was for.

'The legal and constitutional position manages to be very simple and also very complicated, Mr President,' Luntz began. 'Simple first. The governing part of the Constitution is the Twenty-fifth Amendment. Section Two states, and I'm reading here: *Whenever there is a vacancy in the office of the Vice-President, the President shall nominate a Vice-President who shall take office upon confirmation by a majority vote of both Houses of Congress.*'

Theo Carr waved at him irritably. 'Whenever there is a vacancy? That's the damn point, Arlo. Is there a vacancy or not? Help me out here.'

Arlo Luntz refused to be budged from his train of thought.

'Nobody paid attention to any of this for two hundred years, at least 'til Kennedy got shot. The Twenty-fifth Amendment was ratified four years later in Sixty-seven. The Constitution, by this amendment, for the first time provided for filling the vice-presidency. It's been done before. It was first used to elevate Gerald Ford to replace Spiro Agnew. Then it was used to elevate Nelson Rockefeller to replace Ford when Ford himself became President following Nixon's resignation. So, to repeat, the mechanics are simple: you nominate a new vice-president and he or she must be confirmed by both Houses of Congress.'

'So . . .?' Carr wondered aloud. 'I can replace Bobby with whomever I want, whenever I want, just by declaring a vacancy and getting Congress to go along with it? Is that what we're saying?'

Arlo Luntz pulled a face. 'Not quite, Mr President. What I just outlined only gets us halfway. We still have to deal with

237

the question you raised at the start, the vacancy question. Is there or is there not a vacancy?'

'Bobby Black is gone, Arlo,' Stephanie Alejandro insisted. 'Sounds like a vacancy to me.' Arlo Luntz shook his head and a long straggle of hair fell away from the bald patch until he replaced it.

'Just isn't good enough. The legal position is that, should the Vice-President vanish, with no concrete evidence of his or her death, there is no clear constitutional or statutory provisions to handle the case.'

'Meaning?' Carr said. 'Get to it, Arlo.'

'Meaning, it depends.'

'For fuck's sake Arlo . . .'

'It depends for the reason I just stated. Is there or is there not a vacancy? You could not reasonably declare a vacancy if the Vice-President went to the can to take a leak. But is there a vacancy if he goes walkabout for a few days in Scotland? Or a month? Six months? And does the hide make a difference? Nobody knows for sure. It's a matter for judgement. Your judgement, Mr President. I asked around. The AG's office, a couple of constitutional scholars, two presidential historians. They are all scratching their heads. There are no rules.'

Arlo Luntz sighed, then went on. 'The consensus is that, unless we have concrete evidence of death, infirmity, or kidnap, any move to declare Bobby Black dead would have to come first from the family – from Susan or from one of the children. They would have to make the usual legal pleas to have their father or husband declared formally dead. This would then allow the constitutional mechanisms to kick in, letting the president nominate a new Vice-President to be confirmed by the vote in Congress.'

'We can't wait for that,' Kristina said.

'Kristina's right – in cases of disappearance the declaration of death usually takes forever,' Stephanie Alejandro insisted.

238

'Remember when the aviator Steve Fossett went missing? It took months and months to get him presumed dead. We have a government to run. We can't wait.'

'Well, it's not that simple,' Arlo Luntz replied. 'People don't rush into this, for obvious reasons. You would have to ask Susan Black to have her husband declared dead, after what? Forty-eight hours? If she refused, you could go to other members of the family, starting I guess with Alice, who's the oldest daughter, and then Robert. All with fewer than two weeks to go before the elections. Either way . . .' Luntz did not have to finish the sentence.

'Either way, it would be a shit thing to do.'

'Yes, Mr President,' Luntz agreed. 'It would be a shit thing to do.' Theo Carr looked at his chief political adviser. Arlo Luntz had a very high tolerance for doing shit things. If he baulked, it meant something.

'I see,' Theo Carr said, and closed his eyes for a moment.

'Mr President,' Luntz said, eventually. 'I think you need to speak with Susan Fein Black and ask her what she is prepared to do.'

'Yeah,' President Carr said. He stood up and stretched his back, which was still stiff from the flight. 'And bearing in mind the button and thread business, I also have to consider what I am prepared to do.' As the meeting was about to adjourn, one of Kristina's NSC aides knocked at the door. She apologized but said it was urgent, handing Kristina an email. It had been sent by Marian Killick herself. Everyone in the room looked at Kristina.

'Deputy Director Killick says the Scottish police have found a car, Mr President, which they are characterizing as a getaway car.'

'A getaway car?' the President repeated.

'Yes sir. Among other things it contains maps of the area with what Deputy Director Killick calls annotations in a foreign language. The language is Farsi, Mr President.'

'Farsi?'

'Yes, Mr President,' Kristina said. 'They speak it in Iran and in parts of Afghanistan.'

'I'm familiar with where they speak Farsi, Kristina. I'm just wondering at what point we may have to do what Bobby always said we would have to do one day, and go to war with Iran.'

NINETEEN

I was in the shower cleaning up following my fight with the punchbag when I heard the news of the discovery of the getaway car. Anstruther was already at the scene and sent a car which took me to a lay-by on a road about three miles from the whin patch, near the loch shore on the far side of Rowallan village. The getaway car – if that's what it was – was a blue Toyota four-by-four. The area was cordoned off and SOCO teams were crawling over every inch of the vehicle and the surrounding woodland. My hair was still wet from the shower and I shivered as the wind from the hills chilled me.

'The police have been looking for abandoned cars anywhere within a twenty-mile radius,' Anstruther told me. 'This one looks like it's the real thing. Maps of the estate, annotations in some kind of Middle Eastern language that we think is Farsi, empty cola bottles, and something else that we think ties it directly to Black.'

'What?'

'A pair of glasses. They showed them to me. I can't be sure, but they look just like the ones Bobby Black was wearing. He's been kidnapped, Alex. And we're responsible.'

There was nothing more we could do or say standing at

241

the side of the lay-by in Aberdeenshire. I pulled my coat around me and suggested we return to Castle Dubh. We were all in a state of shock, of disbelief. It reminded me of the supposed phases of the grieving process – shock, denial, disbelief, anger and finally, maybe one day, acceptance. I was moving slowly towards the anger stage. How could this have happened? How could I have let it happen? Andy Carnwath called an emergency meeting of the Downing Street team, plus the security service MI5, the secret intelligence service MI6, and senior police officers in Castle Dubh. We met sitting in the conservatory at the back of Castle Dubh, an incongruous emergency meeting of mostly middle-aged white men sitting in wicker chairs among ferns and climbing ivy. The senior MI5 officer, a grey-suited, thin, balding man in his early fifties who introduced himself as Edward Fleming, ran through the latest on the investigation, the forensics and the inquiry. Fleming said that once the kidnappers had got the Vice-President out of the fog and off the mountain to where the Toyota had been discovered, they would have changed cars and, in the words of the MI5 officer, 'They could be anywhere right now, not necessarily in the UK.'

'What are you most worried about?' Janey Masters said. It was a good question. Fleming ran a hand across his chin.

'A backlash,' he said carefully, 'against British Muslims. Some idiot starting a fight somewhere, a BNP demonstration that leads to riots or civil disorder. The police at all levels are most worried about anything that makes ordinary people suspicious of their neighbours. ACPO wants to cancel all police leave throughout the entire country, but they worry that just the announcement of that would be inflammatory. We have to go carefully without alarming people unduly, but equally we have to be aware that almost anything could kick it off.'

ACPO is the Association of Chief Police Officers. The BNP is the British National Party, a fringe far-right-wing group with a neo-Nazi reputation.

242

'Fuck,' Janey Masters said, not entirely under her breath.

'Is there,' I started to ask, choosing my words carefully, 'any possibility that this disappearance might be connected with some British domestic terrorist group? With the Manila bomber Fuad, or with the Khan case, or any of the others we know about?'

Edward Fleming obviously knew what I was alluding to. He answered carefully, without mentioning directly the Heathrow plot.

'We have a number of significant terrorist or proto-terrorist cells under watch,' he said slowly, rather like an accountant going through tax allowances. 'None of the groups we know of is connected to the disappearance of Bobby Black, and there is no connection as far as we know to the figures you named, Fuad or Khan or anyone associated with them.'

Andy Carnwath introduced Vivien Raphael, the representative from MI6, a woman in her late forties with short black hair and a stack of files in front of her.

'The presumed Iran connection,' Raphael said, 'may be something, may be a red herring. We are hearing absolutely nothing – and neither are other foreign intelligence services – about any elements within the Iranian state trying to conduct a kidnapping like this, nor have we heard anything from Hezbollah, Hamas, or Islamic Jihad.'

Foreign intelligence services in this context usually meant Mossad, the Turks, and the Arabs, all of whom were being extremely cooperative, Ms Raphael said.

'We have not found anyone who believes it is credible even for rogue elements of the Revolutionary Guards to be operating in the Scottish Highlands,' she said.

'And yet we have the button, the thread, and the maps with Farsi script,' Anstruther prompted her. 'They must add up to something.'

'Perhaps they do, Lord Anstruther,' Vivien Raphael said very formally. 'The question is not what we have, but what it means. My service is not ruling out an Iranian connection. What we are saying is that beyond so far circumstantial evidence we can find no intelligence source pointing to Iran or its agents or its surrogates, and no credible intelligence agency telling us the Iranians are in this.'

'Then where the fuck are we?' Andy Carnwath wondered aloud. 'We're still in the fucking Scottish mist, aren't we?'

We glanced around at each other and the meeting drew to a close. As the others left the conservatory Andy Carnwath pulled me to one side.

'I'm going to have to talk to the press,' he said, with the face of a man who has just been informed he has terminal cancer. 'Try to calm things down. But there's one other thing you need to know, Alex. Though this must go no further. Not to the Americans. Not to *any* American. You understand?' It was an update on the Heathrow plot.

'What Fleming did not say in the meeting is that his people and the police are ready to make arrests,' he said. 'We're really worried about a backlash when they do. He says it is so big there really could be trouble on the streets, and it is that which has got ACPO spooked.' Whatever the Heathrow plot entailed – and at that time I still did not know – the arrest of British Muslims planning a terrorist attack at the busiest airport in Europe while the hunt for the Vice-President continued would likely cause trouble in almost any British city.

'I can't tell you the details,' Carnwath whispered, 'because I don't know the details, except that Fleming told me tens of thousands of lives are at risk. *Tens of thousands*. And it is vital you do not tell the Americans because—'

I stopped him. 'Look, I understand, Andy. I get it.'

'Because we know about you and Kristina Taft.'

I nodded.

'Of course you do. And I know that you know. So let's cut the crap. I won't be telling Kristina anything. In fact, I doubt

I will be seeing her much for quite some time. Even the fact that she knows me right now could prove toxic for her.'

We stared at each other for a few seconds.

'I'm sorry, Alex,' Carnwath said. 'I hadn't thought about what this must be doing to you. Anyway, Fleming and the security service want a few more days, and they are shitting themselves that their operation on the Heathrow plot somehow becomes confused with whatever has happened to Vice-President Black.'

'Why would anyone think the two things might be connected?'

Andy Carnwath looked at me and took a deep breath, as if trying to figure out the lesser of two evils – telling me or not telling me.

'Just pray that Fleming is right and Muhammad Asif Khan is not involved in any way with Bobby Black's disappearance. You understand where we're going with this?'

I nodded.

'And you have to understand,' I said, 'that over the past few hours I have been hearing all kinds of things about who was *not* responsible for the disappearance. Don't you think maybe you and Fraser need to start telling people about who *is* responsible?'

Carnwath shrugged. 'Yeah, well, right now I've got to go and talk to the press and feed the beasts. I think we've all had enough bad news for one day, right?'

I did not much like Andy Carnwath, but he was good at his job. And I did not envy him.

According to Edward Fleming's security service reports, which formed the basis of the subsequent Heathrow conspiracy trials, Muhammad Asif Khan's cousin Shawfiq Iqbal returned to Twickenham Stadium several times more in the months leading up to the planned attack. Shawfiq's notes, emails and martyrdom video all suggested that he wanted to work through every detail in his head, to check as much as was humanly possible, for error. His own error. The portrait of Shawfiq that emerges is of a competent and willing terrorist, but a man riddled with uncertainty. He was not uncertain about whether it was right to try to kill up to 80,000 people. Shawfiq's doubts were all matters of practicality – could he do it? Was he up to the job? Was he truly God's chosen instrument? Would he go to paradise? At the subsequent conspiracy trial his defence barrister claimed that Shawfiq's doubts proved that he had merely gone along with the idea of an attack on Twickenham, headquarters of the English Rugby Football Union, as a propaganda blow against the British authorities, but at no point did he really intend to kill anyone.

The watchers reported otherwise. They monitored Shawfiq as he checked and rechecked the elliptical shape of the international rugby stadium, paced round it numerous times, as if it were a place of pilgrimage. His notebooks and sketches show that he tried to figure out whether it made a significant difference to the death toll if the impact from the aircraft on Twickenham was on the broader sides facing Heathrow – the East and West Stands – or on the narrower sides to the north and south. The broader sides, obviously, were a bigger and therefore an easier target. To avoid suspicion, as he continued his reconnaissance missions, Shawfiq had shaved off his beard, though he occasionally retained some stubble. He was photographed by the watchers wearing a cheap grey suit and tie. He dressed, he was recorded telling his sister Hasina one morning as she left for work and remarked on his new neatness, 'proper, like a estate agent, innit?'

Each time Shawfiq went to Twickenham he paced around the area in ever-decreasing circles, beginning as usual where he parked his Subaru at Harlequins' ground, The Stoop, and then working towards the giant stands at Twickenham. He took photographs on each occasion. It seemed that he wanted to remind himself of every angle at every location, and he sent JPEGs to the others, most especially to 'the Pilot'. Shawfiq had never met this Soldier of God, this Pilot. He had no idea which country he was from, where he lived, which airline he worked for. All he knew was that the Pilot was the key to the project and he was to be regarded by Umar, Waheed, and the others with the greatest confidence. The plan meant Shawfiq would never meet the Pilot until the very last moment, but he did know that the Pilot depended on him getting everything right, every detail. For someone planning to kill 80,000 people, Shawfiq Khan Iqbal repeatedly demonstrated considerable sensitivity over his own competence, and considerable need of praise.

'The Pilot is most grateful,' one of the emails in response to his JPEGs informed him, 'that you are so rigorous in your efforts, my brother.'

Shawfiq boasted to Hasina about that email and said he was very pleased his contribution was being recognized. Hasina meekly agreed, but she asked no questions. On one of his missions, in the September, just a month before Bobby Black's disappearance, the watchers photographed Shawfiq as he stood under the sign that proudly proclaimed Twickenham as the 'Home of English Rugby'. He was recorded gazing towards Heathrow in the west, watching the planes take off and making notes as he logged the separation between them. In one of his emails, to another of the plotters, Umar, Shawfiq explained in a crude kind of code that a fully laden Airbus or 747 ready for a long-distance flight and filled with tonnes of aviation spirit would hit Twickenham with the force of a giant fist.

'The fist of God shall strike the nonbelievers,' he wrote. Such an attack 'would go down in history forever, my brother, making 9/11 seem like nothing', he wrote. It would be talked of in years – decades – maybe even centuries to come – as the greatest possible blow for freedom and justice. 'Even if the Plan does not succeed in every detail, the attempt will make them think again,' he warned.

'The Plan will succeed, my brother, *inshallah*,' Umar had written back, 'thanks to your work, and by the will of God.'

The thought made Shawfiq smile. He had been spurred on in his efforts for months by the American talk of 'the Spartacus Solution', and 'the Spartacus Programme'. But, he asked Umar, what if the next time the oppressed people of the world rose up, they made it clear they would rather die than be nailed to a cross? What if some good Muslim brothers here in Britain were prepared not just to kill but to die in a glorious martyrdom?

'For people like us, crucifixion is not a deterrent,' Umar wrote back to Shawfiq. 'It is an incentive to a true believer!'

On one other occasion in early October, Shawfiq was again filmed standing under the Heathrow flight path as he timed the gap between aircraft on takeoff and on landing to approximately two minutes. The more he timed, the more occasions he carried out his reconnaissance, the more nervous and worried Shawfiq became. He realized that, despite the confidence of the Pilot and Brother Umar and Brother Waheed, the margin for error really was small. Minuscule. Crashlanding a plane into Twickenham as it descended into Heathrow was far easier than doing the same on takeoff, Shawfiq was sure of it. But a plane on landing would have relatively little fuel on board. It would be far less likely to produce the kind of spectacular event that the Plan called for. Shawfiq tried to bury his doubts when Umar finally told him the date for the attack. It was to be early November, the Saturday immediately after the American mid-term elections, the day of the major rugby match between England and Scotland sponsored directly by the Prime Minister, Fraser Davis.

The idea of this new 'Island Race' championship was to bring together what Davis insisted on calling 'the Home Nations' – including Ireland, north and south, England, Scotland, and Wales – at least partly in a display of 'Britishness'.

It was dressed up as a sporting event, but Shawfiq recognized the political context: ahead of the referendum on independence for Scotland the following May, Davis was desperate to do everything and anything to persuade the Scots to stay in the United Kingdom, and to persuade the English to want them to stay. The rugby match was not just a rugby match, Shawfiq replied to Brother Umar, praising his genius in choosing it as the target. It was a political stunt and therefore a legitimate target for the sword of Islamic revenge to thrust into the heart of those who offered a Spartacus Solution or who supported the Americans in their anti-Muslim madness.

On one further occasion, in mid-October, just before Bobby Black travelled to Scotland for the shooting trip, Shawfiq was again filmed as he walked to the north of the Twickenham ground. This time he entered along a path beside a small channel that ran into the massive complex knows as the West Middlesex Drainage Works. This was a much bigger area, perhaps by a factor of ten, than the stadium itself.

'All this shit,' Shawfiq mumbled to himself, and took a few photographs for completeness, as the watchers photographed him in turn.

All the sewage from the western approaches to London found its way to the drainage works, to be cleaned up by the Duke of Northumberland's river, channelled into a concrete canal which itself eventually drained clean water back into the River Thames. Shawfiq was followed as he walked on. To the immediate east was the Twickenham trading estate. On the Saturday of a big match, as Shawfiq had recorded in his previous visits, the trading estate and the supermarket on its edges would be more or less empty. No normal person would want to shop with so many rugby fans in the vicinity, and all the rugby fans would be inside watching the game. Shawfiq looked up at the sky. This was another worry, as he explained in one of his more nervous emails to Umar, Waheed and the Pilot. Any aircraft that missed the 80,000 people in the rugby football ground might plough into empty buildings, car parks, or stagnant ponds filled with shit.

'Tell our brother that the risk is worth taking,' the Pilot had said in one of his responses forwarded by Umar to Shawfiq. 'Tell our brother that we shall succeed and be covered in glory, *inshallah*.'

Hasina's transfer from the shop in Terminal Five to Terminal One had come six months earlier. It was a formality, but there was a complication. Hasina Iqbal still did not know exactly what the plot entailed, but after Manila she was too sharp not to understand it must have something to do with the hijacking or destruction of an aircraft. Shawfiq told her that her role was to smuggle something – she did not know what – airside at Terminal One. When she requested the transfer from terminal Five to One, Hasina had been expecting questions about her motives, and had rehearsed the answers in her head as she went to see her company's airport supervisor.

'My mother's best friend is a cleaner at Terminal One,' Hasina muttered, reciting her reasons as if memorizing a poem. 'And my cousin Benazir works in Garfunkels. We can travel together from Hounslow. Much better for me.'

In the event, there were no questions asked by the airport supervisor, no answers needed. It was a formality.

Hasina was told she must report to Terminal One at the start of her Monday morning shift and ask for the shop manager, a Mr Dhaliwal. And that was the complication. Hasina later told her police interrogators that she knew Dhaliwal was a Sikh name, and in her head this Mr Dhaliwal was a turban-wearing, pot-bellied, middle-aged Sikh who drank beer and wore bad shoes and cheap clothes. Instead, on her first day at Terminal One, she was welcomed by a clean-shaven, good-looking young man in his late twenties, in a clean and well-pressed dark suit. He was very handsome, this Mr Dhaliwal, Hasina decided. She looked away from him, modestly.

'I am Navdeep Dhaliwal,' the good-looking young man said, smiling from behind the chocolate and bottled water display with the good nature that seemed to come naturally to him.

'I'm Hasina Iqbal.'

'And you are most welcome here in Terminal One, Ms Iqbal. If you have any problems, please let me know. This is a happy place, and I want you to be happy too.'

He seemed to mean it. She particularly liked his teeth, which were small and even.

'Thank you,' Hasina said. 'Thank you very much, Mr Dhaliwal.'

'Navdeep,' he said, and smiled again. 'My friends call me Nav.'

This time Hasina smiled back, and then dipped her eyes again, shyly. Despite herself, Hasina felt something move within her. The man seemed to light up at her presence. He was good-natured with everyone, but with her there appeared to be some special spark that came alive within Navdeep. She shuddered. Yes, there was a spark within her too. She knew it was impossible, but for a moment Hasina wondered if she could be attracted to this broad-shouldered, well-dressed, smiling Sikh. The thought made her shudder once more. No, she thought. Of course not. It is not *halal*. It is not allowed. It is *haram*, forbidden. Nor is it *halal* to think of the future. It is not allowed to think of the future when you know that you do not have one.

TWENTY

That evening in my room at Castle Dubh I saw Kristina on the television for the first time in days and it gave me a strange thrill. It is odd to watch someone that you are close to perform publicly thousands of miles away, for the TV cameras. I tried to pay attention to what was being said but just the sight of Kristina filled me with an indescribable longing to touch her, to talk with her, to feel her breath on my neck and to sleep with my arms around her. I shook myself and listened.

'In the absence of the Vice-President,' CNN was reporting, 'the two most powerful people in the Carr White House, alongside the President himself are both now women: Chief of Staff Stephanie Alejandro who, with presidential adviser Arlo Luntz is coordinating the political response to the crisis and focusing on relations with Congress, and National Security Adviser Dr Kristina Taft who, along with Secretary of State Andrew Baker and CIA Director Conrad Shultz is efforting a massive national security response to the current emergency, amid unconfirmed rumours of an Iran connection. Dr Taft and Mrs Alejandro are with the President at an undisclosed location in the western United States.'

They showed pictures of Kristina with President Carr in Colorado. She looked fresh, business-like, beautiful, thriving in adversity, perhaps a little tired, dressed conservatively in a black suit and white shirt, her hair tied back. I thought of her the way I did that first day we met in the White House, of how she reeked of intelligence and power. They had assembled the White House tight pool of reporters – usually one TV network, one wire service, one newspaper or magazine reporter, with a couple of cameras to report on behalf of the entire White House press corps. As news of the discovery of the getaway car and the obvious inference that the Vice-President might have been kidnapped hit the screens, Kristina held a small news conference outlining what she said were 'precautionary measures'.

The United States 'could not confirm' that a foreign power or terrorist organization had a hand in the disappearance of the Vice-President. Claims of responsibility had been received from various terrorist factions, but none had credibility. Kristina announced that the US fleet in Bahrain was being augmented 'with immediate effect'. The DoD was sending another aircraft carrier battle group from the Indian Ocean.

Kristina also announced that more strategic bombers from the continental United States were being sent to unspecified 'allied countries in Europe and the Gulf region.' Watching her performance reminded me of a conductor in command of an orchestra as the tight pool of journalists threw questions at her. I was also struck by how the disappearance of Bobby Black had allowed Kristina, and even President Carr himself, to thrive.

'We do not take anything off the table with Iran,' Kristina replied when the Reps' questions turned to the Tehran regime. 'We wish to negotiate in good faith about their illegal nuclear weapons programme, about their attempted subversion of other governments, their malign influence in Lebanon, in Syria, and in Gaza. We are not yet making any direct link with the disappearance of the Vice-President, but President Carr has not ruled out any option in respect of our dealings with Iran.'

'People will interpret that as a threat, Dr Taft,' one of the journalists tried as a supplementary.

'People will interpret what they will in the way that they wish.'

'But—'

'For the sake of clarity,' she said, 'let me state our position once and for all. The Tehran regime is pursuing a nuclear programme that will lead to an arms race in the region. Turkey and neighbouring Arab countries cannot be expected to live under the shadow of an Iranian nuclear bomb. Nor can Israel. The United States will do everything – *everything* – to stop its manufacture. Should there be any connection with any foreign power in the disappearance of the Vice-President, then, as the President has clearly stated, it would be viewed as an act of war, an attack on the United States, and we will act accordingly. The Spartacus Doctrine applies to countries as well as to individuals. The United States will not allow others to attack us without penalty.'

The Spartacus Doctrine? How had a flimsy sheet of arguments advanced by an obscure Pentagon general two years ago now been elevated into some military 'doctrine'? Had the rhetoric started to define American policy rather than the other way round? And had Kristina bought into it? The television performance left me uneasy in all kinds of ways. I found it difficult to reconcile in my head the two Kristinas, the one the newspapers had called 'The Vulcan' and who was on display on television, and the other, vulnerable, human Kristina who discussed poetry, novels, and jazz and whom I wanted beside me right now with a longing that felt like a toothache. After my own news conference the previous day, and the encounter with Byrne, I had switched on my mobile and there had been a text message from Kristina.

'Good job,' was all it had said, plus a row of kisses. I tried to dial her cellphone, but the number was unobtainable. I guessed that she was still in her cave or bunker with the

President himself. When CNN moved on to other news I sent her a text in response.

'Good job yourself,' I wrote. 'XXX.'

I waited for a reply, but none came. I lay on my bed in Castle Dubh, exhausted but unable to fall asleep properly. My head was tormented by the uncomfortable feeling that, however bad things were now, they were about to get even worse. I tried to chase the demons away by thinking erotic thoughts of Kristina.

One night the previous spring, about six months before Bobby Black disappeared, I'd turned up as arranged at Kristina's apartment in the Watergate building. She had a strange kind of smile on her face. I kissed her and she pulled me hard towards her. She was clearly aroused.

'I have been waiting for you,' she said. I kissed her again, but she pushed me away. 'A new game.'

She whispered in my ear. When she finished I looked at her and felt my pulse skip. Kristina had a kind of genius for knowing which buttons to push in me, and no doubt in others too. The more I thought about it, her former boyfriend Stephen Haddon had been a remarkable man. Very few people ever said no to Kristina. He was the only one that I had come across. That evening she left the room to change, and when she came back she was wearing sweat pants and a tee shirt.

'Come play,' she held out her hand and led me into the bedroom. On the bed she had laid out three objects – the waist-tie from her towelling dressing gown, her iPod, and the kind of expensive eye-patch that they give you when you fly first class over the Atlantic. 'I have been reading psychology reports,' she had told me. 'The psychology of sensory deprivation. The kind of stuff that turns Bobby Black on more than it ever does me. But some of it hooked me, you know? One study in Canada, they tied up a bunch of student volunteers, put blindfolds on them and covered their eyes so they could not move, touch, hear, or see. Then they left them for a couple of days and the sense of isolation was so intense they did exactly as their captors wanted.'

'And?'

'I want to try it.'

'For a couple of days?'

She grinned.

'Don't get greedy. One hour, max.'

Before I could protest, Kristina strapped the iPod onto her arm, put the phones in her ear, and switched it on. It was Miles Davis. *Kind of Blue*. Then she placed the blindfold over her own eyes.

'Tie my hands tightly,' she instructed me. 'Then do as you please.'

I did.

The Heathrow bomb plot files also show that in the weeks running up to that October when Bobby Black went missing it had become increasingly obvious to Hasina Iqbal that Navdeep, her manager, was attracted to her, and she to him. Navdeep would seek her out, they would laugh and chat, perhaps only for a few minutes at a time, but at least several times a day. He could not hide his interest in her, though she noted in her diary that he always treated her with great respect. In the first week after she switched the location of her job to Terminal One, she had told him that she would need to go for daily prayers, and he nodded.

'Of course.'

Nothing was a problem for him. She had never in her life met anyone quite so positive.

'Problems are just there to be solved,' Navdeep would say when something went wrong, when the newspapers did not turn up on time, or the refrigerator stopped working. And then he would solve them.

They discussed Ramadan, and Navdeep asked if she wished to change her shift for the Holy Month. Perhaps it would be better for her to be away from the chocolate and other temptations while fasting? Hasina laughed.

'That's the whole point of the Holy Month,' she lectured Navdeep with amusement. 'To be tempted. To want. And to resist. I'll be fine. Much worse than the chocolate is the idea of a nice hot cup of tea. Keep me away from that! That is of the devil!'

'I respect a religion that handles temptation,' Navdeep told her. 'To desire something but to decide that you cannot have it.'

She looked at his dark brown eyes, neat white teeth, and soft lips when he said it, and she blushed.

One evening, after the late rush of flights had cleared, Navdeep was completing his accounts and stocktaking in the main storeroom at the back of the shop in Terminal One. He was working late. Hasina was about to come off shift. There were no customers. He struck up a conversation and explained what he was doing with the stock. Suddenly he suggested that Hasina herself could obtain a managerial position with the company by the time she was in her mid-twenties.

'Is that something you might be interested in? You are certainly qualified. You have good school results.'

She felt strange at this conversation, but also grateful. 'Thank you. That is very kind.'

'There are forms we could fill out together to get you on the managerial training programme. They paid for me to get a business degree at Thames Valley University.'

Hasina blushed again. No one, not even in her own family, had ever suggested she might have a career of any sort of her own. Not just a job, but a proper career.

'You know the difference between a job and a career?' Navdeep joked with her. 'When you have a career you take a shower before you go to work. When you have a job, you get so sweaty you take the shower after you've been to work.'

Even his feeble jokes were suffused with such good humour,

they made her laugh. This stranger, this Sikh boy with the little white teeth and the warm dark eyes, he was someone she wanted to spend time with. She smiled back at him.

'Yes,' she said quickly, almost without thinking it through, 'I would like a career. I would like that very much.'

Navdeep was as good as his word. He obtained the forms and she filled them out under his guidance. He wrote her a reference, which he showed her. It said that Hasina Khan Iqbal was a mature, intelligent, honest, and hardworking woman of great potential, and that she could easily move into junior management with the company.

'Even to a senior managerial position after five years or so,' he had written, which pleased her beyond words. If her application was successful they would offer her two years of on-the-job training, day-release classes in management and accounting, an enhanced pay packet and the prospect of running her own store before she was much older. Navdeep kissed the letter for good luck as she put it into the post.

'Would you . . .?' he stumbled. She had never heard him lost for words like this before. Now it was Navdeep's turn to be embarrassed. 'Would you ever come with me for a drive some place? Or maybe out for a coffee or ice cream? I know a place . . .' The proposal surprised Hasina. Astounded her, in fact. 'Perhaps tomorrow? After work?'

Before she could say anything she realized she was nodding in agreement. 'Yes, of course,' Hasina said. 'That would be lovely.'

As she took the Tube and bus home to Hounslow that night, Hasina thought of something Shawfiq and her uncles had said about any of the women in their family ever entering into a relationship with any man not approved by the family, especially a non-Muslim man.

'We have the answer to that,' an uncle had said in Urdu.

Hasina was puzzled. 'The answer?'

The man took his hand, extended a finger and ran it

round his throat from ear to ear. Shawfiq and the other men laughed.

On the day of their first date, Navdeep Dhaliwal and Hasina knew they had to be careful, though they did not discuss it. Navdeep drove to a small village in the countryside about ten miles from Heathrow Airport, close to Windsor. The watchers filmed them as they sat and drank milky iced coffees with whipped cream and talked about their weird families and their lives and the pressures that had been placed on them to get a job and to do the right thing. Navdeep looked at her wide brown eyes and the way they flashed at him from behind the hejab. He liked the black cycliner that she used, and the lightness of her skin. When she laughed it made him feel strange, as if he had been put on earth to listen to this tinkling sound. He smiled at the thought that it was more sexy that she wore a headscarf than if she had been sitting with him naked, and then he smiled again at the possibility he was deluding himself.

'I cannot be seen with a man,' Hasina said, and explained about her family. 'Especially not a non-Muslim man, a Sikh . . . If one of them were to see me here with you, it would be . . . a matter of honour . . .'

Her voice trailed away. They both understood. A death sentence. Perhaps for both of them.

'And I cannot be seen with a Muslim,' Navdeep responded. 'For me too this is difficult . . .'

'Do you sometimes wonder why God puts men and women together to meet and be like this if the relationship between them is . . . impossible?'

He laughed. 'Impossible according to whose rules? Perhaps the rules themselves are wrong if they are so inhuman. No God would be that cruel.'

The iced coffees took them more than an hour to finish and then reluctantly they left. He drove her to within a mile of where she lived. It was already dark. Navdeep parked in the empty car park of a small Pentecostalist church, which had a badly painted sign proclaiming that Jesus was 'THE WAY THE TRUTH THE LIFE.' They looked around nervously, but there was no one in the church or the car park, and no one passing by. When they both decided it was safe, Navdeep touched her chin gently with his hand and drew her towards him. They kissed and the thought crossed his mind that if there ever was to be a paradise, then it could not be any greater than a parked car in a run-down church car park in Hounslow, touching the woman he desired. He ran his fingertips along the smooth warmth of her face and felt her lips upon him. Hasina allowed his hands to hold her and pull her towards him and to explore places that had never been touched by a man before. All at once she felt secure, wanted, and loved. And then she felt suddenly very afraid. He was trying to get her a two-year management traineeship. He talked of her becoming possibly a senior manager for the company in five years. She could not bear to tell him that unfortunately she had chosen another path, and the path she had chosen came with no future.

When I read the reports of the watchers, I was struck by the sharpness of Hasina Iqbal's observations. She was a clever young woman. Personally, I also did wonder why men and women were put on earth to meet if the relationship between them is, as Hasina put it, destined to be impossible. I thought it about Kristina, especially when we were separated in the days after Bobby Black's disappearance. I replayed constantly in my mind the events of our relationship, how we met, how we innocently had breakfast together, the night at Blues Alley where things changed, and then the night we first made love. One night kept coming back to me over and over again – partly, I suppose, out of sexual frustration. It was an evening when I was not supposed to see Kristina at all. I was attending a dinner on Capitol Hill with the Speaker Betty Furedi. It was just a week before I came over to Scotland to prepare for the Bobby Black visit.

'I hear it's kiss and make up time between the Carr administration and the Evil British,' Furedi said over cocktails before the dinner began. She's a tiny, birdlike woman, and she tends to peck out her words in a slightly annoying way, a bit like a sparrow; but her brain is very sharp.

'British prime ministers always do the right thing,' I replied, 'usually after having exhausted every other possibility. It's time we fixed things. Whoever is in power, it is no good if London and Washington are not in sync.'

'Don't fix things too good,' Furedi pecked at me. 'Bobby Black might not be around much longer. We hear Carr is thinking about dropping him. Health problems, or some such. The only pulse that the Carr people check is to gauge the health of the opinion polls, from what I see.'

I spent the entire dinner listening to boring speeches from the chairman of this committee and the chairman of that, all the time thinking about Kristina. No matter what she had said, no matter what we agreed, it was not simply that I wanted her. I did. But I also had come in some way to need her. As we came to the dessert course, I stepped outside the Congressional banqueting room and called her. I had planned just to leave a message, but to my surprise she picked up.

'I don't suppose you're free this evening?'

'You said you had a dinner.'

'I'm desperate to see you,' I said. 'I need you.'

There was a pause on the line.

'What are you wearing?'

My heart pounded.

'A tuxedo.'

'When can you get here?'

'An hour,' I said.

'Good. Surprise me. You'll know what to do.'

Less than an hour later, full of anticipation, I turned the

key in the lock of her door in the Watergate. I called out her name, as usual. This time there was no response.

'Kristina,' I tried again, but still nothing. I walked towards the bedroom and saw her. She was lying on the bed in her underwear with her red airline blindfold over her eyes and the iPod earphones in her ears. This time the music was playing loudly, to block out any noise. She had pushed her hands together into one of those tight bandages used for sports injuries. It looked like a kind of soft handcuff. She lay absolutely still.

'Kristina?' I said one more time, softly, but she could neither see nor hear me. The music was loud enough for me to notice that it was Neil Young. I quickly moved towards her, put my hand hard over her mouth and pushed myself on top of her. She jumped with fright, but I held her mouth tightly so she could not scream. I felt her breath hard with fear. After a few minutes she relaxed. My familiar touch and smell calmed her. I threw myself upon her, and was no longer surprised to find that her body had anticipated everything.

TWENTY-ONE

Sir Hamish Martin, Her Majesty the Queen's private secretary, woke me from my troubled dreams shortly after six o'clock in the morning. He was calling from Balmoral to ask me if I was aware that President Carr had called Susan Black late the previous night at the cottage the Queen had offered her in the grounds of the estate. Mrs Black's son Robert and daughter Alice had flown to Scotland and were staying with their mother when the President rang.

'I'm British Ambassador in Washington, Hamish,' I replied. 'Nobody tells me anything. So thank you for keeping me informed.'

'Well, I think you may wish to know about the content of the call. *Need* to know about it might be a better way of putting it.'

'Go on.'

Sir Hamish told me that since Bobby Black's disappearance the Queen had met Susan Black on a number of occasions. The first time was full of tears.

'A very moving meeting,' was how Hamish described it. 'Her Majesty was appalled, Alex, simply *ap-palled* that Susan Black was having to go through this terrible ordeal, and offered her Craik's Cottage, which is the best on the estate.

It's used for close friends and family. Very private. Mrs Black accepted – though I don't think everyone was too pleased.'

Craik's Cottage was a recently refurbished shooting lodge in the grounds of Balmoral. Johnny Lee and his team had been insistent that Susan Black stay either in a hotel in Aberdeen – no, said Mrs Black; or in Bolfracks Bothy with the rest of the Americans – absolutely not, said Susan Black; or return to the United States. No chance. In her quiet way, Susan Black was absolutely formidable.

'Mrs Black clearly did not want to be under anyone's supervision,' Sir Hamish told me on the phone. 'She is a very strong woman, and I have to say that Her Majesty is really quite taken with her and the way she is bearing up.'

Hamish stopped just as things were getting interesting.

'For example?' I prompted.

'For example, Her Majesty has told me that if Mrs Black calls then I am to put her through, whatever the hour. She says that Susan Black needs to be comforted and looked after and I am to give her every assistance. And to take their minds off things, they have been spending a lot of time at the stables with the horses.'

'Tell me about the President's telephone call, Hamish.'

Sir Hamish breathed deeply.

'Well, we were told that the President wished to talk to Mrs Black, and we made arrangements for him to do so. On a secure telephone, of course. Utterly private. But as soon as the conversation was over, Mrs Black called me, in a dreadful state. I tried to comfort her, but she was making almost no sense. Then she said she wanted to talk with her children and rang off. I telephoned the Queen and Her Majesty asked me to call Mrs Black, despite the lateness of the hour, and ask her if she needed any help. The long and the short of it is that I picked her up in my own car around midnight last night and brought her here, where she sat up with the Queen for an hour or more and then went to bed. At first she was shaking and in tears. The President really upset her. But when she went to bed she was much better.'

I was astonished at the news.

'Theo Carr is – for all his faults, Hamish – a kindly and decent man. I don't understand why he would upset Mrs Black. It is not like him.'

'Well, he did, Alex. Mrs Black told the Queen – I sat in on the first part of the meeting – that the President had demanded of Mrs Black that she move immediately to have her husband declared dead. The Queen was very distressed too. She kept pointing out that the poor man has only been missing for seventy-two hours and it would be presumptuous to reach any conclusion. Stiff upper lips be damned. It was tears and tissues all round, frankly.'

I later heard the other side of the story from Kristina. What Hamish had told me was substantially accurate, but in Kristina's version, as soon as the secure telephone line to Scotland was established, Stephanie Alejandro handed the receiver to President Carr. They were all together in the presidential suite at Cheyenne Mountain – Kristina, Stephanie Alejandro, and Arlo Luntz.

The lack of fresh air and daylight in Cheyenne Mountain irritated Carr more than anything else. He was safe, but tetchy, and full of complaints. Perhaps that made him uncharacteristically harsh on the telephone with Susan Black. He told Kristina that he felt as if he were trapped inside a submarine and insisted that Stephanie Alejandro schedule time to walk the mountains.

'Even Bin Laden gets to go for a walk,' the President muttered.

'Mr President . . .'

'How about Rocky Mountain National Park? Check out the elk herds above Estes Park? I love it up there.'

'We'll see what we can do, Mr President. But walking on the mountains has not been going well for us lately.'

'Just fix it, Stephanie,' Carr snapped. 'I want to get out into the real world before I get back to DC.'

'Susan Fein Black for you, Mr President,' Alejandro said, passing over the receiver to the President. 'In Balmoral.'

'Susan, it's Theo,' President Carr said warmly, switching gears rapidly. 'I am so sorry you are going through this.'

'Mr President . . . Theo . . .' Susan Black could feel the tears coming but she managed to control herself.

'How are you, Susan?'

She was in the main sitting room of Craik's Cottage, sitting by a wood fire.

'I just feel so . . . powerless . . .' she said. 'Helpless.'

'I know, I know. Susan, we are doing everything possible. Everyone is doing everything possible to find him.'

'But how . . .? How could it happen . . .? He can't just disappear . . .'

'Wrong place, wrong time. Do you have everything you need?'

'The people here – Queen Elizabeth – I can't tell you how kind they have been to me, Mr President. We are all together in this, and the Queen has been . . . Like a mother to me, and a best friend. It is such a strange experience to find out someone like that is just human too, you know? But . . . they are saying here it might not be an accident.'

'That's also what I am hearing from our people, Susan. The possibility of hostile forces. Which I guess is part of the reason I needed to speak with you now, beyond hearing how you are. There is . . . something of an emergency here, Susan. We have to . . . plan for the future. I am sure that you understand that.' Susan Black said that she did not entirely understand what her President had in mind.

'I have no future, Mr President, not until we find Bobby.'

'I know, I know,' he repeated emolliently. Theo Carr took a deep breath. He glanced at the six-by-four-inch cards that Arlo Luntz had used to script in advance his side of the

266

conversation. He shifted uncomfortably. This was more difficult than any TV broadcast or State of the Union speech. 'Susan, this is hard for me to say, very hard, but I am saying it to you as your friend and also as your President. We need to move quickly to replace Bobby. The country needs a Vice-President of the United States. I need a Vice-President. I know that it is a great shock to you, and that it has only been a couple of days. It is a great shock to me as well. But whatever has happened to Bobby, this country needs . . .'

She burst into uncontrollable tears. The argument that the President had rehearsed from the six-by-four cards was not working.

'And I need my husband back!' Susan Fein Black screamed. 'Don't give up on finding him, Mr President! Don't give up, Theo! He's here, somewhere! I know it!'

President Carr waited until she calmed down.

'Nobody is giving up on anything, Susan. Especially not me. We will never give up. We will bring Bobby back home if it is humanly possible, I give you my word. But we are facing certain realities here.'

'Realities?' she gasped. 'The reality is that Bobby—'

'Susan, let me tell you why . . .' he interrupted, trying to explain about Furedi, but he knew that Susan Fein Black was not really listening. The Constitutional position, the chain of command, even his own cholesterol and high blood pressure problems were not imperatives to a woman who feared for her husband. Arlo Luntz had told him just before the phone call to remember an old saying of his own and think how it would apply to Susan Fein Black.

'Bad planning on our part, Mr President, does not necessarily constitute an emergency on Susan Black's part. Go easy.'

Luntz had been right. Carr's own political emergency meant almost nothing to Susan Black compared to the enormity of her own problems. He had pushed too hard and too fast. He changed tack.

'What would be real helpful, Susan,' Theo Carr said, 'would be if you would meet with some folks I'm sending over to you there at Balmoral. Some of my people. Maybe . . . maybe we could make things easier for you by bringing you home to Washington?'

Susan Black bristled at the suggestion.

'I'm staying here Mr President. I am staying here until Bobby comes back with me, dead or alive.' She said it with a finality that would brook no argument.

'Well, I guess we all understand that, Susan. The decision is yours. But I'd like you to look over some papers and sign them for me, please.'

'Papers, Mr President? Theo? What papers?' He cleared his throat. The conversation had been far more awkward than he had thought possible. Kristina told me that she and Stephanie Alejandro squirmed in their chairs and tried not to look at the President directly. Luntz did look at him, but sat motionless, trying to figure his way through the problem. He could see that Carr felt frustrated. He could deal successfully with millions of voters as a group, but dealing with a single wilful woman was proving beyond his powers.

'Legal papers, Susan,' President Carr said slowly.

'Legal papers,' she repeated like an automaton.

'Papers to have Bobby presumed dead. I can move to replace him in other ways, but this would be the best. For all of us. I'm sure you understand.'

'B-but he's not dead,' she blurted out. 'N-not . . .'

Theo Carr did not respond. The telephone in Susan Fein Black's hand was like the corpse of an animal. She looked at it for a second, and then said simply with redundant repetition, 'I see, I see, I see, I scc.'

Then she hung up on the President of the United States. Stephanie Alejandro looked at President Carr.

'Well?' she said.

He shook his head.

'I don't think she's going to go for it.'

'No,' Stephanie Alejandro hissed under her breath. 'I guess not.'

Sir Hamish Martin finished telling me his side of the story.

'Poor woman, she seems totally bereft, betrayed, abandoned,' he said. 'She's quick-witted, though. She said that President Carr wanted her to move to have the Vice-President declared dead because it would be better for him, not for her or the family. She told all this to the Queen who asked if there was anything – anything – we could do. Mrs Black shook her head and said, just let me stay here please, and keep these people away from me. The Queen said of course. That we will help in any way we can. Well, I have to say, Alex, it did seem very brutal. What do you think?'

I sighed.

'What I think, Hamish, is that wherever the President is and whoever he is with, he is in a corner and desperately, desperately frightened this whole damn thing is heading for disaster.'

Sir Hamish paused for a second.

'And what do you think, Alex?'

'I think the President may well be right.'

According to Kristina, the telephone conversation with Susan Fein Black triggered immediate moves to replace Bobby Black as Vice-President, but it was only one of two very difficult calls President Carr had to make that day. The second was to the Speaker of the House of Representatives, Betty Furedi.

The office accommodation of the Speaker is the best in Washington, much better than the Oval Office and the cramped facilities in the White House where the President works. The presidential quarters are small. The office space very limited, and the Oval Office is at ground level, looking out on the White House Rose Garden. The Speaker, on the other hand, has a majestic view from what is by law the District of Columbia's tallest landmark, the Capitol building. From her desk by the window you can look right up the Mall towards the great monuments of Washington, all the way to the Washington Monument, the Lincoln Memorial, the Iwo Jima Memorial and Netherlands Carillon on the other side of the Potomac in Virginia. Speaker Betty Furedi told me on more than one occasion that she adored her office. She adored the view.

'Best in the world,' she said. And she very much liked being Speaker too. Furedi clearly enjoyed the influence and power, and she especially liked the idea that she was about to mastermind a mid-term election triumph for her party that would cut the Carr administration off at the knees and set the scene for Carr's replacement by a Democratic president within two years. When the call went through to her office from the President, she was sitting behind her enormous mahogany desk in a leather chair, this tiny, bird-like woman, a finch or a warbler chirping away in a deep pink suit. She was reading papers with her glasses perched on her little beak of a nose when her secretary disturbed her with the news that the President of the United States was on the line. The subsequent transcripts of the Congressional inquiry into the security breaches established that Furedi instructed her secretary to make sure that John Crockett was also across the call.

'He was across all the important calls,' Furedi later testified. 'John Crockett was my right hand.'

This piece of information was used to damage the credibility of Speaker Furedi after the security breaches became public.

'What secrets did you keep from your Chief of Staff Mr Crockett?' Furedi was asked under oath by counsel at the Congressional inquiry.

'Not many,' she replied.

'Any?'

'I said, not many.'

John Crockett is a middle-aged African American from Oakland, California, a man – in my experience – of infinite patience and old-fashioned civility. Crockett hurried into the room and picked up one of the extensions. The White House transcript of the call and the Congressional inquiry testimony show a moment of wary intimacy, typical of Washington insiders circling each other with armed politesse.

'This is Speaker Furedi.'

'One moment please,' the White House operator responded. 'I have President Carr for you.'

Betty Furedi whispered to Crockett. 'What's this about, John?'

He whispered back. 'Must be about Vice.'

Suddenly the President was on the line, full of warmth and good humour.

'Speaker Furedi, how are you? So good to talk to you again, Betty.'

'Mr President, it's been too long. You've been far too busy trying to get enough Republicans elected to throw me out of this fine office of mine. Put me on the street, that's what you'd do. Well, I'm not about to let you do that without a fight.'

Theo Carr laughed.

'Come up and visit with me some evening, Betty, when I get back to Washington,' he said. 'Right now I'm out west where the buffalo roam, but I can't see them 'cos I'm in a hole in the ground. Anyway, maybe you and Arlen'll come on over some night and sit down and watch a movie in the White House theatre. I'd like that. But first let me tell you why I'm calling. We got ourselves a situation here.'

'A situation, Mr President?' Furedi responded. 'Is this about the disappearance of the Vice-President?'

Carr explained that it was. The Speaker had issued a statement calling it a 'human tragedy' and said her 'prayers were with Susan Fein Black and her family.' Then she and John Crockett had summoned several Democrat-leaning

271

constitutional scholars to talk them through her own slightly tricky position.

'As you know,' President Carr said, 'pending the safe return of the Vice-President, which we hope and pray for, you are next in line, Betty.'

'Yes, Mr President. It is a grave duty that has been placed upon me.'

'The Secret Service folks tell me you have already accepted a higher and more appropriate level of protection.'

'Yes, Mr President. Thank you for your concern and your courtesy.'

'And the White House counsel tells me I'm gonna have to send some people over to you to go through some formalities, or maybe you would do me the honour of visiting with my people at the White House pending my return. That would be our preferred option, for obvious security reasons. They have things they need to say to you that are . . . very sensitive.'

'Of course, Mr President.'

'Now, I don't want you to be getting your feet under my desk or measuring the drapes while I am out of town,' Theo Carr laughed, 'but I think for the good of the country you need to be brought into the loop. You're gonna be hearing a few things relating to national security, some of which might surprise you.'

'Of course, Mr President,' Furedi repeated.

'Like the fact that some of the folks doing the investigating over in Scotland think Bobby Black might be in the hands of the Iranians. Or their allies. Hezbollah.'

Betty Furedi sucked in her breath.

'Are you serious?'

'Yes, ma'am. I can't tell you on what basis they have reached that conclusion. That's still confidential. But I would be grateful if you would hear that message yourself in person at the White House later today. You'll get a full briefing in the next two or three hours if that fits your busy schedule.'

'I understand, Mr President. We all have to pull together on this. If ever there was a time to put country above party and above everything, it's now.'

'You are right, Madam Speaker. Thank you. This could get ugly with Iran. I know we have had differences on the subject in the past, but now is the time to put everything between us on hold.'

'I agree, Mr President.'

'This could end up in a war, Madam Speaker.'

'I see, Mr President. Well, I think you know my views on that. Congress will need to be consulted.'

'And I think you know mine, Betty, as Commander-in-Chief.'

In her own subsequent account to Congressional investigators, Furedi said she looked over at John Crockett who was staring at the floor and involuntarily shaking his head. Then he suddenly started scribbling something on a yellow legal pad. Furedi had frequently used what she called the 'Carr administration's warmongering towards Iran' as a stick with which to beat the Carr presidency. She said that the 'failure to engage Iran for more than three decades since Nineteen Seventy-nine' was what she called 'the most momentous strategic failure since Pearl Harbor.' This speech of hers played well with battle-weary Americans, fed up with wars in Iraq and Afghanistan and in no mood to extend the conflict. Now Carr was threatening to trump this argument with the revelation that Iran might be involved in the kidnapping of the Vice-President? John Crockett pushed the notepad towards his boss. It said simply: *HARD EVIDENCE?????* She picked up the cue.

'You have hard evidence that Iran has kidnapped the Vice-President of the United States?' Furedi asked directly.

'No, Betty, I do not,' Carr replied firmly. 'But . . . evidence has been found. You'll get the whole nine yards later today. As you know, I have ordered the dispatch of two aircraft carrier battle groups, one for Bahrain, the other towards the eastern Mediterranean, near Turkey and Syria, plus movements of strategic bombers, Marines, and other combat forces, and I hope I can count on your support in these precautionary measures.'

Crockett stared over at his boss and shook his head. He mouthed something.

'Just like Manila,' he whispered. 'Tryin' to scare us shitless.'

Furedi waved a finger at Crockett to be quiet. She turned back to the phone call.

'Mr President, you have sent two aircraft carrier battle groups to the region before you establish any definitive Iran link. That's exactly why some of my colleagues are wary of—'

'Precautionary action,' Theo Carr interrupted. 'If it amounts to nothing, then nothing will happen. If it amounts to something, then we're ready.' The President stopped talking and the line suddenly felt as quiet as a graveyard.

'And if Iran is really behind this thing?' Betty Furedi could hear the President breathe.

'Then it would be an act of war against the United States of America which will demand a response in line with the Spartacus Doctrine, a response of the utmost prejudice.'

Now it was Speaker Furedi's turn to breathe hard. 'Spartacus Doctrine?' she blurted out.

'If people attack the United States of America, they will be met with overwhelming force, overwhelmingly applied, as a punishment and a deterrent to others. There will be no hiding place, and no mercy. Betty, I am telling you that I intend to make a speech to the American people within the next day or so, probably from Colorado but from somewhere outside of this goddamn mountain hole in the ground, a speech outlining what we know of the disappearance, and announcing the Spartacus Doctrine. I hope that constitutionally as my successor I can count on your full support.'

Betty Furedi did not know what to say.

'I . . . I can't give blank-cheque assurances, Mr President.' She looked over to see John Crockett nodding enthusiastic encouragement. 'But I will of course be honoured to attend the briefing you have organized at the White House and consider what I can and cannot support. Our thoughts and prayers are with Bobby Black's family at this troubling time, and with you and Mrs Carr and the burdens you carry. I will be issuing a statement to that effect later today.'

'Thank you Madam Speaker, much appreciated.'

They said their goodbyes. Speaker Betty Furedi turned to John Crockett.

'He wants me to go to the White House to go through things?'

John Crockett recounted in his own later testimony that at that point her voice had raised uncharacteristically almost to a shriek. 'Iran? Aircraft carrier battle groups? Spartacus Doctrine! What's really going on here, John?'

Crockett thought for a moment. He sat behind the desk jacketless, wearing a striped shirt and bright red braces.

'An October Surprise,' Crockett said slowly. 'Another goddamn October Surprise. He's doing it again. After the way the Manila bombing worked in his favour, it's another Theo Carr stunt. And this time he's trying to co-opt you into his war with Iran.'

'What, so he kidnaps his own Vice-President?' Furedi scoffed. 'Get real, John.'

Crockett snarled.

'No, but it wouldn't surprise me if Bobby Black turned up the day after the mid-terms in Disneyland. Roll up! Roll up! Catch the Second Coming of the Antichrist. It's a stunt, Betty, and—'

Furedi was angry now. 'John, sometimes I worry about you. Sometimes you get so blinded by hatred for these people you can't see clearly.'

'I can see clear enough,' he shot back. 'Two years ago, less than one month before the presidential elections that Carr is bound to lose, well guess what? A bomb goes off in an airliner at Manila killing all the Americans on board. Theo Carr wins the presidency. And now, two weeks before these mid-term elections that Carr is bound to lose, he pulls another rabbit out of the hat, the Vice-President disappears and Carr talks about bombing Iran. Same shit, different Boogie Man. This time it's the Ayatollahs, and he sends the fleet and enough B2s and B52s to turn Tehran into a car park . . . Jeez. What will it be next time? France? Mexico? How stupid does he think we all are?'

'President Carr has not kidnapped his own Vice-President!' Betty Furedi scoffed. 'That's just nonsense. And he did not blow up the airliner at Manila. You're getting paranoid.'

'Betty, I'm telling you that I smell a rat here. He's cranking things up, just like he did last time. He creates the fear so that he can be the one you turn to to take it away. It's like beating your wife so she cries on your shoulder. He's pushing us all into a corner so we have to support whatever he does in Iran, and when he does it . . . He's a son of a—'

'Stop it!' Furedi interrupted him, loudly. 'Whatever he is, he's also the President of the United States at a time when the Vice-President has gone missing. I will not hear you talk about him as if he were some kind of criminal, you hear me?'

Crockett blinked with surprise. 'But . . .' Could she not understand why he was suspicious? More than suspicious?

'Enough!'

There was a long pause. Crockett had never seen his boss so angry with him. He chose his words carefully.

'There was once this French statesman I read about at college – Talleyrand, I think. Anyway, this guy was so slippery that when he died people said, 'I wonder what he meant by that?' Carr and Black are in the same league as Talleyrand, Betty. Even if they die or disappear they mean to get some advantage from it. If they told me I had gotten into Heaven I'd wonder what their angle was, and check out Hell just to be sure.'

She sighed with exasperation. Crockett had gone too far.

'The Iranians or Hezbollah or some of their people could have kidnapped Bobby Black,' Furedi insisted. 'There are plenty of Iranians in England. You saw the pictures on the TV. That guy Khan who we let out because the British whined so much—'

'Khan's British and his family are Pakistani,' Crockett blurted out. 'Not Iranian. How can you complain that Khan was . . .' The look in her eyes made him stop talking. The realization struck him for the first time that Betty Furedi was now, quite literally, just a heartbeat away from the presidency of the United States. If something happened to Theo Carr, then the tiny, birdlike woman in front of John Crockett would take over the most powerful job in the world.

The prospect had changed Betty Furedi already, changed her completely, even if she knew that there was almost no realistic chance of her ever getting to be president. The switch of ambition in her brain was flicked to 'On', and it alarmed John Crockett. It meant Betty Furedi was willing to put all thoughts of an October Surprise, of conspiracies, of mean tricks out of her mind. It meant that her ability to campaign against the Carr administration had just evaporated. Carr had done it again. He did not know how, but Crockett knew that Carr had outmanoeuvred them all.

'Could you fix up so that I get to the White House for this briefing, please?' Furedi asked Crockett with forced politeness.

It was a redundant instruction. As she spoke, the telephone

277

rang. The White House was already on the line, scheduling a briefing for 5 p.m. that same day. John Crockett was not invited.

When President Carr put down the telephone, Arlo Luntz also put down his handset. So did Stephanie Alejandro and Kristina.

'Well?' Carr wondered.

'Her tits are in the wringer,' Luntz replied, clapping his hands together. 'Let's see her wriggle to get them out. And you've given John Crockett something to mull over. He'll be up all night war-gaming it, beating himself up, playing the angles in his head. That guy thinks too much. But there's a danger too.'

Theo Carr sighed. The pig's bladder again.

'Go on, Arlo. Rain on my fucking parade.'

'You have to be seen to extend every courtesy to the Speaker, but without making her appear too presidential. There's ten days until the elections. We need to get a simple message through. This world is a dangerous enough place for the Vice-President to go missing, which means nobody is safe. If you vote Democrat, pussies like Betty Furedi could end up running this country and tackling terrorism. You want to risk that?'

'Betty Furedi couldn't tackle a bowl of Wheaties,' Carr snapped. 'The American people know that.'

Arlo Luntz nodded. 'In case they don't, we have ads that will remind them.'

'Yeah,' Carr said. 'I have some other ideas about that, Arlo.'

Arlo Luntz turned lugubriously to the President of the United States. 'You do?'

'Kristina, Stephanie, leave us please. Kristina, I want the latest from Shultz in an hour. Stephanie, I want to go for a walk in among the elk, like I said, and then to make a speech from the real America, maybe that little place I keep telling you about, Estes Park, on the outskirts of Rocky Mountain National Park. I want people to remember that this country

278

is worth fighting for, and you can't do that from a hole in the ground.'

'Yes, Mr President.'

'Thank you. Now, Arlo, let's talk about how we're going to turn this thing around.'

TWENTY-TWO

It was Jack Rothstein from *The Times* who told me about the first of the postings on the Internet. It was five days after Bobby Black had disappeared and, there being nothing much else to occupy me, I spent time watching the continuing search for clues on the hillside and then turned again to Anstruther's gym, beating a punchbag to death to the best of my ability. I was sweating profusely and out of breath as I turned to the speed bag. My mobile phone went off and I struggled to remove the boxing gloves so I could answer it. I was still panting from the effort when Rothstein told me I needed to get in front of a computer or a TV screen immediately.

'Why?'

'The people who have kidnapped the Vice-President are turning him into some kind of freak show on the Internet. I'd like your comments.'

I told Rothstein I'd get back to him. I switched on the TV in the gym. Rothstein was right about the freak show. The Internet posting looked so amateurish and badly filmed. At first it seemed almost innocent. A crumpled figure stirred under a dark blue blanket on a mattress in a room that you could not see clearly, except that it was small, a prison cell, or – as we were eventually to figure out – a room made up

280

to look like a prison cell. There was no sound on the video, the crumpled figure stirred as if he had become aware of a noise. The man on the mattress stretched out his hand and then moved his fingers awkwardly towards his face. Our PSYOPS people concluded he was probably, instinctively, looking for his glasses, trying to explain to himself why he could not see properly. One hand groped in a circle around where he lay, without success. Then he attempted to pull away the blue blanket and we caught a glimpse of the puffed-up face of the Vice-President of the United States. He floundered on the mattress with the blue blanket like a drunk, with all the coordination of a pile of human jelly. Even to my own untutored eyes it was obvious someone had pumped him full of drugs. His senses worked, his brain functioned, his muscles did not. It made me think of the TV pictures of mad cows with BSE, stumbling around muddy farmyards before they were put out of their misery. The man rocked to the side in a kind of rolling motion, trying to sit or stand up, but again his brain could not get his limbs to obey its commands.

The man rolled back on to the mattress and lay still until a point where the tape was edited. It cut to black. When it resumed there was a blurred vision of other shapes in the room. They wore green combat fatigues and rubber gloves, and had black balaclavas hiding their faces. There was still no sound as they fell upon him. The green combat fatigues cut across the picture and then the screen froze and the picture stopped. There was no commentary, there were no demands, and no explanation on the first of the Internet postings. I called Jack Rothstein to thank him for his tip-off and told him that I could not comment on the record.

'Off the record?'

I took a deep breath. 'Western diplomatic sources,' I said, 'believe that the video may amount to an act of war against the United States. The release of this shocking tape justifies all the precautions and actions taken by the Carr administration.

This could also result in NATO action if a foreign government is found to be responsible and if the Vice-President is not released without further harm immediately.'

'Thanks, Alex.' He repeated the words verbatim in his news story on the front page of the following morning's *Times* newspaper.

'Thanks for the warning, Jack.'

'How bad is this, Alex?'

'I wish I knew, Jack.'

I saw the second Internet posting two hours later while Janey Masters, Andy Carnwath, and I were still trying to draft our official response to the first. We were sitting in the library at Castle Dubh with the television news channels on low in the background. They were showing what appeared to be an almost uninterrupted loop of the Internet video, replaying the pictures endlessly and trying to secure reaction from all around the world. The White House commented along the lines of my own 'Western diplomatic sources', off-the-record comment, but with the strong implication that we were on the brink of war. Who precisely we were on the brink of war with was left to the imagination.

I am not making light of it when I say that in the atmosphere of fear and panic, it almost did not matter. This was our Reichstag Fire. We were ready for The Enemy, the Evil-Doers – whoever that might prove to be. Sandy McAuley, the White House spokesman, read out a terse statement from the press room podium, and then refused to take questions.

'The United States of America demands the immediate return of the Vice-President, unharmed and without further delay,' the statement said. 'The United States of America expects and requires from all nations and all peoples full cooperation in securing the Vice-President's return and in bringing to justice the perpetrators of this evil act. The United States of America will use all available means to secure the freedom and the safety of all its citizens. Statement ends.'

McAuley walked away from the podium and the news channels cut to their reporters on the streets of New York, Miami, and Chicago, stopping ordinary people on the streets to give their reaction and cut through the diplomatic cackle.

'Bomb bomb bomb – bomb bomb Iran,' one worker in a yellow hard-hat sang to the camera, to the tune of the Beach Boys hit 'Barbara Ann'. 'Whoever did it, they deserve to die.'

'Nuke 'em,' another worker said. 'Kill 'em all. The good, the bad and the ugly. Let God sort 'em out.'

'Turn Tehran into a car park,' said a third. 'We're not about to take this shit from a bunch of freakin' towel heads.'

As we watched it together in the great drawing room at Castle Dubh, which was now the unofficial British headquarters, Andy Carnwath started to argue with Janey Masters about how to draft a statement that would make it clear we were shoulder to shoulder with the Americans, without committing us to any action they might take – perhaps precipitately – in terms of attacking Iran, at least without clear evidence.

'Europe,' Janey said, turning to one of the usual British excuses. 'We need to bring in the European Union and NATO. And the UN. Multilateralize it. Say we need meetings to discuss . . . whatever. You know, Brussels. New York. Security Council resolutions. Gives us breathing space.'

Brussels is the Hotel California of British policy. Ideas check in to the European bureaucracy, but they never leave.

'We don't have breathing space,' I said, and turned up the volume on the TV. 'Look at this.'

There was suddenly a big red strap across the bottom of the screen saying: BREAKING NEWS. The TV channels were running a second Internet video from whoever was holding Bobby Black, and this second video seemed to start more or less where the other one ended. What you saw was three or four, perhaps as many as six, people in green combat fatigues, all – apparently – men wearing the same uniform of black balaclavas and rubber gloves. The video started with the men fumbling over the mattress in the Vice-President's cell. They grabbed and pulled at Bobby Black so his mouth was pushed down on the mattress. There was a glimpse of his face which, on subsequent broadcasts, the TV channels froze, to confirm without any doubt the identity of the victim. It was a strange sight because it looked as if he felt no pain. It made me think of the mindless sensation I experienced when I tore a muscle in my back playing tennis and the doctors gave me a cocktail of painkillers and Valium, the face of cognizant helplessness. Four pairs of hands – we counted them – held him down. They pulled up his right sleeve roughly, and you could see a needle enter his arm. I tried to imagine the sensation and assumed it would be like the warmth spreading throughout the body that you get from anaesthetics. Within seconds, Bobby Black would be floating above himself, a spectator on his own life, or possibly death. Then the four pairs of hands dragged him to his feet. His eyes were still open. When we analysed the pictures later it was noticed that he blinked several times, though his legs were almost useless and the men in green combat fatigues held him roughly above the mattress and made him look towards the camera so there could be absolutely no doubt that the Vice-President of the United States was being humiliated, kidnapped, drugged, and held against his will. His eyes were black saucers of emptiness, the pupils dilated by the drug cocktail. The freak show, as Jack Rothstein had called it, was turning into a deliberate act of cruelty. I felt a ripple of fear run through me as I realized that it would be very difficult now to stop a war against the people who had done this, whoever they were. Diplomacy was over.

*   *   *

That day was probably the worst of my professional life, even worse than the day Bobby Black disappeared, because at least then we had for a few hours the comforting delusion that maybe it was all just an accident. Someone – I think it was Janey Masters – had the idea that after the Internet postings we should hold a joint news conference with the Americans at the Rowallan Hotel to show how close we were on everything. It sounded to me like holding a news conference with your wife to deny you were about to divorce.

'What do you think, Alex?' Andy Carnwath said.

'It's always good to be seen to be shoulder to shoulder with the Americans,' I replied, 'except if you are not. And we are not exactly square with them, are we? If they start bombing Iran because of this, are we part of it?'

Carnwath called the Prime Minister to find out. No, Fraser Davis said, we were to make no military commitment until NATO, the UN, and the EU all had a chance to discuss the kidnapping, but yes, we should appear at a news conference with the Americans and explain how close we really were. I was overruled in favour of Janey Masters. She insisted that we all go to see Johnny Lee Ironside. He was sitting in the American Sit. Room – the library – in Castle Dubh, surrounded by CIA, FBI, and Secret Service people who looked at us with disdain. Janey clickety-clacked across the wooden floor on her perilous heels.

'The Prime Minister thinks it would be a good idea if we briefed together on the Internet postings,' Janey began, looking at Johnny Lee. 'Fraser says there is not a cigarette paper of distance between us on this outrageous set of videos and we should show it.'

Johnny Lee listened to every word, carefully and politely, while he up-and-downed Janey, paying particular attention to her bare legs. His gaze was not entirely professional.

'Is the Prime Minister ready to commit British forces to

operations against any country found to support this act of war against the United States?'

I could see Janey bridle.

'We agree about the videos . . .' she began.

'Do we agree about what to do to the people who made them?'

Andy Carnwath, despite his foul tongue, is much more emollient in these situations. Janey put her hands on her hips and looked at Johnny Lee with a face full of truculent irritation. 'The Prime Minister does not give blank cheques,' she snapped back. 'What he does do is give his full support to an inquiry into—'

Johnny Lee interrupted. 'Why don't you just commit all necessary forces to finding the Vice-President, Ms Masters?' he said coldly. 'And then why don't you just hold your inquiries and convene your multilateral meetings or whatever the hell you do instead of fixing things. We'll be holding our own news briefings today and in the foreseeable future. If we stand together the journalists will simply ask all the same questions I have been asking. And when they do, they may find the gap between us is wider than just a cigarette paper. About as wide as the Atlantic.'

There was nothing more to say, and we returned, in silence, to our own operations room, with the clickety-clack of Janey's heels following behind me down the corridor. By the time we arrived back in the drawing room, I had received a text from Johnny Lee.

'Who was that???' it said. He also asked for her cellphone number.

The postings on the Internet came one after the other throughout that long day. The kidnappers knew how to manipulate the cycle of twenty-four-hour news. Just as we were prepared to respond to the first posting, they put out the second. By the time we had regrouped enough to react to the second, there was a third posting on the Internet. They had constructed the day to be a series of propaganda cyber-attacks, and it was working.

The third posting showed Bobby Black taken down a corridor from the room we came to call 'the cell' into another room. His feet barely touched the floor as the men bundled him along. This second room was bigger than the first, like a large hallway, and much brighter than 'the cell'. It was so bright that you could see it hurt his eyes; presumably – as one of our video analysts pointed out – because his dilated pupils would have made the brightness unbearable. Light bounced from the shiny white walls and you could see the Vice-President wince as he tried to move his right hand to shield his pupils. He could not control his arms and they flopped by his sides.

This second room was like a movie set or a stage. As his captors swirled him around you could catch sight of tripods, reflectors, and stands. Suddenly the men let his body fall to the floor. The body crumpled when they no longer held him up. Then hands with rubber gloves were seen pulling at the Vice-President's clothing. There was a cut in the video and it went to black. When it resumed, the Vice-President of the United States was naked on the floor, though the camera did not dwell on his nakedness. Two men were fixing a large jute sack over his head. They tied it at the neck. Why they were doing this was at first beyond comprehension. The Vice-President struggled feebly, his arms and legs moving erratically, like an unhappy baby whose diaper was being changed: naked, helpless, and pointless. Watching the scene, you knew something very bad was about to happen, but it was not clear what that might be. Then the captors stood back and for the first time there was sound on the video. It was the sound of barking dogs.

Our analysts, and those of the Americans, pored over the videos. We asked teams from the BBC to offer their advice about the kind of equipment that was being used and the ability of the camera team or teams. It looked to me like hand-held, amateurish video, but one of the BBC people called it 'deliberate wobbly-vision', meaning that while it was shaky and unprofessional in appearance, the people who shot the video knew how to operate the equipment in a range of lighting conditions, in corridors, in the cell, and the 'stage' room. Our own analysts – and those of the Americans – agreed. They concluded that the Internet postings were shot in a naive way on middle-range Sony equipment, using bottom-of-the-range professional lighting. Some of the postings that appeared later in the day were clearly out of time order, which confused us further, especially since we referred to them in order of broadcast rather than in order of their production. And it was a production.

'It's like some reality TV show,' Janey Masters said. 'Disgusting but unmissable.'

As she said it, her mobile phone rang, and when she picked it up her voice changed tone. She walked away to gain some privacy during the call.

The next release – the fourth within ten hours – began with a tight shot of a door, which looked like the door of a cell. The door opened. It revealed a white-walled prison cell – the 'cell' from the very first posting. This video was more elaborate than the others and you could see, with reasonable certainty, that it was not a real cell but a room in an old warehouse or factory made up to look like a prison cell, with a mattress on the floor pushed up against a wall, and metal bars on the window. The person who took the video walked into the cell and panned around showing that the room was completely bare apart from a single light bulb. Then the photographer turned the camera downwards towards the mattress. A hand came in from the right. Someone pulled the blue blanket from the bed and revealed the form of Bobby Black underneath. He was conscious, but immobile. His eyes were open. He blinked myopically at the camera lens, a stunned animal in a slaughterhouse, waiting for the knife.

The photographer pulled back and panned up and down the body. The picture showed Bobby Black wearing the bright orange jumpsuit associated with the US prisoners held in Guantanamo Bay in Cuba. The camera pulled back further to show Bobby Black lying on the mattress and moving in a way which for half a second could have indicated he was sobbing, or perhaps shaking with emotion. Maybe it was fear. It was difficult to tell. Then the picture froze. On the posting on the Internet a number of names appeared on the screen, moving upwards like the credits at the end of a movie. I did not recognize the names, but it was obvious most of them were Muslim. Eventually one of our team made the right guess.

'Guantanamo detainees,' someone said. 'Black's been kidnapped for revenge.'

We checked. She was right.

'Oh, shit,' Janey Masters said. 'Shit, shit, shit, shit, shit. What next?'

We did not have long to wait to find out. The postings on the Internet were coming out on average every two or three hours, and so, like the worst of soap operas, we waited for the next instalment. In the meantime there was breaking news from Tehran. The Iranian regime responded to the continuing drum-beat of innuendo from Washington by calling up military reservists, mobilizing the armed forces and declaring a state of national emergency. At the same time, Iranian officials continually denied playing any part in the disappearance of Bobby Black.

The Hezbollah leadership in Lebanon also denied involvement. At a mass rally in Beirut, Sheikh Hamza blamed unspecified

'Zionists' and their supporters in the United States. Then a statement was played out on Al Jazeera, which came from someone claiming to be Osama bin Laden. Voice recognition software put it as 98 per cent likely that it was indeed the great bearded wonder himself, no doubt from a cave in the tribal regions of Pakistan. Bin Laden neither confirmed nor denied any part in the capture or torture of Bobby Black, leaving the matter of his involvement open. Instead he ruminated thoughtfully that Allah had ways of punishing those who would seek to harm Muslims, and that British Muslims had risen up to fight the Holy War against the American tyrants and would show 'in coming days the depth of their resistance.' He said all this in a very soft voice, as if it were a kind of love poetry, though the implication that British Muslims were involved in the kidnap and torture of Bobby Black was itself very dangerous and, as far as any of us knew, wrong.

'We need to deny that immediately,' Andy Carnwath said. 'If people start believing that kind of shit on the basis of no evidence, this country is fucked.'

Carnwath put out a statement jointly with British Muslim groups saying there was no evidence of any British Muslim involvement and that British Muslims called on the kidnappers to release Bobby Black from what they called 'his inhumane captivity'.

As the day wore on, I became increasingly uneasy. I never believed in the Iranian theory. There were plenty of Iranians in Britain, but mostly they detested the regime in Tehran, whatever they thought about Carr and Black. And, like the people in MI6, I could not imagine Iranian Revolutionary Guards or their surrogates operating in the Scottish Highlands, where they would be as comfortable as fish in the desert.

'What's the matter, Alex?' Andy Carnwath asked me at one point. I did not know how to answer him.

'Something smells,' I replied, 'but I haven't a clue what it is.'

The next Internet posting of Bobby Black – the fifth that day – showed the large room or corridor that we came to call the 'stage room'. Our analysts again said they thought it was shot on semi-professional Sony equipment with adequate professional lighting, and that the camera shakes were added deliberately for effect rather than as a sign of incompetence. The photographer entered from one end of the corridor, and at the other end there was something in the centre of the frame. It was not at first possible to make out what that something was. The camera approached. As it drew closer you could see a table on which stood the figure of a naked man. The man had his hands tied behind his back. Over his head he had the large canvas bag, the jute sack we had seen in a previous video. The table was far enough out from the wall so that the photographer could walk around the man, and you could see that Bobby Black was not standing of his own volition. He was hanging from ropes tied round his chest and attached to a pulley on the ceiling. The man's scrotum was tight with fear, his cock shrunken with terror, in a knock-off of one of the notorious pictures from Abu Ghraib. There were wires attached to the victim, and it was obvious that Bobby Black could never hope to retain high political office ever again. You can survive hatred and contempt. You cannot survive ridicule. This time the picture froze and the words 'Abu Ghraib' came on the screen. 'In memory of the Martyrs,' it said. 'There will more tomorrow.'

We all spotted that one of the words in that last sentence was missing. Presumably it should have said, 'There will *be* more tomorrow.' The words were written in three languages, English, Arabic, and Farsi. Our analysts said that there were minor grammatical or syntactical mistakes in two of the languages, English and Arabic. There were no grammatical or syntactical mistakes in the Farsi. Whether this was significant or not seemed to depend on whether you wanted to go to war with Iran. Increasingly, I didn't.

The last posting on the Internet was the most troublesome. It came after a break, one day later. Our analysts had been working frame by frame through the Internet postings and had concluded that the photographer was male, 5'7" to 5'9" in height, thickset and physically fit. I was told that some of this information came from basic trigonometry, measuring angles of reflection, the cast of a shadow inadvertently seen in one shot, and some kind of extrapolation from the height of the camera held shoulder-high compared to the door and the door handle, plus the known size of Bobby Black. It all seemed a little too neat to me. I did not understand the reasoning, or the trigonometry involved, but – like everyone else – I lapped up the conclusions. And yet I trust my instincts.

Hour after hour I convinced myself that something really was wrong. Perhaps it was that I was resistant to being sucked into another war. Perhaps it was that I found everything that we were being drip-fed just a little too convenient, like one of those country house Murder Mystery weekends where you have to guess who committed the crime and the clues lead you by the nose, because the actors are playing out a script. That was what this felt like. Actors, and a script. One analyst, for example – one of ours – claimed that an ungloved hand that came into one of the shots was of someone with an olive, possibly Mediterranean or Middle Eastern complexion. Maybe, but a Groupthink takes over on these occasions, just as it did for the intelligence agencies when they decided Saddam Hussein had Weapons of Mass Destruction in 2003, with facts used to support conclusions that have already been arrived at.

There were some facts on which all the analysts agreed. While they were unable to identify any of the locations in which the videos had been shot, they did conclude that the table on which Bobby Black had been standing was cheap teak veneer of the type commonly used in British offices from the 1980s onwards. They identified the light bulb in the prison cell as of Dutch design, Chinese manufacture, forty watts; again commonly available in England. One of the pipes in the background, painted white, was identified as an English foul-water pipe of the type manufactured in the 1920s. The jute sack over Bobby Black's head was thought to be quite unusual. It was eventually identified as being of Pakistani manufacture, from a bag that originally held rice for export, and with a batch number which showed the bag had been exported from Pakistan to Iran.

That final posting led to what people claimed was a break-through. It was the most elaborate and horrific video of all, and the scene was the larger of the two rooms, the one with the table in the background. This time Bobby Black was lying on the bare floor. His eyes were covered with grey duct tape and his hands were taped in front of him. He was again naked. The captors – and for the first time we were able to conclude definitively that there were at least six of them, including the photographer – used dogs which we had heard barking in a previous video nasty. The dogs were identified as pit-bull cross-breeds, low-slung tubs of meanness, muscle, and teeth. They were encouraged to bark and growl and got closer and closer to Bobby Black's face, head, and genitals. This kind of treatment continued for a few minutes and the video was the most heavily edited. We were not sure why. The analysts clucked a lot over the edits because, apparently, what is cut out of a film like this is almost as interesting as what is left in.

I hadn't a clue what they were talking about, and waited for their conclusions. The police and military police dog-handlers were unanimous in their assessment that the men in the video were unused to dealing with dogs. The dogs were a stunt, a show, one said. When asked how they knew this, one of the Met Police dog-handlers said, 'There was no rapport between man and beast.' That word 'rapport' again. And control, of course, of man over beast. Strange, is it not, that the relations between man and dog, between interrogator and interrogated, between master and servant, between lovers, revolve around those same two words – rapport and control – which appear to be among the minimum requirements for a civilized life? The Americans concluded that the dogs were 'not a professional K9 unit', though again what the real significance of all this might be was not obvious to me.

Our own analysts were unable to say how long Vice-President Black had been forced to endure the dogs. From the video, it looked as though the dogs never bit him, but even without any sign of biting, what we saw was terrifying enough. The edited version was full of sharp teeth and flexed jaws, barking, and dog slobber on the camera. From the range of shots and positions it was assumed that the ordeal must have lasted at least twenty minutes, though the Internet posting was just five minutes long. The photographer had to move the lights around several times, apparently, to get all his shots.

There were further clues. The dogs had collars and leads that contained brass spikes and the manufacturer was identified and sourced to a British brand, *Bulldog,* made in China. In the previous twelve months the manufacturer had sold 2,674 lead and collar sets matching the brand used on the film. The editing had removed most of the evidence of the identity of the dog-handlers, but one sharp-eyed analyst spotted a reflection from the white tiles on the wall and with some computer enhancement concluded that at least one of the abusers was wearing desert combat fatigues of the type worn by US service personnel in, among other places, Iraq, and now commonly available for sale on the Internet and in army surplus stores. The face of the abuser was not visible, but his hands were. They were small, dark, and rough, as if he was a man used to physical labour. His race was not clear, however. Pakistani? Arab? Iranian? Hispanic? Mediterranean?

The video stopped. When it restarted, Bobby Black was still supine on the floor. The dogs had gone, and were replaced by a tableau. In this picture of Black on the floor he was surrounded by life-size cardboard cut-out figures, each one of a US soldier. The faces were all recognizable. When the analysts ran their checks they discovered the cardboard figures were life-size blow-ups of photographs taken inside Abu Ghraib jail. The Americans who had carried out real abuse were all identifiable, including a grinning young woman giving the thumbs-up signal and holding an unlit cigarette in her lips, the one who became the poster girl for American imperial abuse. When news of Abu Ghraib first broke, years ago, what really shocked me was not the ill-treatment of the prisoners. Compared to what Saddam Hussein had done, or what the Iranian regime was doing in Evin Prison, or to conditions in dozens of countries around the world, what the Americans did in Abu Ghraib was pretty mild. But what was most shocking about Abu Ghraib was the light it shone on the worst aspects of American society, the narcissism and utter lack of shame of the abusers who sent photographs of what they had done to their friends and relatives, gloating over their actions. The shock from Abu Ghraib was not that they did it, but that they were proud of it. When I was involved in the interrogation of IRA prisoners in Northern Ireland, I did things that I would never wish to boast about. There were five sanctioned interrogation techniques – sleep deprivation, white noise, bagging (putting hoods over their heads), standing up against a wall for hours at a time, and lack of food and water. But I also used a sixth technique, which we called 'special attention', and which formed the part of my military file that was redacted before it was given to the Americans. I was a young man then, and I thought I was doing the best for my country but, even as I did it, I always retained a sense of shame.

At the end of that final posting on the Internet of Bobby Black there was another caption. It said, again in English, Arabic, and Farsi: 'No more pictures for wile. Next time – Waterboarding.' The analysts spotted the error in the English – 'wile' for 'while', and no 'a' before it. This time there was no error in either the Arabic or the Farsi. But there was one other clue. The tape had been wiped clean of sound, but the sound editing was imperfect. One of the geeks the Americans used to analyse the tape somehow rebuilt the sound over part of the sequence of the men with the dogs. The men were urging the dogs to snap and bite at Bobby Black. One man whose voice was restructured was found to be yelling in Farsi, or so the Americans told us. The British government analysts were unable to replicate this reconstruction, and the BBC analysts couldn't do it either.

By the time the last video had hit the screens, it was announced from Washington that Bobby Black was no longer Vice-President of the United States. His replacement had already been sworn in at a ceremony at an undisclosed location. It was General Conrad Shultz, formerly Director of Central Intelligence. President Carr was said to be returning to the White House, while the new Vice-President was to remain at his undisclosed location. American troop movements to the Gulf were stepped up. There were now four aircraft carrier battle groups within striking distance of Iran, more than 1,000 US combat aircraft capable of hitting Iranian targets, plus sea- and ground-launched Cruise missiles and other weapons.

Late that night, as I sipped a whisky in my room at Castle Dubh, I did my own analysis of the TV pictures of the swearing-in ceremony of Conrad Shultz in Colorado. I could see Kristina in the background applauding as he took the oath of office. She wore a fixed smile. I wondered if she was happy.

Shultz was not going to be as assertive or difficult to deal with. I was hopeful that Kristina would call me, and I tried her several times on her cellphone, but the number was now unobtainable. Perhaps things would change when she returned with the President to DC. One other thing happened that remarkable night. At around two in the morning, unable to sleep, I went down to the kitchen to pour myself another glass of whisky. I passed the end of the corridor where Johnny Lee slept and saw Janey Masters walking out of Johnny Lee's room. She gave me a nervous smile and then disappeared in the direction of her own bedroom.

TWENTY-THREE

The only thing more difficult to handle than Bobby Black's disappearance was his return. As Arlo Luntz had told me years ago, there really are no Second Acts in American political life. You get one shot at it and then you are done. Bobby Black's return came on a Tuesday a week after he had vanished on the Scottish hills, and a week before the US mid-term elections. The videos released on the Internet had stopped, mercifully, although for some days we watched anxiously for the promised video featuring waterboarding. It never came. We assumed that the kidnappers had shot much more propaganda footage and intended to release it at some moment of advantage to them, and so we held our breath, but all we saw were the six original Internet postings recycled endlessly on TV news channels. There were gloating commentaries on al Qaeda-sympathetic websites like Al-Eklas, Al-Firdaws and Al-Buraq, but there were some points of light. Thousands – literally thousands – of Muslim preachers and scholars from all around the world condemned the treatment of Bobby Black in Friday prayers, in sermons, in letters to newspapers, and in learned Islamic journals. In Turkey, Egypt, Malaysia, Indonesia, Pakistan – and even in Iran, scholars insisted that the Internet propaganda was 'un-Islamic cruelty'. A prominent Iranian scholar said that Muslims had to show people of other religions 'more compassion than has been shown to us.' Another scholar, from Fez in Morocco, was of the opinion that 'even those using the rhetoric of the Crusades and of ancient Rome should be treated with humanity and decency.'

All around the world, and from every country with a Muslim majority, there were calls for the captors to release Bobby Black. The Iranian Grand Ayatollah actually pronounced a *fatwa* declaring that the US Vice-President must be released. And then it happened, though whether as a result of his efforts we could not immediately establish. It came only after a taste of the backlash that we had all feared. There were mass demonstrations in New York, Los Angeles, Miami, Chicago, St Louis, and even supposedly liberal enclaves like San Francisco, Seattle, Boston, and Portland, Oregon. Mostly they were sombre and peaceful expressions of sympathy for Bobby Black and his family, although there was some trouble on the fringes, with demonstrators calling for a war on Iran. Two mosques were attacked with firebombs, one in Michigan, the other in Illinois, and a handful more were damaged by graffiti or vandalism, plus there was a large pro-war demonstration in Washington, DC. Police estimated 100,000 people marched from Capitol Hill to the Lincoln Memorial and, at the site of Martin Luther King's 'I Have a Dream' speech, a group of political leaders, Republicans and Democrats, called for an immediate strike on Tehran. President Carr said he was listening. He said he was always listening to the people of the United States, but he was also listening to his senior military officers and the CIA, and he would take the decisions about war and peace, not the demonstrators.

Things in Europe were worse. In the United Kingdom there were two riots, one in Bradford, where the British National Party decided to hold a 'Free Bobby Black' rally in the centre of the town and the Anti-Nazi League attacked them, trying to beat them off the streets. The other British troublespot was

Tottenham in north London, where police made thirty arrests, mostly of Muslim demonstrators, after shop windows were smashed and a petrol station looted. Across Europe there were dozens of reports of mosques being attacked – mosques where the imams had generally condemned the treatment of Bobby Black: in east London, Basingstoke, Dewsbury, Paris, Marseilles, Lyons, Munich, Berlin, Dortmund, Brussels, Amsterdam, Rotterdam, Rome, Seville, and Granada. Turkish cafés and shops in Berlin were attacked by small groups of neo-Nazis. A Tunisian pastry shop in Paris was looted and burned to the ground. A busload of French Algerians was stoned in Marseilles. Some British newspapers talked of 'an Enemy Within', and Andy Carnwath was hard-pressed to keep them in line. It took telephone calls from Fraser Davis himself to three newspaper proprietors, reminding them that if there were riots he would publicly lay the blame on inflammatory commentaries in the newspapers themselves, for the coverage to be moderated. Mostly, however, it was low-level stuff, but it was persistent, and I worried that we all risked being swept along by a wave of pro-war sentiment, with the Worst leading the Best into a catastrophe.

For want of something more constructive to do, I spent a couple of days witnessing the search for Bobby Black. It had reached epic proportions, with diggers scraping off the topsoil on the mountain side, and men with chainsaws cutting down the whin bushes and passing the earth and vegetation through metal detectors and sieves of various types.

It was the kind of thing you might expect at a high-tech archaeological dig, except there was no sign of a fossil. Or anything else.

'The excavation of Troy,' Anstruther said to me as we stood together on the hillside in wonderment.

'At least Troy existed,' I replied. Whether Bobby Black did or not was beginning to trouble me. He had become almost a mythical figure, like the Minotaur, Bigfoot, or the Yeti, a myth full of different meanings for different people. I resented that the hillsides of Scotland were being punished for their part in his disappearance.

Everything before Manila and the Black kidnapping belonged to one era, everything after the Manila bombing and the kidnapping belonged to another. Every day, every hour, events speeded up, faster and faster, like water swirling down a plug-hole. James Byrne, my personal demon, turned out to be at the heart of much of it. I cannot tell you how distraught I was at his success. He became a world superstar in the forty-eight hours before Bobby Black was discovered, strutting around Rowallan village, cock of the walk, all because he had written two exclusive stories for the *Washington Post*. The stories were largely true, but for someone in Washington, they were also very useful. The stories put Byrne on every front page, every radio and TV news bulletin around the world, but they also pushed us all even further down the road to war with Iran.

Byrne claimed he had the 'facts'. The first came on Halloween. It asserted that British and American investigators were now 'convinced beyond reasonable doubt' that the Islamic Republic of Iran was behind the kidnapping and torture of the Vice-President of the United States. The story said that 'US sources familiar with the investigation' had told the *Washington Post* there was now 'concrete forensic and other evidence' that nailed the Tehran regime. There were no further details in Byrne's story of this supposedly 'concrete' evidence, and officially we denied it. Our version said that British investigators still had an 'open mind' about the reasons behind Bobby Black's disappearance, although unofficially we confirmed that there was some 'potential forensic evidence' which pointed to a 'possible Iranian link.' We did not specify what that evidence might be. The night of that first story – just forty-eight hours before Bobby Black's reappearance – Johnny Lee, Janey Masters, and I gathered for a late evening whisky in Lord Anstruther's private quarters. Even though it was Halloween, none of us was in a festive mood.

'Exclusive access for a story of this magnitude,' Johnny Lee Ironside said dismissively when Janey raised the subject, 'usually means that someone at the White House has decided James Byrne is a urinal into which from time to time they will piss.'

'But he got the story,' I admitted ruefully, helping myself to a very fine Dufftown Glenlivet. 'More or less.'

'You have to ask yourself why has he got the right story? Who's working him?'

'And the answer?' Anstruther chipped in. We were sitting round a big fire. Johnny Lee and Janey Masters were enjoying each other's company with all the pleasure of new lovers. Their relationship was openly acknowledged among us.

'I have learned in my two years with the Carr administration that the right hand does not always know what the far-right hand is doing,' Johnny Lee joked. 'I mean, who would leak this shit to a liberal columnist on a liberal newspaper that hates us? What the fuck, Alex? I mean, what the fucking fuck?'

'The story means the next pro-war demonstration in Washington at the weekend is only going to get bigger,' Janey said. 'So why are you so cheerful?'

'Hysteria, honey,' he said to her. 'I ain't cheerful, just border-line insane. Fits in with the mood of the country, I guess. Let's go bomb somebody and ask questions later.'

That Halloween night the four of us methodically decided to kill as much of Anstruther's whisky as was humanly possible. It was a maudlin evening and I apologized to Johnny Lee for everything that I had got wrong and all our cross words.

'Hell,' he said, 'us Anglo-Saxons, we have to stick together, don't we? All the rest are unreliable or just plain evil. 'Specially the French.'

'You should be so lucky to be French,' Janey said. 'The French say that the United States has gone from barbarism to decadence without an intervening period of civilization. And in that they are correct.'

I was starting to warm to her. Johnny Lee brought out the best in her.

'So is there going to be a war or isn't there?' Anstruther said, gloomily. 'I mean, I look at the numbers. The British Army just can't fight anywhere else. Iraq, Afghanistan, plus the bases in Northern Ireland and Germany. In the case of a major ground war against Iran we would need to think of conscription.'

'We can't do that!' Janey blurted out.

'I know we can't,' Anstruther said. 'But with more than one in five of our soldiers coming from here in Scotland, if the Scots vote for independence next year, who will do our fighting for us? Do we pull out of Afghanistan? Iraq? We can't do three wars. We can't even do two.'

We looked to Johnny Lee.

'As Alex's good friend Dr Kristina Taft would say: if we screw this up, it won't be three wars. It will be one mother-fucking huge war stretching from Turkey and Israel to India and all points in between, and you'll have to be involved.'

'I need another drink,' I said. So did we all.

That Halloween night before Bobby Black came back was filled with monsters and demons, but it was also a night for exorcizing fears. Until well after midnight we chatted, while Anstruther sat in his favourite battered armchair, sipping from a heavy crystal glass, with a hunting magazine open on his lap, as if the world had not changed much since Victoria was on the throne.

'You British give good calm,' Johnny Lee said to him at one point. 'Maybe that's something we could learn from you.'

'Grace under pressure,' Anstruther retorted. 'The quality for which President Kennedy was famous.'

'More like postcoital exhaustion,' Janey Masters responded, sipping her own malt whisky. We all looked at her and smiled. 'In the case of Kennedy, I mean.'

'Calais Rules apply here in Castle Dubh,' Anstruther said.

'What do you mean?' Janey asked.

'When I was in the army we used to say that anything that happened beyond Calais stayed beyond Calais. As far as I'm concerned, anything that we say or do here,' he looked at Johnny Lee and Janey, 'especially between consenting adults, is subject to the same rules. Anything that happens in Castle Dubh stays in Castle Dubh. You have my word on it.'

Then he looked at me.

'Same goes for you too, Alex.'

The private quarters in Castle Dubh were lined with aged paintings, the faces of Anstruthers from the past 200 years, interspersed with landscapes and Arcadian or bucolic scenes in the style of Claude Lorrain, plus a few hunting and fishing trophies preserved from the nineteenth century.

'If it really is the Iranians, then God help us all,' I said. 'If it is NOT the Iranians, then we need to cool things down as quickly as possible.'

'Kennedy again,' Anstruther murmured. 'Only in a different way. After the assassination of President Kennedy, the world needed a simple explanation. A dupe like Lee Harvey Oswald was a much better explanation than a big-time conspiracy that drew in Russia or Cuba.'

'I don't get what you mean,' Johnny Lee said. 'What the world needed was the truth, and the Warren Commission ensured we didn't get it.'

'The world couldn't handle the truth. If the official explanation for Kennedy's assassination was that Cuba or Russia really was involved, do you think we could have avoided a nuclear war? You really want to risk the whole world for one single life? Then or now?'

'So we sit back and do nothing if we conclusively find

Iranian prints all over this?' Johnny Lee scoffed. 'Is that what you're saying, Dickie? I beg to differ, my friend.'

'"*They made a desert and they called it peace*",' Anstruther said, passing around the whisky bottle again. 'Where did that come from? Some Roman, probably.'

Johnny Lee smiled. 'Always the goddamn Romans, eh? One of my favourite quotes. I used it in my postgraduate dissertation at Georgetown, writing about Cambodia after the US bombing. It's from the Roman historian Tacitus, quoting one of your British chieftains of the first century, Cagacus.

'And I expect you know the full Cagacus quote in Latin, smartarse?' Janey Masters said. The whisky was talking in all of us now.

'Matter of fact I do,' Johnny Lee smiled. 'The benefits of an American education.'

Anstruther shook his head. 'I got a C in Latin,' he butted in.

'"*Auferre, trucidare, rapere, falsis nominibus imperium; atque, ubi solitudinem faciunt, pacem appellant*",' Johnny Lee declaimed.

We all were impressed.

'Yes, I knew that,' Anstruther sniffed. 'Remind me?'

'Translation,' Johnny Lee laughed as Anstruther passed the crystal water jug. '"*They ravage, they slaughter, they seize under false pretences and call it empire; and where they make a desert, they call it peace.*" That's what empires do, at least in Tacitus's version – though, like the Reps today, he was prob'ly making up quotes to suit his political allegiances and paying off scores in Rome in the name of supposed history. The James Byrne of his day, I guess.'

'Empire is Empire,' Anstruther agreed, morosely. 'Power is Power. We did the same when we ruled the world, and so did the French, the Spanish, the Romans, and the Greeks and, God help us, the Persians. Why would Brother Yank be any different? You do what you can to keep it together, Johnny Lee, and when it starts to fall apart, you dress up your own best interests as if they were moral imperatives for everybody else. You make a desert and you call it peace, all the time claiming that you never wanted to be the world's policemen – it's just that you don't want anyone else to be either.'

Johnny Lee laughed.

'A better translation of Tacitus. Screw the bastards. Fuck 'em all.'

I looked over at him. We were back to being friends again. I was grateful.

The second Byrne exclusive story came the next morning, 1 November. The *Washington Post* had found out about the 'hide'. The story explained the location and described the short tunnel under the whins, then went on to say that the 'hide' was of the type used by special forces, including the American Delta Force and the British SAS, but there was again a 'strong Iranian link, believed to be with elements of the Iranian Revolutionary Guards, the al Quds section.' *Al Quds* is Arabic for Jerusalem, Byrne explained, and the Al Quds section of the Revolutionary Guards was the most fanatical of the Iranian units, committed to spreading the Shia revolution around the world, culminating in a triumphant takeover of the Holy City – which, inconveniently, Israel was using as its capital. Byrne fleshed out the supposed forensic evidence linking the hide to Iran. He reported that the button had been found, of Chinese manufacture, similar to that used in Iranian military clothing, and that cotton thread found on the button was of Iranian manufacture. Byrne did have good sources. He reported information that I did not know, sourcing the cotton thread to a spinning mill in the Iranian town of Shiraz. Boot-prints found at the hide were said to match the soles of the kinds of military boots manufactured in the Iranian city of Tirz. Four different boot-prints were detected. Byrne also mentioned the maps found in the supposed getaway car and that they were annotated in Farsi, and he identified the jute sack over the head of the Vice-President in one of the Internet videos as being from a consignment shipped from Pakistan to Iran.

'Each piece of evidence taken on its own, according to US intelligence sources, is circumstantial,' Byrne reported, 'but taken together, fingers are now being directly pointed at Tehran. So too are American missiles.'

From the moment of this second exclusive story, Byrne's smug face and his croaky voice were everywhere, on every radio and TV channel, his views reproduced as fact even though the words 'credible' and 'believed' kept appearing in his stories, giving them the gloss of faith rather than fact. TV news was all James Byrne, all the time. For me it was a taste of purgatory, for obvious personal reasons, but also because I continued to have my doubts about the Iranian story. Revolutionary Guards? In the Scottish Highlands? Byrne struck me as a willing dupe.

Like some ambitious newspaper reporters in the run-up to the war with Iraq in 2003, he was paving the way for a conflict that most people did not want, based on evidence that he could not justify, manipulated by people whose identity he refused to reveal.

'I never reveal my sources,' he told the BBC. His smugness made me feel physically sick. I started to recover when he was arrested.

It came the next day, very early in the morning. It was the same day that Bobby Black was finally discovered. I was still at Castle Dubh, with yet another hangover following yet another late-night drinking session with Anstruther, Janey, and Johnny Lee Ironside. I had heard nothing from Kristina despite the fact that she was back in Washington, and my numerous attempts to contact her through the White House switchboard, her home telephone, and on her cellphone. I asked Johnny Lee to help and told him – in this new atmosphere of frank talking – all about our relationship. He knew much of it already, but he listened to the details as if he did not. He made a few calls and told me that Kristina was indeed back in Washington, but she had no time for anything – or anyone – except work. Theo Carr was about to make an address to the nation, which Johnny Lee said was to be an ultimatum to Iran to release Bobby Black. Secretary of State Andrew Baker was already in the Gulf, and Johnny Lee said he was to go to Tehran before the address and tell the Iranians plainly that if Bobby Black did not reappear, then, in Johnny Lee's words, 'Persian civilization was about to be set back three thousand years.'

I considered things from Kristina's point of view. With her country on the brink of war, she was busier than at any time in her life, but it was obvious that I was also probably best avoided. I was toxic, mixed up in the disappearance of Bobby Black in some way not easy to explain. It was better for her to have nothing to do with me. I missed her more than I would have believed possible, missed her talk, her wit, her insights. I missed her smell beside me in the morning. I came up with the fantasy that one day sometime soon – maybe after the inquiry had reported into my supposed incompetence over Bobby Black's disappearance – I would leave the Foreign Office and set up a business bottling the smells of lovers. Imagine if you had a few drops of scent that reminded you exactly of the hair or neck of the one you loved? How much would you pay to sprinkle those drops on your pillow?

'Ambassador Price,' I was told when I phoned the White House and asked for the National Security Adviser, 'the National Security Adviser is still at an undisclosed location.'

'I thought Dr Taft had returned to Washington?'

'I am sorry, Ambassador Price. I have no further information on the whereabouts of Dr Taft.' And no, there were no messages.

*　　*　　*

308

President Carr's broadcast to the American people took place from the Oval Office at 9 p.m. Washington time, 2 a.m. in the UK. The four of us sat up to watch it, more than marginally drunk. Carr talked about what he called 'the Iranian threat to our national security and the Iranian dimension that we suspect may be linked to the disappearance of the Vice-President of the United States.' He used his words carefully but firmly. American and British investigations had 'not yet' conclusively established who was behind the kidnapping, or the motive for it, but the treatment and public humiliation of the Vice-President was 'despicable, cowardly, and clearly could not be tolerated by those who believe in any of the great Abrahamic religions – not Jews, nor Muslims, nor Christians, nor people of any of the world's great faiths. I call on the people holding Bobby Black, in the name of humanity and in the service of the God that looks down on us all, to release him now, without further harm or humiliation.'

Then the President turned even more serious.

'Let me be clear. There is some evidence of possible Iranian involvement. If any foreign power contributed in any way to the kidnapping of the Vice-President of the United States,' Carr warned, wagging his finger at the camera, 'that will be considered an unprovoked act of war against the United States and its allies, and it will be met with the maximum response of which the United States is capable. The United States is pursuing something that was very dear to the heart of Vice-President Black. We call it the Spartacus Doctrine. As you know, it takes its name from the harsh treatment meted out in Rome to those who tried to overturn and subvert the order of the greatest civilization of the day. We can promise the enemies of freedom, of liberty and justice, a similar fate. I announce today that any state, any power, which attacks the United States or its citizens, or condones such an attack, can expect overwhelming force, overwhelmingly applied, to be used against it. Secretary of State Andrew Baker is in Tehran tonight conveying the message to the Iranian regime that we will respond and, when we do, it will be a maximum response.'

I stopped at the words 'maximum response' and looked at the television set, and then at Johnny Lee. The words had only one meaning. President Theo Carr was telling the government in Tehran that if they were behind the kidnapping of Vice-President Black, then he was prepared to use nuclear weapons. It was the ultimate threat a president could make.

In the flurry of news reports and analysis that followed the President's statement, American officials – I supposed Kristina among them – briefed that the United States had now invoked Article Five of the NATO charter, which regards an attack on one NATO member as an attack on all NATO members. If the US declared war on Iran, it would expect the rest of NATO to follow suit, and that one of the military objectives of any war would be to ensure that 'a new Iran' was incapable of producing a nuclear weapon, ever. This future 'new Iran', one 'high-ranking US official' said, would be a 'beacon of democracy in the Middle East.'

It was a long night, with reports of troop movements in southern Russia along the Iranian border, and panic in the Gulf states, with the richest Arab citizens turning up at the airports, desperate to fly as far away as possible. In Iran itself the government of the Islamic Republic yet again denied any involvement in the disappearance of Bobby Black. Iranian TV and the IRNA news agency showed pictures of 'Islamic volunteers' – including women – operating anti-aircraft batteries and cleaning their rifles ready to repel the American invader. IRNA called President Carr's speech an 'American neo-imperialist ploy to further destabilize the region,' and the Iranian president invited television cameras to see him conduct prayers in which he claimed that the disappearance of the Vice-President was a 'pretext for war conjured up by the American

Zionist lobby and the warmongers of the illegal regime in Israel which must be swept from the map.' At that moment, I would have put the chances of an American strike against Iran at higher than 50 per cent, but events that morning moved much more swiftly than any of us could have anticipated. As I shaved after just a couple of hours' sleep, at seven in the morning, Johnny Lee called me on my mobile.

'You wanna come down with me to Rowallan village?' he asked. 'Get some breakfast down at the hotel?'

'Yes,' I said, slightly puzzled, 'if you can face seeing all the reporters camped out down there.'

'Sure can,' he said. 'There's one less Reptile to worry about. James Aloysius Byrne has been arrested and is in custody, awaiting deportation.'

Johnny Lee had a car waiting outside, a big Chevy truck which he drove himself. He told me the story as we hit the main road to Rowallan.

'You know your friend Byrne had been boasting to anyone who would listen that he was "unable to name his sources" for his exclusive stories?' Johnny Lee said. 'Well, I guess I am unable to name my sources either, but Scotland Yard detectives busted him at five o'clock this morning in pursuit of a warrant from the FBI.'

'Jesus Christ.' I tried not to smile, but could not stop myself. 'Nothing serious, I hope?'

Johnny Lee kept driving but for a second looked over at me. 'Listen, Alex, I know about him and Fiona.' He turned back to the road.

'I see,' I said.

'It's okay,' he said. 'Nobody is going to talk about it. Specially not me. Calais Rules, right? But the reason I'm bringing it up is our people think Fiona is one of the sources for Byrne. She's been talking to him a bunch lately. There have been wiretaps on him which have picked up . . . her voice.'

I felt my stomach sink to the floor. 'Talking about what . . . ?'

''Bout you and Northern Ireland twenty years ago, among other things. All I got is the headlines. I don't have the details. I thought you should know.'

I looked out of the window at the bright autumnal colours. Kristina's elusiveness began to make more sense.

'Our people . . . listened in,' Johnny Lee said. 'I guess you need to know. The British security service was . . . very helpful about Byrne. Cooperation at the highest level between NSA and GCHQ, and no problems from the Prime Minister's office, even though it's his sister. Fiona told Byrne a whole pile of shit about you.'

I looked over to gauge his reaction. Johnny Lee smiled.

'Personally, Alex, I'm proud of you. But I guess you'd better brace yourself. It'll all come out, sooner or later. You can't tell a Rep anything and not get it in the paper one day, and when it comes out, not everybody's gonna be so happy.'

I nodded, and said nothing. We were now in Rowallan and Johnny Lee parked the car. I was still in shock.

'C'mon, let's go get breakfast and find out a little more about Mr Byrne.'

'I just want you to know,' I said, grabbing at his sleeve, 'that I did what I did in Northern Ireland for a reason.'

Johnny Lee laughed and slapped me on the back.

'Tell you what, Alex. Now I know what you're capable of, I won't ever fuck with you again, you hear me? Not even in fun. I'm just glad we're on the same side, is all. I always knew the British were ruthless; it's just that you hide it so well.'

The Rowallan Hotel looked like a cross between a major crime scene and a media city. Media encampments all look the same, wherever they are – Washington, Goma, Rowallan – a forest of satellite dishes, trucks, earnest people with note-books, puffer jackets, jeans, trainers, and a few reporters with suits and ties standing in front of bright lights constantly talking onto microphones. Outside the hotel, a dozen British

312

and European reporters were babbling into breakfast news programmes, plus two or three from Japan and the Far East delivering what for them must have been the late-night news. Johnny Lee pushed through and up to the main stairwell. He checked a message on his Blackberry.

'Byrne was in room one-three-two,' he said. He bounded up the stairs on his long legs and I followed.

The corridor was sealed off. Uniformed British police were at both ends, Scotland Yard detectives were in the middle, but inside the bedroom itself the work of going through Byrnes' clothes, files, and notebooks was being conducted by the FBI, supervised by Deputy Director Marian Killick herself.

'Good morning, Deputy Director,' Johnny Lee said with a sprightly tone in his voice. 'I guess you all had an early start.' She looked up from a sheaf of papers she was studying.

'Why, yes, good morning, Johnny Lee.' It was obvious Johnny Lee had charmed her – just as he had charmed most people, including me. I was still slightly wary of Killick, but tried not to show it. 'And good morning, Ambassador. Good to meet with you again.'

'Good morning.'

'Can you give us a run-through?' Johnny Lee requested. Killick explained that, in pursuit of a warrant obtained by the FBI overnight in Washington DC as part of an investigation into the leaking of top-secret information, at five o'clock in the morning British time, British police – with the assistance of the FBI – had arrested James Byrne in his bedroom. He was now facing extradition to the United States. His computer, cellphone, and flash drives had been taken away and were being studied by FBI technicians at Bolfracks Bothy.

'Of course, he was not alone at the time of the arrest,' Deputy Director Killick said, arching an eyebrow. 'He had company.'

'You're kiddin' me,' said Johnny Lee, clapping his hands

313

together in delight. 'This is the gift that just keeps on giving. Tell me it was a male escort? Make my day.'

'He was found in bed with one of the hotel chamber-maids, a twenty-three-year-old Polish woman called . . . Katya something.'

'Duprowska.' One of the other agents helped out his boss.

'Whatever. A quantity of marijuana was also discovered. British police are questioning the girl, though I guess she's just collateral damage in all this.'

Johnny Lee grinned widely. 'Sex, drugs, and rock and roll. Deputy Director, I do believe we just spoiled Mr Byrne's day, not to mention the day of one or two folks in Washington.'

Killick did not respond. She nodded and returned to her files. ''Scuse me,' she said. 'I have work to do.'

Johnny Lee took me by the arm and steered me to the breakfast room, full of good cheer.

'I don't understand,' I said. 'Whose day in Washington has been spoiled by all this?'

He winked at me. 'After we order.'

I settled for orange juice, coffee, and cereal, and Johnny Lee said, 'What the heck?' and ordered a complete fried breakfast.

'They timed the raid for five o'clock this morning,' he said, 'because midnight last night Washington time was when the Bureau went in and arrested John Crockett.'

I was astonished. 'Crockett? Betty Furedi's Chief of Staff? What on earth for?'

Johnny Lee laughed. His breakfast arrived and he cut open one of the fried eggs and dipped toast in the yolk.

'Passing on secret information to unauthorized persons, namely Byrne and the readers of the *Washington Post*. Speaker Furedi got a classified White House briefing because she was next in line. The FBI think she told Crockett all about it, and Crockett couldn't wait to spill the beans to his liberal friend Mr Byrne.'

'You are kidding me? Betty Furedi's no leaker.'

Johnny Lee was grinning so widely he could hardly eat his breakfast. 'Oh, yes she is,' he said in a pantomime voice. 'She tells Crockett everything. Always has done.'

Johnny Lee was irrepressibly cheerful. A phone call had been traced from the Speaker's office on Capitol Hill to the Rowallan Hotel.

The caller – an American male – asked to be connected to Mr Byrne's room. The following day a second call was made to Byrne on his US cellphone from the same land-line, allegedly in Speaker Furedi's office. The FBI claimed that this telephone was located in the office of John Crockett, an office right next to the Speaker's own. Crockett said he was in the gym on Capitol Hill at the time the call was made and he angrily denied leaking the Iran link.

'Either way, Betty Boop's in the doo-doo,' Johnny Lee smiled in triumph. 'In fact, that gal's in so deep she might never come out. Mid-term elections are looking a lot rosier for the President than they were twenty-four hours ago.'

We had all seen Speaker Betty Furedi on television a couple of nights previously, after her first security briefing as next in line. She had been standing outside the White House press stakeout position saying that she was 'honoured and humbled' to be invited to discuss the 'national security of this great country of ours' with the President's advisers. After Byrne's arrest, Speaker Furedi's office denied that she or any of her staff were the source of the leak, and at first she appeared to find an ally in the White House. The Communications Director Sandy McAuley refused to comment 'on Justice Department matters', beyond saying that the classified White House briefing to Speaker Furedi was 'a highly sensitive national security matter on the subject of Bobby Black's disappearance.' McAuley then said it would be 'inconceivable' that Speaker Furedi – or indeed 'any patriotic American' – would leak such matters.

'Our democracy depends on trust,' McAuley had said. 'President Carr wants it to be known that he has absolute faith in the integrity of Speaker Furedi.'

You could hear a pin drop in the White House press room.

'How would you characterize someone who leaked such a story?' one of the White House reporters asked McAuley. He took a breath.

'As a traitor,' he said softly. 'Beneath contempt. Unfit to hold any public office. The modern equivalent to Benedict Arnold.'

I marvelled at McAuley's brilliance. He had set Betty Furedi up perfectly. And now it all had a point. The Carr administration looked as if they had trusted Furedi and been betrayed. It was a catastrophe for the Speaker, and for the Democrats' election campaign.

Johnny Lee and I finished breakfast and found a TV in the hotel bar. A group of journalists were watching the screen and finishing their coffees.

After a few minutes it cut to a report from Washington. It was the early hours of the morning, Washington time, just after John Crockett's arrest. He was led away in the darkness, shamefaced and in handcuffs. A spokeswoman for Speaker Furedi was asked repeatedly if the Speaker had told anyone about the contents of her top-secret briefing. The spokeswoman read from a statement written by the Speaker:

'Following a private White House meeting about the circumstances surrounding the disappearance of Vice-President Black, I turned for advice to my Chief of Staff John Crockett. In order to secure his advice at this most difficult time, I found it necessary to give him some of the details I had learned at the White House. I regret this error of judgement. I have not discussed the contents of the White House briefing with anyone else. Mr Crockett assures me that he did not pass on the information to James Byrne of the Washington Post *or anyone else. I will cooperate fully and await the outcome of the investigations.'*

Politics, like football, is beyond fiction. You can be three goals up with five minutes to go and still lose. Around the bar I could hear the journalists scoff into their coffee.

'She's toast,' an American voice called out. Against all the odds, and all the polls, the Democrats were being neutered. They could no longer attack Theo Carr for warmongering.

'Toast is right,' Johnny Lee Ironside agreed.

The latest Pew Research tracking polls showed that for the first time in almost two years, the Democrats' lead had narrowed to single digits. It would shrink even further thanks to Furedi and the arrests. And then my mobile and Johnny Lee Ironside's phones rang simultaneously. On mine was Andy Carnwath.

'We've found him, Alex,' he said. 'There's an RAF plane on standby at Aberdeen Airport to fly you to Lakenheath in Suffolk. He's in a hospital in Norfolk. You have to drop what you are doing and leave right now.'

'How is he?'

'Alive,' Carnwath said. 'That's all I have.'

TWENTY-FOUR

We left the Rowallan Hotel immediately and climbed back in the Chevy. Johnny Lee gunned it up the road towards Castle Dubh. He had received a little more information than I did. A man thought to be the Vice-President of the United States had been found by dog-walkers on a beach near some place . . . he had written the name down and fumbled for his notes as he drove . . . Wells-next-the-Sea on the north Norfolk coast. The man was on his way to hospital at King's Lynn. We had to get there as soon as possible.

'They have a plane for me at Aberdeen.'

'Me too. You want to come with us?' Johnny Lee offered me a ride.

'You sure?'

'Yep,' he replied, with a return to his old generosity and warmth. 'We're heading to the same place. We've got the same problems. We've even got the same hangovers.'

'Okay.'

'Shit, there's a catch,' he said, suddenly. 'Helicopters. I have a Chinook taking me to Aberdeen airport. Susan Black and the family will meet us there. We can't wait for a car.'

I swallowed. I could make my own way, avoiding the helicopters, arriving a couple of hours after Johnny Lee.

318

Or I could accept his offer of a ride-along and climb on to a helicopter for the first time in twenty years.

'No, it's okay,' I said. 'I'll come with you.'

I could feel the knot of nervousness tighten in my stomach and the saliva swim into my mouth.

'You sure?' he said. 'I understand your problem.'

'No. I mean, yes. Yes – I'll be fine.'

A Chinook is the least helicopter-like of the beasts: ugly, overweight, massive, more like a fixed-wing aircraft than the helicopters I had used in Northern Ireland. I called Downing Street and told Andy Carnwath my travel plans.

'Good,' he responded. 'Up their arse and stay there. I'll tell Fraser.'

I grabbed a travel bag, just in case, and ran back downstairs to where the Chinook was waiting. Johnny Lee followed me on board. I felt my heart and stomach turn somersaults as the twin rotors started. I strapped myself in and closed my eyes. Chinooks can carry more than forty people. They are fully enclosed, and as we lifted off I felt the knot in my guts slowly unclench, though I clasped the sides of my seat in white-knuckled fear.

'You hear any more details?' I said.

'Some,' Johnny Lee confirmed. 'Unidentified male in confused state found naked or near naked on a beach. Unidentified male matches the description of the Vice-President. Thought to be suffering from hypothermia, among other things.'

We reached Aberdeen Airport less than ten minutes later. I was relieved I had not disgraced myself on the helicopter. On the tarmac next to the American plane we were joined by Susan Fein Black, her daughter Alice and son Robert Junior, both in their twenties, plus three American women from the Secret Service. Mrs Black wore dark sunglasses and a heavy overcoat with the collar turned up. She said nothing to Johnny Lee or to me and seemed almost in a trance as she sat at the front of the plane staring at the seat back ahead of her. Johnny Lee and I were placed towards the back. Susan Black looked as if she had aged twenty years in the week or so since her husband had gone missing. Her finely boned face was grey and taut with strain, like a woman in mourning.

We took off immediately for Lakenheath RAF Base in Suffolk. When we got there a little over an hour later, we transferred to another Chinook to take us to what we were told was the Queen Elizabeth Hospital on the outskirts of King's Lynn. The USAF Colonel I had met before at Castle Dubh, the bullet-headed Martinez, and half a dozen other American military personnel joined us. Susan Black and her party kept separate from the rest. Colonel Martinez sat with me and Johnny Lee, and confirmed the details – that the man in hospital at King's Lynn had now positively been identified as the Vice-President. He was under armed police guard and his condition was still being assessed by British doctors. American military doctors were arriving ahead of us at the hospital.

'We will make our own assessment of the Vice-President's condition,' Colonel Martinez insisted, in a tone that suggested the British National Health Service could not be trusted with diagnosing the common cold.

'Of course, Colonel. Whatever you need, let me know.'

I looked out of the Chinook window at the little farms and villages of Norfolk and dreamed of a normal life among normal people when this was all over. If it was ever going to be.

The QE2 hospital in King's Lynn is modern, sprawling, and dotted with enormous lawns on a green-field site on the outskirts of the town. The Chinook landed in the grounds, but the second we stepped from the helicopter it was clear we had flown straight into a diplomatic incident. I was met by a delegation of hospital managers and consultants.

'They have taken over,' one of the consultants complained of the Americans. 'Incredibly arrogant people. It's as if we're under military occupation.' Being called arrogant by a British hospital consultant is a bit like being called ugly by a frog.

'As soon as the patient was identified as the Vice-President, we were big-footed by a team of American military doctors,' another chimed in.

'It's supposed to be a British hospital,' the chief administrator added. 'Not an American military facility.'

'Let me introduce the Vice-President's wife, Susan Black, his son Robert and daughter Alice,' I said, silencing them. 'And his Chief of Staff, Johnny Lee Ironside.'

'Thank you so much for your assistance,' Susan Black said with grave courtesy. I admired her politeness in the face of the British doctors' rudeness. The doctors stopped whingeing, at least for a moment.

'Yes, thank you,' Johnny Lee said politely. 'Thank you all.'

We walked briskly away from the Chinook towards a private hospital wing. There were about forty armed Norfolk constabulary and Metropolitan Police officers and a dozen or so American military personnel in uniform ringing a low-rise modern hospital block. We stopped in the reception area. It was my turn to do something for Anglo–American relations.

'Now listen,' I said to the British doctors and managers, in a loud voice so everyone, including the USAF Colonel, Susan Black, and Johnny Lee, could hear clearly. 'This may be your hospital and your patient, but he is the American Vice-President, and he is Mrs Black's husband. We appreciate everything you have done and everything you are going to do for Vice-President Black, but this is now an American matter. It is up to our friends here how to handle it. We are here to help in any way we can. I am speaking to you with the full authority of the Prime Minister. Any problems, I can call Downing Street. Am I being clear?'

It was agreed that I was being clear.

'May I see my husband?' Susan Black said in a firm voice.

One of the British consultants led the way. Johnny Lee followed with the family and the Colonel. The rest of us stood around the reception area and made do with coffee and biscuits. We kicked our heels for an hour until Johnny Lee reappeared. One of the British consultants came up to me and complained again about what he called the 'heavy-handed actions of the Americans.'

'It's a British hospital, for goodness' sake! Who do these people think they are?'

I tore into him.

'I thought I had explained the situation, Dr . . .'

'Allen. Tobias Allen.'

'Well, Dr Allen, if anything bad happens to Bobby Black in your hospital, I think you might find it would be better if the American military doctors were to discover the bad news first. For example, if he was about to die? Don't you agree?'

'Oh,' he said, flustered. 'I hadn't thought of it that way. I mean, yes. I see.'

Fear, as I was never short of repeating nowadays, really does work.

When Johnny Lee returned, he stood in the middle of the reception area and talked to the British doctors and administrators just as I had done.

'Thank you very much ladies and gentlemen,' he said loudly. 'Thank you for your care and your hospitality and your help. Mrs Black asked me to pass on her personal gratitude.

'Our military doctors tell me that the Vice-President is well enough to be moved. For security reasons we believe that this is necessary. It will also be better for the smooth running of your excellent hospital, I am sure you will agree, if this patient goes somewhere more suitable to his condition and the armed guards can be removed. We have decided to move the patient to Scotland, where he can recover from his ordeal and be

322

treated. This is Mrs Black's wish also. We are making arrangements for all facilities that we may need to be taken to Castle Dubh and the Bolfracks Bothy. Thank you.'

With that, the meeting was over. I could see the British doctors looking at one another and a few, hurried, whispered conversations. I buttonholed Dr Allen.

'You have a problem with this?' I said.

'N-no,' he said, in a voice which suggested the opposite. 'I see his point.'

'Tell me what you really think,' I demanded.

'Well,' he shrugged, gaining a little in confidence, 'from what I and my colleagues saw of Vice-President Black, he is unable to speak, unable to stand or even sit up, unable to respond to simple commands. It's as though he had some kind of epidural. His limbs are all intact but he has limited sensation below the waist.'

'In layman's terms?'

'He's in a terrible state. Best not subject him to any more ordeals, like getting on a plane. He should not be moved. That's my judgement. For what it's worth.'

'Thank you, Dr Allen.'

Within half an hour I was in the Chinook again, this time at the back. US military personnel carried Bobby Black, wrapped in blankets and on a wheelchair, up the steps. He had a drip alongside him, held by a USAF nurse. Susan Black fussed over her husband attentively, though I noticed she did not appear to be speaking to him. Maybe he had been sedated. Perhaps there was no point in attempting a conversation.

I wasn't able to see the Vice-President at any point during the journey back to Scotland, though I took it as a good sign that he was in a wheelchair rather than lying on a bed or gurney. I asked Johnny Lee how he looked.

'I saw him for a few minutes until the doctors told me to wait outside,' he replied. 'He was conscious but . . . but not all there, y'know? Like he has been drugged or something. He looked like a blob of a man.'

'That's what the British doctors told me. What do yours say?'

'Hypothermia, exposure, shock for sure. Probably some kind of psychotropic or other mind-bending drugs were used on him.'

'Is this journey altogether wise?' I wondered as we waited while they bundled the Vice-President off the Chinook and on to the waiting plane for Aberdeen. Johnny Lee shrugged.

'The British doctors didn't think so,' I persisted.

'Wise? What is wise any more? It is inevitable, is all. We can't risk . . .'

'Anything more happening to him?'

'Yeah. And neither can you.'

That much was true. Johnny Lee told me that two women walking their dogs in the early hours of the morning had seen a naked man chained to a beach hut on the strand at Wells-next-the-Sea. The area has a nudist beach among the dunes, but even Norfolk nudists are not brave enough to risk exposure at the end of October. There are a hundred or so beach huts all along the strand, and he was manacled to one, lying in a heap, naked except for a rough blue blanket.

'He couldn't talk properly,' Johnny Lee explained, 'just mumbling and making sounds, but the dog-walkers recognized him.'

'Why not fly him immediately back to the US if he's fit for travel?' I suggested.

'Officially,' Johnny Lee replied, 'because of medical advice about a long journey, and because Susan Fein Black wants her husband to remain in Scotland until he is definitely fit for a transatlantic flight.'

'Unofficially?'

'Unofficially, because no one at the White House wants him back in the United States until the mid-term elections are out

324

of the way Tuesday. In Washington he'd be the ghost of Christmas past. Things are going the administration's way. Why spoil it?'

'You make it sound like political quarantine,' I suggested, 'imposed by Arlo Luntz's focus groups.'

'Arlo had an input. Arlo always has an input. But we also have to check for contamination: physical, mental, spiritual, sexual. Whatever the big guy has already gone through, he's gonna get it twice over. He took it in the ass once from Them, whoever They are, and now it'll be once from Us, poor old fella.'

On the last leg of our journey, the Chinook from Aberdeen Airport landed in the grounds of Castle Dubh nearest to Bolfracks Bothy. I looked out of the window as we landed and could see Dickie Anstruther, perhaps a dozen of his staff, and what looked like more than a hundred American personnel, uniformed Secret Service, soldiers in combat fatigues, doctors, nurses, and others on the edge of the grass where we set down. I unbelted myself and let out a deep sigh.

'You did good,' Johnny Lee said to me as they began to take Bobby Black out from the front of the plane, 'for someone who spent the entire journey shitting himself with fear.'

I was surprised at what it is possible to overcome.

'No helicopters for twenty years and then four flights in one day,' I replied. 'That kind of broke the ice.'

I watched through the window as the wheelchair, draped in a blanket, was carried down the steps and then wheeled across the grass towards Bolfracks Bothy, with Susan Fein Black and her children walking alongside. Her face was still etched with pain and worry. Dozens of the American personnel enveloped them and the wheelchair was lost in another fog, this time of uniforms and people. It occurred to me that I probably would not see Bobby Black ever again.

'I need a drink,' I told Johnny Lee. 'Whisky?'

He nodded. We headed again for Anstruther's private

quarters and Johnny Lee texted Janey Masters, who greeted him with a kiss.

We helped ourselves to whisky and sat around watching the news channels deliver live and at full-length congratulatory news conferences from both sides of the Atlantic. Downing Street announced the Prime Minister's pleasure that the Vice-President was now safe with his wife in Scotland.

There is a well-known political principle that you leave bad news to underlings but corner the good news yourself. Fraser Davis appeared wearing an overcoat in light rain at the stakeout position outside Number Ten and congratulated everyone involved, as if the previous week had been a triumph rather than a disaster.

'This has demonstrated the best of Britain,' Fraser Davis intoned, 'from the north of Scotland down to the south and east of England.'

He praised the police and emergency services in Norfolk and all those agencies that had been part of the biggest manhunt in our history. He ended by saying that 'this magnificent United Kingdom of ours' was 'worth preserving, even if some people are intent on breaking it up.'

I looked at Janey, and she loyally kept a straight face.

'D'you know,' Fraser Davis said with a pouty grin, 'there's an old saying from Tin Pan Alley. You never rewrite a hit. Let's just bear that in mind when it comes to this United Kingdom of ours.' Davis did not mention Dougal Hastie by name or the SNP-inspired referendum on independence for Scotland but, like all good politicians, he did not have to. He was taking an event and jumping all over it. 'And that is why I am glad to say that I shall be attending next Saturday's extraordinary celebration of British sporting achievement with the Island Race rugby at Twickenham. There is always a special spice in our Home Nations when England play Scotland, and Ireland, as you know, will be playing Wales in Dublin on Sunday. These events are not a time for politics.

But they are a time for reflection, a time to remember the ties of affection – and, yes, of rivalry – that bind us. I am pleased to say that the first minister of Scotland has accepted my invitation to attend, as has the Taoiseach. I look forward to a unique experience and a great day at Twickenham as we celebrate the common culture of these great islands.'

'Is there going to be a war with Iran, Prime Minister?' the BBC political editor, John Coxon, could be heard yelling out. Fraser Davis smiled and waved and went inside Number Ten. He did not answer.

Shortly after Fraser Davis finished talking, President Carr walked out into the Rose Garden of the White House and read out a prepared text in which he said that his prayers and the prayers of the American people had been answered. He wished Bobby Black a swift recovery from his ordeal, hoping to welcome him back to the United States soon. Carr also praised the great efforts of the British people in finding the Vice-President, then he turned to leave for the Oval Office and his next meeting. Before he could do so, one of the smarter reporters called out: 'What will Mr Black's role be in future, Mr President?'

Theo Carr pretended he could not hear the question. He made no attempt to answer it.

Other reporters were more pointed.

'Is Mr Black returning to any kind of job or role in the White House?'

'Is there going to be a war with Iran?'

'Was it the ultimatum to the Iranians which led to the release?'

'What future does Bobby Black have now?'

Carr smiled affably, waved, and walked away. There was no answer to any of the shouted questions from President Carr either.

*　　*　　*

327

The news bulletins that evening also showed a series of full-scale FBI raids in Washington: one on the offices of the Speaker of the US House of Representatives, the other on Betty Furedi's home near Capitol Hill. Someone had tipped off a camera crew and all the networks had pictures of several hundred US federal agents running into the Capitol and taking away filing cabinets and boxes of material. It was not disclosed what had been taken. A source close to the Speaker said she was 'saddened' by the developments. Constitutional historians claimed that never in the history of the American Republic had the Speaker of the House of Representatives been the target of such an investigation.

TWENTY-FIVE

Over the next forty-eight hours, the version of Bobby Black's condition put about by Johnny Lee Ironside and others was that he was physically stable, but extremely ill. He was said to be 'disturbed' by his experiences. It was not clear what his illness or condition really was, or what those experiences were, beyond what we had seen in the Internet postings, but the speculation was that Bobby Black had suffered a nervous breakdown. A team of doctors had been flown to Aberdeenshire from the Bethesda Naval Hospital in Maryland.

Privately, I was told by Johnny Lee, the doctors were puzzled. There appeared to be no obvious source of paralysis or physical incapacity. Instead it was concluded that Bobby Black had suffered mental trauma linked to the abuse he had received from the kidnappers and to the drugs he had been given. Johnny Lee said that he personally was now 'out of the loop'. The former Vice-President was being interviewed by psychologists and other specialists who were working for the FBI, CIA, and Pentagon.

'Is he speaking?'

Again a shrug.

'Dunno. In policy terms we are assuming that anything he has ever known, ever, about anything, is now also known to the people who did this, which means it is all compromised.'

In US embassies all over the world, staff had already been ordered to take defensive steps to minimize the damage. Papers were shredded, computer hard drives wiped, agents of influence offered new positions, even new identities.

The day after Bobby Black was discovered on the Norfolk beach and flown to Scotland, our intelligence services had a breakthrough on the Heathrow plot, although for a time it was an unwelcome breakthrough that threatened to disturb everything. The surveillance cameras inside her family home in Hounslow showed that Hasina Iqbal dressed for work with special care that morning, as she always did when she was preparing for something important. She sat in her bedroom applying eye make-up and looking at her image in the mirror. She brushed her hair and pushed it carefully behind the hejab so not one strand was showing. Her brother Shawfiq had long gone from the family home, a month before.

At the beginning of October, the watchers logged Shawfiq telling Hasina and the rest of the family that he was planning not to be around in London for a few weeks. He said he was travelling to Pakistan, though Hasina admitted later that when she watched him pack his clothes it did not look as if that was where he was going. Shawfiq stuffed clothes for cool and wet weather in a suitcase, plus two cheap but new business suits he had recently purchased, a couple of stiff white shirts and three ties. Hasina was puzzled. Why would her brother need shirts and ties and business suits for Pakistan? Why was he going there anyway? She suspected that he was lying to her and in fact was staying somewhere in England. She also suspected that the moment of decision was coming close, that the attack was imminent, although she did not know the details.

Shortly before he left, Shawfiq was recorded instructing

Hasina that she was to do exactly as one of his devout friends from the Green Mosque in Slough, Waheed Hussain, told her. This unnerved Hasina still further. Waheed Hussain was someone unknown, a stranger to her and the family. On the day Shawfiq did leave, he brought Waheed to the family home in Hounslow for the first time. Hasina disliked him from the start. She disliked almost everything about him – from the way he looked to the way he spoke; to his unbending views on their supposedly shared faith. Shawfiq kissed his mother and grandmother and then Hasina herself. There were tears in his eyes.

'Goodbye, little sister,' he said, and then he was gone. And Waheed was still there.

Hasina later told the police from Counter Terrorism Command that her faith was based on the Holy Koran, on the example of the Prophet, and on the idea that God wanted her to help others and to bring them the joys and the peace of the one true religion. She knew that Waheed was different. He was, as Hasina put it, 'the kind of man who thinks that the word of God is identical to whatever is in his own best interests.' The surveillance teams followed Shawfiq not to Pakistan but to a house in Slough, used by the conspirators for the final four weeks of training before the attack. It was also the place where they filmed their martyrdom videos. While the stakeout of the Slough property continued, Waheed began to turn up every few days without invitation at the Iqbal home. He had been given a list of Hasina's shifts by Shawfiq so that he was always able to arrive when she was at home, and that compounded her dislike of him day by day.

She did not like his brush of a beard. She did not like his arrogance. She especially did not like his dark-eyed certainty that what he wanted was also the Will of God, a phrase he intoned repeatedly and with absolute conviction. It seemed to Hasina increasingly unlikely that the Will of God, would be identical to the Will of Waheed. Throughout that month of

October, throughout that month that Bobby Black came to Scotland, disappeared, and then reappeared, Waheed was filmed and recorded repeatedly travelling from the safe house in Slough and turning up with new instructions for Hasina, and new items for her to smuggle into the airport.

'These are the first items necessary for the Plan,' he said, as he was filmed handing her a small package wrapped in plastic sandwich bags and clingfilm. 'God be with you, sister. You are an instrument in the furtherance of His Will.'

Hasina took the items and blanched. She loathed the word 'instrument'. She was a woman of flesh and blood. A human being. The Prophet, May Peace Be Upon Him, treated women with courtesy, humanity, and dignity, listening to their views and acting upon their advice and wisdom. Anyone who had the wit to read and understand the Holy Koran could see this. So who was this bristle-faced Waheed to tell her what to do? What had she allowed herself to become involved in? And then, most discouragingly, she worried why her brother Shawfiq had left her like this.

'It is the Will of Allah that we serve Him,' Waheed said repeatedly, by way of encouragement, not recognizing that his words had the opposite effect. Again and again it sounded more like the will of Waheed, with Allah being invoked to make sure Waheed's instructions were carried out without argument. On each occasion Hasina and Waheed spoke throughout that October they were alone, as her brother had arranged. They sat in the kitchen of the tiny terraced house but, for the sake of propriety, the door was always left open. Since her father's death, Hasina's mother had worked at a catering company that made food for the airlines at Heathrow, but her deaf and yet not entirely blind grandmother from Sind would sit in her usual place on the couch in the living room, watching (when she could stay awake) to ensure that nothing infringed the girl's honour. With Waheed, Hasina knew that nothing ever would, at least not in the way the phrase was usually meant.

'What exactly are we doing this for?' she asked, as he handed over the second consignment of sandwich bags to be smuggled into the airport, a few days after the first.

'Sister,' Waheed answered her, as if shocked at the impertinence of any question, 'the Chosen Instruments of His Will do not need to know.'

Waheed gave a bow of false humility. If she had been braver she would have pulled his beard and slapped his stupid face. Instead she sat meekly as Waheed lectured that the most difficult thing she would have to do was not smuggling the goods into Heathrow. That would be easy. The difficult part would be to make sure the items were not discovered once they were airside. There were numerous security checks. Staff were aware of the constant scrutiny. Lockers were repeatedly searched by hand and with sniffer dogs.

'You must listen carefully,' Waheed instructed repeatedly, as if talking to a child. 'You must follow the Plan. It is God's Plan.'

Some men do this with women, Hasina thought. Keep them in a state of infancy. Navdeep does not do this.

'Navdeep treats me as an equal,' she whispered to herself as Waheed went on with his idiotic lecture. 'In some ways he treats me as better than him. Whereas Waheed says the same things over and over as if I were a child . . .' No, she thought. Not a child. A donkey. Sometimes when she looked at his pale face and brush of a beard she wanted to laugh or bray exactly like a donkey, but she was fearful. She understood Waheed. He was a man who wanted nothing in this life, only in the next. He could kill without compunction because he lived without compassion. Throughout October, Waheed said, she was to tape the things he gave her to the inside of her upper thigh inside her underpants. He said this without any salacious sense of delight. The inside of her thigh was nothing to him. The items were small, tiny bits and pieces, fragments, innocuous by themselves. She would take them to prearranged drops inside Heathrow Terminal One and leave them airside. She would leave them exactly where he instructed – *exactly where he instructed*, he repeated several times.

'Our brothers and sisters will take up the challenge of the next stage of the Plan,' Waheed said. 'You need not know who this will be.'

Hasina listened in her accustomed silence, her heart pounding. She had made tea and offered him homemade cakes. He sipped the tea and ate nothing. She would do as he said, at least for now, all the time aware that there was a decision to be made, and she knew she would have to make it soon. Very soon. Navdeep had asked her to marry him.

'This is all plastic,' Waheed said, handling Hasina the next small bundle. She turned it in her hand and saw some metal parts, which she held towards him. '*Mostly* plastic,' Waheed corrected himself. 'But not a problem.'

Not a problem for you, Hasina thought. In fact, not much of a problem for her, either. Waheed had once worked at the airport as a driver for one of the food preparation companies, and he was aware of the security measures and how Heathrow operated. Throughout the months of preparation for the bomb plot, he did not work. He existed on incapacity benefit and housing benefit, paid for by the British taxpayer, and occasionally he boasted that they were paying for him to bring about their own destruction. Heathrow, he lectured her, was a city within a city, with its own catering, security, and internal transportation facilities.

'And its own weaknesses,' Waheed said, 'because there are always weaknesses in any system devised by man. Laziness, familiarity, stupidity. We shall exploit them all.'

The metal detectors at the security screening stations for airport staff were one of the weaknesses that he had identified. The detectors could be set with different degrees of sensitivity, but mostly they were fixed deliberately so as *not* to be set off by small metal items such as watches, jewellery, belts, and shoe buckles. Setting the screening equipment too sensitively slowed down the process of bringing in the workers at every shift change.

'Time,' Waheed repeatedly pointed out, licking his pink lips above his beard, 'to the Western decadent mindset, is money. To us, it is opportunity.'

In preparation for her smuggling, Hasina had watched the screening of passengers as they passed through into Terminal Five or Terminal One, and had compared the procedures to those employed on staff like herself. She marvelled at the inconsistencies.

Sometimes she would watch the ordinary air travellers remove their shoes in one line while in another line a metre away they were told to keep their shoes on. Why would a shoe bomber get into the line where his shoes were screened? It made no sense. Sometimes passengers were told to take their laptop computers out of their bags, while on other occasions they were told to keep the computers in the bags, and on still other occasions they were told to switch them on. Waheed was fond of saying it was a system without any coherence, built on whim, for social control rather than security.

'And being England,' Waheed observed, his stiff beard bouncing with delight at his own intelligence, 'people fall into line and no one ever complains.'

'Like sheep,' Hasina for once agreed, 'happy to walk to the slaughter.'

At Heathrow she was screened by people she saw almost every day of her working life, and she had become friends with the security staff. Sometimes they flirted a little or indulged in banter, talking about a television programme or some major development in the news.

'What did you think about the Vice-President disappearing in Scotland?' one of the security men was heard asking her one day that October as she passed through the metal detector.

'I have not heard much about it,' Hasina commented. This

was untrue. She had been transfixed by the news reports of the search on the Scottish hillsides.

'Idiot probably wandered off,' one of the other security staff, a Polish woman, added. A Sikh woman chipped in, 'Shouldn't be allowed out without a babysitter.'

They all shared a laugh and Hasina passed through the scanner, the plastic bag Waheed had given her securely fastened inside her knickers with gaffer's tape. For the security staff, she decided, the screening was mostly a matter of appearing to go through the motions rather than actively searching for dangerous or illicit goods. She was trusted, and she felt her abaya and hejab helped prevent people from searching her more intimately. Day by day she grew increasingly confident that she could do as Waheed instructed, and smuggle all the equipment airside, undetected – unless, of course, she herself chose otherwise. And she was beginning to choose otherwise. She realized she would have to talk to Navdeep. To tell him. It would be the most difficult conversation of her life.

'There will be metal items now,' Waheed told her after she had carried the first three loads of plastic and gels success-fully into the airport. 'But the drop-off point is the same.'

He had given her a plastic tool, like an Allen key, to open the back of the panel behind the women's toilet in the staff area, airside Terminal One. He instructed Hasina to unscrew the panel, place it carefully on the lavatory seat so no one peeping under the door could see it resting on the floor, and then to put the items inside the opening, behind the piping. She was then to screw the panel back on the wall. On each occasion the trip had been a success. Easier than she had predicted. Waheed told her that the items she had taken inside had been successfully removed from behind the panel by another Instrument of God and placed somewhere safe, ready for 'the Day'.

'And when is "the Day"?' she had asked, but Waheed refused even to listen to such a question.

336

'Now, sister,' Waheed said on this, his fourth visit that month, 'now we have a more difficult challenge. Some metal parts.'

'What are these things?' she asked him, blurting out the question even though she knew he would never answer it.

'Sister, it is better that you do not know.'

The metal parts included what the Americans called 'box cutters', and the British call Stanley knives. But these were not the fat and rounded Stanley knives favoured in England. Instead they were flat versions.

'These,' Waheed held up a bag containing what looked like a number of fat little fuses with a thread coming out of them. 'Be very careful with these.'

'Why?'

'They are detonators for causing explosives to detonate, sister,' Waheed instructed her. She must have looked alarmed and nervous. 'They are harmless provided you treat them as I will instruct.'

Waheed disassembled everything so that they were in the smallest possible pieces, and distributed them among three more plastic sandwich bags, one for each of the following three days. He hinted to Hasina that she was not the only courier operating in Heathrow, and that the other courier was also a devout woman.

'In Terminal One?' she asked. Waheed shrugged.

'Now, for the metal parts,' he said by way of an answer, 'we will use a different system.'

Hasina felt nothing but contempt though she did gradually discover a way of enticing information from him by expressing an oblique interest. If, for example, she hinted at Waheed's devastating wisdom, his beard would bristle upwards, his lips would moisten, and his tongue would loosen.

'You must have planned things very well,' she said on one occasion, lowering her gaze modestly, 'to keep everything hidden inside the airport. I am on my sixth load tomorrow. That demands cleverness to hide.'

Her eyes flickered back to his face in time to see the brief smile of pleasure that split the brush of his beard; his slack lips opened showing yellow and misshapen teeth.

'There are ways,' he beamed. 'There are places.'

Waheed volunteered the information that everything Hasina took airside was taken from the cavity in the woman's lavatory and transferred into a hollowed space in the brickwork in another of the staff lavatories, in a building used to house the trucks that pull the baggage trailers to the aircraft. Hasina assumed it was a men's lavatory, although Waheed did not confirm this. Again she praised his intelligence and creativity.

'And you yourself came upon this idea,' she commented, 'that in itself is a clever and masterful thing.'

'*The Shawshank Redemption*,' Waheed explained, with a grin. Hasina did not understand. It was a Hollywood prison escape movie, he said. Hasina was even more puzzled.

'I have not seen this film.'

Waheed told her that it was good that a devout Muslim woman did not see such a movie, or indeed any movies based upon the kind of decadence found in American society and culture. He revealed that in the film one of the prisoners escaped from the cruelties of the jail by digging out a false wall in his cell.

'The idea of the false wall inspired us,' Waheed confirmed.

It was one of the very few times Hasina remembered him laughing out loud, amused at the idea of using a Hollywood movie plot against Western interests and decadence. Waheed saw an irony. Hasina saw an irony too, though it was a different irony; the idea that Waheed's supposed creativity derived from a Hollywood scriptwriter. When it came to the others involved in the Plan, Waheed occasionally spoke of 'brother Umar', 'the Pilot', and of 'brother Ibrahim' and 'brother Assad' and 'sister Rasheeda', but it was not clear which of these people were connected directly to the plot and which were merely sympathizers. When Hasina asked him about her own brother, he said simply that 'brother Shawfiq' was also 'an instrument of God's will and was in a safe place waiting to play his part in the Plan.' Waheed talked with particular fondness about brother Umar and 'the Pilot', who appeared to have some kind of position of leadership within the movement.

'Brother Umar asked me to tell you that he is pleased with your successes,' Waheed told her on one occasion. She looked away so he could not see what she was thinking.

Each day, when she was carrying her contraband, Hasina would say a short prayer as she taped the bag of parts to her crotch under her abaya and inside her underpants. She would pray not to be caught, and then she would pray to be given the wisdom to know what she should do about telling Navdeep. She grew in confidence, though she wrote in her diary that still expected true wisdom about what to do next to come to her like a wave of knowledge that would guide her in her big decision; but the wave stubbornly refused to come. On the day she was due to take the first of the box-cutter blades into the airport, she was especially nervous. Metal parts of the size she was expected to carry would almost certainly show up on the detectors. But Waheed had a plan. Waheed always had a plan. He had borrowed an old pair of Hasina's work shoes and returned them to her with new brass buckles fixed, he said, by a brother who worked in a cobbler's in Hayes. Waheed instructed Hasina to wear the shoes with the new buckles but also to take a pair of trainers so she could change when she got to work.

'Leave the buckle shoes in your locker, not in the usual drop,' he said. 'They will be dealt with.'

'But you said the lockers were not safe,' she replied, puzzled.

'Sister Hasina, do not worry. The blades are under here.' Waheed turned her work shoes over so she could see that new soles had been put on each one. When she put on the shoes the soles felt stiff, but otherwise appeared normal. 'The metal is small and so low, right on the floor, it will not show up on the metal detectors, god willing, and, if it does, blame it on the buckles. When you get airside, please to leave the shoes in your locker and change into trainers. The shoes will be returned to the locker the next day. Bring them back here. We will place new soles on them, and repeat what we have done.'

Hasina did as she was told, trusting that someone with access to her locker would remove the blades and place them with the other equipment, which is what happened. Waheed was very pleased.

'This is indeed a great mission,' she told Waheed. Again, Waheed's eyes flashed with pride. He replied that what they were planning would 'set the world alight.' They would be great heroes as well as great martyrs.

'What we will do will make the events in New York on September the eleventh seem like nothing,' Waheed instructed her, wagging a bony finger in her direction. Hasina smiled modestly and looked at the floor. The word 'martyrs' made her feel sick.

When she returned from her shift on the day that Bobby Black reappeared on the beach in Norfolk, Hasina had made up her mind. Wisdom had not come to her as she had hoped in a big sweeping wave, but it had come, drop by drop, in a series of small events. There was her loathing for Waheed, her separation from her brother, who no longer guided her, and who, she had concluded, had used her for his own ends. And then there were the videos she had seen on the television, of the torture of the old American, the man Waheed called 'Satan Black'. Hasina understood why people hated the policies of the United States, and she did too. But she could not understand why people would do terrible things to a man old enough

340

to be her grandfather. And above all there was Navdeep. She had grown used to his smell, his touch, the gentle warmth of his skin.

She had grown used to his kindness and laughter, his ability to see the best in anyone or anything – exactly the opposite of the profound pessimism of Waheed and her brother. Some days Navdeep would bring her a flower that he had plucked from a garden. Other days it would be a square of chocolate, or a toy, or a postcard or something childish, perhaps a not-very-good poem that he had written while on a late-night managerial shift. They would escape for a few hours to have coffee or a meal. They would slip into a lay-by near Windsor or Slough and sit together in his car. She hungered for his hands upon her and the beauty and pleasure they brought. She knew that his touch made her melt. She would bury her face in his hair and his smell, and she wanted him in a way she had never wanted anything in her life.

'I want to . . . inhale you,' she said once, with a passion that made him laugh. They broke apart from an embrace.

'You want to what?' he smiled.

'Inhale you. Breathe you in. Eat you.'

'Cannibal!'

'I am serious, Navdeep. I want you to be a part of me.'

'I am a part of you,' he said softly, and kissed her again till she felt her insides yearn for him. She had made up her mind. Or her body had made it up for her. She would have Navdeep, and she would have a life. She would choose. She had already chosen. Wisdom, of a sort, had come to her.

The following day, exactly twenty-four hours after Bobby Black's surprising reappearance at the end of October, Hasina Iqbal had a day off from work. She told her grandmother that she was going out to see friends for a few hours. She took with her a small suitcase filled with clothes, jewellery, her copy of the Holy Koran, and her savings. She telephoned

Navdeep and asked him to come to meet her. When his car came into the corner of the car park at the Hounslow Tesco's, Hasina felt her heart turn in somersaults and her breath come in gasps. In that instant, walking towards his car and seeing his smile split his face with happiness, she knew she had made the right decision. He helped her put the small suitcase in the boot.

'You going somewhere?' he said with a grin.

'You once asked me to be your wife,' she said to him. 'And I said it was impossible. You asked me again, and I said that I would think about it. We both know what it means. Moving away. Finding a new life. Not seeing my family. Or yours. Well, I have thought about it, Nav. I will be your wife.' In the car, he leaped towards her and kissed her with joy, but she pushed him away. 'I will, Nav. I will marry you. But first there is something I have to tell you. And there is something I have to do. I will need your help and your patience and your courage and your love. It may take me some time to tell you it all, and when I have finished, you may no longer want to have anything to do with me.' He looked at her stern face, beautiful under the hejab. 'In which case I want you to drop me off at Hounslow Police Station and I will do what I have decided to do, alone.'

'Go on,' he said, brushing his lips on hers quickly. 'Go on, Hasina. I'm listening.'

She licked her lips and began to speak. Once she had begun, it was as if a dam had broken within her, and she could not stop.

'There's this thing going on at the airport,' she began. The watchers were listening to every word, and they grew alarmed. There were emergency calls to the Counter Terrorism Command. The girl was changing sides, and that was not what anyone wanted.

TWENTY-SIX

There are so many versions of what happened next, I don't know which to rely on. Perhaps there are really just two versions, the one of my dreams and the one of my nightmares. Both versions have a great deal in common. Both involve the conclusion of the investigation into the Heathrow plot in the most remarkable way. Both involve Bobby Black, and a scandal – of sorts – that sucked me in. First, the facts.

A brave twenty-year-old Muslim woman – Hasina – and her Sikh boyfriend, Navdeep, went to a west London police station and exposed what would have been the worst terrorist act in British history, perhaps in world history. The plotters were hoping for up to 80,000 dead, although the difficulties of successfully doing what they were attempting – hitting Twickenham rugby ground during an international match with an Airbus taking off from Heathrow – should not be under-estimated. For more than two hours after she arrived at Hounslow police station, specialist female officers from Counter Terrorism Command and the security service MI5 talked with Hasina and persuaded her – at first against her will – to go back home, to go back to work, to say nothing to anyone, and to pretend all was normal for a few days more so as not to alert the plotters.

'It's under control,' Hasina was told. She prayed repeatedly that what she had been told was correct. For obvious reasons no one told her that her every move was being watched and recorded.

As for me, well, two days after Bobby Black's return, while he was still being held incommunicado in Bolfracks Bothy, I checked with Downing Street that my presence in Scotland was no longer necessary and I returned to the United States. I wanted to witness the remarkable turnaround in the midterm elections, to see first-hand how much damage Betty Furedi had done to her party and how much good President Carr had done to his. Of course I also wanted to try to talk with Kristina, if that was ever going to be possible. I knew I had some explaining to do. A lot of explaining to do. Andy Carnwath said that I was not to return to Washington without a face-to-face meeting with Fraser Davis in Downing Street.

It was partly official business, but mostly family matters. The Prime Minister started with praise, telling me that he thought I had handled things in Aberdeenshire 'very well, all things considered.' There was great relief in the United States that Bobby Black was alive and that he was now safe. The immediate sense of emergency with Iran began to recede. There were unattributed news reports from Washington that 'rogue elements within the Iranian Revolutionary Guards' were thought to be behind the kidnapping, and that Secretary of State Andrew Baker had received 'unequivocal assurances' that the Tehran regime would 'bring these elements to revolutionary justice if they can be identified', although officially the Iranian government continued to reject the idea that the kidnappers were Iranian 'unless we are provided with some evidence.'

Fraser Davis was enjoying an unaccustomed good press on both sides of the Atlantic, and taking the credit for doing something right, even if there was still considerable mystery about what exactly had happened to the Vice-President.

'Do we think there is any connection with the airport plot?' I asked him when we sat having coffee in his small private study in Downing Street. It was, unusually, just the two of us. He shook his head.

'Not as far as the security service is aware,' he answered carefully. 'The big question is where Black was held. They tell me that if they can crack that, they might get somewhere on the who and why.'

The search for where the kidnappers had tortured Bobby Black was continuing, while on the Internet the conspiracy theories and questions piled up. The usual suspects – al Qaeda, the Iranians, Mossad, the CIA, the Russians; everyone short of the Freemasons and the Illuminati – were named in one place or another as being behind the disappearance. Whatever the truth, and numerous investigations and inquiries had been launched on both sides of the Atlantic, things between London and Washington appeared to be back on track. Theo Carr publicly congratulated the British for everything they had done to find Bobby Black, and seemed to forget his previous anger that we had somehow lost him in the first place. Carr also announced that his new Vice-President Conrad Shultz would be visiting the United Kingdom, Europe, and 'other destinations' within the next few weeks 'to review the security situation and make recommendations and to thank the government and people of Great Britain.'

'General Shultz is not going on any grouse moors,' Davis lectured me, pushing aside his coffee, a moist lip prominently pouting in my direction. 'You got that? No more smart ideas on your part.'

I nodded. 'Yes, Prime Minister.'

'Probably best that you are not anywhere around Shultz for this visit. We don't want any reminders of disappearing predecessors, do we?'

'No, Prime Minister.'

There was a short pause while he changed gear.

'Now, what about Fiona?' he said.

'What about her?'

'Well?'

'I . . . she and I haven't talked much, if that's what you mean. There's not been time.' That was a lie. I had nothing but time in Aberdeenshire, waiting for Bobby Black to be found. One of my least appealing characteristics is that when I hate dealing with something in my personal life, I pretend it does not exist. My shattered relationship with Fiona most certainly did exist. A divorce would soon be a formality.

'You two need to talk. You need to make time. And I need this saga to come to a conclusion before the newspapers pick it up again. Happy or otherwise.'

'I know, I know. I'll call her.'

He knew I was lying, and if Andy Carnwath knew about me and Kristina, then so would Fraser Davis. Perhaps he had known from more or less the start, though when there is a clash between public duties and private lives it is sometimes necessary for everyone involved to engage in various levels of deceit. He gave a little cough and then pouted his lip.

'I'd like to invite you – and Fiona – to be my guests at the Island Race rugby matches at Twickenham on Saturday.'

It was not actually an invitation. It was an instruction. Given the guest list – the Irish Taoiseach, the Scottish First Minister Dougal Hastie and the Leader of the Opposition – it was also an honour.

The idea of spending hours watching a bunch of big men in shorts smash each other up has never appealed to me, but it was necessary to pretend otherwise.

'Of course, Prime Minister. Thank you very much. I'll look forward to it.'

Unlike previous Prime Ministers who manufactured an interest in sport to forge a bond with ordinary voters, Fraser Davis was genuinely a fan. He had played rugby at Eton and Oxford, and the fact that the Irish Taoiseach Siobhan Kinsella and Scottish First Minister Dougal Hastie were also attending demonstrated he was correct in assuming the political import-ance of the matches.

'I want you to talk with Fiona,' Fraser Davis insisted, 'and decide by the end of the weekend whether you are going to make it work and get reconciled, or end it all and get divorced. Piss or get off the pot, Alex. I want it sorted by Sunday. Andy will announce it on Monday.'

'I . . .' I did not know how to handle a personal ultimatum from my brother-in-law. His lips were pouting towards me in a way I found insufferable.

'I mean it Alex,' he pouted some more. 'Sunday. You have to manage things or they will manage you. You can get away with more or less anything in the newspapers as long as people think you have moved on. By Monday you will have moved on, at least in the pages of the *Daily Mail*. Fix it or finish it.'

'But this is my marriage, Prime Minister.'

'And it is my sister,' he snapped back, 'whom you married shortly before I announced you were to be Ambassador to Washington, which, in case you have forgotten, makes your marriage my political problem. I went out on a limb for you, Alex. All I can promise you is that it should prove to be a good weekend to bury bad news. You got that?'

'Yes.'

'One more thing, I hear from Andy that Janey Masters has been doing her bit for Anglo–American relations.'

I raised an eyebrow.

'What did you hear?'

'What is there to hear?'

'She . . . has formed a friendship with Bobby Black's Chief of Staff, yes.'

'Good. He's on his way up.'

'Is he? How do you know?'

'Janey. She has what you might call an impeccable source. Enjoy your trip.'

Davis returned to his paperwork without saying any more. I left Downing Street and was driven to Heathrow Airport, my cheeks still red with embarrassment and anger. How dare he tell me how to run my life?

'Because he can,' I muttered to myself.

I took the plane to Washington and sat drinking too much champagne, pondering whether there was anything salvageable in my relationship with Fiona. The answer became more obvious the more I drank – No. Then I wondered whether there was any realistic chance of resurrecting what had been my relationship with Kristina. This was more difficult, but after even more champagne I concluded probably not, and yet I would refuse to give up on Kristina until I had no choice but to do so, at least in part because I could not bear the thought of another relationship ending in failure.

I arrived back in Washington that Tuesday night, the day American voters went to the polls. It was an astonishing moment. You could sense that Theo Carr was about to do it again. He – and the emergency over Bobby Black – had turned the campaign around in the closing two weeks, just as the Manila bombing had done two years previously. I sipped a few bottles of Sam Adams alone, in front of the TV, and watched the screens of the American networks turn red – red – red – as Theo Carr, underestimated at every turn, for a second time snatched victory from defeat. Democrats complained of unspecified 'dirty tricks', but it was clear that Betty Furedi's reputation had been permanently damaged by her own missteps. She was taking her party down with her. FOXNews – which tends to operate as the publicity arm for the Republican Party – turned into a gloat-fest. It showcased one of its many hyperactive commentators shrieking that 'the writing was on the wall' for Betty Furedi.

'The biblical writing on the wall said: *Mene, mene, tekel upharsin*, which translates as: "You have been weighed in the balance and found wanting." Betty Boop, your time is up. This is Mickey O'Hanlon, and that's the Unvarnished Truth.'

I felt like calling Mr O'Hanlon and suggesting he stick to decaffeinated coffee.

Betty Furedi held on to her own House seat in San Francisco – just – but the red TV tide meant she was no longer going to be Speaker. Republicans made gains all across the country and Furedi was forced to concede control of the House of Representatives in an historic shift, one of the few times ever in American history that a sitting President, after two years in the White House, had seen gains for his party rather than losses at mid-term. The Senate also swung the Republicans' way, even though only a third of the seats were up. It ended evenly balanced 50-50, but the Vice-President has the casting vote in the Senate in the event of a tie, meaning there, too, effective Republican control. From dire political difficulties and even the possibility of impeachment a couple of weeks back, that November night things really were looking good for Theo Carr. He had a mandate for his party, for the first time a compliant Congress, and a new Vice-President content to work in the shadows. God was in his Republican Heaven. All was good with the world as President Carr defied the laws of political gravity, yet again.

The following morning Carr appeared at the White House, beaming.

'The people have spoken,' he said, 'and with a loud and clear voice. They want this administration to work with Congress to do the business of America. My first task will be to ask the new Congressional leadership to finance America's armed forces with the weapons systems they require for the dangerous world of the twenty-first century.'

Conrad Shultz was nowhere to be seen. He had already been nicknamed 'Mr Invisible' by some newspapers. From Theo Carr's point of view, perhaps that was no bad thing compared to his predecessor. The Wednesday morning

US newspaper headline-makers called Carr 'a political Houdini', the 'Comeback Kid', and 'the great escape artist', the man who constantly looked as if he was about to lose elections and then turned things around at two minutes to midnight. Comparisons were made with President Harry Truman's turnaround victory in 1948, the Midwest haberdasher who confounded the pundits and pollsters, while internationally things really began to ease. The President of Iran offered public congratulations to President Carr on the success of his party, and said that 'the people of the Islamic Republic of Iran' were delighted that Bobby Black had returned to his family. He repeated that he had 'no evidence' of any Iranian link in the kidnapping, but he promised to punish any perpetrators of the kidnap if they were ever found. In the meantime he offered to hold talks 'at the highest level and without preconditions' with the United States to resolve 'remaining differences between our two great peoples.'

The Americans rebuffed the suggestion of direct talks, but they did so politely, and while a military attack on Iran still seemed possible, it no longer looked inevitable or even likely. Privately, the White House briefed the Reptiles that the evidence against the Iranian government being involved in Bobby Black's disappearance was 'circumstantial at best', but 'rogue elements' of the Revolutionary Guards were still being sought, along with their supposed accomplices in Great Britain.

The French President offered to mediate between Washington and Tehran; though, in my experience, French presidents always offer to mediate because it helps confirm their existence to the rest of the world. American forces remained on high alert, but stopped short of any further movement towards Iranian waters. Even so, these were nervous times. Six motorboats with armed Iranian Revolutionary Guards approached an American Aegis class cruiser in the middle of the night in international waters sixty kilometres from the Iranian coast. The Americans opened fire from the cruiser and from helicopters, killing at least twenty Iranians and capturing twelve. There was talk of the prisoners being returned to Iran, 'in due course', as part of a wider *rapprochement*, though this detachment of Guards was definitively branded a 'rogue element' by the Iranian government. It all seemed quite convenient.

The *New York Times* congratulated President Carr for his cool demeanour. Their lead editorial said: 'We should not go to war with Iran based on a button, some Internet videos, a couple of maps, and a slender piece of thread. We could not convict someone on such circumstantial evidence. We cannot launch a circumstantial war. George Bush made that mistake in 2003 in Iraq over Weapons of Mass Destruction. We are confident that, to his credit, President Carr will not make the same mistake.'

The Pew Research Centre showed 73 per cent of American voters agreed with this sentiment.

As for Bobby Black, well, as I was preparing the following Friday night for the red-eye back to London and the Twickenham 'Island Race' rugby match, we were told that he and his family had set off in a US military aircraft from Aberdeen to the United States. The timetable of the homecoming was dictated by Arlo Luntz, who decreed in the hours after the extraordinary election victory that it was safe to bring Bobby Black home. He and Susan Black returned to the family ranch in Montana for the long process of recuperation. But that week stories started to emerge, first on American political blogs and then in the newspapers, referring to Bobby Black's 'flaky' past, with hints that he had conspired in his own disappearance.

Unnamed former colleagues claimed on the Drudge Report and The Huffington Post that for years Bobby Black had suffered strange mood swings and had abused prescription drugs. More or less every day in the late afternoons, the

351

bloggers claimed, at four o'clock precisely, Black locked himself away in his White House office for an hour or so to 'feed his habit.' I read the Internet stories with growing disbelief. It made me feel as if the fog in Scotland was as nothing compared to this new fog of information being leaked in Washington. Some of these unsourced stories seemed just crazy, but once the hints of mental instability appeared, they multiplied like bacterial culture in a Petri dish. Bobby Black's odd behaviour, the stories said, included 'abusive and threatening language to junior staffers and members of Congress', plus the threat of punching one staffer who dared to question the Vice-President's opinions.

'Bobby Black was a man who liked to be loathed,' one person, identified only as a 'senior former staffer', explained. 'He revelled in the hatred of others. He had political Tourette's – he used and abused people without mercy.' The anonymous staffer went on to talk about Bobby Black's 'Ego Wall', covered in prized examples of the hatred for him on Capitol Hill and elsewhere. As I read the quotes, I realized this account was almost an exact reprise of the conversation I had had months before with Johnny Lee Ironside, even though the source was not named.

The *coup de grâce* to Bobby Black's reputation was delivered on television at the end of that week by his oldest political friend, Paul Comfort. I was sitting in the British Airways first-class lounge at Dulles Airport getting ready to board my flight back to London, when I saw Comfort on FOXNews.

Any interview with Paul Comfort was a rare event. Despite being regarded as one of the top five business people in the United States, he was habitually invisible in public. He had not done any TV network interviews since the shooting incident on the Texas quail hunt the previous year, and then suddenly here he was, sitting on his porch on his Texas ranch in an open-necked designer sports shirt, sipping iced water, chatting with FOX's chief national correspondent, a doe-eyed bleach blonde with a stiff helmet of golden hair. The bleach blonde reminded viewers that it was the very same ranch that had been the scene of the unfortunate shooting incident. Comfort smiled as he spoke of his delight that Bobby Black had returned to the United States, and was recovering. He spoke at first warmly about his old friend and said that he wished Bobby and Susan Black well.

'I'm glad he is on the road to wellness,' he said. 'But Bobby – well, he still has problems.'

The doe-eyed bleach blonde cocked her head sideways to listen attentively. 'And what kind of problems are they, Paul?' she asked with great concern.

They were calling my flight, but I stayed in front of the TV to hear the rest of what he had to say. Comfort suddenly gave a remarkably different account of the shooting incident on the quail hunt from the story he had offered more than a year before.

'Bobby changed,' Comfort said, shaking his head regretfully, 'and the White House changed him.'

'In what way?'

'For the worse. Bobby wanted power but could not handle it . . . It made him . . . mean. Unstable. Sick, in a way.'

'For example?'

'For example, that time he shot me . . .' There was a long pause.

'Yes?' Doe-Eyes prompted. Comfort looked at his hands.

'Well, I said at the time that I walked into his line of fire, and that it was my fault. That was the way it appeared to me at the time. But . . . the more I think on it, the more I guess it was deliberate. Bobby'd done that kind of thing before.'

There was a cutaway of the interviewer with a face of astonishment, mock astonishment I thought, like the outrage in a Bateman cartoon. I stood back in awe.

'Ambassador, we need to board you now,' one of the BA cabin staff said.

'One minute!' I responded firmly. 'This is dynamite!'

I could not make up my mind what I was seeing. Was it a phoney interview on a phoney news channel with a phoney TV presenter offering up . . . well, what was it offering up? A phoney view of the past? America's equivalent of Stalin's purges with some old political leader being suddenly airbrushed out? Or just a different view? A recantation? The Truth? A rewriting of history now that Bobby Black could no longer defend himself? The interviewer knew what was coming and led Comfort through it like a seductress pulling her willing partner into bed.

'Are you saying, sir, that you believe Vice-President Black shot you deliberately?'

Paul Comfort nodded. 'That's the way it looks to me now. Like I say, the facts don't change, but the way I think of them does. The one thing not out in the public domain is that we had a fight that day, Bobby and me, right as we set off on the hunt. He had popped pills, and as a friend I was always on his case to get help on that, and he got mad with me and . . . and I always wondered whether he made a mistake or really meant to . . . you know . . . *do it* . . . Bobby had a mean temper. Way back when we were kids . . .'

Paul Comfort's voice trailed away. Doe-Eyes helped out again.

'Of course as everyone knows, you grew up together,' she prompted.

'Yes, we did,' Comfort agreed, pulling himself together. 'Back in Billings, Montana. Well, one time Bobby 'n' me had a serious falling out. We must've been like ten years old or so. And I am cycling home when Bobby comes at me with a brick, hits me in the side of the head and near kills me. The look on his face when he filled me full of buckshot was just the same. I love him like a brother, but sometimes I just fear for what is going on in Bobby's mind. It's a dark place.'

The interviewer mumbled a few thoughts about the former

354

Vice-President's condition. Comfort ended with a smile to the cameras.

'All I would say is that, Bobby, if you're watching this, or any of your family are watching this, we just want you to get *well*.'

The way Comfort said the word made it sound as if the former Vice-President of the United States was an escaped lunatic, capable of anything and suffering from a profound mental illness.

I watched the report open jawed. I did not know what to believe. Everything was turned on its head. I walked on to the aircraft and we took off for Heathrow, but my head was back in the fog on the Scottish hills once more.

When I stepped off the plane at Heathrow first thing that Saturday morning I was told that Bobby and Susan Black were now at the family ranch, in total seclusion, resting and recovering, and there would be no further bulletins about Bobby Black's condition 'for several weeks.' It was rumoured that he was under twenty-four-hour suicide watch, though officially it was a 'twenty-four-hour observation of his condition.' In Britain, one tabloid, with the good taste for which it is famed, had a blurry picture of Bobby Black wrapped in a tartan blanket and sitting in a wheelchair, with the headline: '*Wacko Blacko*'. They claimed that the man who was 'once one heartbeat away from having his finger on the nuclear trigger has now been certified nuts by American doctors.' Well, that was one way of putting it. Paul Comfort's interview changed everything, and allowed every prejudice about mental illness to be replayed in public. The White House, at least, appeared to play it straight.

'Former Vice-President Black is now a private citizen,' White House Communications Director Sandy McAuley said when asked at a press briefing about his condition. 'We wish him well, and we respect his desire for ongoing privacy. I will take no further questions on the subject.'

'What is the White House view of Paul Comfort's statement that he was shot deliberately by the Vice-President and that while he was in office he popped pills every afternoon at four o'clock?'

'We have no information about that.'

'None, Sandy? Come on.'

'None.'

'Did Paul Comfort and Bobby Black argue about the Vice-President's drug habit?'

'I have no information beyond what you already know.'

'How compromised is our national security by the Black kidnapping?' AP's chief correspondent Dan Weiss asked. McAuley took a deep breath.

'We have every confidence that the national security of the United States has not been impaired by the disappearance,' he responded. He was obviously well prepared to answer this question. 'Quite the opposite. The wide-ranging security review being conducted by Vice-President Shultz, plus the resolute response from US forces and our allies, and the moves towards compliance by Iran, all suggest that in the long term our national security has been enhanced, particularly now that we have a Republican Congress committed to passing a new Defence Appropriations Bill.'

'Why can't you just tell us, Sandy, who was it who kidnapped the Vice-President and made the videos on the Internet?' Weiss persisted. 'What are your theories?'

McAuley shook his head. 'We are not doing theories. We are doing facts. The President intends to announce a bipartisan Commission of Inquiry, alongside the inquiries already being conducted by the Secret Service, the FBI, and other agencies, and those in Great Britain. I do not know the answer to your question, Dan. If I did, I would tell the investigators.'

An official car and driver picked me up at Heathrow and took me to one of the airport hotels. I was not staying at my

London apartment, which I had left to Fiona, at least until we could come to some kind of final decision about our marriage and the division of assets. In the hotel room I showered, shaved, and changed into warm clothes for the rugby game at Twickenham, but I kept the TV on because the news from the United States was coming thick and fast. While I had been flying across the Atlantic the White House announced a reshuffling of key staff. Janey Masters was right. Johnny Lee Ironside was to be promoted to replace Stephanie Alejandro as the President's Chief of Staff with immediate effect, a very significant promotion. Alejandro was to return to her husband and legal practice in Albuquerque. There were rumours of more changes at the top, but Sandy McAuley said he had 'no further announcements scheduled at this time.' As for Kristina, all through the previous few days, even when I was in Washington, I had continued to call and email, but still nothing, until I stepped out of the shower in the hotel room, at noon British time, seven in the morning in Washington. My cellphone rang. It was an unfamiliar number.

'Alex?'

'Yes.' My heart suddenly pumped. 'Hello, stranger.'

'You back in London?'

She obviously knew I was.

'Yes.'

'We need to talk.' All business.

'I . . . yes. Of course.'

'But not right now,' Kristina informed me. 'I need time. I have big decisions to make about my life and my future, and I don't want you around me when I make them.'

'But—'

'No buts. Being around you distorts my mind, my thought processes and—'

I interrupted. 'That's what happens when you get emotionally attached to someone.'

'Stop it,' she snapped. 'I do not want to hear any of this.

It's not useful to me. I have decisions to make and I will call you when I have made them, right?'

'But—'

'It may not be for a few days or even weeks. I have things . . . to think about.'

'Kristina . . .'

'Alex, look, you were right that you cannot draw straight lines in your heart but I do not want to talk to you for a while. Stop calling me. Just stop, okay? Respect this. Respect me.'

'I need to tell you about Northern Ireland.'

'Damn right you do. You missed your chance. I will call you when I am ready to listen. Goodbye.'

She put down the phone. I mashed my fist in my hand with exasperation.

An hour later a car picked me up to take me to the match. I was in no mood to waste several hours of a November day in the cold in the stands at Twickenham, and I was also in no mood to be part of Fraser Davis's stunt to help retain the Union or to talk with Fiona, but I needed to do as I was told. I called her.

'Fiona Davis,' she said as she answered her mobile phone.

'Ah,' I said, 'I see you have gone back to your maiden name?'

'Now, look, Alex,' she said defensively, 'Listen . . .'

'Sorry, sorry.' I apologized. When things break down, every word can be an offence. 'We need to talk, Fiona.'

'Yes,' she agreed. 'We need to talk.'

'Dinner after the game?' I could hear her sigh. I guessed she had received a similar ultimatum from her brother and wanted to see me as little as I wanted to see her.

'How about a drink instead?' she offered. 'An hour in each other's company might be enough.'

I agreed and we made arrangements.

'Where are you?'

'In the box at Twickenham with my brother and all the Big Knobs. You?'

'On my way. Twenty minutes in this traffic I would guess. See you soon.'

We rang off. At least we had managed a conversation without exploding into anger, which was a kind of progress, I suppose.

I arrived at Twickenham an hour before kickoff. I was led into the new corporate hospitality seating at the South Stand for drinks and canapés. There was a short welcoming line – Fraser Davis, Dougal Hastie, the Taoiseach, Siobhan Kinsella, and a Welshman whose name I did not catch. We shook hands. There was much beaming and joshing for the cameras. I needed a drink. Next to the canapés and the champagne glasses, I saw Fiona, and I went over to be polite.

'I am glad we can talk tonight,' I said.

'Yes,' she agreed. 'We need to be civilized about this.' There was something different about her.

'There's someone else, isn't there?' I asked, even though I could see the answer written all over her face. In truth I did not care.

'You're the one to talk,' she said. 'From what I hear.'

'What do you hear?'

'More than enough.'

'Good,' I added. 'Well, I am pleased for you. As long as it's not Byrne.'

'It's not Byrne. He's . . . it's not Byrne.'

'But you have been talking to him.'

Her face flushed red. 'Who I talk with is my business.'

I could not tell her everything that I knew. She turned her face quickly away from me, and I realized that everything really was broken between us and could never be fixed. Fine. A few minutes later we were escorted to our seats in the VIP area as kickoff time for the game approached. I was pleased to see that Fiona and I were not sitting together; we were not even in the same row. I was sitting next to the Irish Finance minister, who had the manner of a spectacularly dull accountant and who tried to engage me in discussions about inflationary pressures on the European economies and the future of international lending in the years after the credit crunch. I nodded and smiled. On my other side was the Deputy Leader of the Scottish National Party, a fizzy Glaswegian woman who confessed to me that she was a Rangers supporter and had no knowledge of, or interest in, rugby. I liked her immediately.

'Me neither,' I whispered conspiratorially. 'Shall we just get drunk instead?'

She laughed. 'When we are independent we might need a Scottish ambassador in Washington,' she responded. 'Maybe you should apply.'

'Maybe I will.'

I also chatted inconsequentially to the man from the Welsh assembly whose name I never caught. I checked my watch. Two thirty in the afternoon. We stood for the national anthems. As soon as we sat down ready for kickoff, I noticed the arrival of a tall man in a grey suit, Edward Fleming, the security service officer who had briefed us in Aberdeenshire. Fleming was standing where Fraser Davis was seated and whispering in his ear. Fleming whispered for a long time and I watched Davis's face drink in the information with some satisfaction. He kept nodding, pleased. It was something he had been expecting, I decided. Good news. A smile crept over his face. Fleming was telling the Prime Minister that the first of the police raids on the Heathrow conspirators had already begun.

A combined police Counter Terrorism Command, MI5, and SAS team, with regular army backup, had taken control of Heathrow Airport, principally Terminals One and Two. The Gold Commander was in the control tower.

All flights throughout the entire airport had been stopped as armed police boarded an Egyptian Red Crescent Airways 747 scheduled to take off for Cairo and Muscat at around rugby kickoff time. Six passengers were arrested. Two passengers put up a struggle, one managing to discharge a crude firearm, rather like a home-made, or zip gun. The bullet from the gun hit the cabin bulkhead but did not penetrate the skin of the aircraft. No one was injured, except the gunman who was shot dead. The other violent passenger tried to slash one of the arresting police officers with a knife, but missed and was shot in the chest. He was on life-support at a west London hospital. They were the only two casualties that day.

There were simultaneous raids at seven different locations in west London and Slough in Berkshire. Among those arrested on the plane was Hasina's brother Shawfiq Iqbal, who was travelling under his own name, with a British passport. He was in business class, clean-shaven and dressed in a suit and tie. Plastic explosives of a type similar to Czech-made C4 were found in his attaché case, plus half a dozen detonators. The hijackers had a total of two zip guns and four box-cutter-type knives. Waheed was picked up at his home in Slough. Hasina Iqbal and her fiancé Navdeep Dhaliwal were taken into protective custody, then brought to a safe house outside London where they slept together for the first time. Their consummation took place under the protection of Her Majesty's Government and UK Crown Forces.

The rugby match continued in front of us. I kept looking over towards the Prime Minister and saw that Fleming was coming up and talking to Fraser Davis throughout. It was obviously a big deal, though how big we did not know until later. I watched the Prime Minister's face, marvelling at his capacity for grace under pressure. He did not share any information with me, or any of the other guests, but at one point he walked out of his seat and conducted whispered consultations with Andy Carnwath, who had suddenly arrived on the scene, and was standing with Edward Fleming and a woman whom I also took for someone from MI5. While they were talking, England scored a try. The stands around us erupted with cheers and the singing of 'Swing Low, Sweet Chariot'. Fraser Davis was asking Fleming and the MI5 woman a series of questions, deep in animated conversation.

I seized the moment to get up and sidle over to Carnwath, who was scribbling notes on the blank pages of a book, preparing for the press briefing he would give within the hour.

'What's up, Andy?' I asked.

He had the look that you have when you are inside the loop and do not care to share information with someone who is not.

'Those who need to know, know,' he answered laconically. 'If you don't know . . . well, you don't need to know. Or not yet.'

'Very Zen of you, Andy, now stop being such a twat. You want me to read about it in tomorrow's Sunday papers?'

He nodded. 'You will. And it's good news. It will run all week. If you and Fiona are splitting up I need to announce it tomorrow. Trust me, nobody will care.'

'I might,' I said.

He looked at me as if he doubted it. I went back to my seat. The crowd was roaring. Scotland were pressing on the English line, but could not quite break through. At half-time we headed back to the hospitality area. Fraser Davis had another briefing with Fleming and the MI5 woman, then he called us all together. He said he had a short announcement.

'There has been a major terrorist incident,' he said grimly, 'or at least the threat of an incident, broken up by the Metropolitan Police, the security services, and the Secret Intelligence Service, with assistance from the armed forces. I cannot go into details for now, but what I can tell you is that it involved a plot to hijack an Egyptian airliner and fly it into this stadium at around this time. The police, backed up by the SAS and other military units, have made arrests. We are not proposing to make any public announcement of the target of the attack until the stadium is cleared, for obvious reasons. Public order and safety are our top priority. The threat has passed and I think we can return to our seats and enjoy the rugby. Perhaps we should thank our lucky stars for the way things turned out, but we should also thank the police and security services. The target was to murder 80,000 people here at Twickenham today, and we have thwarted the plan.'

There were murmurs of 'hear hear' from around the room. Even Dougal Hastie looked, for once, slightly impressed; or perhaps relieved.

I noticed to my surprise that a television crew from the BBC had been allowed in to the hospitality suite and were discreetly filming Fraser Davis's little speech for posterity, or at least for the evening news. Terrorism, as we were always told in Northern Ireland, is a kind of theatre. So, of course, is politics. And Fraser Davis was in command of the stage.

Under interrogation over the next few days, the Red Crescent Airways hijackers cracked. They had little choice. They had left martyrdom videos boasting about the plot, plus there had been months of emails, SKYPE conversations, telephone messages, and print-outs amounting to three million words of text, all monitored by MI5 and GCHQ. The plan had been to book two business-class seats – one for Shawfiq, one for 'the Pilot' – so they were as far forward in the aircraft as possible. The Pilot, a Pakistani national called Rashid al-Haq, had flown military aircraft in Pakistan and was thought capable of seizing control of the Red Crescent Airbus. The other hijackers travelled in coach class and had taken aisle seats, and were there to terrorize the other passengers and crew while Shawfiq and the Pilot brought the plane down. Each of the hijackers had picked up their weapons and equipment from those items smuggled airside by Hasina and 'sister Rasheeda' into the Heathrow terminal. One hijacker, Shawfiq, had been handed a briefcase with the explosives, detonators, and other material by one of the other airport workers involved in the plot. That airport worker was caught on CCTV and had also been arrested, as was 'sister Rasheeda'.

The plan, as far as MI5 could unpick it, was for the hijackers to move immediately after takeoff, while the Egyptian Red Crescent Airbus was still climbing out of Heathrow. The hijackers were supposed to rush towards the cockpit, Shawfiq would place a small charge of plastic explosive on the fortified cockpit door, blowing it open using the detonators Hasina had smuggled through. Once inside the cockpit, the plan was to force the pilot at gun- and knife-point to crash the plane on to the Twickenham ground, or for Rashid al-Haq to do so.

The best guess of our aviation experts was that, even if the plotters succeeded in gaining control of the plane, the chances of hitting Twickenham rugby stadium with a fully laden Airbus were very slim, but it was not impossible. When asked why they had chosen to attack Red Crescent Airways, Waheed said that it was because the Egyptian government 'was a puppet of the Zionist Imperialist Americans.' Shawfiq said it was because Red Crescent was deemed to have lax security. You can choose which version to believe, although I assumed it was a little of both.

Halfway through the second half of the rugby match, England were up ten points to three. The Scots had just secured a penalty – idiotic play by England, refusing to release the ball after a tackle. The Scottish fullback was lined up to take the kick and my mind was wandering. I looked up and could see that the skies leading to Heathrow were empty. All flights to Europe's busiest airport were diverted. Coincidentally, that same day, Norfolk police found the place where Bobby Black had been held. It was a disused infantry barracks near

Thetford, and inside they found the makeshift 'cell' where Bobby Black had been held, and also the larger room where he had been abused. They also discovered a pile of burned materials including a jute sack, a mattress, a blanket, and an orange jumpsuit. Forensic tests showed that in among the burned material were the bodies of four pit-bull-type dogs. Each one had been killed by a single gunshot to the head.

An old terrorist saying from Northern Ireland came into my head: 'We only have to be lucky once,' the IRA used to boast, 'the British government has to be lucky every time.'

We were lucky, that day. Lucky to find the Norfolk infantry barracks and very lucky to prevent potentially the worst terrorist incident in history. My own luck, however, was about to run out.

TWENTY-SEVEN

Politics, like physics, has its own Chaos Theory. There are rules – gravity, for example – which cannot easily be overcome, but occasionally there comes a point when so many events happen simultaneously it is almost impossible to see what the rules are, to separate cause and effect, or – to use Johnny Lee's word – Clusterfuck. Bobby Black's disappearance, the videos on the Internet, the arrests of Crockett and Byrne, the discrediting of Speaker Betty Furedi, the resurgence of the Republicans, the possibility of war with Iran, which receded almost as quickly as it began, and the uncovering of our own terrorist plot in London hit rapidly like a series of blows. There was some kind of relationship between all these events, though they were not directly connected, except in that they shape the world we live in nowadays.

All of this helps explain why conspiracy theories are so comforting. They give us the delusional sense that someone is in charge, that there is order in the chaos, that a person or a group – even if they are Evil – have some kind of plan, and if we could only nail those Evil-Doers then life would be fine. I wish it were that simple. In the days that followed the arrests, Andy Carnwath also announced that Fiona and I were getting divorced and, as he rightly predicted, there was so much news around about the Twickenham and Heathrow plot that it was buried under the weight of far more important events. Still, it was to be a difficult time for me. Some people find solace in prayer, others in history, but for me, as Kristina had discovered, it had always been poetry. As I visited lawyers and began the divorce proceedings against Fiona, I discovered I had been carrying the book of Wallace Stevens poems that Kristina had given me, almost as a love token. I started to read it through, and it fell open at a well-thumbed page, with Kristina's annotations in pencil in the margin. It was a poem called *The Man with the Blue Guitar*.

> They said, 'You have a blue guitar.
> You do not play things as they are.'
>
> The man replied, 'Things as they are
> Are changed upon the blue guitar.'

One word written was written beside the stanza in capital letters followed by several exclamation marks: 'SPIN!!!!' I started to think of Carnwath and McAuley and Johnny Lee and Kristina and even of myself as players of the blue guitar, but it did not comfort me very much. Instead, yet again, I planned to return to Washington, and to what I was good at. My job. As I arrived back at the embassy I was informed that James Byrne had been released on bail. The charges against him had not been dropped, but lawyers for the *Washington Post* said Byrne would 'exercise his First Amendment privileges' and insist on his constitutional right to freedom of speech.

'No court in the land will convict my client on these trumped-up charges,' his own lawyer, Dan Feingold, argued at a televised news conference. 'Mr Byrne will not implicate anyone else. He will not name his sources. He will not point the finger at anyone from Speaker Furedi's office. These charges were politically motivated and convenient for the Carr administration. My client has a story to tell, and he will tell it in his great newspaper.'

'Oh, fuck off, you asshole,' I screamed at the TV when Feingold's self-satisfied face went through the words. Now everyone was playing the blue guitar, even people who were tone deaf. Byrne celebrated his release by appearing on various television talk shows, labelling himself as a Freedom of Speech martyr, and it made me think of him as the American equivalent of Shawfiq and Waheed's martyrdom videos, which were also made public. They were all super-confident, self-satisfied, self-obsessed people with some kind of grievance, acting out their psycho-dramas for the benefits of the TV cameras.

It took another ten days for Byrne's attempt to destroy me. Even though I knew it was coming, it still unnerved me. He wrote two more front-page, exclusive stories on consecutive days, one of which was about me. The stories could only have come from sources inside the Carr administration, although, of course, one of them was rooted in what Fiona had told Byrne.

I had been trying to pick up the threads of my job, and I had arranged to call on the Republican leadership on Capitol Hill, the people who would take over in the new Congress. I paid particular attention to Representative Harry Bunning from Kansas who would replace Furedi as House Speaker. It took me a few days to get an appointment with him but we sat and talked through the recent events.

'You're going to have to do something about your Muslims,' he said at one point. 'Fuad in Manila. The Khan case. Now this gang of crazies at Heathrow. Your country is becoming the place the terrorists like to hang out.'

I protested politely that his comments were unfair, and that a tiny minority of British Muslims, mostly young Muslim men with their family roots in Pakistan, were so disaffected they were becoming involved in violence, but that we had – so far – successfully contained them.

'You did not contain the ones who kidnapped Bobby Black.'

'No, but I don't think any of us fully understands who did kidnap the Vice-President.'

'I agree with you on that, Ambassador,' Bunning said. 'But I need to tell you that when I am Speaker we are going to do something that was very close to Bobby Black's heart. We are going to bring to the floor a bill along the lines he suggested to require all British citizens of Pakistani origin to have background checks and obtain special visas before flying to the United States.'

I thought I had killed off this monster, but apparently not.

'With respect, Congressman, I do not think you can discriminate—'

'Well,' he interrupted, 'I know where you are going with this, but where we are going with this is that we'll have to target all British citizens; all sixty million of you will need the special visas. Is that what you are telling me the British government wants?'

'No, but . . .'

We talked on for another ten minutes, but before the meeting ended one of Bunning's administrative assistants came in with two sheets of paper and a strange look on his face.

'What is it, Clyde?'

'It's from the *Washington Post* website, sir,' the assistant said. 'I thought you and the Ambassador should see it. It's a story by Mr James Byrne about the War on Terror which will be appearing in the print version of the *Post* tomorrow morning.'

He handed Harry Bunning one sheet of paper and me the other. The Byrne story claimed that the Red Crescent Airways plot at London's Heathrow Airport had been disrupted because of 'valuable information' disclosed by Muhammad Asif Khan while under interrogation by the United States.

Foiling the plot, the Byrne story claimed, was a victory for US policy, for the Spartacus Doctrine, the Carr administration, and robust US interrogation methods in the teeth of 'strong protests from the British government which set back the programme.' The Byrne story said that unnamed 'US intelligence sources' claimed that saving up to 80,000 people from death at the Twickenham rugby ground in London was a 'total vindication' of Spartacus as created by Vice-President Shultz.

'A senior White House official told the *Washington Post* that the information delivered by Muhammad Asif Khan while part of the extraordinary rendition programme and the exceptional interrogation programme authorized by Spartacus had saved tens of thousands of British lives, the lives of innocent civilians in a key American ally. "This comes despite fierce British government and diplomatic opposition," the senior official said, speaking on condition of anonymity. "We saved the British from themselves. If the British and others had not resisted the programme in its entirety, who knows what might be achievable? We prevented a terrorist holocaust at Twickenham, England, and we are preventing attacks every day in the United States, despite the efforts of some of our supposed allies."

'British sources have refused to comment.'

I read the account with a feeling of sickness in the pit of my stomach.

'You see where we're coming from on this?' Harry Bunning said, waving the paper towards me. 'The people I represent in Kansas, Ambassador, would think we were crazy here in Washington – hell, they think we are crazy enough already – if we do not pass laws to keep Khan, Fuad, this Shawfiq Iqbal guy and his gang of crazies out of the United States. Thank you for visiting with me, Ambassador. We're going to need to keep in touch on this. But it will happen.'

I had so many things that I could have said to contradict the Byrne story, but I could not say them without checking with London. I had one parting shot.

'Congressman, I appreciate your time, but I have to tell you I know some things about the Heathrow terror plot from the inside, and they do not square with Mr Byrne's report. If you will allow me, I will talk to London and then brief your staff on what really happened.'

'You do that, Ambassador. And, in the meantime, we'll be drafting the new visa requirements. You can bet the farm on it.'

I was picked up by the embassy Rolls Royce and, as we headed back up Pennsylvania Avenue, I called Andy Carnwath immediately. I told him that I thought we should respond forcibly to the Byrne story.

'We need to point out that the Red Crescent Airways plot had absolutely nothing whatsoever to do with Muhammad Asif Khan. We need to get the truth out, to say that the British security service had been tracking the plotters for months and that British Muslims themselves had provided the key information that led to the arrests. This was a major success for MI5, and for British Muslims.'

Carnwath said it wasn't going to happen. 'Forget about it.'

I grew irritated. 'We need to get out in front of this, Andy,' I said. 'It was a British success, right? Without naming the young woman, we need to say that a British intelligence source from within the Heathrow plotters themselves was the—'

'No, Alex,' he cut me off firmly. 'Absolutely not. You are not to talk to any American journalists or anyone else about this.'

'But just think how good it would be for community relations in Britain to know that a British Muslim woman and other British Muslims—'

'No, you fucking dickbrain,' Carnwath screamed at me. 'Fraser has ruled on this. The Americans want Khan to be the source. We say, fine.'

'But it's not true,' I protested.

371

'It's true enough. Fingering Khan means he is completely compromised, incapable of any future political activity in this country or anywhere else. We'll leave him twisting in the wind. Plus, it shows that the Americans can break these people.'

'But that's not true either,' I protested.

'It is fucking true now,' Andy screamed at me. 'More important, it's useful. So stop being such a fucking naive twat. It screws Khan, right? And it takes the spotlight off Hasina Iqbal, plus it justifies Spartacus and takes the heat off for your fuck-ups over Bobby Black. Everybody wins.'

'But—'

'Khan is fucked, the girl protected, the Americans happy, Fraser Davis and Theo Carr best of buddies, Vice-President Shultz as nice as ninepence when he met the Prime Minister earlier today. For Chrissake, Alex, we nearly ended up with thousands dead during Fraser's big day of national unity at Twickenham. Right now, if the Americans proposed crucifying every potential terrorist on the road to Rome, Fraser would ask how high they want the crosses. You know that he's thinking about a General Election to coincide with the Scottish independence referendum in May?' I did not know that. 'Yeah, well, he thinks he can win both. That's what our polls say. That's the only truth that counts. Scottish independence is fucked, Dougal Hastie is fucked, and Fraser gets to win the next election. If this doesn't suit, you have the choice of go fuck yourself.'

He slammed down the phone before I had the chance to tell him the visa bill was back on the agenda in Congress. When I got back to the embassy I went to my private study in the living quarters and wrote an email about my conversations with the Republican leadership; then I tried to concentrate on the files about the new members of Congress. I wanted to look through them all and figure out who my allies might be to derail the new legislation. Thirty-three new Republicans would be arriving in January and I would want to call on all of them as early as I could. I made a list, in order of precedence. A little flattery from me at the start of their first month of their first term in Washington usually cemented relationships.

As I was just finalizing the order, my secretary called saying that I had a telephone call from a Mr James Byrne.

'Put him through.'

The croaking voice was raspy and unpleasant. That gave me some satisfaction.

'Yes?' I said. 'What can I do for you, Mr Byrne?'

There was almost a chuckle in his voice as he responded.

'I want to discuss on the record, Ambassador Price, the interrogation procedures you used when you were a Captain in British Military Intelligence in Gough Barracks, Armagh city, Northern Ireland, twenty years ago. I am recording this call. I have evidence which proves that you personally participated in acts that could be considered torture under the United Nations definition, and might even arguably be considered to be war crimes.'

I had expected the call, but I felt my breath squeeze out of me like air from a tyre.

'Are you still there, Ambassador Price?'

Oh yes. I was still there.

'You'd better tell me what you've got, Mr Byrne,' I said calmly, 'and then I will respond if I am able to do so.'

TWENTY-EIGHT

Gough Barracks, County Armagh, Northern Ireland.

I was twenty-five years old, a Captain in a British infantry regiment, on secondment to Military Intelligence. I had been in the army since I'd been eighteen years old. I remember the day that they brought in four IRA suspects, two of them well known to me from our surveillance operations. The four had been picked up at gunpoint by the SAS near Pomeroy after their car was held at a roadblock. The SAS were disappointed. They had been hoping for some resistance so they could shoot all four of them, but there was none; the IRA gang surrendered without a struggle.

The SAS searched the car and found no weapons, or explosives, just a couple of copies of *An Phoblacht,* the Republican newspaper also known as *Republican News*, but they knew who they were dealing with, and so they brought them to Gough Barracks. And to me. To call them IRA 'suspects' sticks in my throat, because that suggests an element of doubt. There was no doubt. The four arrested men had been up to their necks in Provisional IRA terrorist activity for years. Two of them were donkeys, Michael Taggart and Patsy O'Hara, PIRA footsoldiers from Coalisland, the kind of low-level men who did the dirty work and who did not do much of the thinking. Or any of the thinking.

The other two were different, which is why they were brought to me. They were the McBride brothers from the Moy, County Tyrone. I guess no one much remembers them now, but at the time the McBrides were famous, or notorious, depending on your sympathies. Either way, they were in a different class from most of the IRA suspects I saw. In another life, or another war, the McBrides could have risen to become senior officers in the British Army, or the US Army, or they could have embraced a political career. But when I saw them, they were killers, terrorists, dangerous men, no different from the 9/11 bombers or Fuad, Shawfiq, and Waheed – except that the McBrides were in the terrorism business for the long term. They killed not once, but time after time, and they had no plans to leave a martyrdom video. As an enemy, I respected the McBrides. Within British Military Intelligence we were taught, tongue slightly in cheek, that Irish Republicanism was a genetic defect, and the McBrides were often used by our Colonel as a good example.

'They get it from their mothers,' the Colonel told us when I first arrived in County Armagh at the start of an eighteen-month tour of duty. It was a long tour, but I was unmarried, unattached, and ambitious.

'I am not sure I understand you, sir.'

'The mother is the Typhoid Mary of Irish Republicanism, Captain Price. Don't forget that. These people would kill you as quick as look at you, but mention the mother and they start to cry.'

I was not sure of this as a general principle, but in the case of Sean and Brendan McBride it was more or less true. Their mother, Mary McBride, had been an activist in the Old IRA in the Fifties. Their grandmother and great-grandmothers had been activists too – in the case of the great-grandmother she had known, apparently, Countess Markievicz and some of the

Easter Rising conspirators. Or so we were told. And so the McBrides boasted. It could have been bullshit, but it suited everyone, on both sides, to believe a myth that was close enough to the truth to be acceptable. As I remember it, there were five McBride children, three boys and two girls. One of the girls had blown herself up in a car bomb which went off prematurely in Newry. Another was on the run somewhere in the Irish Republic after setting up two British soldiers in a honeytrap. The two soldiers had gone to a house in a supposedly safe area off the Lisburn Road in south Belfast with two women who promised them a good time. The women led them to a flat where instead of sex the men were kidnapped at gunpoint, taken to west Belfast, beaten, tortured, castrated, and murdered. We found their bodies at the side of the road in a lay-by on the Cavehill, their faces beaten to a pulp, their ribs smashed and their legs broken. I looked at the photographs of the corpses and wondered how one man could do this to another in pursuit of a political cause. Forget the romantic songs, the Irish ballads and the great *craic*, these were not nice people. Okay, so the IRA did not carry out suicide bombings, but McBride's sister was able to look into a man's eyes, kiss and fondle him, and then lead him off to where they knew his cheekbones would be smashed to jelly, his legs broken, and a single shot to the back of the head would put him out of his misery.

The oldest McBride brother, Finbar, had been shot dead by British soldiers while he was attempting a sniper attack in Dungannon. We think Finbar had more than twenty kills to his supposed credit, but again, that could have been an IRA exaggeration. Or one of our own. The truth in Ireland has always been fungible, but you could say that we were working our way through the McBride family with admirable consistency.

The only two who were left active in the North were Sean and Brendan, and now we had them in custody, though they had been in and out of jail and on remand on charges of membership of the IRA for years, but nothing stuck. We used special no-jury Diplock courts, but still could not obtain convictions. The McBrides were known in the Moy as the Teflon Terrorists, always getting away with it. Until now. A breakthrough. Twenty years ago we had our equivalents of Hasina Iqbal, and one of them was codenamed Whiskey Alpha. This was a man – or possibly a woman, I never found out which – at the top levels of the IRA, and he provided the tip-off about a planned attack in March 1988 on Gibraltar. Three IRA bombers were going to blow up the British Army marine band as it marched through the streets of the Rock, and it was the softest of soft targets. After the SAS killed them, the three bombers became known as the 'Gibraltar Three' – Máiréad Farrell, Sean Savage and Danny McCann. They were committed Republicans, and they were, I suppose, good at what they were doing. But then so were we. We had turned enough PIRA people, like Whiskey Alpha, to have the IRA as porous as pumice stone. We knew where Farrell, Savage, and McCann ate, slept, breathed, and when they took a piss. Whether we could make charges stick in court was another matter, but thanks to Whiskey Alpha we launched Operation Flavius. It had one aim: to take out Farrell, Savage, and McCann. They were shot dead on the streets of Gibraltar by the SAS in circumstances that were disputed. Some say they were killed without warning, others that they were challenged and offered resistance. To the credit of the IRA, while they mourned their comrades, they did not whinge about it. Whingeing about the killings was a matter for the Left in Britain, in Ireland, and their sentimental fellow-travellers in the United States of America, the kind of people who passed the hats around for dollars in bars in Boston and New York not caring who was being killed in Belfast and elsewhere.

What happened next was chaos. After the Gibraltar Three were killed, there were days of rioting all over Northern

Ireland, and warnings that the IRA would 'retaliate', a threat we took very seriously. We were desperate to find out what they were planning. Whiskey Alpha told his handler that the Army Council of the IRA had tasked the McBride brothers with planning the revenge attack, and it was to take place some time in the month of July 1988. The IRA active service unit that was to carry out the attack was, Whiskey Alpha claimed, already in position in England.

It was that information which led us to pick up the McBrides and the two donkeys in Pomeroy, and that was why I was told I had to choose one or other of the brothers and break him within forty-eight hours. I chose Sean.

I had two things going for me. Even though I was young, I had a reputation as someone who could get through to the IRA activists. I was not from the usual British infantry officer class and I was more like the McBrides than either of us would care to acknowledge. The other thing I had going for me was that, if something went badly wrong during my interrogation of Sean, I was young enough not to question orders, not to ask for them to be written down, and to be expendable if something very bad happened. One of the other Captains, Jack Lucas, who was two years older than me but nowhere near as good, was given Brendan. We separated the two brothers and began.

There are two ways to break a man: fear, and rapport. Fear works, as Bobby Black says, but only sometimes. When it does work it can be quick, but a terrified man will tell you anything to escape his terror. Rapport is far more difficult to establish, but it works more often and more reliably. I was good at rapport, but I did not have time. I had forty-eight hours before we had to hand the McBrides over to the Royal Ulster Constabulary, who would hold them for a few days under the Prevention of Terrorism Act and then release them.

Sean McBride was brought to me by two thickset NCOs whom I had worked with many times before. McBride was handcuffed and slumped down in the chair with a fuck-you look on his face. I ignored him and pretended to write on the notebook in front of me. Sean McBride was thirty years old, a hard case, with chilling blue eyes and a heavy mat of greasy brown hair. The biggest difference between us was that he had killed people, and I had not. He was staring at me with contempt, but I ignored him and left him sitting impotently and in silence while I wrote in longhand in a notebook. I had to write something and had nothing to say, and so I wrote out some attempt at poetry. It was the last poetry I was ever to write. It was, of course, doggerel.

> *There was a man*
> *His name was Sean.*
> *I asked him*
> *What was going on.*
> *Said Sean to me*
> *Why can't you see*
> *What's going on,*
> *Is me.*

Pure tripe. The poetry was not to my liking, but I still needed something more to write to pass the time and make Sean see that I was in no hurry. I decided to write out the five techniques that had been permitted to army interrogators in Northern Ireland in the 1970s. I looked at my list and realized that none of these five techniques would work with McBride. He and his brother had been deprived of sleep since he arrived. We had offered him no water or food. The other techniques had been avoided, so far, but making him stand against a wall for hours had not worked in his many arrests in the past and I doubted it was going to work now. I decided on a sixth technique and began doodling on my pad but, before I could fully formulate the idea, McBride broke into my thoughts.

379

'When you've finished writing your novel, wee lad, why don't you either ask me questions or let me go, you fucking English cunt.'

I looked up at him and smiled. There was a fat Yellow Pages phone book on my desk that I kept for such moments. I snatched it up and hit McBride hard in the face with it and then a dozen times on the head until he fell on the floor, blood trickling from his nose. When he hit the ground I kicked him in the guts and continued the beating around his head, and then I stopped. I rearranged my uniform and threw the phone book down on my desk. I sat back on my chair and watched him writhe in pain as I caught my breath.

'You got some place better you want to go?' I said softly. 'Something else you want to do? Tell me about it.'

McBride glared back at me from the floor with his fuck-you eyes. He said nothing. I looked at the pad in front of me where I had been doodling, and I realized that what I had drawn was a helicopter.

The idea of the sixth technique had come to me, almost into my subconscious. I signalled to the two NCOs to drag McBride back up to the chair, then I turned the pad towards him.

'You recognize this?' McBride looked at the helicopter doodle and said nothing. 'You should do. Your fellas have been popping RPGs at them for long enough. It's a British Army helicopter, Sean. And what I am going to do is take you for a ride in one. A special ride. You are going to be tied up with a bag over your head, but with just enough room so you can wriggle. We are going to fly to five thousand feet and, when we get to that height, a mile high over Lough Neagh, if you have not told me what I want to know, and *exactly* what I want to know, I am going to let you wriggle your way by accident out of the helicopter and into the lough. I don't know if you can swim, but I wouldn't worry. The fall should kill you.'

I spoke in a calm soft voice as if I organized this kind of milk run every day, but my heart was beating fast. I did not think I could out-bluff such a hard case, and I was not even sure whether I would be permitted to do what I needed to do, but something about McBride's face changed and encouraged me. I saw a flash of fear.

'Why don't you go fuck yoursel'?' McBride said. I ignored it.

'Did you know, Sean, that from five thousand feet, water on a lough surface is like concrete. Your mother won't need a coffin. Old Mary can bury you as a liquid in a Tupperware.'

He glared back at me and blinked his yes. The fear again. Either for himself or for his mother's grief.

'Don't go away,' I added as I stood up and left the room. 'I'm going to arrange our transport.'

I left McBride for an hour with the NCOs, and watched him occasionally. He stood up after ten minutes, his hands still cuffed behind him. He paced the room. The two NCOs glared at him but stood against the walls, saying nothing. McBride looked concerned. He had a pudgy, boxer's face, with scar tissue from fights, from Gaelic football and from hurley sticks.

The McBrides came from a small hamlet on the outskirts of the Moy. The family were hill farmers, tough as bejasus, but every man has his fears. The question was whether fear of heights was something that scared Sean McBride? I thought it might. After the hour had passed, I walked back into the room. He was sitting upright on his seat. I nodded at one of the NCOs to let him have a cigarette. He puffed at it gratefully. I sat facing him and we talked.

'You and I are in the same business, Sean.'

McBride scoffed and puffed smoke. 'I am not in the business of occupying other people's countries. I am in the business of freeing my people.'

I smiled. 'Your people occupy Cricklewood, Balham, and half of Glasgow,' I said. 'And Liverpool and Boston and the northeastern seaboard of the United States. But that's not what I meant. They say that you are the best interrogator in the IRA.' McBride showed no emotion. I went on. 'I hear that when you found a tout in Cookstown you broke his legs with breeze blocks before he confessed.'

'Tout' is the IRA word for informer. The McBrides had taken the son of a farmer, Damien O'Neill, to a patch of woodland, tortured, and then shot him. McBride did not respond.

'So, as one professional to another, what was that like with Damien O'Neill, Sean?' I wondered. 'I mean, did it work?' McBride returned my gaze in stony silence.

After Damien O'Neill's body had been found, both McBrides were arrested by the Royal Ulster Constabulary, but they could obtain no usable evidence or witnesses prepared to testify against them. The trial collapsed. Even O'Neill's family, who had watched their son taken away from their farmhouse and returned to them in such a mess that the burial was in a closed coffin, said they could not recognize the people who did it. To my surprise, McBride began to speak.

'I was arrested, charged, and then acquitted in a Diplock court of anything to do with the Damien O'Neill case,' McBride said. 'But Damien O'Neill was a tout so he got what was coming.'

He licked his lips. I offered him another cigarette, which he accepted.

'The way I understand it, you tied him to a tree, gagged him, but made sure he could see everything that was going on. Then you piled up the breeze blocks beside him, smoked a cigarette so he could think about it, then you smashed one leg, and waited a while, then you smashed the other when he passed out with the pain. But I am interested to know at what point did he talk? At what point did he confess? Y'see, here's my theory. I bet he confessed after just one leg, and you did the other one anyway. Out of badness. Or to see if he was holding something back. I'm right, aren't I?'

McBride stared back at me. I had hit a chord with him, somehow.

'I'd have done it differently with O'Neill, Sean. I'd have told him you were going to torture his brother or his sister Sheelagh. I think that would have been his cracking point. Family. Like yours. Your mother.' McBride took a deep breath. I was on to something. I could feel it. 'Well, anyway, I don't do breeze blocks.' I looked at my watch. 'But if you do not tell me within the next hour what the target for the Gibraltar Three revenge attack is going to be, you will be attempting to escape from a helicopter at a time and place of my choosing. Then once you and Brendan are done, we're going to make sure the UVF know when your mother is all alone at the farmhouse, so they can pay their respects. Maybe have three family funerals. Save duplication.'

The UVF were Loyalist paramilitaries who would murder McBride's mother without a second's thought once they had the address. Sean McBride looked at me for a full minute of undisguised hatred and I returned his gaze.

'Go fuck yourself,' he said, but not with as much spirit as before.

I stood up abruptly. 'No, Sean. It's you who's about to be fucked. And your ma.'

I left the room and we prepared the helicopter. Twenty minutes later the two NCOs, along with four squaddies, bound, gagged, and blindfolded McBride. He put up token resistance but he was never going anywhere. I suppose if I had known about waterboarding at the time I would have tried that on him first and saved the expense of the helicopter, but these were less sophisticated times.

The NCOs trussed McBride like a turkey. He stood in front of me and I held the bag that I was about to put over his head in my hands. I looked into his eyes.

'Last chance, Sean. Personally I don't give a shit whether you talk or not, because you falling into Lough Neagh would make my day. I have a bet with my sergeant that you won't float. He says you will. What do you think?'

McBride said nothing but I could see he was now pale with fear.

'What's the target, Sean?'

He tried to glare back at me but the sound of rotor blades starting up outside unnerved him.

Pocka-pocka-pocka.

'The target, Sean?' I shouted in his ear.

Pocka-pocka-pocka.

'In England, Sean? London?'

No answer.

Pocka-pocka-pocka.

'Goodbye, Sean.'

I put the bag over his head and tied it tightly at the neck, then had him carried to the helicopter. He was shoved on the floor and I sat above him with my boot hard on his back, just so he knew I was there. We took off. It's a short helicopter flight from Armagh to Belfast. The pilot climbed fast, in case of RPG and sniper fire. He turned and wheeled and headed towards Lough Neagh, climbing all the time. The pilot then swooped and turned until I lost control of my senses and at one point almost lost control of my stomach. The pilot put the helicopter into hover. My heart was beating hard with anticipation. I did not know what was about to happen, and I did not know what I was capable of. Perhaps McBride would tell me what I wanted to know. Perhaps he would not. Then the decision would be all mine. And what would I do? I knelt hard on him as he lay on the floor of the helicopter and I loosened the hood so he could hear me. I screamed in his ear, with my mouth as close as that of a lover.

'This is it, Sean. Decision time. Target for the attack? Who will be carrying it out? You give me the full details and you will be safe. You fuck up, and you and your brother better know how to fly. We'll take you back to your ma in a Tupperware.'

I could see him attempt to swallow but he was so scared the saliva would not come. I felt something on my left knee, through my trousers.

'Piss,' one of the NCOs yelled out, 'he's fuckin' pissed hissel'.'

There was a stain on his trousers at the back too, though there was no smell. The air rushing through the cabin ventilated everything.

'Well?'

'N-no,' he said.

'Last chance. Yes or no?'

'N-no.'

I did not really take a decision. My instinct knew exactly what to do. I pulled the hood down on him, moved behind and kicked his body across the floor of the cabin.

'Goodbye, Sean,' I screamed. Then I kicked him as hard as I could out of the side of the helicopter.

TWENTY-NINE

The moment I finished talking with Byrne on the telephone, I called Andy Carnwath to warn him what was coming. That night I slept badly, got up at five thirty and walked over to the embassy to pick up the first delivery of the papers. The *Washington Post* had dug up a picture of me in my army uniform and ran it alongside another photograph of me at Chequers with Fraser Davis and Bobby Black. I knew that the army picture was in my apartment in London, and I assumed Fiona had handed it over to Byrne. In the article he described me as 'the Prime Minister's brother-in-law, adviser, and confidant,' a description which would have been hilarious if things were not so serious. The story began like this:

> The British ambassador to the United States, Alexander 'Alex' Price, has been implicated in serious allegations of ill-treatment, torture, and potential war crimes while serving as a British Army officer in Northern Ireland more than twenty years ago.
>
> At that time, according to informed intelligence and other sources, Price was serving as a Captain in British Military Intelligence based at Gough Barracks, County Armagh.

The allegations refer to the mistreatment of an alleged IRA commander, Sean McBride.

McBride was, according to senior US intelligence sources speaking on condition of anonymity, repeatedly thrown from a helicopter as part of an interrogation process allegedly devised by Captain Price. McBride was told that if he did not offer information to the British he would be thrown out of a helicopter as it flew at 5,000 feet over a local lake, known as Lough Neagh. His death, he was told, would look like an accident, and that he was about to join the IRA 'Mile-High Club'.

McBride refused to cooperate and was taken on the helicopter ride. McBride claims he was thrown from the helicopter by Captain Price, but that the aircraft was flying just a few feet above the ground. McBride landed on soft grass and was physically unhurt, although the psychological damage was, 'incalculable' McBride said in an interview with the *Washington Post*.

McBride said that he has suffered from mental problems for twenty years as a result of his experiences at the hands of the British and that he intended to pursue a claim for damages against the British government in the European courts. US intelligence and diplomatic sources said the Captain who brutalized Sean McBride is now the British Ambassador to the United States, Alexander Price, a diplomat who has repeatedly denounced the alleged use of torture by the United States in the War on Terror.

Price declined to comment, but late last night the British Prime Minister's office issued a statement. 'We are investigating the allegations made against Ambassador Price. Ambassador Price has asked to be given leave of absence from his duties until the investigation is complete. Pending the outcome, the chargé d'affaires in Washington is to be the Minister Counsellor Peter Hogarth.' Price intends to leave Washington for London within the next few days to assist

in the inquiry. It is not know when – or if – he will return
to his post in the United States.'

Almost immediately I became a prisoner in the British Embassy
and the Great House, under media siege. Irish American groups
also staged protests outside, a twenty-first century reminder
of the kinds of demonstrations that had gone on years before
over British policy in Northern Ireland, in those good old
days before Americans had woken up to the idea that a
terrorist is a terrorist is a terrorist, whether the cause is Islamic
revolution, social revolution, or the unification of Ireland.
Killing civilians is the same thing: wrong.

The Irish American demonstrators were noisy but peaceful,
a dozen or so middle-aged Irish-Americans who chanted and
in one case played the bagpipes, some of them holding up
hand-painted signs talking about 'British Brutality' and urging
'Brits Out of Ireland'. I kept out of their way, inside, hidden.
I had thought of writing to the *Washington Post* to remind
them of the IRA bombings on Bloody Friday, or of the Omagh
bombing, or of the numerous other murders of civilians
conducted by the IRA and other terrorist groups, but I was
expressly forbidden by Downing Street from making any public
statements on any matters whatsoever. Like Bobby Black I
was about to become an ex-person, politically incorrect for
these new times, silenced and purged. That day, however, was
full of surprises. The first was a phone call from Lord
Anstruther from his office at the Ministry of Defence.

'Alex,' he said, laughing, 'who knew?'

'What do you mean, Dickie?'

'Who knew that you were a hero.'

I paused. 'You mean . . .'

'You know what I mean, Alex. I've now seen your whole
file. All of it. Not just the bits given to Byrne. I know what
you did and what you saved us from. If you want help, you
can count on me.'

'I . . .' I was lost for words. Pathetically grateful. 'Thank you, Dickie.'

'And something else. I was told about the story last night by the Defence Secretary himself. He said there might be a bit of bother, that's why I ordered your file. Once I read it I decided to ask some friends of mine to lend a hand.'

'Friends?'

'In . . . another Service. I think you might be interested in what they found.'

'Another Service,' is Whitehall-speak for the Secret Intelligence Service, MI6.

'And what did they find?'

'Enough information to sink James Byrne for ever. Details to follow.'

Anstruther rang off.

That same morning a letter arrived, hand delivered by a courier company to the embassy residence. I recognized Kristina's handwriting immediately. I was packing my things, on the assumption that I would not be back from my imminent exile from the United States for some time. Perhaps I would never be back.

I gave instructions about my files to the *chargé d'affaires*, Peter Hogarth, and arranged for my personal possessions to be crated for shipment home. I was contemplating resignation from the Diplomatic Service. That did not bother me so much as the deep sadness I felt about leaving the United States under such a cloud, and leaving permanently. Outside the embassy I can see the statue of Winston Churchill, standing like a bulldog on the edge of the embassy grounds, one foot on American soil, one foot in the embassy itself. Churchill once observed that the people of the United States always do the right thing, usually after having exhausted every conceivable alternative. I felt as if I was one of the alternatives that was about to be exhausted. I was also very angry. Byrne had obviously been helped by Fiona, as Johnny Lee had told me, but I also assumed he had received help from someone in the White House. From whom?

Surely not Kristina? Or Johnny Lee? Could it be Shultz? Who else would have access to my files? Presumably someone in London had decided to lift the 'UK EYES ONLY' classification at the Americans' behest, but if Anstruther had seen the full file, I wondered who had weeded out every shred of evidence that showed me in anything approaching a good light? Byrne? Or someone before it got to Byrne?

The more angry I became, the more I wanted to get even. My mood was made even worse when I switched on the TV. I was being called a hypocrite on the talk shows, my harsh conduct against McBride weighed against my being 'soft' on people like Khan, Fuad, and other terrorists of the twenty-first century.

I cannot tell you how distressing it is to have your character analysed and destroyed by people you do not respect and who know nothing about you, except what they have read in a highly partial newspaper report. I looked at the telephone and thought about phoning in to one show to say that the real hypocrisy was that if I had tortured a Muslim like Muhammad Asif Khan and claimed it was part of the Spartacus Programme, I would have been a hero, but because I took a good Catholic lad from Northern Ireland and threw him out of a helicopter on to grass from a height of ten feet, I was given the treatment you might expect if they had discovered I was a concentration camp guard.

Jack Rothstein called me from *The Times*. His was one of the few calls that I did take that day. I had to tell him that I was not allowed to say anything on or off the record.

'You've been silenced like a heretical bishop of the church,' he laughed, with a degree of sympathy.

'Like you would know, Jack.'

He laughed again.

'All us Rothsteins are big-time Catholics. When are they going to let you defend yourself, Alex?'

'Maybe never.'

'Well, if you ever want to get out your side of the story, call me first.'

I said I would think about it. In the meantime Byrne himself was on FOX, hitting me as hard as it was possible to do.

'I am not saying Ambassador Alex Price is another Himmler or Milošević or Bin Laden,' Byrne croaked. 'But I am saying he has the same mind-set. He dehumanized Sean McBride and treated him like an object. That's the way Nazis and Islamofascists think.'

'The hypocrite of Embassy Row,' was how one FOX commentator described me. 'Lecturing America on how to conduct the War on Terror while throwing an innocent Irishman from a helicopter.'

Innocent? Sean McBride? Then the courier arrived with Kristina's letter and I forgot about the TV pillorying of my reputation. I opened the envelope with a wave of fear and excitement.

'Don't trust your telephones, any of them. Especially the cellphone. Assume everything is compromised. Stay long enough in Washington for us to meet. This is important. Get a bicycle and go on Saturday afternoon to Great Falls, Maryland, along the C and O canal towpath. Be careful you are not followed. Do not bring your cellphone or any electronic devices. I will meet you at 2 p.m. where the canal widens – you remember the spot? – a mile short of Great Falls. You can't miss it. Tell no one. Do not text, call, or try to contact me. This might be the last time we can talk. Be there. Destroy this letter.'

The letter was unsigned, except for one word that was as good as a signature.

'Aloha.'

I finished packing and squirmed with nervousness at the thought of seeing Kristina again. It had been a month, the most chaotic month of my life. I booked my seat on the plane out of Dulles for the last flight on Saturday night, then I dug out an old bicycle from one of the embassy garages and made sure it worked. Kristina had planned it well. Following a man in a car or on foot is simple, but following a man on a bicycle is extremely difficult for the news cameras, reporters, or anyone else. The speed of a bicycle is too slow for a car and too fast for a pedestrian. I spent the forty-eight hours until Kristina and I were to meet packing, briefing my supposedly temporary successor, and hiding. I also did something I had not done much of in the previous four or five weeks. Thinking.

On the Friday before our meeting, I received an email from an address I did not recognize. It contained material about James Byrne that the sender thought 'you might find interesting.' I read it through at first with a sense of disbelief and then total delight. It would come in very handy. The next morning, the Saturday, as I prepared to meet Kristina for the last time, Dickie Anstruther called me again.

'Well? Did you get anything?'

'Thank you. Very interesting information indeed, Dickie. Thank your friends for me too.'

'Least I could do for a fellow veteran,' he said. 'What damages one of us, damages all of us. This is not over yet for you, Alex, you know that?'

I knew that.

'Here in the United States they consider me a torturer, Dickie.'

'That's because they do not know it all,' he replied. 'And soon they will. Brace yourself. It's going to get very bumpy for a while. But I'm always here if you need me. You are a good man, Alex.'

I thanked him and rang off. I checked my watch and it was time. I put on my cycling gear, a tight fleece and a cycling helmet with goggles. I knew precisely the spot Kristina meant. In better times we had cycled to Great Falls together several times, both on the Virginia and Maryland sides. It is one of Washington's finest landmarks, massive waterfalls as the Potomac River makes its final sprint to the sea and the Chesapeake Bay. When I was ready to go I opened one of the side gates from the embassy compound, like a thief or burglar making his escape, and then shot away so quickly I do not believe any of the press pack would have spotted me, even supposing they recognized me under the cycling gear. I hit Massachusetts Avenue and pedalled as fast as I could for Dupont Circle, looking behind me to make sure I was not being followed. Nothing. I planned to turn through the back streets of Georgetown and slip down to the canal. It was a chill early winter day, but with plenty of brightness and sunshine, precisely the kind of Washington day I most love. I stopped in Georgetown and picked up a sandwich, and munched it joylessly, looking at the crowds of tourists on M Street. I would miss America very much, and the anger stirred more and more deeply within me.

I wanted to punch something or someone as assuredly as I had punched the bags with my boxing gloves in Anstruther's gym, and the someone I most wanted to punch looked very like James Aloysius Byrne. I climbed back on my bicycle and slipped down to the canal towpath. I rattled the old bicycle westwards towards Foxhall, where the pocked asphalt on the path gave way to smooth red dirt. I checked several times for signs that I was being followed, but there was nothing and no one. I pedalled hard until I reached the spot Kristina intended, where the canal widens among a series of big rocks. I got to the spot about half an hour early, as I had planned. I was now increasingly suspicious of everyone and anything and I wanted to check the location before Kristina arrived.

The C and O canal – the Chesapeake and Ohio – runs westwards from Washington some 200 miles and follows the route of the Potomac River. It was constructed to navigate from the Atlantic coast to the Ohio River by avoiding the rapids and waterfalls of the lower Potomac. The canal is a magnificent, beautiful construction, and it is now a national park. In summer it is full of hummingbirds and turtles. The part where the canal widens is like a water-filled red rock canyon where you have to carry your bike fifty yards or more over the rocks as the track peters out.

I hitched the bike on my shoulder, climbed above what was left of the track and found a split in one part of the canyon ramparts where I was able to hide the bike in bushes. I took off my helmet and goggles, walked in a series of circles to check that no one was close enough to observe us, then I hunkered down and waited. Twenty minutes later a familiar figure appeared down the trail in tight cycling clothes and on an expensive mountain bike. Kristina. It was a cold day and I watched her breath steam into the chill air, then when I was sure she was alone I stood up and waved to her. I clambered down over the rocks to help her carry her bicycle to where I had put mine. I checked and double-checked. No one followed her. Or at least no one I could see. We had found the perfect spot for lovers, or for an illicit meeting, with views both ways along the towpath. We sat down behind the rocks and looked at each other.

'It's good to see you,' I said.

She nodded. 'And you.'

'How much time do you have?'

She shrugged. We had not touched each other for a month. We had not talked face to face since before Bobby Black disappeared.

'Enough.' She leaned over and kissed me, then pushed me away.

'Did you do it?' she asked me suddenly. Her voice was flat. She just wanted an answer.

'Did I do what?'

'I read the files on you a couple of weeks ago. Did you throw an IRA prisoner from a helicopter?'

'Yes,' I admitted. 'Into wet grass from about ten feet. Repeatedly. I did it five times with McBride. I would have done it fifty times if I thought it was necessary.'

'Did he talk?'

'You didn't see the whole file or you would know the answer.'

'Oh,' she said. 'Maybe not.'

'Yes, he talked. And the IRA know he talked because I made sure of that. I wanted the McBride brothers fucked forever, and they were. Sean McBride was taken out of IRA active service just as efficiently as if I had shot him. Better. They never trusted him again. You can't come back, as Bobby Black himself now knows. There are no second chances in the IRA either.'

Kristina sucked in a deep breath. She looked at me for a full minute.

'How could you do it?' Her tone was not accusatory. She just wanted to know the answer. I started to explain, but I don't think I made much sense. I consider myself a civilized person. I read novels. I like jazz. Once upon a time I even wrote poetry. And yet I was capable of throwing a man out of a helicopter, threatening him with certain death. I wondered what less civilized men – or more desperate ones – might be capable of.

'The Nazis thought they were civilized too,' she said. 'They liked Wagner, Goethe, Mozart, Italian opera.'

'What I did, well, it worked with Sean McBride because he was scared of heights,' I went on. 'It would not work with someone else. I got lucky. When I threw him out of the helicopter for the first time we jumped onto the grass alongside him and bundled him back in. He was already broken, a shivering, quivering wreck. Snapped like a stick.

'I held him down and he yelled out to me the target for the revenge attack right away. Told me who was going to do it. Told me in which part of London they had rented a safe house. Names, places, dates, everything.'

'What was the target?'

'The Proms.'

Kristina had never heard of The Proms. I explained about the Henry Wood Promenade Concerts, held every summer in the Royal Albert Hall, one of the great events of the British summer.

'The IRA planned to put a bomb in the Royal Albert Hall on the night of a royal performance at the Proms. Hundreds would have died. The Albert Hall holds three thousand people. It would have been the IRA's 9/11, but we stopped them. McBride stopped them, with a little encouragement from me. Told me it straightaway. I never killed anyone. We saved hundreds, maybe thousands, of lives, perhaps including those of the Queen and Prince Philip.'

I could see some of the certainties about me drain from Kristina's face.

'But . . . but why did you throw him out of the helicopter four more times? Why was that necessary?'

I sucked in my own breath. It was the most difficult question of all to answer.

'It wasn't necessary,' I said. 'But I had started, I wanted to finish. To make sure. Leave nothing to chance. Everything McBride had of value – names, dates, places, faces – he told me straightaway. But I did not know that. He could have been holding something back. I decided – *I decided* – *me* – that we should do it again. And again. In fact it was counter-productive. He became so . . . fucked up that he stopped talking altogether. Maybe there is a lesson in there somewhere, but once you start it is difficult to stop. Once you cross the line, you just keep on going.'

I sat back on the red rock and look at the waterway in front of me. A family of two adults and three children were squabbling noisily along the track.

'Did you know that under conditions of extreme stress and terror you can plant false memories in suspects?' I asked

Kristina. 'You can get people to remember things that they have done – when they really never did them.'

Kristina nodded. 'I read the papers on this. I told you.'

'Yes, of course.'

Of course. She had read everything. Everything. But I had actually done it. We looked at each other for a few minutes in silence. I did not understand what I saw in her eyes.

'I don't know what to make of it,' she said eventually, shaking her head slowly. 'I don't know what to . . .' She stopped for a moment and then caught herself. 'President Carr wants me to stay on,' she said, returning to her flat business voice, 'if he gets a second term. *When* he gets a second term. He's not to be underestimated, is he? Andy Baker is going to be out. The President wants me to move to State.'

It was a big promotion, about the biggest possible. By the time she was forty years old, Kristina would be the most powerful woman in the administration, and possibly in the world.

'I see. And what did you say?'

She breathed out and did not look at me.

'I said yes,' she replied, her eyes fixed on an interesting rock lying between us. 'What did you expect me to say? To turn down Secretary of State? No way.'

'You know that I wanted to give you and me a chance to have something of a normal relationship?' I responded by way of an answer.

'Yes, I know that.'

'It won't happen now. I am recalled and there is no chance I will come back.'

She sighed. 'Alex, sometimes I think you are more in love with the idea of me rather than the reality, and I am not sure either of us knows what normal is any more.'

'I thought that you came to the brink of loving me, Kristina, though you hid it better . . .'

She said nothing.

'My career is over,' I said. 'My divorce has begun. My reputation – such as it was – has been messed up. But I am not going to take all this shit, Kristina. I am going to fight back and I am going to fight back to win.'

She looked at me with a flicker of alarm in her grey eyes. I had predicted this moment but I had not realized how much she meant to me.

'Fight who?' she said, sounding alarmed. 'Win against what? Fight how?'

'I will be leaving the diplomatic service soon,' I said. 'One way or another it's over for me.'

She nodded.

'And for us, you and me,' she said. 'It has to be over too. I can't be seen to compromise my career by . . .'

'By being the lover of a torturer? Even if it saved a load of people?'

'Something like that,' she said.

I shook my head. I wasn't interested in her career any more. In the collision of public versus private, I recognized that private life would always lose out for Kristina Taft. I just hoped she would be happy with the result.

'Who was it in the White House who leaked it about me to Byrne?' I said. 'It's a partial leak – just the stuff you saw. But it comes from my file, and I would guess it had to be an American.'

She shrugged. 'I don't know. When they found out about you and me, Marian Killick ran some checks. So did the Secret Service, with assistance from the CIA, and ultimately with the assistance of the British. They cleared your files for us, or most of them. That's why I kept my distance. I was told you were toxic.'

'Am I?'

'I'm not sure. Either way, I don't know who leaked it to Byrne. It wasn't me. And the word is that for all his valiant journalistic efforts this year, James Byrne is a shoe-in for a Pulitzer Prize.'

'I doubt it,' I said.

'You doubt it?'

'I haven't finished with him yet.'

'Don't do anything crazy,' Kristina looked at me, alarmed once more.

'Why not? You got something against crazy?'

She nodded. There were tears in her eyes.

'I told you straight from the start,' she said. 'Fuck-buddies. That was the best we could do. Not get attached. I was always only trying to be honest. And you had to go spoil it by getting too involved.'

'I don't regret it. I don't regret any of it. Except that it has ended.'

She laughed bitterly. 'You don't regret throwing a helpless prisoner out of a fucking helicopter, Alex. Your regret response leaves something to be desired.'

She started to pull together her things, clipping her bicycle helmet on.

'So, I guess this is goodbye,' she said. 'Men! What a waste of time. At least my career is something I can rely on. Something I can plan. Do for myself, without surprises. I've even been talking with . . . with people about running for office. A Senate seat in California will be open in four years. If I do well at State . . . well, who knows?'

'Who knows,' I repeated. 'Yes, who knows?'

She stood up and I stood with her. I put my hands on her arms and held her roughly. In the pattern of our games, perhaps I could have forced her to do something intimate, and I knew she would have submitted, but power games only worked when I knew she wanted me. Now was different. She didn't.

'Before you go, there is one thing you need to tell me. One thing, and then if it is over, I will never bother you again.'

She shrugged. I held on to her arms, tightly.

'You're bruising me. Make it quick.'

'What really happened to Bobby Black?'

'I don't honestly know,' she responded, and tried to break away. 'We don't think it was the Iranians.'

'Neither do I. But who, then?'

'We think he conspired in it himself. That's the way the Kidnap Commission is leaning.'

I let her go and she leaned back on a rock and looked down the path beside the canal.

'That's bullshit and you know it.'

There was a group of half a dozen bikers coming past. They stopped at the rocks and began to clamber over them towards Great Falls. When they'd passed, she started talking again.

'He wandered off because he had some kind of breakdown,' she said without intonation, in such a way that it was obvious she did not believe it either. 'Isn't that what they are pointing to now? All this Paul Comfort stuff about how maybe he meant to shoot him last year? That Bobby Black somehow conspired in his own disappearance because the strain of the job had got to him?'

'And the videos?'

'The psychologists have diagnosed him with some kind of martyr complex. He wanted to go down in history, wanted to provoke a war with Iran – which fortunately wiser people like the President stood out against.'

'I don't believe a word of this.'

'Oh, is that right? Well then, maybe the Iranians did it and we should bomb them to fuck. Or maybe the British did it, Alex. Maybe it was you. You've shown you will do just about anything for Queen and Country.'

'Just about anything, Kristina,' I said. 'Including saying goodbye to you. And keeping our secrets.'

THIRTY

When I arrived back in London, Andy Carnwath informed me that my career as a diplomat was over. On occasions like this, Carnwath acts as Fraser Davis's chief hitman rather than spokesman, and he stood hulking over me when we met in a tiny room I had been given in the Foreign Office to clear up my things and prepare to leave. Because of my pariah status with the Americans, I was now banned from Downing Street.

'Fraser says if you go quietly, all will be well. So you had better go quietly.'

'What does that mean, Andy?'

Carnwath explained. If I cooperated, which he defined as leaving the government service 'without making any waves', then I would receive a substantial lump-sum payoff, plus a full pension, and the new inquiry into my conduct in Northern Ireland would be a formality.

'You'll be cleared,' he said. 'Dickie Anstruther is arranging it.'

The anger that had been boiling inside me since Byrne's story suddenly broke out.

'Of course I will be cleared and it will all be fine, Andy,' I snapped back at him. 'You have no choice but to make it fine unless you intend to dump a pile of shit on your own doorstep.'

Now it was his turn to ask me what I meant.

'Check the files,' I suggested, 'check the report of the original inquiry years ago, the one that cleared me.'

'What the fuck about it?'

He was still looming over me, as if his physical presence could intimidate me into doing what he wanted. I found it almost laughable.

'Mr Justice Proctor, he was called. A High Court judge who was told to look into allegations of the mistreatment of IRA prisoners by the British Army. He spent a year and a half doing it, some bits in public, other bits in secret, and in the end he cleared me and the others involved. Now, if you happen to find something different this time round, then every inquiry up till now including his one will look like a whitewash. You will have to reopen every case of alleged army or police brutality going back to 1969. Despite the impersonation you are doing right now, Andy, of a complete twat, I don't think you are stupid enough to pour forty years of shit onto Fraser Davis, but I suppose you might.'

Carnwath looked at me as if I had just punched him in the guts. My success with Sean McBride led to 'helicoptering' of high-value IRA suspects becoming common for a few months until the complaints of human-rights abuses caused a big political fuss. It took a few years for the government to set up the Proctor Inquiry but, by then, the 1990s, the IRA's political wing, Sinn Féin, were groping their way towards an IRA ceasefire. No one wanted to rock the boat.

I was by that time a junior diplomat in Washington during the Clinton administration, and I was recalled to give evidence anonymously as 'Captain F'. Proctor's report cleared 'Captain F' of serious misconduct, although he did acknowledge that I had 'exceeded direct orders', used 'excessive force', and 'instilled fear' into a leading member of the IRA. In his conclusions, however, Proctor asserted that 'Captain F' had used 'inventive techniques' to uncover 'extremely valuable intelligence

402

information which saved numerous civilian lives and which at least in part justified the methods he used.'

The British government was so desperate to secure an IRA ceasefire they kept secret the fact that the target of the IRA attack was to blow up the Queen at the Proms in the Royal Albert Hall, because if that had become known it would have sunk any chance of any British government negotiating with the IRA for a generation. All the inconvenient information was buried in my file, but Lord Anstruther's second inquiry could hardly dissent from the findings of the first without questioning the credibility of everything that had gone on before. I could see from Carnwath's eyes that he was alarmed. Instead of standing over me he slumped back into the only other chair in the office and sighed deeply.

'Are you going to cause trouble, Alex?' Carnwath said, quietly.

'I haven't decided yet.'

'When will you decide?'

'I have no idea. In my own time. I will do the right thing, Andy, but I will not be bullied into it. Bullying doesn't work with me.'

He seemed to regain some of his courage, leaned forward, and wagged his finger in my face.

'If you publish anything – anything – without clearance from the Cabinet Office, then we will fuck you, Alex,' Carnwath threatened. That part was of course true. You cannot have ambassadors going around writing books and telling the truth about what they do. That kind of thing throws the world of power-politics into disrepute.

'Well, then,' I said, 'it seems that we could be on a path to Mutually Assured Destruction, which neither of us wants. So here's my suggestion. You make sure that I am cleared of all torture and brutality charges, and you do it quickly: let's say within three months. Then you fix it with the Americans so I can work and travel there if I need to. That will improve my mood greatly. And I will quit the Diplomatic Service as you want, provided you pay me what you have agreed. You will not get a better offer.'

I tried not to smile, but it struck me that for the first time in years I was actually having fun, real fun, and that I was remarkably calm for someone who was taking on the entire British establishment and also, probably, the Carr administration and human-rights groups too. At least watching Andy Carnwath's quick brain ticking over in front of me gave me the confidence to realize that they were as frightened of me as I was of them. Unless, like Bobby Black, I disappeared to the wilds of Montana, I could make a lot of trouble.

'I'll see what I can do,' Carnwath said. He stood, picked up his papers, glared at me and prepared to go.

'It will happen to you one day, Andy,' I said. 'It will be different in the details, of course, but the feeling will be the same. All political careers end in failure. Fraser will lose an election or he will tire of you or you will overreach yourself and the newspapers will start writing about how you bully people and what an arsehole you are. Whatever it is, Fraser'll get rid of you in a heartbeat, and then you'll be just another Out of Work Antichrist.'

Carnwath looked at me but he said nothing, not even goodbye. When he left the room he slammed the door behind him, and I started to laugh out loud.

The second inquiry into my conduct in Northern Ireland took just eight weeks. It was also chaired by a High Court judge, Lord Gibbons-Walters.

He reviewed the paperwork, I gave evidence, and so did Sean McBride, but I was helped immeasurably by the fact that someone leaked to Jack Rothstein details of my case which changed completely the way I was seen all around the world. Rothstein reported on the front page of *The Times*, with remarkable accuracy, that by throwing Sean McBride from a helicopter I had forced him to confess that an IRA Active Service Unit had been planning to blow up the Royal Albert Hall during a royal performance, with the Queen and Duke of Edinburgh in attendance. Rothstein cross-checked and discovered that, soon after the allegedly helicoptering of Sean McBride, an IRA active service unit had indeed been arrested in a safe house in Shepherds Bush, West London, with several kilos of plastic explosive, firearms, and other bomb-making equipment. They had been charged with conspiracy to cause explosions, and all four members of the active service unit were sentenced to prison terms of upwards of twenty years. They were eventually released under the Good Friday Agreement amnesty. Rothstein's story said that none of the men would speak to him on the record, but that sources within Sinn Féin confirmed that the Albert Hall was indeed the target of the revenge bombing for the murders of the Gibraltar Three. The day the story was published, British newspapers stopped treating me as a torturer and started treating me as something of a hero.

'The Man Who Saved the Queen', was one *Sun* headline.

'Who Dares Wins', was another.

I refused to speak to any of the journalists, of course. I was forbidden by my agreement with the Foreign Office from doing so. But the newspapers seemed to have good sources. They found that the programme that night at the Proms had been Beethoven and Mozart, and they tracked down the conductor, a wonderfully opinionated Israeli, who said that anyone who tried to bomb the Promenade concerts, or to attack Beethoven and Mozart, was 'by definition not just a terrorist but in fact a barbarian.' *The Times* also contacted the soloists who'd played that evening, who said that I had saved their lives and that they were extremely grateful. Then people who claimed to have been in the audience wrote letters to the newspapers thanking me for what I had done. The good headlines just kept on coming.

'The Best of British', was how one tabloid saw me, reusing the picture of me in my army uniform which had found its way into the *Washington Post.*

The Sun even began a campaign for me to be given an honour by the Queen in recognition of my service.

'Arise, Sir Alex – whatever the Americans think', agreed the *Daily Express.*

'True Grit', said the *Daily Mail.*

'Prime Minister's Brother-In-Law Saved Hundreds from Bomb Death', said *The Guardian.*

The newspaper coverage helped tip the balance. After weeks of being treated by Downing Street as a political leper, Andy Carnwath called me to say that Fraser Davis wanted me to know he was 'very pleased your difficulties are over' and that he would be inviting me to a meeting at Downing Street. Carnwath said Davis wanted to know if I would consider running for Parliament. He talked about a seat in Kidderminster where the sitting MP was about to retire at the next election, and ('but keep this under your hat, Alex') the election was probably going to be called for the following May, to coincide, as Fraser Davis wanted, with the Scottish referendum on independence.

'Thank you, Andy,' I said. His tone could not have been more different from the meeting in the Foreign Office. 'And please thank Fraser for me. That is much appreciated. I will think about it.'

Suddenly I had a lot of choices to make. Publishers on both sides of the Atlantic tried to outbid each other for my memoirs. Universities – including Georgetown and the Kennedy School of Government at Harvard – offered me well-paid visiting professorships. I was snowed under with offers to appear on television and radio programmes – all of which I declined, although I did employ a literary agent, who told me he was confident I could sell the movie rights to my autobiography if I chose to do so. Three big-name film directors – one Irish, one English, and one American – were all interested in a potential biopic. I could not believe it. I was stunned by the remarkable turnaround, as extraordinary in its way as that of Theo Carr. As I tried to make sense of it all, of my personal circumstances, and of what I might do in the future, a plan did form in my mind. It was helped immensely by a series of problems that befell James Byrne, and which also cheered me up.

Stories started to appear in the British press, beginning again with Jack Rothstein in *The Times*, who seemed to be having a good run of exclusives. Rothstein had found out that the 'star American reporter and Pulitzer-prize nominee James Byrne' had 'twisted' details of my military career because I had caught him having sex with my wife, 'Fiona Davis, sister of Prime Minister Fraser Davis.'

'This was not journalism,' *The Times* quoted an unnamed British government source speaking about Byrne's reporting. 'This was a personal vendetta by an adulterer. Byrne should not receive a Pulitzer. He should receive an Oscar.'

Byrne's heroic status as press martyr began to disintegrate further when the Defence Correspondent at the *Daily Telegraph* revealed that Byrne's career in journalism had begun in Boston in the 1980s, where he wrote a regular column for the Sinn Féin IRA newspaper *An Phoblacht/Republican News* under the pseudonym 'American Patriot'. Byrne's family came originally from County Donegal and he wrote in one of his columns, reproduced in the *Telegraph*, that 'every true American patriot is behind the IRA's struggle for freedom.' Writing about two British soldiers murdered and castrated by a Republican mob after the deaths of the Gibraltar Three, 'American Patriot' said: 'Seen from here in Boston, what do you call two dead and castrated British soldiers? A GOOD START! *Erin go Bragh!*'

Byrne's editors at the *Washington Post* were appalled and he was immediately suspended. They withdrew his entry to the Pulitzer committee citing "ethical questions". His wife, who had apparently forgiven him for the lapse with the twenty-three-year-old Polish chambermaid at the Rowallan Hotel, was outraged by the details of his affair with Fiona two years before. She threw him out and filed for divorce. There were even suggestions in the *Columbia Journalism Review* that Byrne had been used by the Carr administration to help change US public opinion and 'soften up' Americans for a possible war with Iran, by printing stories that were 'by their nature uncheckable but pointed in only one direction – towards war'.

I refused to comment, of course. So did Fiona, although it must have been painful for her to be reminded of what she had done. Still, in the interior design business a bit of notoriety never did anyone any harm. I heard that her phone never stopped ringing with people desperate for her to redesign their homes. No doubt the bedrooms were a big feature.

Downing Street, however, was less than happy. Andy Carnwath phoned to tackle me about who was responsible for the leaks. I had by this time left the Foreign office for good and was sitting in my new rented apartment with my laptop on a cheap desk, beginning to write the first of the books I had been commissioned to produce, about the fight against the IRA and its lessons for the War on Terror now. I was irritated by the interruption.

'You know Rothstein well,' Carnwath said.

'So do you.'

'But I am not forbidden to talk to journalists, Alex. You are. Did you leak the stuff about Fiona to Rothstein?'

'Does it matter?' I responded.

'Of course it fucking matters. It matters to Fraser, who has gone apeshit. You have made his sister look like a—'

'Like a what, Andy? And is Fraser Davis upset in his capacity as Prime Minister? Or in his capacity as Fiona's brother? Either way, I don't see he has much responsibility for who

Fiona chooses to commit adultery with, though I suppose for her to be having sex with a Boston Irish American who thinks British soldiers should be castrated might prove to be a bit of a problem. For him, not for me.'

Carnwath offered a tirade of expletives and threats. He said – deleting the swearwords – that Fraser Davis was not happy that the Prime Minister's sister had been made to look like a cheap whore and that it contradicted everything he had been trying to say about Family Values and moral responsibility. I tried not to giggle.

'Then he should talk to Fiona about being so off-message, Andy. Now, since I don't work for you any more, here's a suggestion. Why don't you just fuck off and leave me alone?'

I put the phone down while he was still swearing in response. Over the next couple of months I wrote my account – as far as I could recall it – of what had happened in Northern Ireland, and at every stage I made sure I not only saved it and backed it up but also emailed it to an account I was sure would be safe. And then I waited for the moment I knew would arrive.

I waited until Fraser Davis did as he always supposed he would do and won the Scottish independence referendum and his own re-election in the British General Election held that same day. Davis had a tidy majority in both votes. Dougal Hastie, bitter in defeat, announced that he was quitting as leader of the Scottish National Party and leaving politics altogether. Fraser praised him for his 'great contribution to our national debate.'

The day after the election was when I had planned to begin. I contacted the offices of the IRA's political wing, Sinn Féin, in Dublin. I told them who I was, and the line went quiet.

'The helicopter man?' a voice said darkly. 'The Who Dares Wins fella?'

'The very one. Formerly Captain Price. And Ambassador Price. Now just plain Alex Price.'

409

'And what can we do for you, Captain Price?' the man at the other end of the line said darkly.

'I want to meet Sean McBride,' I said, 'if he is prepared to meet with me.'

I could hear breath being sucked in.

'Would you mind telling me why?'

'I want to tell him that I'm sorry for what I did to him. No strings. I will travel to Ireland to do it. I will put myself in the hands of Sinn Féin. Or the IRA. I'd prefer it to be a private meeting. No cameras, no reporters, no publicity.'

The line went quiet for a moment.

'We'll get back to you,' the Sinn Féin spokesman said.

I gave him my details. I knew the risks of what I was planning, but I have never been frightened of risks, only of inactivity. It took twenty-four hours, but the response from Sinn Féin was positive, almost enthusiastic. After all, they now had their own political agenda. They had done well enough in the British General Election, winning two Northern Ireland seats, and were gearing up for elections to the Northern Ireland Assembly and the Dáil, the parliament in the Irish Republic. Kevin Quinn, the Sinn Féin President, had the extraordinary prospect of being leader of the only party in coalition government in two European countries, on both sides of the Irish border, simultaneously.

Sinn Féin was also running on a reconciliation ticket, with the slogan: 'Remember the Past – But Build for the Future.' My phone call played to their deepest desires just as much as their cooperation played to mine. Within a few days I flew to Dublin. The meeting with Sean McBride took place in the Sinn Féin offices in O'Connell Street, and the content of that meeting will remain private, though it was very emotional, for both of us. We were left in a room together, just the two of us, for an hour. What I can say is that I cried, and McBride cried too. We hugged each other, a thin wiry ex-British soldier and a thickset boxer of an Irish Republican. We talked of old

410

times and fallen comrades in the way that I suspect British and German veterans of World War Two might have talked about El Alamein or Dunkirk.

Because that meeting passed off so well, I stayed in Dublin overnight. Sinn Féin – with my consent – announced that McBride and I would hold a joint news conference dedicated to reconciliation the following day, under the chairmanship of Kevin Quinn, the Sinn Féin President. This time Sean McBride and I embraced for the cameras. We slapped each other on the back. We held each other's hands in the air as if in some kind of mutual triumph.

'A victory for common sense and for peace,' I said, and Sean McBride agreed. Our reconciliation was cheesy, but genuine. We talked of forgiveness and redemption. He was asked how he could forgive what a journalist from the *Irish Press* called 'your torturer'.

'No problem,' Sean McBride said, looking at me. 'Alex Price and I have talked it through. No problem at all.'

'But why, Mr McBride? At the very least you could ask for compensation.'

He looked embarrassed. He put his big farmer's hands on the table in front of him, the same hands that had smashed informants' legs with bricks and breeze blocks.

'I did some bad things myself,' Sean replied. 'I did them for Ireland, but I regret . . . regret the people I harmed. I pray to God, and to those that I have wronged, to give me forgiveness. How could I not offer forgiveness to the man who wronged me?' He nodded his head towards me. 'Alex was doing his job for his country, and I was doing my job for mine. You do things you hope for the greater good, and sometimes it turns out it's the greater evil.'

'How would you characterize your relationship now?' someone from RTE asked.

'Friends,' Sean said.

'Friends,' I said. We shook hands and slapped each other

411

on the back. There were tears in many eyes at that news conference, though I looked over and saw that there were no tears in the eyes of the Sinn Féin President, Kevin Quinn. His brain was counting votes. I might as well have had a 'Vote Sinn Féin' sticker plastered across my forehead. Quinn was fit for government now, and he knew it. Before I left Dublin I shook his hand and said, 'When you are Taoiseach, Mr Quinn, I expect an invitation to hear you speak at Dáil Éireann.'

Quinn grinned. 'I'll see what I can do,' he said. 'Captain Price.'

The news conference with Sean McBride was, of course, carried around the world, and it resulted in a number of phone calls to me. One was from the Endowment for Peace in Washington, who offered to host a twenty-city tour of the United States for Sean and me to talk about reconciliation and the War on Terror. I agreed, and so did Sean. Then two days later the new US Secretary of State Kristina Taft called.

'Happy birthday,' I said.

'Thanks.' Even with her birthday she was still the youngest US Secretary of State in history.

'I didn't send a card.'

'I didn't expect one. But it's nice that you remembered.'

Kristina told me she was calling because President Carr wanted Sean and me to visit the White House, to receive some kind of citation or award, as living proof of the kind of reconciliation, encouraged by the government of the United States towards the people of Ireland, and in conflict zones everywhere. Irish American groups – the very ones that a few months previously had been demonstrating against me – were now pressuring their Congressmen for McBride and me to be rewarded, and a Nobel Peace Prize was talked about. Ridiculous, I thought. No, apparently not. I suspected Arlo Luntz's hand in all of this. We were now eighteen months away from Carr's re-election and forty million Americans claimed Irish roots. They would be interested to see Sean McBride and Alex Price kiss and make up alongside Theo Carr in the White House, especially after all the bitterness over Spartacus.

'It's nice to hear your voice, Kristina.'

'And yours. It's good to know that you are not a war criminal after all. Luntz got it wrong.'

'Luntz never gets it wrong. What do you mean?'

'There *is* life after political death, for you at least. The last few days we have just witnessed a total resurrection of Alex Price. You can have any job, do anything you want now.'

There was an awkward pause on the line.

'What is it you want?'

'Could we meet again, Alex? Just you and me? The way it ended, I . . . well, right now I . . . miss your conversation, your wit. Your advice.'

'Is that all?'

'No, but it's all I'm prepared to say right now.'

'Your career is flourishing . . .'

'In the nunnery. There's no one . . . what about you?'

I had dated a few people in the previous months, but nothing serious.

'I decided I could do with a period of . . . limited excitement,' I said. 'Although that period may be coming to an end.'

We left the idea of meeting together at 'perhaps', but I knew I would hear from her again.

The next few days were confusing. After the United States and Iran had come almost to the brink of war the previous October and November, things had slowly eased.

US forces were withdrawn from the Gulf and the French President's mediation produced a new series of talks. Congress announced a major inquiry into the leaks from Speaker Furedi's office, and President Carr's bipartisan commission on Bobby Black's kidnap held the last of its public and also private hearings with the intelligence agencies and others. Bobby Black was too ill to attend, though he had given some kind of garbled account to lawyers for the commission. The model was the Warren Commission into the death of President Kennedy, or the 9/11 Commission, or the inquiries into the Reagan administration's Iran Contra affair, and what all these inquiries had in common was that they never quite put to rest the public disquiet about what had happened, who had been behind it, and how wide a conspiracy was involved. I expected the same on Bobby Black.

On the eve of my visit to Washington to receive my citation with Sean McBride, I switched on CNN and there was a big red strap across the screen that said, BREAKING NEWS: IRAN. Kristina was at the White House with President Carr announcing that the economic sanctions imposed on the Tehran regime by the United States were to be lifted. She was in discussions with the Iranian government about a possible high-level visit. The CNN correspondent said he had been told that Ron Gold of Goldcrest had already personally visited Iran and met with the President and also with the Supreme Leader Ayatollah Hashemi.

'Goldcrest is said to have negotiated a new licence to pump oil from a massive new field in the north of the country,' the CNN correspondent said. 'An announcement is expected this week.'

Paul Comfort had also been in Tehran. He signed a deal to build a new oil refinery, a construction project that was hugely important to the Iranians because they had plenty of oil but very limited refinery capacity. They pumped millions of barrels of crude but still had to import refined petroleum products from abroad. Plus he was in negotiations to build an American-designed pressurized-water reactor which, at a

414

stroke, would give Iranians the nuclear power programme they claimed to want while putting all the most contentious parts of it in American hands. The series of business deals amounted to tens of billions of dollars, dwarfing any of the agreements Warburton and Goldcrest had signed in Iraq.

The Tehran regime announced that they were pleased to be dealing with the United States 'at a businesslike level – one sovereign country to another', and they looked forward to welcoming Dr Kristina Taft, who 'does us the great honour of speaking our language as well as the language of the Holy Koran.' It was also announced by Tehran that 'all Iranian nuclear facilities' were to be open to IAEA inspection.

That evening my mobile phone rang and a familiar voice was on the end of the line: Johnny Lee Ironside. I had not heard from him in months.

'Good afternoon – I guess where you are it's good evening, Ambassador.'

'Just Mr Price now, Johnny Lee. Though you can call me "sir". How is the White House Chief of Staff today?'

He laughed. 'Just fine and dandy. I hear that you are flying over tomorrow on some kind of peace tour and you'll be with us the day after at the White House.'

'Correct.'

'Could I add some social engagements to your calendar?'

'If I can fit them in, yes.'

'Let's have dinner some night, Alex,' he said. 'I'm on the wagon. I decided I could not mix drinking with this job, so the drinking can wait until we're out of the White House.'

'Sure,' I said. 'It will be good to see you.'

'And one other thing. There's somebody who would like to see you. He lives on a ranch on the outskirts of Billings, Montana. I think if you can you should make time for Bobby Black.'

415

THIRTY-ONE

Sean McBride and I walked into the White House to a hero's welcome. President Carr had invited the Congressional leadership, Muslim groups, and selected diplomats to witness the handing over of a presidential scroll to McBride and me in the Rose Garden, symbolizing what Carr in his speech called 'our personal journey from war to peace.'

From the White House, Sean McBride and I hopped around the country, beginning in New York and then heading west, for the series of meetings organized by the Endowment for Peace, talking about our time in Northern Ireland and of the lessons we had learned, drawing whatever conclusions were possible for today's War on Terror. When we finished the tour, in Chicago, Sean flew back to Ireland. We said quite fond goodbyes and promised that we would meet up again and perhaps collaborate on one of the many book projects we had been offered, *A Soldier's Guide to Peace*. Then I flew to Montana to see Bobby Black.

I spent the flight thinking about how crazy my life had been since that first meeting with him at Chequers three years before. I was also curious as to why Bobby Black had been so keen to see me. He was apparently living the life of a recluse. The preliminary report on the Presidential

Commission of Inquiry into his disappearance had concluded – though they put it more eloquently – that he was crazy as a result of what had happened and he might even have been crazy beforehand. They did not appear to rule out that he had somehow connived in his own kidnapping. How convenient. Like the abusers at Abu Ghraib, or like me years ago in Northern Ireland, or Lee Harvey Oswald, it is so much easier to deal with one bad apple, one rootless crazy person. The alternative, some kind of systemic rottenness, is not in anyone's interest to uncover. And yet. And yet . . .

The plane landed at Billings. As I collected my bags I decided that I wanted, as Arlo Luntz would have put it, to hear a convincing narrative from Bobby Black, a story that would thread together all the pieces and make order out of the chaos of what had happened. I wanted him to play the blue guitar, to tell me the truth, or at least a convenient fiction that I could accept as near enough the truth. I had been to Montana only once before, and I remembered driving south with Fiona from Canada through Glacier National Park down to Billings, and I could recall almost nothing about the experience except that in summer the national park was full of grizzly bears eating berries and looking – from a distance of 200 metres – like cuddly teddies, as they sat on their capacious rear ends and ate themselves fat for winter.

Bobby Black had sent a US Secret Service driver to meet me at the airport. We headed towards the mountains on a two-hour drive from Billings. I knew that Bobby Black had grown up poor, his father had been in the US Navy and had died in active service, and that his mother had moved up from Colorado to find work in Montana, a single mother in the 1950s holding down two jobs, one as a waitress in a diner, plus a little house-cleaning on the side. It was a hard existence. As soon as Bobby Black made any money, he came back to Billings, looked around for a ranch nearby and bought

417

himself 5,000 acres of forest and lakes with a further 3,000 acres of pastureland, which he named the Peggy Ranch in his mother's honour. We turned off the main road through a massive archway made of tree trunks and bearing the 'Peggy Ranch' sign. My driver, an otherwise silent middle-aged white man, muttered something about a serious storm on its way.

'Any chance I might be stranded up here?' I wondered.

He laughed. 'There's always a chance of being stranded in Montana,' he replied. 'Welcome to the Big Sky country.'

From the main road to the ranch buildings turned out to be more than a mile on an asphalted private road, between the pastureland and forest. There was a series of buildings, the main ranch house, which was a massive log and stone cabin, plus three other houses, including a bunkhouse for male ranch staff and one for guests.

Susan Fein Black walked out to meet me. She wore a heavy down jacket, jeans, and Timberland boots. She looked ten years younger than when I had last seen her in Aberdeenshire.

'It's good to see you, Alex.'

'And you, Susan. How is he?'

'He's taking a nap. He tires real easy. Come on in and have hot tea and cookies and we'll talk.'

We sat by a log fire in front of the stone fireplace. She offered me homemade chocolate chip cookies and then explained that one of the lingering consequences of the ordeal was that her husband was often very tired.

'His speech . . . is impaired. He can think lucidly, mostly, but he talks real slow and real quiet.'

'Can he . . . move around?'

'Only in the wheelchair,' she replied, 'but the feeling is coming back in his legs. The doctors are pleased. They say that even a man of his age after being subjected to trauma has scope for recovery, although much of his memory of what happened has been blanked out. He doesn't remember being kidnapped. He doesn't remember being abused or filmed, and he doesn't remember being found. What he does remember is shooting the grouse – well, he would, right?' She laughed a little at the thought, though her face was taut and drawn. 'And he also has a new thing, a fear of dogs, which he couldn't understand, though I think the rest of us probably can.'

'Has he seen the videos?'

She shook her head. 'No.'

She put her teacup down and passed me some more cookies. 'Delicious,' I said. 'Why did he want to see me?'

'I will let him explain himself, but when he read your story about Northern Ireland and saw you and that Irish man . . .'

'McBride. Sean McBride.'

'McBride. Well, that did it. Now, why don't you go freshen up and maybe the two of you can go down to the lake and talk.'

I did as I was told. I washed and changed into jeans and pulled on a down jacket and went back to the main house after about an hour. Bobby Black was waiting for me, in his wheelchair, warmly dressed in a heavy wool shirt and down parka with a tartan blanket on his knees.

'He-llo, Am-bass-a-dor,' he said. Every syllable was an effort, but he was getting there.

'Mr Vice-President.'

'Bo-bby.'

'Alex.'

It was as if we were meeting each other for the first time. Susan Black gave me instructions. They had laid a path of wooden decking which led down to a small lake about a hundred yards from the house.

'It's where he likes to sit,' she said, 'and look at the fish rising and the birds. But no longer than one hour before supper, you got that? And no excitement. We're having steaks and corn on the cob, so I want you here in one hour, sharp.'

I told her I understood. I pushed the wheelchair down to the lake and we started to talk, Bobby Black and me, to talk

419

I suppose for the first time. Maybe it was everything that we had gone through, shared sacrifice. Maybe it was because we no longer wanted anything from each other. Or from anyone else.

'I'm sorry for my part in everything that you had to go through,' I began as we sat together by the edge of the lake. There were egrets in the shallows and a blue heron on the rim where the lake spilled towards a small river over a dam.

'No ne-ed to ap-ol-o-gize,' he said. 'Not your fault.'

'Whose fault was it then?'

'Still fig-ur-ing that out,' he responded.

'The bipartisan Commission of Inquiry will let us know once they finish their final report,' I suggested, but Black just laughed bitterly.

'Yeah, my ass,' he said. 'Like the War-ren Comm-ission, what-ever is con-ven-ient. They think I'm cra-zy.'

'Are you?'

'No.'

I sat on a wooden bench overlooking the lake with his wheelchair beside me. There was a chill in the air but it was clear and fresh and it made me think of our time on the Scottish mountains.

'Who or what do you think it was?' I asked. 'The Iranians?'

'No,' he said.

'But who, then?' I pressed him.

'All of them,' he said, this time without hesitation. 'You remember that Agatha Christie story about the dozen people who might have killed someone, and when the detective figured it, turns out it was all of them, every one of them did it. Same here. All of them. They needed to get rid of me, so that's what they did.'

'You don't sound bitter?'

A smile played on his face.

'In their position I'd have done the same.' He started to

laugh. 'Winning isn't the most important thing. It's the only thing. I always believed that. You don't get into this business and want to finish second. You know that. At least you did in Northern Ireland. Tell me about it.'

I did as he asked. When I finished he said, 'So I was right all along. Fear works. Spartacus works.'

'With some people,' I admitted. 'But you can't tell with which, and once you start abusing people you never know when to stop. I know that much.'

'No,' he contradicted me, 'fear works with all of us. More than love. More than hate. It works.'

Suddenly Bobby Black went quiet and let the thought die over the lake, lapsing back into his chair. I thought he was tired and soon afterwards I wheeled him back up to the main house. I spent that evening and the whole of the next day with the Blacks.

Over dinner that night, Susan Black helped feed her husband, cutting his steak into small pieces. He was able to direct the fork towards his mouth with reasonable accuracy. He said nothing whatsoever over dinner, but Susan Black asked me about Kristina.

'We all knew you were close,' she said.

'We split up after . . . when it all happened.'

She nodded.

'These things are difficult when you are in the public eye.'

'Impossible, sometimes.'

'And now?'

'We have been in contact,' I said. 'I admire her. There is . . . still something between us, but I don't exactly know what it is.'

'She's one ambitious lady,' Susan Black said, and then told me that Paul Comfort and Ron Gold were promising to fund Kristina's campaign to run for the Senate in California, if she chose to do so in a couple of years' time. 'There's talk she could run for the presidency herself one day.'

'Pro-vided she gets her-self a hus-band,' Bobby Black chimed in, opening his mouth as he said it so I could see bits of chewed-up steak. It was the first and only time he said anything during the meal.

'Is a husband necessary?' I wondered.

Susan Black nodded. 'Oh, yeah. Single woman candidate for the Senate is never going to make it. People will think it's not normal. Or worse. She needs to be married with kids. Or at least married.'

'Is she serious about the Senate?'

Susan Black nodded. She told me that Comfort and Gold had promised Kristina as much as $50 million in campaign contributions. Arlo Luntz would work for her with Theo Carr's permission, but Kristina needed to have what Luntz called 'a normal family life.' Susan Black looked at me as she said all this.

The following morning Bobby Black and I went trout fishing. Well, we returned to the lake at the end of the path, I tried to fish and he watched. He said that he felt his strength returning a little more every day and hoped he could hold a rod within a year.

'Can I ask you something?'

'Sure,' he said.

'Why did Theo Carr pick you as Vice-President, and why did he allow you to overshadow him?'

Bobby Black laughed again and told me the story, though it was sometimes an effort for him to say it all. It started because there was a long-term relationship between Bobby Black and the Carr family. He explained that when Governor Theo Carr finally decided to follow his father and grandfather and run for the presidency of the United States, his first step was to hire Arlo Luntz. But the next step was to call on a trusted family adviser to help him – Senator Bobby Black from Montana.

'I was always the "Man to Know" in Washington,' he said.

Top of the list of Black's tasks was to raise money for the Carr campaign, which he told me was fairly easy 'when your friends include the guys who run Goldcrest and Warburton'. Tens of millions of dollars from Friends of Bobby flooded in, mostly of the soft-money kind that does not cause problems later. Then the Carr family asked Bobby Black for another favour: could he find the perfect vice-presidential running mate for Theo Carr? Not someone disastrous like Sarah Palin or comedic like Dan Quayle, just a regular meat and potatoes kind of running mate?

'Sure,' Bobby Black said. He applied himself. He sought advice. He met the greybeards in the party. He asked Governor Carr's father, former President Andrew Carr, for his thoughts. Then he interviewed a dozen potential candidates. He tried out the Governor of California, Felix Hart, to help secure the West. He spent time with Senator Stevens from Illinois, who might help capture the Midwest, the Governor of Florida, Roberto Baez, and so on. Bobby Black explained to me that he sent out questionnaires asking all the potential vice-presidential candidates to tell him – in total confidence – about their private lives, to detail intimate business connections, fund-raising activities, guilty secrets, adulteries, anything which might embarrass Theo Carr.

'I demanded total disclosure,' he said, and he got it.

After weeks of searching for the ideal man or woman, after reviewing the questionnaires and consulting the party chiefs, imagine Bobby Black's astonishment when, out of 300 million Americans, the best-qualified candidate to be Theo Carr's running mate as Vice-President of the United States turned out to be the senior Senator from a tiny state of 'Flyover People' of no particular significance and with very few electoral college votes, Montana.

'I chose myself,' Bobby Black laughed. He was to become Vice-President of the United States on his own recommendation. He also explained that he had amassed a treasure-trove of dirt on political rivals, and when one – the hapless Florida Governor Baez – stepped out of line, and criticized Bobby Black publicly over some minor political difference, the Vice-President told reporters that he and Governor Baez would 'just have to agree to disagree.'

'A week later the *Miami Herald* discovered that Governor Baez had conducted a five-year sexual affair with a Cuban-American lobbyist from Fort Lauderdale,' Bobby Black said with a lopsided grin. 'Secretly paying for her to bring up their love child.'

Bobby Black said Baez apologized to his wife and family and announced he would not seek re-election as Governor of Florida when his term expired the following November.

'I never had much of a problem after that,' Bobby Black said. 'People, including President Carr himself, just kinda did what I told them, until . . . Well, until . . .'

He stopped talking and looked back out over the lake. It was starting to get chilly and we returned to the house. We had dinner that night and I talked mostly to Susan. Bobby Black seemed lost in thought, or perhaps it would be more accurate to say he was just lost. He was present at the table, but for most of that evening he was no longer there. I can only imagine the darkness and the demons that flooded his mind. The following morning we said our goodbyes after breakfast. As my case was loaded into the back of the car to return to the airport, I kissed Susan Black on both cheeks and then bent down to shake hands with the former Vice-President of the United States. He gripped me hard and pulled me towards the wheelchair.

'She'll be pre-si-dent one day,' he said, his voice strained with effort, his hands holding my shirt with an old man's ferocity.

'Who will?'

'Kri-sti-na. If you mar-ry her, she'll be pres-i-dent.'

I climbed into the car and left the ranch. As we drove away

I turned and looked behind me as Susan Black wheeled her husband into the ranch house. She was pushing the wheelchair with one hand and stroking his thinning hair with the other.

THIRTY-TWO

I returned via Chicago to Washington where I had meetings with the faculty at Georgetown University. It seemed to go well, and the Dean offered me a position, a house in Georgetown, a place to write, and what sounded like a considerable sum of money. I was staying in a small and discreet Georgetown hotel and walked back from the university through the streets, picking up some wine and beer on the way. I returned to my room and waited for Kristina. We had talked a few times on the telephone and had arranged to meet. It seemed the natural thing to do. I tried not to feel excited, but I was like a teenager on a first date, unable to settle, not sure exactly what I wanted to happen. I showered and changed, opened a beer, and sat watching CNN's reports from Tehran on what they were calling 'the new, businesslike mood' of relations between the two countries. Iranian officials had allowed CNN to visit the site of the new pressurized-water reactor, which would be constructed over the next few years with American help. It was near Natanz, where for years we had assumed the Iranians were trying to develop their nuclear bomb. But not, apparently, any more.

'The biggest worry,' CNN reported, 'is not the bomb, but the safety of the American workers and the pressurized-water reactor in a region prone to earthquakes.'

Kristina arrived at my hotel room, alone, shortly after seven that evening. She left her security detail and driver outside. When she knocked quietly on the door, despite myself, my heart leapt. You can tell yourself what to think, but you cannot successfully tell yourself what to feel. I did not want to be excited by her, but I was. I always was. I opened the door and she walked in, with a smile on her face, as if we had parted just an hour ago. 'Hello, Alex,' she said, and then held me to her and kissed me on both cheeks. Her lips lingered on my skin and her hands stayed on my waist. 'It's been a long time.' I put my hands on her hips and just the touch aroused me. I broke away.

'Drink?'

'White wine.'

I poured. She sat down on the sofa, crossed her legs and looked at me. Despite everything, despite what I had told myself, she had the same effect on me as she always did, perhaps even more. Power suited her.

'So,' she said softly, 'you managed to go from Hero to Zero and back to Hero in a matter of weeks. That's against the rules. I talked to Arlo and he says he might do a chapter of his book just about you. I don't know how you managed it, but you surprised us all.'

'And you surprised me, Kristina.'

'In what way?'

'Well, for instance, what was your role in the disappearance of Bobby Black?'

'Oh,' she said with a chuckle, putting the wine down. 'No more Mister Nice Guy. So this is to be one of those interrogations for which you're so famous? Is the helicopter warming up on the lawn? Am I about to join the IRA Mile-High Club?'

'Not exactly, but I thought you might fill in a few blanks for me. I went to Montana to see him.'

She looked surprised. 'Bobby Black?'

'Yes.'

'And?'

'He doesn't remember anything of the kidnapping, but he does think his disappearance suited a lot of people in Washington more than the folks in Tehran. He thinks you all conspired to get rid of him and, because you are all in on it – you, Luntz, Shultz and maybe even the president himself – it will never come out.'

'I had absolutely no role in the disappearance of the Vice-President of the United States,' she replied firmly, 'except to respond to the emergency which you helped create, Alex. Maybe you should tell me more about your role in the disappearance of Bobby Black, Alex. You organized it. You were there.'

'I was there,' I agreed, 'and I put into place some ideas for repairing relations between our two countries that were in my head because you put them there.'

She looked startled.

'Don't look surprised Kristina. We both know it was your idea to invite him to Scotland, not mine. I have never mentioned it to anyone that Alex Price's "great idea" was actually placed in my head while my head was lying on your pillow and after we had been making love for a few hours. Do you think I should start mentioning it now?'

She looked at me coldly.

'You will do what you have to do,' she said. 'Although your recollection is very different from mine, Alex. It was your idea. That's what you said.'

I smiled. She was a very fine player indeed. A world-class act.

'Besides,' she went on, reaching for the wine again, and suddenly looking a lot more relaxed, 'you seemed happy enough to take the credit when things were going well. It would look odd that it has taken you all these months to decide it was my idea. I doubt if anyone would believe you. With the commission reporting soon, it is case closed now, anyway. Why did you not mention it to Killick? Or the British security people? You might even look like a spurned lover. I think it was you who taught me over breakfast two years ago that when things go badly we all look for someone to blame. I do not know why you are trying to blame me, except that we broke up.'

'I am blaming you because I know you wanted rid of Bobby Black, because you told me. Because you suggested the shooting trip. And because you are one of the main beneficiaries of his disappearance – along with Shultz and Johnny Lee and, I suppose, Luntz. You have all emerged from his shadow.'

Kristina picked up her wine glass again, took another sip, and laughed. 'You are the guy who said we should not go to war with Iran based on a button, a piece of thread, a few maps and some videos on the Internet, yet you want to go to war with me based on this bullshit? Please, Alex. I thought better of you.'

We sat looking at each other for a few minutes.

'The Presidential Commission of Inquiry . . .' I began.

'The inquiry into the disappearance will do as it is damn well told. It will report next month. While the Vice-President's mind was disturbed he concocted some kind of plot to disappear, wandered off, and was a willing partner in everything that happened to him. The psychological evidence for this is, apparently, very compelling. Bobby had been seeing a therapist for years about his mood swings, his anger, and a martyrdom complex. The stories about prescription drug addiction are true. There is . . . a lot of it around. Now are you and I going to fight all evening? In which case maybe you want me to go.'

'No,' I said. I moved over and sat next to her, then I cupped her face in my hands and kissed her on the lips. 'No, I don't want to fight, Kristina. I am not sure that I trust you. I am not sure that I will ever trust you again, but there is something almost chemical that you do to me . . .'

429

I kissed her again and my hands ran over her body. Just the memory of the pleasure we had enjoyed aroused me.

'I have been a long time without a man,' she said. 'Perhaps you should show me how much you miss me.'

'Perhaps.' I stood up and poured myself another drink, not because I wanted more wine but because I wanted to look at her from a distance. I wanted to mess up the perfect picture of power dressing; I wanted to grab her and to hurt her. I put my arms round her, and she pulled me towards her on the couch. Just as at the start there was a desperation, a brutality, in our love-making, but that evening I went over the edge of violence. I did not hit her but I pulled at her until she squealed, and I tore at her expensive clothes with a fury of expiation for my own sins and for hers as I ripped the buttons from her silk shirt and pulled at her underclothes. She slapped me, hard, and I turned on her and held her down. We were like mating carnivores, big cats not knowing whether they want to mate or to attack one another. We decided no longer to attack. When we finished we lay exhausted together on the couch and then eventually I pulled her to the bed.

'I need to call some people,' she said, taking off the remains of her clothes and staring at the damage I had done to her designer suit and shirt.

'Max Mara,' she said, holding up a torn piece of cloth. 'Agnès B.'

She started to laugh and then dialled the number of her security detail, saying that she would not need them until morning and that she was staying with me at the hotel. 'But I need fresh clothes.' She instructed them what to find and where to find them in her apartment and when to bring them to the hotel.

'I don't remember asking you to stay,' I said, when she put the phone down. 'Part of me wants to throw you out, naked and bruised.'

'It's me that could have you thrown out – out of this country as an undesirable alien,' she replied, lying beside me on the bed. 'But you are desirable.'

That night we made love again, talked, and lay in each other's arms with her breath on my neck as it had been when we were together conducting our clandestine affair. Suddenly, without warning, Kristina said, 'Do you still love me?'

The question took me completely by surprise. I did not know the answer any more, but I told her that probably I did not.

'Could that change?'

I sighed.

'When we split up I deleted every email, threw away every letter and photograph of you, and tried to forget you,' I said. 'I did not expect – ever – to talk with you or to be in bed with you again. There are no second acts in emotional life either. You need to give me a bit of time to come to terms with all this. I am not sure what I think of you any more.'

'Well, while I have got you confused, can I ask you something else? How's the divorce?'

'It came through last month. Fiona was a complete bitch about the money, and I wanted a clean break so I gave her pretty much everything she wanted. I am a free man, but a poor one.'

'But you have the book deals?'

I nodded, and told her I was thinking of accepting the visiting professorship at Georgetown, which would enable me to write.

'It also gets around a little technical problem with the British government over the Official Secrets Act,' I said. 'If I write and publish here in the United States, I don't need to clear anything with the Cabinet Office. And I am looking forward to living in Washington again.'

Kristina sat up in bed and her hair fell over her bare shoulders.

'When that happens,' she said, 'will you marry me?'

* * *

I spent the night with my arms around Kristina, inhaling her scent like some kind of narcotic. I admit that – despite the warning from Bobby Black and Susan Black – I was still shocked by her question about marriage. And yet I slept better than at any time in the months since we had broken up. She said that she was young enough to have children, and she knew that this was a longing in my own life. I said very little. She had thought it all through, and outlined how our lives might work in the future, like a business proposal or a political manifesto, rather than a proposal of marriage. I felt a peculiar numbness as well as a sense of shock.

'You want me as a sperm donor,' I said at one point.

'If that's how you want to put it,' she laughed. 'But the hours are not bad, the conditions are good. You might even enjoy it.'

'I might not. I still have to figure out who you really are, Kristina.'

'But you'll think about it?'

'Of course I will think about it.'

'Don't think for too long.'

'No. I won't. I am supposed to return to London on the overnight flight tomorrow. I'll have a day here and walk around and think it all through.'

Kristina's security detail turned up with fresh clothes at 5.30 the next morning, as they had been instructed. She put her torn designer clothes in the trash. I made a pot of the dreadful hotel coffee while she showered.

'So when can I see you again?' she said.

'I don't know,' I replied.

'When you come back to Washington,' she said, 'if it suits you, you can stay with me at the Watergate while you look for your own place. It's safer than a hotel, although I enjoyed the grubbiness of meeting you here.'

'Kristina, are you sure you want to marry me?'

'Yes,' she said. 'I'm sure.' Then she kissed me on the lips

432

and wound her body into mine. As she was leaving, I handed her a sealed hotel envelope which I had prepared while she was in the shower.

'What's this?'

'Two hundred and fifty dollars, in tens and twenties, plus a fifty-dollar tip for extras. I believe it is the price we agreed.'

She laughed. And put the money in her bag.

Even though it was very early, the moment Kristina left I went out for what I knew would be one of the longest walks of my life. I started in Georgetown, snatched a breakfast in a coffee shop and then walked down Pennsylvania Avenue. I passed the White House, walked through Lafayette Park and past the old Riggs bank, down to the Treasury. Then I continued down Pennsylvania Avenue until I got to Capitol Hill. I did not go inside, but turned and started to walk back the way I had come, past the Ulysses S. Grant fountain and up the Mall towards the Washington, Lincoln and Jefferson monuments. My head was buzzing with ideas and possibilities. Looking back over the past couple of years, I had seen my marriage collapse and the development of a new relationship with someone who now wanted to marry me; the disappearance of Bobby Black and the collapse of my career. I had, I suppose, come close to death. The Heathrow plotters would cheerfully have blown me up alongside the other 80,000 at Twickenham. And I had lost my career. Now, I was undergoing a resurrection. I was faced with the real possibility of a Second Act to my life. I could write, and I knew my books would sell, although I also knew I would not be able to tell the whole truth. I could marry Kristina and live a life at the top of the political tree in the United States as the husband of the US Secretary of State and then the spouse of the junior Senator from California. Possibly Bobby Black was right that she had ambitions to get to the very top, and one day would take me with her. I would have to adopt American citizenship, but that would not be such a difficulty. In some ways I am more American than I am British. And Kristina would give me something that I always longed for, and which she apparently needed, the blessing of children.

I had now walked all the way to the Washington Monument. To my left I could see the Jefferson, my favourite of all the monuments and memorials. It's large, with a neoclassical cupola dedicated to the great thinker and intellectual who helped shape the American Republic on the path of liberty and justice for all and as a beacon to people all over the world. And yet Jefferson was famously a hypocrite, pondering questions of liberty while being served and catered for by his black slaves.

To my right I could see the White House, where Jefferson's most recent successor, Theo Carr, would be huddled with Arlo Luntz figuring out how to win re-election. I felt a smile across my face. I knew the flaws of Carr and his team, but I wondered how long it would take for him to be transformed from just another grubby politician to an elder statesman and international hero in the footsteps of Jefferson? It suddenly occurred to me that what we hated about people in power was not that they were different from you and me, but that they are the same, unfortunately. They have the same human weaknesses and frailties: sex, money, love, power, drugs, alcohol. We want them to be better than us, and they are not, until they are safely dead, when we can forget Clinton with Lewinsky, Nixon and Watergate, Jefferson and his slaves, Churchill with his brandy bottle, and concentrate on what they achieved.

I started to walk back towards the White House and then to Georgetown to pack my bags for the plane. What had really happened to me over the past three or four years as I played with those in power at the very highest levels? What had really happened to Bobby Black? And did it matter that we would never know the truth, only the convenient fiction served up by the media and the Commission of Inquiry?

I was no longer sure how much truth I could handle. I wanted a convenient fiction, a narrative, a story or a myth that made sense of what had happened and meant I could file away the past and concentrate on the future and the here and now. At that moment, as I stood outside at the south side of the White House, my cellphone rang. It was Kristina. She was looking for an answer. So was I.

ACKNOWLEDGEMENTS

I would like to thank a number of people for their help and encouragement. Most of all I would like to thank my agent, Toby Eady, and editor at HarperCollins, Susan Watt, for their advice, wit, conversation and sharp observations, and their colleagues at Toby Eady Associates and HarperCollins. Max McElligott helped talk me through grouse shooting in the Scottish Highlands. Robert McGeehan and Professor Gary McDowell of the University of Richmond were as intrigued as I was with the constitutional implications of a disappearing Vice-President, and helped explain the consequences. Professor Anthony McElligott of the University of Limerick eloquently alerted me to the civil liberties implications of emergency security measures and the potential parallels with the Weimar Republic. Kevin Sullivan, co-bureau chief of the *Washington Post* in London read the manuscript for failures in my American English, and I would also like to thank Mina al Oraibi, Agnés Poirier, Jamie Coleman and Jennifer Joel for reading the first draft and offering suggestions and guidance. Any remaining mistakes are mine. Behind the scenes, British and US diplomats and government officials over the years have suffered my curiosity about their jobs and their lives, and have been unfailingly helpful and courteous. My colleagues at *Newsnight* have also been supportive. Above all, Anna has put up with my many idiosyncrasies, and made me smile.

What's next?

Tell us the name of an author you love

| Gavin Esler | Go ▶ |

and we'll find your next great book.